To Ma

Enjoy!

Chroma

Imogen's Secret

Book 1

B FLEETWOOD

B fleetwood

First published in 2016
Copyright © B Fleetwood 2016

BECKY FLEETWOOD

The moral right of the author has been asserted.

www.bfleetwood.com
ISBN: 1537074393
ISBN 13: 9781537074399

In memory of my brother, Jonny.

Acknowledgements

There are a few key people I would like to thank from the bottom of my heart for their encouragement, help and enthusiasm: my son Rik, daughter Katie, hubby Julian, great friends Val and Alison and Jonathan Moseley. These are the folk who have allowed me to bash them over the head with raw ideas, troubleshoot problems and, in the case of Val, thrown a bag of commas at my manuscript! Many thanks to you and also to family members: Ben, Laura, Adam, Hannah, Ruth and Judy and supportive friends: Shirley, Liz, Louise, Mary and Liz E for giving me the 'thumbs up'.

A huge thank you to the talented animator, Jonathan Moseley, who designed the front cover and the Chroma pendant.

Finally, to the late Anne McCaffrey, thank you for your inspirational heroine, Lessa, from the Dragonflight Series. The inception of Imogen and Chroma stems from my early love of these books, which had me enraptured.

Becky

IMOGEN

The scream at the back of her throat would not surface.

They were coming.

Shouts - angry indecipherable - rang out from the back of the church. Footsteps pounded down the aisle. A draft of cool air blew out the candles and darkness enveloped her. Shards of torchlight began to criss-cross in all directions. They flashed across empty pews, marble columns and elevated statues. Large shadowy figures rushed towards her. She cowered below the church dome.

She could only watch in horror as they reached her grandfather, now on his feet by the front pew. His arms flailed as he tried to beat them back. They were too strong; they had him.

Caught between beams of light, he turned his head to her. "Run!" he mouthed, eyes wide and imploring.

Faceless shapes bore down upon her. Forcing her body to mobilise, she clambered up the marble flight of steps to the altar table. It seemed that she ran in slow motion, her heart pounding with each step. Giant arms swung at her and angry voices shrieked as she twisted, dodged and dived around the solid table to escape their grasping clutches.

Terrified, she leapt towards the colossal crown that hung, like a canopy, above the altar. The jewels in the crown rim glittered, amongst them a small circular black sphere pulsed eerily.

Hands lunged, ready to clamp around her feet.

Time slowed.

The crown, the sphere, drew her up and she was swathed in a blackness so impenetrable, it swallowed every sense. Suspended, unable to breathe, lungs about to burst. She heard a cry: a slow, droning, desperate call of her name, as she struggled to take a breath…

And then, in an instant, her eyes sprang open and she was awake in the cold, grey light of dawn.

Wiping beads of sweat from her brow, Imogen sat up breathlessly in bed. She reached for the glass of water. Her heart was racing and the panic of her nightmare remained a clenched fist in her stomach. A glance through her open door to her mother's bedroom reassured her that nothing had changed. The heart monitor silently winked in the background. Her mother's sleeping form lay, as it had for nearly ten full years, in a deep and persistent sleep encircled by a soft halo of pastel colours.

Focus.

Biting her lip, the drill kicked in and Imogen forced herself to take a deep breath. Sipping the water she gradually slowed her heart and soothed her sparking colours until they dulled to a slight glimmer and finally to neutral.

She checked the clock, less than three minutes. *Not bad.*

Her childhood nightmare had resurfaced and begun to disturb her sleep regularly in the last few weeks. At least she was getting faster with the drill and, as she had been taught, she could already put her mind to analysing what she had seen. More clarity this time, although she could still not see the church in its entirety, or gain any clues that would identify its whereabouts.

Turning on the bedside lamp, she slowly reached out to smooth Sadiki who was lying luxuriously at the bottom of her bedding. The small rust-striped cat awoke instantly and recoiled, baring its teeth and giving her a warning hiss before jumping down. Grandad had always said he was wild at heart. "Leave him well alone," he had cautioned. When awake, the cat was mistrustful and wore a permanent melancholy expression, which made her think he was yearning for something he couldn't have. By contrast, he looked so relaxed and soft in his sleep, that she couldn't stop herself trying to give him a gentle stroke each day. *One day he will let me.*

With a sigh, Imogen took her sketch pad and pencil from next to the bed and added more detail to the latest drawing of inside the church: the altar table; the grasping hand of a shadowy figure; the pulsing sphere in the crown. Critically examining the picture she had built up over the last fortnight, she knew it was an accurate representation. The small, frightened depiction of herself in mid leap sent a shiver down her spine.

Determined she would not be sucked into its power again, she flicked the page and leafed through her other sketches. Her mother's face appeared everywhere: smiling, laughing, eyes wide open. These disturbed her almost as much as the nightmare illustrations. They were just as dreamlike, just as unreal and totally without assurance.

The sound of the alarm on her clock interrupted her thoughts, which she filed away for reflection at a future time or date. *Stay focussed and practical*, she told herself, and with resolve she got up and set about the morning routine before college.

Imogen rose early each day, to spend precious time alone with her slumbering mother before the first of a chain of carers arrived. The start and end of each day was her time to share her innermost thoughts and fears; to trace the fine features of her mother's beautiful face with her fingers, soothing her sleeping brow; to stroke the faint birthmark next to her right eye and to watch the corona of colours for any slight flicker or change. When she touched her fingertips to connect to those on her mother's dormant open hand, she mentally described the intensity of the nightmare and she was sure there had been a hint of grey filter into her mother's normally unchanging stream. It was nearly imperceptible, but it was there: the colour of worry.

She may seem lifeless to others, but Imogen knew that her mother was aware; she could feel the pulse of her being, it was beyond words or physical expression. She sensed the immeasurable love, no matter how distant, each time she made the connection; it flowed deep within. It was her greatest comfort.

Annie was the first carer to arrive, a quiet, gentle lady of advanced years with a calm blue-white radiance that spoke common sense and efficiency. It always reassured Imogen to see the shine of silver interwoven amongst Annie's colours; the silver thread she had come to associate with those in the caring and nursing professions. 'Check for the silver,' were Grandad's words. 'Silver is safe.'

Knowing all was secure, she got ready for college and by the time Chrissie called at 8.15am, she had showered, grabbed some breakfast, fed Sadiki at arm's length and kissed her mother goodbye. She routinely activated the bedroom camera and switched her phone to *standard & silent,* as she did every time she left the house, and descended the stairs to grab her college bag and step outside.

Imogen loved Chrissie; she had earth colours of brown and green, complemented with a blue calm. She lacked bright yellow and was therefore not overly inquisitive or intrusive, but had a sprinkling of dreamy orange tinged with soft white showing her warmth, honesty and purity. Chrissie was a friend who would not pry, who would take Imogen at face value and who could be trusted implicitly. They set off together, opting to walk on such a pleasant, and untypically British, May day.

"Gen, I've been thinking, we could make my party night a joint one, as your birthday is only a few weeks after mine... and I know with your mum that you, well you may not be able to..." Chrissie trailed off feeling embarrassed, but Imogen could see the sincerity and affection behind the offer, as chromatic glows of white-blues and reds accompanied the suggestion.

She hurriedly said: "That's really nice of you but honestly, Chrissie, you know me. I'd rather not; I hate all that fuss."

"Yeah – I know you do!" Chrissie answered with her usual good-humour, carefully changing the subject as they walked. "Did I tell you that my brothers have finally agreed to play at the party? I had to let them choose most of the music but it's going to be so good. I told them they should form a band but Callum reckons the 'brother thing' is dead cheesy so won't hear of it."

Imogen smiled as she noted the spectrum of hues in Chrissie's Chroma as her emotions flickered through frustration, excitement, and calm acceptance. Her friend was very easy-going and it was taken as read that she was not required to respond as Chrissie continued to chatter cheerfully.

"Wish this morning was over with," Chrissie grumbled as they crossed a road, "I know I haven't done enough revision."

English Literature! The exam leapt to the front of her mind as Imogen immediately quelled the grey surge that threatened to surface as anxiety.

How did I forget that? She acknowledged, internally, that the nightmare had unsettled her more than she cared to admit. Chrissie continued, oblivious to any change in Imogen, bemoaning aloud the difficulty of remembering excerpts and passages, which 'did not stay in her brain'.

Imogen let Chrissie witter on as she mentally switched her thoughts to preparation for the exam. In her mind's eye she summoned the main text, flicked pages and memorised quotes. Layer upon layer of notes, essays and discussions assembled themselves in multiple tiers of perfect recall: Shakespeare, poetry and the set books.

Satisfied with the odd nod and smile, Chrissie babbled all the way to college unaware she did not command Imogen's full attention as she silently completed a month's worth of revision.

Arriving in the crush outside the main hall, Imogen's focus came back to Chrissie who suddenly nudged her, urging her to look down the crowded hallway towards a dark-haired student standing against a far wall, his black leather jacket thrown over one shoulder. He was slowly scanning the numerous faces that passed him as they joined the exam line.

"Now that's enough to take your mind off an exam!" exclaimed Chrissie, sparking scarlet attraction, "Not seen him before... Mmm! This way!" Chrissie pulled Imogen forward as they headed for the end of the line right opposite where he stood.

Imogen briefly sharpened her vision on the impossibly good-looking face of the stranger as they approached. Something triggered an instant defensive response deep within, causing her stomach to shrink.

Danger.

It was a combination of signs: the confidence he exuded as he held his head high, the undulating reds and golds in his Chroma which drew admiring glances from the females nearby, the intermittent peaks of dazzling yellow as he appeared to study each person in turn, but the overwhelming sense of disquiet came from his strong chromatic black edging: the indicative sign of power and authority.

As they got closer, Chrissie's scarlet tones began to jump wildly and Imogen quickly brushed her own colours with a swathe of dull neutral shades. Looking left and right, he began to walk down the corridor directly towards them. Imogen stared listlessly ahead subduing every response. Passing within inches, he gave them only a cursory glance.

"Swoon!" exclaimed Chrissie as her eyes followed him until he disappeared beyond a huddle of students entering the hall.

"Out of our league." Imogen quipped to her friend who was oozing colours of attraction that matched the flush in her cheeks. Inwardly Imogen sighed and thanked her grandfather for the drills.

So what or who was he looking for?

"I hope we haven't seen the last of him," sighed Chrissie.

Imogen, who could only think the opposite, encouraged her friend to turn her thoughts to the exam as they filed into the hall and she put her unease to one side in preparation for the test.

"Turn off all mobile phones please and place them in the box at the end of your row," called the invigilators.

"Gen, we have to get you a new phone," scorned Chrissie, as Imogen placed a rather bulky handset into the box next to the latest slim line model that Chrissie had put in. "Yours belongs in a museum!"

"I like my phone, even if it's a bit old fashioned," responded Imogen good-naturedly.

"Old fashioned? Look at it - it's a brick!" teased Chrissie with a shake of her head as she crossed to her exam desk.

Some brick! Imogen smiled to herself as she went to her numbered seat near the centre of the hall. Chrissie would never know its hidden capabilities, another of her grandfather's amazing inventions.

"No more talking please," announced the examiner. "Put today's date at the top of your answer sheet: May 23rd 2016. You may now open your papers and begin."

Imogen loved the silence of exams. The forced concentration guaranteed she would not be in anyone's focus and she could temporarily drop her shield for a few hours, a rarity in her life of concealment.

The exam had a tedious start with nothing to tax her. She answered two questions with precision and accuracy but the last question on her favourite book, set in wartime, filled her with thought and contemplation: the meaning of true love. She mulled over the relationships between the heroine and her two suitors, the childhood sweetheart to whom she was betrothed and the handsome, intelligent member of the enemy forces. *Who would I have chosen?* One deserved loyalty; the other evoked feelings of a deep and forbidden passion. *Which man could she truly love?*

Imogen pictured the beautiful Greek island where the story was set; imagined walking amongst olive groves dappled in sunlight, where a peaceful world had been turned upside down by an unwanted violent war. *How would I have felt?* Her pen flowed as she experienced the conflicts of the book's characters and tried to grapple with the meaning of a true and deep love. Lost in the storyline and totally absorbed by the changing bonds between the characters, she wrote her last line just as the invigilator called time and placed her pen on the desk with a heartfelt sigh. It was only then that Imogen became aware of the tell-tale prickling sensation, the feeling that always accompanied a threat to penetrate her aura. Annoyed she had lost track, she tentatively looked around the room for the cause of the intrusion.

Her heart skipped a beat. At the back of the exam hall, the dark-haired newcomer sat staring straight at her.

THE CHRONICLES OF TANASTRA THUT – A FOREWORD

*I*f you are studying these chronicles, then two things are absolutely clear. Firstly, you must be a friend, not a foe, as I ensured that only a trusted minority could lift the encryption. Secondly, I must, alas, be dead!

Do not mourn me. I have died in the cause of progress and freedom and have been lucky enough to live to a ripe old age. It matters not if my death goes unmarked. Besides, I have already had a funeral. Yes, it may have been seventy years premature, but I am told it was a glorious and elaborate affair. A state funeral with pomp and ceremony, presided over by our great leader herself. Images were broadcast across the land, where a national day of grieving was declared. My relatively short life history was re-played to all along with numerous tributes to my lasting contribution to scientific advancements. Some even said I had been destined to serve as a senior leader alongside her greatness, but was – alas – taken away too soon. Coverage of my untimely death was relayed to a shocked, and I am told, tearful audience. I had no idea I was held in such high regard.

The destructive explosion that took out my laboratory at the government headquarters made for spectacular, if chilling, viewing. The blast had blown away my lab, my equipment and myself - sky high. Not an identifiable fragment left! I chuckle at the very thought of it. The key thing about being blown to bits is that it allowed me, and my research to escape undetected. I was finally free and there was no possibility of turning back. I remember I felt sick with both fear and excitement...

But I digress. This account is not about me; it is about the bravery of others who joined the cause on a much more dangerous basis. They did not have the advantage of being thought dead. They had to weave a complex web of secrecy and subversion in order to join me.

Whilst my exit was final and unsuspected, their service was perilous and they lived, and still live, in constant fear of discovery and reprisal. Some even paid the ultimate price. It is about this group of brave individuals that I wish to give testimony and make you aware of all the facts.

Goodness, there is so much to tell and it is difficult to know where to begin, but begin I must. The enemy closes in and you need to know what you are up against.

Examination

The moment, though measuring mere seconds, spoke volumes. His black edging, so dominant in the corridor was now hardly noticeable, a mere twinkling in his dark gazing eyes. Whilst still irradiating bold hues, Imogen could also discern a surprising combination of undulating oranges and soft yellows, mixing imagination with enquiry. As he stared, Imogen quickly looked away, shocked, and toned her riotous colours down to muted, pale and then neutral.

How long has he been staring?

With the last paper collected and the silence finally broken, Chrissie rushed over to her side.

"Are you alright Gen? You don't look so good? Do you feel sick? You must have done ok, you didn't stop writing." As Chrissie fussed, Imogen glanced to the chair at the back, which was now empty. There was no sign of her watcher.

"I'm fine Chrissie, honestly. Just need some air."

Where has he gone? Imogen felt deeply troubled as to why he should turn his attention to her. Had he breached her armour? Was she compromised? She would need to ask Grandad. As they retrieved their phones and made to leave the exam hall, she again felt a prickling awareness but this time, less intense.

"Watch out Gen. Reef alert!"

A plump suited woman with large heavily rimmed spectacles blocked the doorway of the hall, as her cold eyes stared at Imogen. She wore a large official badge: 'Mrs R Barrier: Head of Pastoral Care' and a simpering patronising smile. The 'R' actually stood for Regina, but Danny, one of their friends, had dubbed her 'The Reef', in honour of her formidable size and obstructive manner.

"Imogen, can I have a quick word dear?"

Imogen recognised her sparks of prying yellow and black spiky veins of assumed authority. The stout woman took a zealous interest in the personal lives of all of her students. The knowledge she acquired, confidential or otherwise, was shared readily with others and gave her a sense of supreme power. Imogen was a particularly intriguing subject as her home circumstances were so unusual. But, to date, the girl had not succumbed to her interrogative techniques. Determined to wear her down and thereby gain information, Regina Barrier frequently sought out Imogen for questioning, but was constantly frustrated with her lack of success.

It took all of Imogen's powers to project a bland and uninspired persona in order to deflect the woman's interest and resist her probing. Whilst she knew her colours could not be 'seen', she also knew that by altering them, she could project different characteristics, which could be detected by those around her.

"Of course, Mrs Barrier… See you later, Chrissie," she said as she was led to a small office. She prepared for the verbal onslaught by steadying all waves and presenting pastel blurs of compliance and disinterest. With her back to the glass-panelled door, Imogen was unaware that the gazing eyes from the exam hall were now staring in from a bench in the college atrium. From here Imogen's stooped shoulders and changed humble state were clearly visible.

Oblivious that she was being observed, her full focus and concentration were required to divert 'The Reef', now perched at the front of her desk looking over her glasses, from her latest mission.

"Imogen, we are still awaiting your birth certificate. We need it for the examination boards and without it you cannot be validated."

Imogen nodded, staring down at the floor.

Invalid. Faded brown.

"I have, not without some difficulty, managed to persuade the college to allow you to sit the mock examinations, but we shall need your birth certificate for the external papers. Now I do realise it's not your fault that the original is lost, but we really must have a replacement and I have to insist this is done immediately."

No response.

"Goodness, girl! You can't get by in life without a birth certificate, I mean, really! Your last school should have sorted this out and your mother should have..." Mrs Barrier then petered out.

Imogen lowered her head further.

Subdued – tinges of tawny sadness.

Mrs Barrier stuttered with an irritated tone, "I mean - that is - I didn't mean, er, look Imogen, goodness knows, I have been patient enough, but perhaps I had better contact the public records office myself. Yes, I suppose I will have to give up some of my free time, what precious little I have, to sort this out."

Beige.

"So," she continued, as she picked up and read from a typed sheet, "your entry form says you were born in Birmingham, June 1999 – I see your seventeenth birthday is coming up soon then?" she looked over the sheet at Imogen, who remained blank, before returning to the transcript.

"Then you moved here to the North-West... no date there... Mmm, all this should have been checked. Very sloppy work! Your mother, Elizabeth, only scant details here, name and unspecified medical incapacity, but nothing else. Dear oh dear..."

Mrs Barrier sighed and pushing the paper to one side, reached for Imogen's hand, as she said, with affected concern, "And your poor mother, how is she, my dear?"

Imogen squashed the automatic urge to pull her hand away, as Mrs Barrier's thoughts flooded, unwanted, through her fingertips. With her head still down, she whispered: "The same."

Pale beige.

She had to quell the urge to smile, as the Reef's thoughts revealed just how important she believed herself to be and how, in her eyes, Imogen was a pale pathetic figure, barely worthy of attention. It confirmed that her facade was working well.

"No change then? Poor woman! All those years in a coma, with no sign of recovery. What did you say caused the blackout?" The yellow-black prickled, wasp like, as the thoughts seized greedily on the hope of knowledge without a trace of empathy.

Quiet. Nearly imperceptible shrug. *Washed out.*

When the pause did not prompt a response, Mrs Barrier changed tack. "And how do you manage my dear? It really can't be easy without a mother to care for you."

Silence. *Translucent.*

Mrs Barrier leant forward, patting Imogen's hand with her own chunky fingers, so the thoughts strobed as their fingertips touched and, dropping her voice to a low conspiratorial tone, she added: "You know Imogen, it sounds a harsh thing, but it would probably be better for all concerned if the situation were, you know, terminated." The black spikes flared.

"Yes it would, of course, be very sad. But then it would give us all closure, all done and dusted. So much better for you; better for everyone." A flickering image from the woman flashed across Imogen's nervous system into her mind: Mrs Barrier presiding over weeping multitudes as a flower bedecked coffin was lowered into the ground, the mourners revering her eloquent and moving words. Imogen used all her powers not to react, as she pulled her hand away from the woman's grasp and back into her lap.

Mute. Anger can come later. Stay calm. Transparent.

Mrs Barrier sat back and with an overly concerned voice, utterly inconsistent with the frost in her eyes, concluded: "You do know, don't you, Imogen, that you can always talk to me. I have helped a vast number of students and have a great deal of experience and expertise. You can confide in me at any time…"

A faint nod, as Imogen projected only the palest, dreariest colours she could muster, and with which the woman finally lost interest.

"Such a dull, lifeless girl," she confidently announced later to another tutor, cornered in the staff room. "I suppose it's just as well; anyone with a modicum of personality could not possibly cope with such dire home circumstances. It's lucky the poor wretch can turn to me for help and support."

Freed from the office, Imogen sighed with relief and allowed a surge of purple rage to rise and fall, releasing her anger. *Terminated indeed!* At least the interviews were becoming less frequent. The drill was certainly paying off. As she headed hastily for the main door, a dark figure suddenly stepped out in front of her, nearly knocking her over and sending her bag thudding to the floor, its contents scattering.

"Oh sorry," said the rich voice, with a somewhat unfamiliar accent. "I didn't see you."

It's him!

Imogen, flustered to be in such close proximity to his muscular physique, hurriedly reverted to her calm, insignificant guise and said nothing. Head down, forcing her hand not to quiver, she bent to pick up her things only to find he had got there first and was already holding an escaped workbook, slowly scanning the cover. She noted with alarm that he was surrounded in an explosion of red, yellow and gold-edged black barbs, a sinister display of intrigue and power of a strength that she had not witnessed before. In another part of her mind she could not help acknowledge the vaguely hypnotic effect of his musky scent, teasing her nasal senses.

Calm – quash it! What is he up to?

Suppressing her anxiety, she looked away and held out her hand for the return of the book. Keeping her eyes to the ground, she used the drill to still her heart rate and subdue every outward reaction. Acutely aware of how close he was, she avoided his touch as he placed the book back in her hand and she quickly shoved it back in her bag, conscious that her neatly handwritten name was starkly exposed at the top corner. In silence, she continued to pick up her pens and other items.

"Nothing damaged, I hope," said the voice, now resonating above her and with a trace of mockery.

Imogen shook her head silently and, keeping it bowed, she closed her refilled bag, rose and headed for the door. When she had nearly got to the exit, she dared to glance back, but was baffled to see that there was no sign of him. She took a deep breath and was alarmed to note that a red sparkle like electricity shuddered through her body, as her stomach churned.

Chrissie, unaware of the encounter, bounded up, leading Imogen outside where she was unable to spot him amongst the crowds of moving students.

"You got away from the Reef then?"

Without responding, Imogen distractedly scanned the hoards of pupils filtering out into the sunshine.

"Gen? Come in, Gen! So, have you seen him again?"

"Who?"

"Don't give me that! I can see you looking out for him too. Katie says he was in the exam, but I didn't notice him. She said he was avoiding everyone. Oh and get this - Leanne tried to chat him up in the corridor and he just blanked her, mind you, Leanne's so blatant!"

"Chrissie, I'm not in the slightest bit interested."

"Ooh! So you're not interested I've found out his name? No, of course not..."

"Which you're going to tell me anyway!" smiled Imogen.

"Course I am! Apparently he's called Araz Vikram. Araz - never heard of it before. Dead exotic though, and those dark brown eyes… dreamy… Gen? You're really not interested, are you, Gen? Unbelievable! Come on then, let's grab lunch and then it's History revision – aren't we the lucky ones!"

"Look, Chrissie, will you cover for me? I need to get home. Just say I had a dental appointment."

"Sure, no worries, is everything ok? You seem a bit distracted…"

"Everything's fine. Got to go, don't worry about me. I'll see you tomorrow."

"Ok, well text me later."

Imogen set off, as if in the direction of home, but once out of sight of the college, she turned down a side road, checked no-one was following and put her colours to camouflage.

After a further detour to the edge of a wooded copse bordering on open wasteland, she concentrated on increasing her heart rate and blood flow to her leg muscles, as she took a deep breath and broke into a fast run. Racing down paths and walkways, dodging in and out of the trees to avoid any passers-by, her speed, which would be a match for any Olympic sprinter, went unnoticed, as she headed away from the town centre towards 'The Manor', the name 'Araz Vikram' and his deep voice saying: 'nothing damaged, I hope', buzzing in her head.

THE MANOR

*I*mogen arrived at 'The Manor' within fifteen minutes of leaving college, slowing to a walk and barely showing any signs of exertion as she approached the large rambling house. It had once been a row of four sizeable properties, now poorly linked together with mismatching materials, and bricked up doorways. In a dilapidated and neglected state, the building was covered in wild ivy and stringy climbing plants rendering many of the windows invisible and giving the impression that the entire place was being swallowed up by the advancing foliage.

She picked her way through the weedy pot-holed drive, rang the bell and waited outside the large double doors. The paint on the partially rotted door frame was blistered and peeling, affording a poor welcome to visitors and deterring most from enquiring on behalf of prospective residents.

After several minutes, a bulky breathless woman with short streaky dark hair, dressed in a grubby blue uniform and white plastic apron, eventually unlocked the door and with a fond crooked tooth smile, let her in, before routinely re-locking the entrance.

"Hiya, Im'gen. We don't often see you at this time?"

"Hi, Lisa. Just thought I'd pop in and see Grandad. How is he?" Imogen could see from Lisa's heaving chest and gently throbbing rustic brown colours, threaded with safe silver that she was bustling around in a busy but happy manner.

"Oh, you know yer Grandad, dear old Harry. Lord knows what 'e's on about, full of daft ideas and fancies, but 'e's a proper gentleman, bless him, and 'e's one of my favourites, not a bit of trouble."

"Show yerself up. Gotta get on, just clearing up after lunch," she called, as she waddled off down the corridor.

Imogen climbed the stairs and passed the upper lounge. Although the first floor residents were not as disabled as those downstairs, most were seated around the room in shabby chairs, heads either lolling to one side with their mouths wide open, or slumped on their chests; all fast asleep, unaware of the television blaring out mindless noise from the corner of the room and a cleaner slowly vacuuming the threadbare carpet around them.

Grandad's room was at the end of the corridor, beyond Margaret's room. Margaret always called as she passed and today was no different. A frail little old lady, infused with sad sepia tones, she was propped up in her wheelchair near the doorway, twisting the edge of her shawl repetitively with her small thin hands. Imogen felt a strong connection with her, as if she had known her for far more years than the five that had elapsed since Grandad moved into the home. When she saw Imogen, her crumpled old face erupted into a bright beaming smile, which hinted at what must have once been an attractive visage, now masked by infirmity and deep wrinkles.

"Iris, it's good to see you," she croaked. "Have you come to take me home?"

"Not today, Margaret," smiled Imogen, as she always did. "Maybe tomorrow…"

It was obvious from her faded blurred colours that swirls of confusion clouded Margaret's comprehension and Imogen knew intuitively that she would be greatly alarmed, rather than enlightened, if she ever attempted to explain that she was not Iris. It was kinder to comply with the old lady's view of the world and not cause unnecessary agitation.

Margaret's response would usually have been: "That's fine, I think I'll wait until tomorrow," but this time her face abruptly changed, taking on a troubled and frightened look, as she motioned urgently for Imogen to come closer. Imogen, puzzled, tentatively approached the wheelchair when Margaret's hand shot out and grabbed her arm, as soon as she was within reach.

Margaret's frail bony fingers tightened with surprising strength on Imogen's arm and her sharp, yellowed nails bit into her skin. Imogen winced with the stab of pain, but Margaret, unaware of inflicting this, pulled Imogen closer and her eyes bored into hers with a desperate plea.

"They're coming," she croaked, "they've seen you and they're coming. Iris, you must escape," she hissed at Imogen. "You must flee!"

Imogen had never seen Margaret so alert and animated. Vivid surges of blood-red fear rushed around her wizened frame. Imogen placed a reassuring hand on her thin little shoulder, giving it a comforting squeeze.

"It's okay Margaret, it's okay," she soothed, and Margaret's eyes suddenly glazed over. Her colours diminished and she released her grasp, dropped her head and resumed her slumped stance, again fumbling with her shawl.

Imogen looked down at her arm. Four nail-shaped semi-circles of blood rose, congealed and closed as she watched. The pain subsided and the small wounds scabbed and shrank. She gently rubbed the area, as Margaret's words sank deep into the troubled areas of her mind. *They're coming.*

"I'm not feeling so good today," Margaret said in a subdued voice. "I think I'll wait until tomorrow to go home, if you don't mind, Iris."

Imogen, disconcerted by the encounter, nodded as she backed out of the room. She noticed, with sadness, that Margaret's washed out colours had dramatically dulled and gained an ominous blurred edging.

"Thank you for visiting, do come again."

"Will do, Margaret," said Imogen, as she stepped past the door to her grandfather's room. Her arm now temporarily showed purple bruises in the shape of Margaret's fingers, which turned brown, faded and disappeared as she watched. She had no idea why she naturally healed so quickly, another aspect of her life that she had to hide but was very grateful not to have to carry the scars.

Imogen gave a quiet knock on her Grandad's door and entered. A tall, thin, grey-haired man stood by the window. The room was heaped with books, newspapers, files and folders in a haphazard fashion on every surface, including the floor. Harold Reiner was staring up at the sky, lost in his thoughts. To the staff at 'The Manor', he was an old frail befuddled gentleman, quite submerged in his own world and prone to flights of fancy. They thought this to be the result of Alzheimer's, but Imogen knew that his cloak of confusion was a deliberate ploy to divert the attention of others. She could see the pure white layers that spoke of his truth and honesty and the deep blue veins of logic and reason were, to her, crystal clear.

Sensing Imogen was there, Harold turned to greet her with a glowing surge of palpable affection.

"Imogen, what brings you here in the middle of a college day?" He did not need to wait for a response, to realise Imogen was sparking yellow-mauve shades of worry.

"What's happened?"

As she recounted the events of the morning, starting with her recurring nightmare, the encounter with Araz and then Margaret's ominous warning, Harold watched Imogen's swirling colours, noting all the subtle changes with each description and new emotion. When she had finished, he was quiet for some time, and then escorting her to the bed, he pushed aside a pile of papers and sat her down next to him, placing a protective arm around her shoulders.

"Margaret is not in her right mind, she is declining very quickly," he said sadly. Shadowed only momentarily in shades of sombre lavender grey, Harold's colours brightened to bold blues, greens and whites as he passed Imogen a plate of sandwiches, untouched by him.

"Here, eat, these. They shouldn't go to waste," he said kindly. As Imogen began eating in a distracted way, he turned his attention to her other concerns.

"This stranger, edged with gold, I am concerned, but not overly so. I think it is highly unlikely that we have been discovered. I have covered every track and he would have to have been incredibly lucky to find you. And you know what I say about luck…"

Imogen immediately chimed in, as he repeated his old adage: "There's no such thing as luck, you make your own luck in this world!"

"It's true," continued her Grandad. "And, Imogen, you are exceptionally gifted and extremely good at concealing your true identity."

Imogen swallowed a mouthful of sandwich and bit her lip. This was her grandfather's mantra and she was unable to demand what he meant by 'her true identity', as he always diverted enquiry with phrases such as 'not now' and 'all in good time'. She trusted him, above and beyond any other person in the world. He was her guardian, her teacher, her protector, but she had so many questions and was tired of getting no answers.

"Besides," he said, as he nodded towards the mirror on the dressing table opposite the bed, "you're a very beautiful young lady and it may just be, that this, what's he called? Araz?"

"Araz Vikram."

"Well, this Mr Vikram may just have taken a shine to you."

Imogen looked at herself sitting next to her Grandad in the mirror. No colours here, just a clear picture of what must be the norm for everyone else in life. She regarded her reflection: a rounded smooth face with clear complexion and gentle nose, shoulder-length auburn hair untidily scraped back behind the ears, soft full lips and sharp blue-green eyes looked back at her.

"You look just like your mother!" he added, with a hint of sadness.

Imogen gave a weak smile. The tenderness in her grandfather's words and his surge of deep red shades of affection, told her he missed her mum almost as much as she did. Stuck in the edge of the mirror was an old grainy black and white photograph of her mum as a small girl, wearing a white dress with a circle of flowers over a light veil on her head. She was giving a shy smile to the camera. As Imogen's thoughts turned to her mother, she took the phone out of her pocket, ran her finger round the edge, which caused it to reduce to a flexible thin sheet and briefly flicked an edge, so the entire area became a screen which displayed her mother's bedroom at home. Annie was reading aloud from the bedside chair, the monitors all registered calm with no change. As she gazed at the scene, she remembered to tell her Grandad the most important news she had.

"Mum's colours, they seem to be sharpening. It happened the other day, when I was talking about you. Then this morning, I'm sure she sensed my alarm at the nightmare, but I could be mistaken..."

"Imogen, trust your instincts. You will rarely be mistaken. You are a uniquely talented young lady. You are on the same chromatic plane as your mother and I am sure there is a connection between her imminent awakening and your vivid dreams. She will revive, and soon, take my word for it, and we must make ready for that day." He took the device and looked pensively at the image on the screen. His colours burnished red with flickers of white gold, an intensity of love apparent.

Imogen rose, put the empty plate on the dressing table and walked sadly to the window. Her grandfather had spoken of this so frequently that she could hardly bear to listen, as he spoke with fervour about the day her mother's 'temporary state' would come to an end and everything would be alright again. At first, she had been comforted and reassured, but after years of watching her mother's sleeping form and the lack of any change, she found it difficult to share her grandfather's faith.

Sensing her despair, Harold joined her at the window and in soothing tones said, "You too were ill; you recovered; you came back."

Imogen subdued the urge to say irritably, 'But I was not ill for ten years', and instead decided to question him further about her childhood infirmity.

"What was wrong with me, Grandad? You have never told me."

To her surprise, he did not give the usual stock answers that deflected from the question, but instead asked her, "Tell me what you remember, right up until the time of your illness? Use the drill – go back."

Imogen had not done this for some years, but nodded agreement, sat back down, cleared her thoughts and then concentrated, delving back into the depths of her mind to recall her infancy. Images formed in multi layers: sounds; smells; pictures and colours.

She described to him sections of what she saw: her mother laughing and swinging her tiny baby form in her arms; feeding her in a high chair; singing her a lullaby. A faint image of her father reading her a bedtime story; kneeling with open arms as she took her first steps; rocking her to sleep. Her small hand pressed against her mother's fingers, overwhelming her inner being as her mum transmitted waves of saturating love. Happy memories flooded her mind and she felt her heart yearn for a lost age; the security of being surrounded by a loving family, her mother awake and well.

Then her focus turned to her first day at school. The shabby collection of soot-blackened buildings sat in an area of derelict and half demolished houses. Rows of grimy terraced properties adjacent to large rubble piles covered in wild poppies and weeds bordered the school. Unkempt babies cried in their prams, as their brothers and sister kicked tin cans around the road.

She recalled the horror of witnessing desperate poverty around her, which forced children to wear the same dirty clothes, day in and day out, and the sight of one or two of them with no shoes on their blackened filthy feet. She saw her five-year-old self, playing a game of Oranges and Lemons: touching the grubby fingertips of a feral looking girl, Oonagh McKiernan, as they made an archway. She had instantly 'seen' Oonagh surreptitiously taking money from the teacher's purse, in an empty classroom that morning, and, in her innocence had reported this aloud when the head teacher had addressed the whole class. An image of the disbelief turning to hatred on Oonagh's face was rooted deep in her mind, along with the shock at the girl's public punishment: five strikes of the cane to her open hands, each blow forcing tears in shiny clear channels, as they poured down Oonagh's dirt-engrained cheeks.

From that time on, Imogen had worn gloves at school to prevent her 'seeing' more than she should. Her fellow pupils, already jealous of her lively mind, clean clothes, brushed hair and bright smile, merely added this to their growing list of her abnormalities. As she assembled the images in her mind, Imogen recalled the anger and suspicion she had prompted when it was clear she already knew how to read and write. On one occasion, she had corrected Miss Green's maths example, pointing out the error on the blackboard, for which she got sent out of the room, her accuracy clearly unwelcome. Gradually she had stopped raising her hand to answer questions and slowed down in the games lessons, deliberately missing catches of the ball, as the unwanted attention from the teachers when she excelled was nearly as bad as the distrust it provoked from the rest of the class.

Imogen's mind then paused on a day embedded in her memory. This was the day she had realised, without doubt, that her peers could not see the Chroma she saw; that they were colour blind. She had declared that the school bully was a liar; the violet smudges of his boasting being so glaringly obvious. Sure her classmates could see this too, she had just gawped at their obvious incomprehension as it dawned on her that she was the only one able to 'see' the falsehoods. As the bully pushed her to the playground floor, the others ganged up on her too, united by their ignorance and a fear of her strangeness. As they encircled her, they prodded, poked and kicked her, charged with red-black sparks of spite and hatred, and chanting: 'She's not a fighter – she's a dirty little blighter!' Again and again, louder and louder. A tear came to her eye with the recollection. The rhyme, unlike her bruised arms and grazed knees, which healed almost instantly, still hurt even though she didn't know what it meant.

Then she recalled her mother's consoling hug and insistence that she kept the colours 'hush hush' and told no-one. It was not difficult to comply with this, the start of a lifetime of secrecy. But the taunts and bullying continued and remained a scar on her memory until she hit 'the fog'. This was the point where there was a blank – no images – no recollections – nothing. She had not focussed on this for a while. She looked up at her grandfather.

"Go on, what can you recall after the fog."

"Crying, I heard crying." The sound surfaced harshly in her mind. "It was mum, wasn't it?" His sad nod confirmed her deduction, as she forced the hazy pictures into sharper focus. "She was also shouting, screaming my name and then..." Imogen swallowed hard. "Then she was quiet – asleep – gone."

"Tell me about you," Harold asked kindly.

Imogen, glad to turn away from the distressing start of her mother's incarceration, concentrated on her other recollections.

"I was in a different house, in a new bedroom, with my very own television; it had colours," she smiled at the childish recollection of this detail, "and there was no more school, not for a long time. No more bullying. Mum was asleep and couldn't look after me. There was an older lady, I called her auntie." Imogen's memory homed in on the pleasant smiling face and for the first time it dawned on her who she was. "Margaret! Margaret was auntie!"

Harold smiled and nodded in accord.

Imogen added, "She wasn't mum, but she was kind and she looked after me for a while." Imogen recalled her sudden departure: there one day, absent the next. "She couldn't stay. She... she got ill." A younger vibrant face stood, side by side, in her mind, next to Margaret's now aged face, her main features now almost completely hidden by wrinkles and years of wasting. "She's aged so much Grandad."

"She suffered a terrible loss, my dear. Tragedy unhinged her and she has been ailing ever since. Now keep concentrating," he said.

Imogen filed this new information away as she tried to bring to mind what else she remembered.

"Let me see… Dad. He was, was no longer there…" She felt a deep sense of yearning, but nowhere near as strong as her need for her mother. It somehow felt wrong to voice this feeling, so she just continued: "…and everything seemed new. My whole world was changed and altered. Then I remember you. You nursing me, making me well. You teaching me, showing me the drill; coaching me, reassuring me." Imogen looked into her grandfather's eyes as a tear escaped hers. "Grandad, what happened?"

"You were very ill, my dear, and we moved to a new place so you could recuperate. It took a few months, but your memory was affected and it is possible you blocked out what happened, as a psychological defence mechanism." He shook his head sadly. "None of this was ever meant to happen. It all went wrong. Oh Imogen, if only I could turn back time…"

Grandad's favourite saying would not put her off her questioning; not now she was finally getting some answers.

"So, Grandad, what did happen?"

Harold Reiner paused before saying, "You and your mother, how shall I put it? You were involved in the same incident, but you were younger and recovered quickly. Your mother needed more time, but she will recover, Imogen, just as you did."

This was more information than her grandfather had ever given to her and before she could ask 'what incident?' the shutters came down in his eyes, as he turned the conversation to other matters and she knew the moment had gone.

"Now, we need to stay practical and focussed. I want you to take extra care with this Araz person. Analyse his mood, his character, his intent. From a distance, if you can. Keep to the drills. Ensure you conceal your Multi-Com," he said pointing to her phone, "and only use it from here or at home, we cannot risk it being intercepted. In the meantime, the next part of your training is to commence and for this you will need a new instructor. There are some things I cannot teach you."

Before Imogen could ask who or why, Harold continued: "The training will be very intense and will need to make use of every spare moment you have. Because of this, your new mentor will be moving into the house." Imogen went to protest, she hated sharing the house with strangers and had had to put up a huge fight to get her grandfather to agree to removing the overnight carers last year, when she had reached sixteen, but Harold put a hand up to quieten her, saying, "It's just temporary and anyway, I think you'll like him."

"Him?" Imogen responded in dismay.

"His name's Leonard and I trust him."

"Well, who is he?"

"He's only just moved back to the area, but Imogen, I know him from long ago and I trust him with my life. It is my wish that he stays in the house to train you. He will also protect you and your mother. Besides, he may be able to answer some of your many questions."

"I don't suppose I have a choice in this? When does he arrive?"

"Today!"

Imogen allowed herself an annoyed, "Grandad!" before he reverted to the inevitable phrases: "Trust me," and: "It will become clear - all in good time."

Imogen sighed.

As she set off for home, she realised she had gained no answers and yet more riddles, and with an unwanted tutor to be installed at her house, she would lose the peace and quiet of her only sanctuary.

As soon as she had gone, Harold Reiner sent an urgent message using his device.

ARAZ

*B*ack at the college, Araz had waited for his moment outside the main office. He hid in the shadows until the last of the office workers, a Mrs Harris, left the room and rummaged in her handbag for the key to lock the door.

Having watched her for the past week, he knew she was always the last to leave. In fact, he knew a lot more about the secretive Mrs Harris than she would ever realise. He could not always read Chroma, the whole concept was new to him and he was still learning, but her dancing purples and flickering reds were an obvious clue to the combustible state of her emotions. His observations had confirmed that she paid meticulous attention to her appearance before she locked up and that she always checked no-one was watching, as she then headed towards the Science block, rather than the college exit. It had not taken long to discover the focus of her attention was the smarmy head of Physics, with whom she had embarked on a passionate affair. Discovering her sordid liaison was as easy as child's play to Araz, as was intercepting her mobile messages and listening to her inane conversations; he could track anything he liked.

Mrs Harris would have been shocked to know the Physics master had already had numerous extra-marital affairs but that was utterly unimportant to Araz; she was merely a means to an end. Araz quietly pressed the send button on his handset and her phone gave a short beep from within her bag. Flustered, she abandoned the key search and groped for her phone. The text read: Come quickly. We need to talk.' Instantly worried that the cryptic message from a withheld number was the presage of the discovery of her guilty secret, she rushed to the Science block, forgetting all about locking the door.

Araz sniggered to himself, as he let himself into the office and started up the main computer. These people are so pathetic, he thought, as he waited impatiently for the antiquated device to boot up - all so transparent and stupid. He was tired of them, tired of his fruitless search and his lack of success. Months and months of travel, searching so many different towns, so many schools and colleges, so many dull uninteresting people.

But today - for the first time - something new. The girl was so distinct and appeared to be able to exercise real self-control. And to think he may not have noticed her, had he not sat behind her in the exam hall. Was that what these people called 'luck'? He had looked around, bored, to catch her swirl of vivid colours. They had been magical, mesmerizing. Then she had detected his scrutiny and had been able to transform, instantly, and again in the pastoral office. Fascinating. Could she be the one? The prize would be great if he had found her, but he would have to be sure. A few of these people were unpredictable and could demonstrate surprisingly sophisticated traits. He had learnt from previous disappointments that first impressions did not necessarily mean success.

He had tried to follow her, but could not believe how quickly she managed to disappear outside college, or that there was no type of device visible in either the bag he had knocked out of her hands, or on her person. He found this strange, as he was fairly sure she had placed a phone in the box at the start of the exam and now he was frustrated he was unable to track her. Well, he told himself, she's a good-looking specimen, even if she tries to hide it, and what if she is nothing more than a gifted native? I could still have some fun with you, Imogen Reiner, he mused, as he summoned the photographic image of her handwritten name to mind. After all, I deserve a break.

Within seconds of the computer finally kicking into action, Araz had overridden the security screens, found his scant college records that he had placed there just the week before, and falsified a number of details to make them look genuine: previous addresses, past exam results, school reports. He ticked the 'verification' sections, which would ensure he was now considered a full member of Forrester College, who did not need further corroboration. He would be able to remove these at a later date, without a trace, when he was done. He then brought up every piece of information held on Imogen Reiner and transferred it to his device. It did not seem much, compared to other students. Annoyingly, it did not even have what subjects she was studying. He noted she had changed school several times and had not gone to a local primary school. However, he would study the details when back at base, as he needed to shut down and leave without being seen.

It had been a good day's work. He felt a renewed sense of purpose and had gained an invigoration he could not explain, as he kept to the shadows of the empty corridors and slipped away unseen.

Returning to the small bedsit he rented in a large multi-occupancy apartment block, Araz was careful to avoid any contact with the other residents. They were unaware they even had a new neighbour.

He uncovered a miniature tablet-shaped appliance that jumped into life at his touch and then loaded up Imogen's scant records, which he perused with interest. Her birth date made her just under seventeen years of age. Her current address and previous exam results were listed; bright girl, he noted, she seemed to excel in everything. There were only two other pieces of information: Imogen's mother was classified as disabled, disability not given, and all correspondence was to be sent to a secure address 'for the attention of Mr H Reiner', listed as her Legal Guardian. A quick scan for the meaning of 'post office box' set him thinking. Interesting, he pondered. Why the confidential address? Well, at least he knew where she lived, which was as good a start as any.

A message suddenly flashed up, bringing him to alert immediately. It was coded double red and written in his native tongue. After reading its contents, Araz smiled to himself. The enemy was getting careless. An unofficial communicator had been detected in the vicinity. The transmission could not be pinpointed precisely, probably had a deflector fitted to it, and whilst it was brief and undecipherable, it proved he was right to have concentrated his search in this area.

Araz gave a wry smile. The task had seemed impossible at first, like searching for a needle in a haystack. But he had studied the previous sightings and the scattering of reports made over the years, and used predicative methods of analysis. Basically, he had put himself in the shoes of those he pursued and had second-guessed their movements, meticulously combing all possible locations. A combination of information, logic and intuition had led him to the current area and he was delighted that he may yet be proved right.

Now to go and locate the target, he thought. Address committed to memory, he quietly left the premises, went a few blocks to a small lock up garage, under a little-used section of the viaduct, and got out his motorbike before setting off.

LEONARD

*W*hen Imogen arrived home, a small rusty red hatchback car was parked opposite the house. The driver, a young man with a mop of curly fair hair, appeared to be asleep at the wheel, but as soon as she stepped onto the front path of her house, he leapt into life and flung open the car door. A passing van swerved and honked angrily at the near collision and he gave an apologetic shrug, as the driver shouted an obscenity, made a rude gesture through the open window and drove off. The young man, dressed in jeans and t-shirt, slammed his car door shut with such force that the wing mirror, which had been held on with masking tape, dropped down. He clumsily tried to press the mirror back, but with no success and eventually shrugged his shoulders and left it dangling at the side of the car, as he crossed to Imogen with a huge smile on his face.

A glow of orange, yellow and white engulfed the wide smile and Imogen, having neutralised her own colours, could not avoid responding with a grin as he exclaimed, "Whoops! Nearly lost the door!"

"Lucky the other car saw you," she said, terminating contact and turning to the house. But instead of walking away, as she had expected, he followed her up the path. Immediately on her guard, she turned to face him.

"Now, didn't Harry tell you about that thing called luck and how you make your own..." he began, as it dawned on Imogen who he was.

"You're... you're Leonard?" she asked incredulously, scanning him up and down.

"Leonard Newall at your service," he said with a nod of his head. "Well, there's no need to look so shocked," he beamed, clear blue eyes sparkling amusement.

"It's just that Grandad, I mean Harry, said he had known you for years so I was sort of expecting someone, well, someone a bit older?"

"So, you thought I'd be at least eighty?" he teased. "Yes, Harry is full of surprises! So, you're the famous Imogen! Harry's told me so much about you that I feel like I know you already." He stared straight into her eyes, his full of fascination and wonder.

Imogen felt awkward, he could only be a year or two older than her. *What was Grandad thinking!*

"Hardly famous," she said in irritation and hurriedly turned away from his admiring gaze, unlocking the front door. She reluctantly indicated for Leonard to follow her in and he gave a surprised whistle, as he entered the hallway.

"This place hasn't changed at all."

"You mean you've been here before? When was that?" she asked suspiciously.

"Er… good few years back now," he said quickly as he spotted the carer descending the stairs and leapt past Imogen to greet her. He didn't notice the hall rug, ruckled on the floor and tripped theatrically, landing on his knees at the bottom of the stairs with his hands outstretched to save himself. Rendered in a bowed posture as if paying homage to the surprised person whose feet were under his nose, he looked up at Annie and raised his arms high, then low, up and down, saying, "Greetings, oh mighty one!"

Imogen stifled a laugh, as he then got to his feet and offered a hand to the lady on the stairs.

"Whoops! Hi! I'm Leonard. I'm the new member of the team. And I nearly fell for you there!"

Annie didn't bat an eyelid, although a small smile played on her lips, as she shook his hand serenely, nodded and proceeded to the kitchen, showing him into the living room.

Imogen was taken aback at Annie's complete acceptance of this new person. All the carers were trained to grill any stranger and prevent admittance to the house. It was as if she had known Leonard was coming. Although, on reflection, Imogen should have known who had told her. *Grandad!* With a sigh, she closed the front door and followed them into the living area, throwing her college bag on the settee, as Annie made them a drink.

Imogen was not ready to let her guard down and she slipped upstairs to check on her mother, whilst Leonard tucked into a packet of biscuits with his tea.

Annie left after being relieved by Cath, the late afternoon and evening carer, who commenced the daily physiotherapy exercises up in the bedroom. Reassured by her mother's calm aura, Imogen took a deep breath and descended the stairs to find out more about her unwanted guest.

He was sprawled across the settee, quite at home and having eaten a banana from the fruit bowl, the skin abandoned on the table next to the empty biscuit packet, he had started noisily munching on an apple. Bitten apple held in one hand, he was thumbing through the paintings in her artwork folder with the other. Many of the pages were now spread across the floor and chairs.

What the hell!

Without speaking, she gathered all the sheets together; took the last from his hands, brushing a stray piece of apple off the corner, placed them all in the folder and snapped it shut, finally sitting down with her hands firmly on top of it on her lap.

Stay calm – use the drill.

"I was only looking," he said apologetically, as she looked at him steely-eyed. "You have quite a talent there." His praise was genuine, she noted, from his sapphire glints.

Sadiki chose that moment to enter the room and, to Imogen's amazement, Leonard clicked his fingers and the cat leapt into his lap and began to nuzzle into his hand and chest.

He's never done that to me.

Leonard's colours flushed a deep russet recognition, as he tickled him under the ears and chin and, looking up, slightly sheepishly said: "Nice cat… Er… what's he called?"

"Sadiki," she replied, thinking with annoyance that the creature would have taken her hand off if she'd attempted to touch it in the same way.

How did he know the cat was male? And just look at its rapturous expression – not a hint of wildness or dejection.

Forcing herself to ignore the traitorous feline as it purred furiously whilst being pampered, Imogen calmly began, "So Leonard…"

"Please, call me Leo. Leonard sounds so formal. Mind, I promise not to call you Imo, unless you want me to," he said, taking a last mouthful of apple and tossing the core onto the table, as he continued to pet Sadiki.

Ignoring the twinkle of his colours, as he attempted humour, Imogen gave him a stern stare and deepened her serious blue hues, as she asked him to give an account of himself.

"Well, I came to this area when I was, er… About eight or nine years old and Harry, was, well, like a father to me."

Imogen noted, with satisfaction, that his aura not only demonstrated a white honesty, but also surged with a warm glow at the memory.

He continued, "Then I, well, moved for a while…" He rubbed behind his ear with a finger, in an absentminded way, and she could see he was concealing something here; a violet tinge had been briefly visible.

"And here I am, back and ready to give you some advanced training. Love the grave blues by the way."

Imogen maintained her composure and internally added a clear spark of bright yellow curiosity to test the effect.

"Whoa! Should have known I said the wrong thing. Now I have prompted a beautiful yellow flash of inquisition! 'Nobody expects the Spanish Inquisition'!"

"What?"

"The 'Spanish Inquisition'? Monty Python! Priceless! I studied it as part of my training. Love classic comedy… but never mind that. Look, Imogen, I can see that whilst you want to probe, you're also just checking if I can read *Chroma* too?"

Imogen was dumbfounded and nodded, unsure how to react. The only person she knew who shared her ability was her Grandad and she was bewildered to find herself exposed in this way. "And can you?" she managed to murmur.

"Well I have some ability, but nothing like you. You know how to shield your true colours; how to project artificial ones and I can't see the subtleties you can see. According to Harry, you're a true expert."

"Look, I am at a real disadvantage here," Imogen said in frustration. "You seem to know a great deal about me and I know nothing about you." She felt exposed and defenceless and was determined she would get some answers. "Why are you here? What sort of instruction are you supposed to be doing with me? And who in hell studies comedy as part of their training? Not any training I've heard of!"

Before Leo could say a word, she exclaimed, "And anyway, if you are a long-time friend of my grandfather, how do you explain why I have never heard of you until now?"

"Whoa! That is one huge heap of questions!" Leo responded good-humouredly, as he sat upright, Sadiki moving off his lap and settling down on the seat next to him. "Look, I can see that this is a bit weird for you, but the truth is..." he paused.

"Yes? The truth is..." prompted Imogen.

"The truth is… complicated, but Harry has told me that it can only be revealed in a strict order and I promised I would honour his wishes. Tell you what, why don't I get my stuff, I'll take the front room down here, and then I'll rustle us up something to eat. You carry on and go and tend to your mum like you usually do."

Imogen looked quizzical, as she started to say: "How do you know what I usually…" before petering out, as they both said in unison: "Grandad!" and "Harry."

With a sigh, Imogen agreed to defer further conversation and gladly escaped to the security of her mother's bedroom, where she helped Cath to manoeuvre her mother's limbs and flex all her muscles in preparation for the body therapy. Between them, they raised the sleeping form in a barely visible hoist to her feet and placed her in a special device, a light meshwork exoskeleton, that when unfolded, encompassed her body like a transparent glove with no visible means of support. This held her upright and 'walked her', exercising her legs and arms and stimulating her nerve endings as she slept. Imogen loved watching the process and if it were not for her closed eyes, her mother looked every bit awake and alive.

Imogen knew there was nothing like this in the hospitals, but then all the carers demonstrated a complete acceptance of the superior apparatus and never asked questions. As she watched her change the bed, Imogen observed Cath's gentle colours: orangey browns and greens threaded with the usual silver filaments. Not for the first time, she wondered why she and the other carers showed no sign of curiosity at the advanced equipment being used. She did not know how it was accomplished, but she did know that this, like everything, was down to her grandfather. Her thoughts turned to the 'new member of the team' downstairs and she shook her head, as she realised that there was something she had missed, something that definitely did not add up.

With the session complete, and her mother back in bed, Imogen sent Cath for a break and relayed the day's events to her mum.

"So, mum, who is this Leonard Newall?" she whispered as she gently brushed through her mother's silky hair. "Have you heard of him?" She searched the corona of dreamlike colours, but there was no perceptible change to indicate recognition.

"You see, what worries me mum, is that there's no silver fibre, not a trace, and yet Grandad says to trust him. I mean, I do trust Grandad, but he is getting older and what if he's made a mistake? Oh, I don't know. I just don't feel comfortable about him being here; something isn't right." Scanning intensely, Imogen was sure there had been a small pulse of grey on the fringe, as there had been earlier in the day, and this resolved her to remain on her guard until she could find out more about this 'Leo'.

Imogen arrived in the living room, as the kitchen door opened and Leo emerged, amidst billows of smoke, bearing two plates of congealed baked beans on blackened toast, an acrid smell of burning filled the room.

"So, this cooking lark, it's not that difficult," he announced, as he placed the offerings on the table. Seeing the repugnance on Imogen's face, he added, "Sorry it's a bit burnt. Okay – more like cremated! Guess I won't make 'Masterchef' for a while!"

Imogen sat opposite him. "Er, you go ahead," she indicated, "I'm not that hungry."

Leo slid the contents of one plate onto the other and proceeded to tuck energetically into the mound, not seeming to notice it was carbonised. Between mouthfuls, he answered Imogen's questions. "How old am I? If I told you I was younger than you, would you believe me?"

"No! For starters you drive a car, and then you look at least eighteen."

"Fair point! Well I will, apparently, be nineteen in October."

Imogen could see blotches of violet in his Chroma. This was not the truth. "What do you mean, apparently?"

"Look Imogen, I know I can't lie to you. I grew up without knowing my birth date; there was no-one around to celebrate my birthdays…"

Imogen saw both the blue-white truth of his statement and a small spark of red anger, combined with navy-blue hurt, which flared and faded almost instantaneously.

Leo continued: "Such things were not considered to be important. After all, the number of years you have been in existence does not, in itself, mean a thing. It is what you have been doing in those years that age you."

"You're not making sense."

"It's just that there's no conclusive way of telling a person's true age. I mean… well look at your mother. She's been unconscious for nearly ten years, but has not aged at all in that time."

Imogen was about to object, but into her mind there flashed an array of photographic images of her mother – layer upon layer - over the years. She realised with a start that her mother's face had altered subtly during her infancy, had aged a fair amount when she awoke after the fog, but had not changed at all since being in the coma. No wrinkles, no more fine lines. She looked exactly the same as she had ten years before.

"That's… not normal is it?" she whispered, unable to quell the grey trepidation rising inside.

"No, not what most people would call 'normal'," he said with a reassuring tone. Pushing the now empty plate to one side, he flicked the blonde fringe of his curly hair to one side; crossed his arms on the table and leaned forward on them, looking her straight in the eye.

"But you have surely realised that a lot of your life is 'not normal'?"

It was true. She had lived under a cloak of secrecy all of her life. Bound by rules and drills; hiding all the adaptations and technology her grandfather had introduced; guarding her every move and word; veiling her chromatic skills; hiding her ability to receive thoughts by touch; concealing an identity even she did not understand.

She returned Leo's stare, watchful for any variations in his colours and quietly asked: "Why hasn't my mother aged?"

"Well, putting it simply," he responded eagerly, "she is in something like a state of suspended animation, an induced state of unconsciousness. But this will allow a full recovery from the trauma she suffered."

"Induced? You mean she's deliberately being kept asleep?" Imogen reeled. *Why did I take it for granted that mum was ill and in a coma?*

"It's not as straightforward as that," Leo responded with a small flash of copper indignation. "Her treatment is one of the most sophisticated processes in existence. It took Harry years to refine it. His knowledge and skills are un-believable." A deep emerald green surge of awe and pride accompanied this assertion. "The system is the most amazing synthesis of biology, medicine and technology developed just for her. It is completely attuned to her DNA and has been constantly repairing and renewing her cells, which were severely damaged. She will only regain consciousness when she has completely healed and the process has come full circle."

Imogen knew instantly this was the truth. Leo's colours said it, Grandad's remarkable technical prowess, which had produced the complex equipment upstairs, said it and, most importantly, her heart said it. She felt a surge of op-timism she had not felt for years and a new sense of certainty and anticipation of her mother's recovery.

"She **is** going to wake," she said softly to herself as she looked up to the ceiling and seemingly to the room above. "It's true!" Imogen's eyes glistened, as she embraced this newfound security and, for a brief moment, allowed the longing in her heart to pulse through her entire body.

Leo, resting his head against one hand, quietly took the opportunity to surreptitiously take a photograph with a microscopic camera in his watch, as he looked on, witnessing the striking chromatic change in Imogen. Her intense love for her mother blazed and sparkled in multiple hues and shades. It made her more beautiful and alluring. A storm of mixed emotions, including a strong magnetic pull towards her, threatened to overwhelm him. Flustered, he quickly stood and took the plates out to the kitchen, so she could not detect his response and he could calm himself.

Calling from the other room, he said "Imogen, I have to go out, so we'll continue tomorrow after college, okay? Harry gave me a key, so I can let myself in. See you tomorrow."

Imogen, unable to repress her feelings, did not question the abrupt end to their conversation and was just relieved she was to be left alone to take stock of it all.

"Okay, see you tomorrow," she called as she went back upstairs, a fresh buoyancy in her steps.

Leo left soon after and would not slip back into the house until the afternoon of the next day.

On the other side of town, Araz had arrived in the fading light of dusk, at a building site in the middle of an industrial estate. Dismounting his motorbike and removing his helmet, he stood in the rubble of the unmade street, looking all around. He instinctively took a step back, as a guard dog started barking angrily at him from within a wire perimeter fence. Not a residential building in sight. A false address, a clumsy mistake, he chuckled. This meant it was even more likely that his instincts were right. He would have to employ other methods to discover her whereabouts. He rubbed his hands together, as he conjured up the clear eyes, soft skin, full lips and entrancing colours of his trophy before driving off.

TWENTY YEARS EARLIER

The church was cold and dark. It had been locked for the night. A figure stepped out of his hiding place and, after checking he was completely alone, he swiftly walked to the end of the aisle, and sat in the front pew, waiting. A small round object delicately covered in facets of opal and shell-like mother of pearl was cupped in his hand and he anxiously held it up in the gloom to see the ever changing colours brighten as they heralded the imminent activation of the marker.

His mind swirled with fear and worry, and to calm himself he briefly closed his eyes and focussed on her face and the day they had first met. He had been barely twenty years old and she was just eighteen. It was fixed in his memory how the room had lit up when she walked in, nervous and full of an excited anticipation. He had been drawn to her enchanting green eyes, full lips, sleek auburn hair and bright bubbly spirit. There was a magnetism deep within and he could not take his eyes off her. His heart fluttered at the memory of that moment when she had shyly smiled at him, her eyes eager for adventure and love and he knew she felt the same allure.

Within no time they became inseparable and despite the danger of their mission, or even because of it, they became ever closer. They thrived on being constantly in each other's company and developed an intimacy neither had experienced before. Their feelings had deepened to a strong and immovable love and it was only this that had sustained him throughout the long years of her absence.

He gave a sigh as the memories flooded back. Such happy years, experiencing a freedom they had never had. The child had not been part of the plan, indeed it was expressly forbidden. But nonetheless, he could not be sorry; he would not apologise for something that had, after all, made them complete. Who would have thought it was possible to feel such an overwhelming love? They were filled with joy but that was cut short in one foul swoop after just seven years.

He blinked back a tear as he thought of their loss and the events of that fateful day, thirty years in the past. Deeply imprinted in his mind; it could have been yesterday. He steadied himself on the front of the pew, as his mind was taken over by unwanted thoughts. Regardless of any guilt, he had always blamed himself for what happened and it was agonizing to see his lovely wife disintegrate when he had told her that their child was gone. It was too much for her to bear. She was taken over by a grief so strong that it led to a kind of madness. She had gradually sunk into its depths and despite everything he had done to console her, he had barely been able to reach her. He swiftly opened his eyes and clenched his fist to stop these thoughts. They would not help him now and he was determined he would concentrate and stay rational as time got ever closer.

He stood, bit his lip and waited the key moment, which came with a hovering glow of yellow above the altar and ended with a sudden flash. Momentarily blinded, he heard a loud cry, then a series of gut wrenching sobs in that oh-so-familiar voice, long before he could see her in the glimmering light. His stomach dropped, he knew what this meant in an instant. Failure - again. Rushing to the crumpled figure on the floor, he stretched his arms around her and drew her close to him.

"My darling," he soothed, breathing in her scent and pressing his brow against her clammy forehead, overwhelmed to have her with him again.

"I'm going on," she choked.

"You can't, you know you can't. You've already done two vaults. You're too weak – it will kill you. I'll go..."

"NO!" she screamed, "I can't stay here – not alone – I can't do it – I have to try again." She stared into his eyes and in doing so, he was both alarmed at the wildness that shone in her pupils and completely unnerved to look into her impossibly young and beautiful face, the face he had missed and so longed for all these years.'

"Don't go," he pleaded. "I need you, I love you."

"I know and I love you too," she responded, as she momentarily touched her fingertips to his and connected, expressing a deep and unwavering love. But then she shook her head, kissed him tenderly and started to pull away.

"I have to go on, whatever the cost." Silent tears rolled down her cheeks as she pleaded with her eyes.

"Then I will come too..."

"You know that's not possible. You have to remain here; we cannot risk both our lives."

"Please don't leave me again," he urged, as she got to her feet unsteadily. He knew, as the words left his mouth, that he was defeated; he would be unable to stop her. He clasped her to him in a brief embrace, whispering "this should help," as he placed the opal object into her hand and looked deep into her eyes, nodding an unspoken message of love and trust. She tightened her fingers around the device, kissed it to her lips as she indicated understanding, with her eyes boring into his. Then she turned, walked forward opening her arms and in a flash, disappeared into the light.

He stared, as the light faded to blackness. He had not stopped her. The moment was lost. She was gone and possibly forever. There were no guarantees the device would work. The enormity of the situation speared him to the core and, drained of all strength, he sagged to his knees. Deep moans wrenched from his throat as he openly wept and beat his fist to his forehead. He felt his heart breaking, as his tears splashed the cold marble floor beneath him.

College

$\mathcal{I}$mogen had slept badly again. She now knew, without doubt, that the screaming voice in her recurring dream was that of her mother, as she was being relentlessly sucked further into an airless blackness. It was so dark there was nothing, not even the comforting glow of another person. She had woken gasping for breath. The words: *'They're coming – they've seen you,'* echoing around her head, along with the rhyme: *'She's not a fighter, she's a dirty little blighter,'* getting ever louder. Even using the drill, she was unable to completely quash the deep grey veins of anxiety that still coursed through her Chroma.

She had been glad to spend a while curled up next to her mother, transferring her concerns by fingertips.

Why did Grandad put you into an induced coma? Why didn't he tell me?

She was relieved there was no sign of Leo before she left the house. She had knocked at the door of his downstairs room and, when there was no response, looked in, but could see nothing suspicious, other than the fact he had not slept there. The room was a complete mess; thrown over the large sofa bed were clothes and bedding in a heap. Sadiki was curled up on top, and looked up briefly to give her a small hiss. *I wondered where you'd gone – traitor!* Cables, papers and boxes were strewn all over the floor, just like her Grandad's room, she noted. The only surprise was the large TV in the corner, still switched on. The screen was split into multiple smaller screens all playing different channels simultaneously, showing old movies, comedies, and cult dramas and shows. She had grabbed the remote and switched it off, slightly irritated he was not thinking of their electricity bill, but also amused that one of the screens was showing a vintage episode of Monty Python, with a sketch where the characters repeated the words: 'my brain hurts'.

If only they knew, she said to herself wryly as she left.

Imogen was further relieved that there was no sign of Araz at college. She needed time to calm and think.

'The Reef' had managed to intercept her on the corridors between lessons, and had ranted on about the stupidity of the public records office, whilst Imogen cloaked her colours with a dumb disinterest.

"Completely useless!" Mrs Barrier had fumed, as sparks of black, yellow and purple, the colour of bruising, darted in all directions. "They said they had no record of anyone named Imogen Reiner being born in Birmingham since 1959! They had the cheek to ask if I had made a mistake. Outrageous! I told them in no uncertain terms that I, Regina Barrier, do not make mistakes and that furthermore I would be reporting their poor record keeping and incompetent staff to higher authorities. The girl was obviously an imbecile and started blubbering down the telephone. I told her to pull herself together and that this was no way to run a government department. Mark my words, Imogen; I will get satisfaction from them. They are dealing with a professional here. Imogen? Did you hear me?"

Imogen had nodded limply. *1959?*

When it was clear she would get no further response, Mrs Barrier had said, "Yes, well, as you can see, I am doing my utmost on your behalf." Quite undeservedly, she thought to herself. "Now I must get on," and she'd marched away in a bumptious manner, chest puffed up to an inflated size, full of the sense of her self-importance.

Imogen was further troubled by this strange piece of information and was barely able to concentrate in class, her mind a muddle of conflicting thoughts.

Her friends proved a welcome distraction when they met at lunchtime. She was her happiest in their company. Having changed school so many times in the past, Imogen was immensely grateful to have finally stayed at one place for more than a term or two, and found friends with whom she felt at ease.

With her grandfather's help, she had chosen to study subjective subjects like Art, which would not draw attention to her unparalleled knowledge in the disciplines of Maths and Science. Her brilliance now hidden and colours subdued, she had chosen her friendship group slowly but carefully, with the advantage of being able to test their honesty and trustworthiness, by observing their Chroma.

Today the talk was all about Chrissie's seventeenth birthday party on Saturday. "What're you wearing?" "Who's coming?" they buzzed. Katie said she was planning a surprise for the disco, but wouldn't be pressed to give more away.

Richard, the lanky, quiet and studious member of the group, wanted to know what time Chrissie would be at home in the afternoon. Imogen saw from his bright yellow sparks that whilst the question appeared innocent, he was intently interested in her answer and the tremor of indigo, visible only briefly, hinted that he was planning something he wished to keep secret. She also knew from his flaring reds, which she had noticed on an increasing number of occasions that he was besotted with Chrissie, who was completely unaware of his feelings. She observed him critically for a moment. He was quite serious. He had insisted, with a degree of anger, that the group stopped using his old nickname: 'Big Bird'. Chrissie had explained it was given to him at a very early age, when he had shot up in height and towered over his classmates. She had been very surprised that Imogen had never heard of the TV programme it had come from. Well, she thought, Richard may be serious, but she was satisfied to see the snow-white depth of his honest character and his underpinning sage veins of trustworthiness. He would make a good match for Chrissie, she thought approvingly, if she would just notice him.

Chrissie was lost in a haze of dreamy oranges and pinks, as she chattered on about the party plans. Her brothers were playing in a band at their local church hall and they had hired an impressive set of disco lighting that came with the DJ. She explained that her parents had booked the hall on the promise that there would be no under-age drinking, but she was working on them to allow some alcohol, although she was sure that if they did agree, they would insist it was under their supervision. As Leanne sneered a loud:

"Huh!" Chrissie added that she wasn't that bothered about drinking anyway, and Imogen noticed a grey shudder in her colours that accompanied this remark, guessing this was linked to a bad experience in the past. Chrissie did not dwell on this, but bubbled on about who was coming and how brilliant her brothers' new band sounded. Her excitement and warmth was contagious and helped to settle Imogen's unease.

Danny proudly announced, in a loud voice, that he would be making a guest appearance, playing harmonica in the band. The group applauded him but were careful not to slap him on his broad back or nudge his arm, as they would any other friend. Highly intelligent, but diagnosed with a form of autism, Danny hated physical contact. The friends had all learnt to keep within his defined boundaries of friendship, but loved his bright and incisive comments, always delivered with volume, which often had them helpless with laughter. Imogen was always intrigued to see the predominance of deep azure in his colours, with very few signs of the warmer shades. His astounding aptitude showed as sparkles of white-edged blue, but these were speckled in a haphazard fashion throughout his Chroma, denoting the random nature of his thought processes.

"So, who are you bringing, Gen?" asked Leanne, a flash of red-black spite briefly surfacing amidst her prying yellow and confirming to Imogen that Leanne really didn't like her and was jealous of her, though she had no idea why.

"No-one, just me," she responded calmly.

"Well, Callum will be pleased," laughed Chrissie, oblivious to the edge in Leanne's question. "He keeps dropping hints about when you're coming round again!"

"That's too gross," said Katie. "Never palm your best friend off with your brother. If it goes right, they end up being more interested in your brother than you, and if it goes wrong, you end up in the middle of a mess. Either way, your friendship is ruined and that's much more important." Whilst Katie's tone was light and teasing, Imogen could see that there was a navy-blue tinge of hurt around her words.

"I agree," announced Imogen. "And anyway, I will be too busy celebrating with my friends to be bothered with any of that."

"Well, maybe you should ask the new student, what's he called? Araz!" added Leanne, in a malicious tone. "Good luck though, thinks he's too high and mighty for the likes of us."

Richard attempted to change the topic of conversation to the remaining exams, but the other girls launched into an infatuated appraisal of Araz's good looks and mysterious arrival. Imogen listened with half an ear, as she reflected on Araz, not seen since yesterday. Her mind then turned to Leo. It was strange why she felt intrinsically uncomfortable when her thoughts strayed to either of them. Both faces flashed next to each other in her mind, in stark contrast. Blonde, blue-eyed comedian and supposed trainer - dark brown-eyed stranger and possible threat. They were equally puzzling and the attention of either was just as unwelcome. Her thoughts were interrupted again, as she felt the prickle of infiltration and, switching her Chroma to obscure, she looked back to the refectory door and saw that Araz himself was there, swiftly turning his head away from her, as he went to the counter.

"Talk of the devil," nudged Chrissie, a few minutes later. "Hey, Gen, don't look now, but he's coming this way!"

Calm. Pale greens. Disinterest.

The table went quiet, as Araz approached with his drink. Leanne, Katie and Chrissie all sparked deep cherry colours, in varying degrees, whilst Richard maintained a cool steely blue. Danny did his usual strange camera imper-sonation, involving framing the face of the advancing foreigner by making a square with the forefingers and thumbs of each hand, and moving his head left to right, as if judging when to take a shot.

Araz, surrounded in seductive shades of gold and scarlet, smiled and spoke directly to Chrissie.

"Hi, are you Christine?" he asked in his deep voice with the foreign ac-cent. Chrissie just managed a shy blushing nod in response.

"I hope you don't mind," he continued, "but Mrs Barrier pointed you out. I need a timetable and they can't get the printer to work. She said that

I'm in the same classes as you, so if you don't mind, perhaps I could copy your timetable?"

Chrissie positively cooed agreement, much to Richard's disgust noted Imogen, and groped in her bag to retrieve a crumpled sheet which she handed to him, doe-eyed. "It's a... a bit creased," she stammered apologetically, "but you can have it – I... I know it off by heart."

"Thanks, Christine."

"Please, call me Chrissie."

Imogen had to hold back a smile, as she observed Richard's stiff body language being intensified with violent surges of purple-red anger directed at Araz.

"Do you want to join us?" Chrissie fluttered.

"Thanks," came the rich deep voice. "I'm Araz, Araz Vikram."

"We know," gushed Leanne, who had attempted to coolly sip her drink, just before speaking, and so ended up spluttering it all over the table.

Danny glared at the proximity of the newcomer and moved dramatically to the edge of the table, to keep him at arm's length, before holding up the imaginary camera to his face again.

Imogen watched with amusement, as she observed Araz's colour reaction: a brief glint of burnished-mauve disdain, surprisingly bordering on hatred, which was totally absent in his smile and gracious nod. She also suppressed a laugh, as Leanne's Chroma flashed a violent crimson when Araz sat down next to her, the colour matching that in her cheeks, as she hurriedly mopped up the spillage and added in a faltering voice, "I mean… that is, we only know because..."

Katie stepped in and added apologetically, "Thing is, everyone notices when someone new joins near the end of the term and I'm afraid we peeked at your name on the exam seating plan. Anyhow, I'm Katie – this is Leanne, Richard, Danny and Gen."

Politely nodding at each, he only paused when he got to Imogen to say: "We already bumped into each other, didn't we, Gen?"

Imogen didn't react to his fiery glints that sharpened when he looked at her, eyes gleaming. Chrissie gave Imogen a questioning 'You didn't tell me that!' look, before launching into conversation about her forthcoming birthday and celebrations, which inevitably ended with an invitation for Araz to join them. Imogen, appearing outwardly calm and unflustered, unlike her female friends, struggled to subdue the rising rush of sparking sensations and maintained a dull and lacklustre hue.

How does he have this effect on people?

Richard stood, a bit too abruptly, and announced class was about to start. As they all headed out of the canteen, Richard jumped into a gap that appeared, to get ahead next to Chrissie, forcing Araz to fall behind next to Imogen at the back of the group.

He let Richard go forward – why does he want to be next to me? She steadied her colours to those of natural indifference.

As they went through the door towards the Humanities block, Chrissie called "See you later!" to Imogen, who went to carry straight on down the corridor.

Araz stopped and put a hand on her arm. She was unable to completely suppress a small red flicker, but quickly smothered it in earth shades, as she was forced to look into his dark eyes.

"Not in Law?" he questioned as the others went ahead.

"No, I do Art," she said quietly, as she freed her arm from his touch and went to move off, noting a brief surge of purple annoyance in his rich colours.

"So, perhaps I'll see you at this party?" he asked, without a trace of the vexation that was clear in his Chroma.

"Er, perhaps," she said, with some hesitation.

"I mean, really see you," he added cryptically.

Imogen looked away.

"But you don't want that, do you?" said the rich voice teasingly.

She froze. "Wh... What?" she managed to murmur.

"…To be seen."

Imogen turned back, startled, and suddenly off guard. She hastily subdued a rush of crimson and managed to say: "I don't know what you mean," forcing a blank look into his amused and very striking face.

My stomach is not going to knot. Stay focused – calm – unimpressed.

"Clever," he observed as his dark brown eyes briefly penetrated hers, before she looked to the floor.

He walked a slow semi-circle around her and then turned to go, but at the last minute swivelled back towards her and leaned his head into the side of her neck, lips within a fraction of her ear and whispered, "I will see you on Saturday, Gen."

Electricity sent a shudder through her inner core as she dared to look up and watch him swiftly exit through the door. She felt unnerved, alarmed, and something else… Energized!

How does he do that?

Realising she was, again, being watched, she turned to find Danny leaning against the wall looking at her through one cupped hand, as he rolled an imaginary camera with the other. Rippling a deep azure, he said loudly: "And cut!" before dropping his arms and edging past her.

"Powerful," he muttered, "but then he is an invader." Without elaborating further, he headed off.

Imogen shook her head at the strange, yet oddly perceptive remark, before following Danny to the Art block.

The First Chronicle of Tanastra: Firas Lateef

ow, let me tell you about each member of our team, and goodness, what a team we were! Our ages and abilities covered a broad range, young and old and all so talented and so different. Everyone was utterly committed to our cause, down to the last man and woman, quite a force to be reckoned with, that is before all our troubles began...

So, I will begin with Firas, the eldest of the group, that is to say: the eldest after me.

Firas Lateef. A man of learning and principle, he paid the ultimate price for what he believed in. It is a crime that he died in such a brutal, horrible way... but forgive me, I have jumped to the end and first things first, I must tell you about Firas; who he was and the contribution he made.

To call him a great inventor would not do justice to his amazing technical prowess. Without his extraordinary mind and his capacity to think in a multi-dimensional way, this history would not even exist. It is because of him that I discovered the truth and was able to fake my own death and ultimately, my escape. His name may never be placed in the record books or given the honour he deserves; indeed, he may be decried and admonished by those in power, but this gentle giant of a man made all things possible and it is thanks to him that we all embarked on this irreversible mission.

Oh dear, now I have gone off on a tangent; the effects of old age. Let me try to summarise this astonishing person. He arrived here with the others, ten years after me, in the mid 1950's. I always had him down as a loner, but it was necessary for protection to pair up the team members, so Eshe seemed the natural choice. Had I been able to read Chroma, something I never quite got the hang of, I would have seen the chemistry that I am told had long sparked between them and would not have been so surprised when they announced their union in later years. Perhaps I was too busy with my research to notice these things, but they did, in reality, make a rather wonderful partnership.

So, Firas: he was, above all other things, an artist. That may surprise you, as he is generally known as an inventor and engineer, but he was able to add character, beauty and clarity to everything he made, which wouldn't have been possible without his artistic spark. No ugly, functional, 'make-do' gizmos, not with Firas. When he invented something it had depth and finesse and was a joy to behold. Think of the pride the Victorian engineers took in the polished and chromed steam engines of the era: the sounds and smells; the fluid movement of the wheels, cogs and pistons; the sheer magnificence of the machinery was just 'poetry in motion'. Add to this our advanced technology, his genius and delicate touch, and it was no wonder that the things he created were so beautiful and extraordinary.

The 'Tractus', for which I had done the mathematical modelling, could so easily have been a drab, featureless device, but Firas made it into a remarkable and subtle wonder. And so powerful! We soon realised that it must not fall into the hands of the enemy. They would have claimed it for their own and put it to uses that can only make me shudder. I mean, look at the technology developed here during the Second World War. I arrived right at the end of this dreadful conflict but it was immediately apparent there had been an accelerated development of intricate and sophisticated technology, whose sole purpose was to be used as weapons of mass destruction. The driving force behind the guns, aircraft and communication was entirely for the purpose of wielding power and killing others.

The Tractus could not be allowed to go down that route. On that we were all agreed. It had been Firas who realised that this was indeed a real risk and that the elite of the empire was taking an extreme and irreversible step towards complete power. He had seen the evil seeping into our otherwise perfect society and corrupting those in authority. He warned us; he helped to make plans and he gave us the means to escape. Thanks be to Firas!

My part was relatively small in the design. I had to firstly retrieve the marker buried in a Cairo museum, of all places, and then set it up in a new location. Whether by chance or planning, I ended up in the northern hemisphere in the industrial area known as Birmingham. A sprawling conurbation, filled with noisy and smoking factories that had produced ammunition, aircraft and arms for the war effort, it was still recovering from the terrible blitzes of the Luftwaffe.

It had been Firas who suggested using a church; the space was rarely altered and only occupied for a few hours each day. Anyway, I found the perfect one. It had thankfully avoided major bomb damage and whilst the outside was large and uninspiring, the interior was, rather surprisingly, beautiful. Ornate, opulent, gilded with 'Michelangelo' inspired paintings within the high dome, the building was a hidden gem and known locally as 'little Rome.' Of course, it meant I then had to masquerade as a member of the clergy to gain the full access to the premises that I required, but sixty years on, I no longer feel as if I am an imposter. In fact, I am quite at home as 'Father Jonathan.' I not only assumed the identity, I ended up living it and, I must say, becoming a better man for it. Alleluia!

Whilst my 'prayer time' was spent furthering our cause and research, I also played my priestly part in full, and had the privilege of sharing so many intimate moments with my flock, celebrating their births and marriages and giving the last rites on their deaths. I have spoken with families, the brotherhood of fathers, elderly folk and children; I have heard their confessions, witnessed their deepest fears and shared their greatest hopes and I have learnt, above all, not to judge them. Indeed their spirit is unquenchable and it has taught me to know that our only hope lies with these people, regardless of what we conceive to be their primitive state.

Oh dear, I'm wandering again. Yes Firas… he, like all of us, was also disguised and posed as a professor of engineering: Professor Colin Wallace of Imperial College, London. Goodness, he looked the part with his long beard and authoritative tone. Everyone forgave his professorial eccentricities, which mainly consisted of a refusal to be photographed and an appalling lack of historical awareness, on account of his brilliance in his field of expertise. What did it matter if few knew what he looked like and he didn't know which country had invaded Poland, when he could split the atom and mathematically model it in less time than it took to say 'Ernest Rutherford'?

Dear Firas. How we miss him. Even now, I find it hard to accept he has gone and I cannot bring myself to relay his appalling end. I am sick at the very thought of it and so it will have to await a later report, but please remember, we all owe Firas Lateef, the great Professor Wallace, an incalculable gratitude. His death, unlike my own, is a tragic and lamentable loss to all humankind. He was, quite simply, irreplaceable.

Training

$\mathcal{L}$eo was waiting in the hallway for Imogen when she arrived home, a surge of excited anticipation clear in his colours, but she resolutely ignored him and went up to her mother's bedroom without speaking, where she checked everything was in order before going to her own room to call her grandfather.

At least he was unable to see her colours on the screen that linked their devices. She did not need to camouflage her sparking dark bronze frustration and greys of worry, and only had to check her body language and the tone of her voice to convey a fabricated serenity as she spoke.

"Tell me the news, Imogen," Harold's kindly face enquired.

"Well no change in mum, but it **is** going to happen, isn't it Grandad? I just want it to be soon. I need her back," she added, the ache clear in her voice.

Why didn't you tell me you had put her to sleep?

"Me too, my dear, me too," he replied earnestly. "I'm sure it will not be long now. So what's happening at college with this Araz?"

"Well, he seems determined to get in with my group. The girls are just delighted he's there! But his interest seems focussed on me..." Imogen was grateful her grandfather could not see her rush of scarlet that shuddered in her aura at the thought of Araz's lips almost on her ear. Harold's brow furrowed as she continued.

"And, well, he said some very odd things. Sort of... trying to wind me up. I'm not sure, but I think he can read Chroma. And as for Leonard, Grandad, you must know he can. I just don't understand. Where has he come from? And how can you have known him from long ago? He's only a bit older than me."

"Leonard might have some of your gifts, but he is nowhere near as skilled as you, Imogen. He is a mere novice in comparison," Harold snorted contemptuously. "Anyway, he will be explaining where he fits in, all in due course," Harold replied. "But just remember Imogen, it was essential that you were unaware of certain things for your own protection. Concealing your identity has always been of paramount importance. Your very life has depended on it."

Before she could ask more, he changed the subject.

"Now, this Araz, I am feeling more concerned and, if your suspicions are correct he could be very dangerous. If he can read Chroma, he may realise that you are suppressing your true colours. It could have triggered his interest. Hmm." He paused as he thought, before continuing: "You need to be very careful and must stay alert. In fact, it may be an idea to lead him on a false trail. Instead of shielding your identity, you could project a new one, like a regular girl of your age."

Imogen held her tongue and could not help but think to herself how she would love to be a 'regular' girl, without all this subterfuge.

Harold, pleased with his plan, continued enthusiastically. "Take on the behaviour and Chroma of your friends. Fool him into believing you're just like one of them! You're more than clever enough, Imogen. Copy your peers and maybe he will be thrown off course. If it transpires that he is indeed the enemy, which I doubt, it is then that we will need to take action," he added cryptically.

Imogen knew that behaving like a simpering admirer would be straight-forward enough and it could be just what he wasn't expecting. She began to warm to the idea of acting like Leanne, she would not have to subdue the inevitable red sparks that Araz seemed to trigger within her when he was near. She could easily slip into this role at Chrissie's party. She thought this through as she continued to listen to her grandfather on a completely different subject. He told her that Margaret was growing weaker and was going downhill very rapidly. She wanted to see Imogen again, in fact, she seemed quite desperate to do so, so he asked her to call in as soon as possible. Imogen's heart sank as she subconsciously rubbed her arm and recalled in a different part of her mind, Margaret's warning: *They've seen you - they're coming...*

At the end of the conversation, Imogen circled her multi-com with her fingertips, which closed and flattened and then shook her head.

Who is the enemy and why do I need to hide?

Her thoughts were interrupted when Leo called from downstairs and she determined that this time she was going to get some answers and she would not be thrown off track.

He was waiting at the bottom of the stairs, face bright and eager as he absentmindedly pushed a loose curl of blonde hair away from his eyes. "Ready for the training?" he asked in an excited fashion. "You'll be glad to hear it's not a cookery lesson!" he added, as he turned to head out of the front door.

"No! I'm not doing anything until you tell me a few things," she announced as she marched past him into the living room. He paused and then meekly followed, slumping into the armchair as she sat on the edge of the settee, arms folded, a determined cold yellow permeating her aura.

"I need some answers, Leo."

Leo closed his eyes for a moment. His bright sunny reds of excitement began to quieten and he gradually quelled them with pale blues and greens.

Calming himself in preparation, she noted with approval.

A black vein of authority then crept around the newly composed spectrum and he sat upright in the chair as he stated decisively: "Okay, you are allowed just three questions, for now, which I will answer as truthfully as I can, and then we must get on with your training. Deal?"

"Okay," she replied tentatively, "I want to know who sees Chroma."

Leo pursed his lips in thought before starting the explanation, fully aware that Imogen would be able to see if he lied or glanced over the truth.

"Where to begin? Okay, we – you, me, your mum, Harry - we are what's known as tetra-chromatic." Imogen looked blank.

"Most people are tri-chromatic, that is, they have three colour receptors in their eyes, but we have four! It's quite neat really; birds, reptiles and some spiders share the same genetic make-up," he added with a grin and making spider shapes with his fingers in the air, but seeing Imogen's serious face, he dropped his hands down and reverted back to his solemn explanation.

"The result of having an extra receptor is that we have the ability to make what is technically called 'enhanced colour discriminations', in the right light, that is. Basically we see colours others don't see. Visible light is split into twenty-one distinct colours for us, instead of the seven colours for them. So, whilst tri-chromatics can see just red, then orange, we see two other colours in between. Anyway it's the same for all the other colours of the rainbow. And, as you know, we can perceive the colours of thoughts and emotions, although reading them is quite an art. I mean the red of anger is a shade different to the red of excitement or the deeper shade of love, for example." He coughed nervously before continuing. "Or the red of fear... Anyhow, it takes quite some mastering."

Leo noted Imogen's intense concentration as she absorbed this information and the way her full lips pursed in a very appealing quizzical angle as she mulled it over. Quick to smother any outward glow of attraction she might detect, he summoned up more clear blue facts for her.

"Oh yes, and as a female you also have additional retinal pigmentation, so your ability to distinguish colours is even greater than that of any mere male. Plus, a few women can detect the Infrared wavelengths beyond visible light. Harry says you have this gift." Imogen gave a slight nod of her head, waiting for more.

"So, you can detect heat, that's why you can 'see' people in the dark. This, combined with other genetic differences makes our kind quite different to those around us."

"Our kind? Explain."

Leo shuffled on his seat. "You have always known you were different, haven't you. That you needed to hide this from others? Well we have, er, evolved over a long period of time, with a different genetic make-up."

"I don't understand."

Leo gave a deep sigh before he answered. "Harry advised me to explain it like this: eons ago, a group of individuals, greater in intellect to anyone around them, sealed themselves off in a place hidden to the rest of the world.

They separated from the masses, cutting off all ties and contact and set up in a secluded area, far away from their peers."

Imogen could hear her grandfather's words in this account and could see the basic white truth of Leo's Chroma, but it was edged with a pale flutter of violet - not so much a lie as an embellished half-truth. She chose to overlook this for now, as she seemed finally to be getting some answers.

Leo continued as if he was reading from an internal script. "They found and mined new materials, unknown even now to humankind. They synthesised biology, chemistry, physics, and communications systems. They developed technologies superior to anything else on earth. Your mother's apparatus, our devices, these are all examples of the advanced systems they created. They found cures for illnesses, ways of preventing inherited diseases, an effective way of strengthening the body's immune system… in fact, enhancements in every biological sphere. This enabled 'our kind' to have stronger bones and strengthened muscles that increase our agility, cells that self-repair and do not age so quickly, an ability to use more of our brains and respond quickly to every situation. The additional colour receptors in the eyes are just one tiny detail of all the improvements that were made."

Leo noted Imogen absorbing all the facts and admired the radiant white flares in her Chroma as he continued in his own voice: "Harry is a relatively recent addition to a long line of eminent scientists involved. He's advanced our knowledge even further, in massive leaps. He really is ace!" Leo's warmth for her grandfather was undeniable, but Imogen wanted to hear more and maintained a steady intense yellow concentration, forcing him to continue.

"Anyhow, he told me to tell you that 'we' grew and flourished into a superior civilisation; a complete utopia." The narrative returned to words that were clearly not his own, but Imogen could not hear her grandfather's voice either.

"Our focus on intellect and higher aspirations means there is no discrimination or prejudice in our society. Unlike here, individuals grow up to reach their full potential. There is a real peace, as social solutions have been found to the many problems still evident here. Criminality was eradicated for us, along with poverty and war, and we are truly free. We do not mix with the rest of humanity and can only look on in horror, as it develops technologies it can't understand, let alone control, and continues to follow paths of conflict, famine, global mutilation and self destruction." Leo then found his own voice as he concluded: "You, and I, are both from this separate group of people. It's just that... well... you have grown up not knowing this and hidden deep within this heaving mass of primitive humanity."

Imogen could not help noting the gold-black scorn and superiority he assumed when he made his last statement. She observed that, in that brief moment, his colours matched those of Araz.

She sat still and thought long and hard about Leo's explanation, searching for evidence and immediately layering all the truths in her mind's eye. She could read Chroma; she could see Infrared images; she had a photographic memory and a thirst for knowledge she did not detect in others; she could read thoughts by touch, although Leo had not mentioned that as being a feature of 'her kind'. She was physically stronger than her peers; she could easily do several things at the same time, and all well. She knew she assimilated new information almost instantly, with a natural understanding of even the most complex theories and concepts, and she could multi-task on a far higher level than any of her friends. She had never been ill other than the time of 'the fog'; she had had the usual childhood accidents but had never broken a bone and didn't have the smallest scar. Cuts and bruises healed almost instantly; she had never required hospital treatment; in fact she had not even had a cold. The truth was stark: she was more different than even she had imagined and it turned out that this had all been designed by others.

As she sat deep in thought, Leo quietly admired the glints of crystal blue and white logic sparkling like quartz in her colours.

"So let me get this straight," she said eventually, "you're saying I am the product of a highly developed form of genetic engineering, which is why I am different to everyone else and why I can read Chroma?"

"Yes, is that so bad?"

"Bad! It means I'm a total freak!"

"Well if it's any consolation, you're not the only freak! And you're a very pretty one!" he added with a wink, before nervously dropping his eyes.

Ignoring his last remark, Imogen persisted, "and why am I not with the rest of this so-called 'superior civilisation'? Where are they? And what are we doing here?"

"Out of questions!" chirped Leo, as he stood and indicated for Imogen to follow him into the hall.

"No I am not..." she began, pulsing with bronze frustration, as she caught him up at the front door.

"Oh yes you are! One: 'who sees Chroma'? Two: 'explain our kind'? And three: 'have I been genetically engineered'?"

"That wasn't a separate quest..." she started to protest, but was overruled as he continued.

"Now fair's fair! I do have the same power of recall as you, Imogen. Apart from which, that's plenty of heavy stuff for now and my brain hurts! Besides, it's time for your first training session," he said as he opened the front door and beamed a huge orange-red grin.

As it was clear she would get no more out of him, Imogen called upstairs to the carer that she was going out and went through her exit routine: camera on, Multi-Com to standard and silent.

"All this is quite a lot to take on board you know," she complained grumpily as she followed him outside.

"You'll cope, you have a superior brain," he retorted, as he closed the front door behind her, went down the path whistling the tune: 'Always look on the bright side of life', and opened the driver's door of his car indicating for her to get in.

"And now for something completely different! Ter-raaa!" he grinned, eyes sparkling, as he handed her a key with a mock fanfare.

Imogen looked blank.

"The key to my car! You are about to have your first driving lesson," he announced.

"I'm not old enough," she answered, her colours blurring with confusion.

Ignoring her protests, Leo insisted she got in, shut her door and went round to the passenger side. Once in, he opened the glove compartment and got out and unzipped a document wallet, producing a small credit card sized driving licence in her name.

Imogen scanned the licence bearing her photograph. It was taken yesterday, she noted in the back of her mind. "This can't be right! It's a full licence, which puts me a year older than I am and anyway it can only be issued if I have passed all the driving tests..."

"Oh, you don't need to do those. That stuff is the primitive way. No, this permit will suffice and... this!" Leo then produced a small flat black oval shape, stroked it around the edge so it sprang into an egg-shaped object and placed it in her hands.

"This is known as a DE: 'Data Encounter', and you are about to have your first lesson," he explained.

Imogen reluctantly cupped the object as Leo closed her fingers over it, pressing her thumb and fingertips into five equally spaced indentations. As the connection was made, her mind instantly flooded with animated drawings, diagrams and film clips showing explanations of engines, gears, the theory of combustion, maps, rules of the highway and driving techniques, layer upon layer. After just five minutes, she opened her hand and Leo took if from her palm and returned her stare.

"Now your brain hurts too?" he quipped and when she didn't respond, he added: "Sorry, Monty Py..."

"What... what was that?" she mumbled to herself, ignoring his witticism and looking from his face to the black object. She wasn't sure how, but her mind now had a firm grasp of everything to do with vehicles and driving. She had been swamped with knowledge and saturated with information about every aspect of how to operate and manoeuvre a car. She could not help smiling as she managed to say: "Well I've no idea how that works, but I do know that I can now drive!"

"You're going to love this," cooed Leo "Let's go!"

Imogen put on her seatbelt, tested the gear positions and the clutch and the brake pedals for feel. She then adjusted her rear mirror and checked the angle of the re-glued wing mirror before taking a deep breath and turning the key. As the engine spluttered into life, she could see the ignition from the spark plugs, the movement of the pistons and rapid firing of the engine in her mind's eye. She knew exactly how this worked and felt a surge of intrepidation and excitement, which Leo could behold in multi-coloured glints in her Chroma. Without hesitation, she engaged the gear, knowing it would transfer the power of the engine to the wheels, and, using the throttle with one foot, she gently released the clutch with the other as she disengaged the handbrake and moved off smoothly and proficiently, as if she had been driving for years.

It felt a bit strange to begin with, but after several minutes of busy rush hour roads, traffic lights, dual carriageways and roundabouts, Imogen was handling the vehicle as if she had been born to it. She had a natural spatial awareness and found she could judge distances and anticipate hazards intuitively. It gave her a buzz of excitement, which translated as shining warm hues infusing her colours. Leo tried to keep his eyes fixed on the roads in front but could not help glancing at her in satisfaction, as she sparkled competence and happiness.

"So where are we going?" he asked.

Imogen summoned up the road map that the 'DE' had imprinted on her mind, and plotted her route in an instant.

"The Manor," she said decisively, as she took a left turn and wove expertly in and out of the traffic towards Grandad's home.

ARAZ

*A*fter college, Araz sat and reviewed his day from the privacy of his bed-sit. He was cross that he had been unable to follow Imogen. Her inane friends had swooped down on him at the end of classes and he had only been able to see her wave to Chrissie from a distance at the college entrance, before hurrying off. By the time he managed to get to the main road, there was no sign of her. He was more furious with himself for assuming Imogen was in the same lessons as her dumb friend. He should have known better; facts, not assumptions, were the sign of a good agent. It was a clumsy mistake. The only classes they shared were English Literature and History, and these were suspended during the exams. To maintain his cover, he was now forced to sit through the tedium of other lectures, unable to observe the target.

This could, of course, work to his advantage, he thought and he chuckled when he summoned the flushed faces of Chrissie and her friends when he had taken a seat near them in class. They so easily succumbed to his polished charm, the trait that had given him the edge over the other candidates for this job. As he had smiled seductively back at them, it was with a recognition that, without Imogen in the room he could be confident in the knowledge that they were totally blind to his chromatic thoughts which would betray his utter disdain for them all.

He mused over Imogen. Could she read Chroma? She had not reacted in the same way as other females. Of course, he could still have made a mistake. The girl may not be the one. However he resolved to look on the positive side and reminded himself with self-satisfaction that he had entered her friendship group and was now close to confirming if he was on the right track. He was sure he had detected some anxiety in her pretty face, if not her colours, when he had tried to get a reaction with his cryptic remarks, and now the prospect of the party on Saturday promised to be very interesting.

Araz's fingers hovered over his Multi-Com. He should really report his findings, but something stopped him tapping in the code for 'possible sighting' and he merely entered the regular 'search continues' code, as he had for the past few months.

He puzzled over his hesitation. He knew that mistakes and failure were not tolerated and was determined he would not be accused of either, making one hundred percent sure he was right before revealing his find. He was also aware that the subject held an immense attraction he had not been prepared for, and this caused him to feel strangely unnerved and not completely in control. It was not acceptable for anyone else to detect this and the delay was as much to get these emotions under control as it was to be sure of his facts. What was it about this restrained young woman? The image of her green-blue eyes, silky hair, soft neck, and alluring fragrance flooded his mind, uninvited, as did her astonishing array of colours he had witnessed on his first sighting. He quickly reminded himself that she could just be an ordinary girl. No more, no less. And even if his instinct was right and she was indeed the one, he should be able to control his feelings. He could not afford to be emotionally involved. It was against all his training.

He reached for a guitar, standing against the wall, and strummed a few chords before picking out a melody he had heard earlier on the radio. Amongst all the mindless claptrap, he had to concede there were some incredible compositions. He was able to reproduce the song note for note and even embellish the tune, making a richer sound. The playing soothed and relaxed him. After several minutes getting lost in the music, he felt calm and refreshed.

Replacing the instrument against the wall, Araz resolved to recover his sense of duty and discipline, and retrieved a metallic box from under the bed and selected one of the small oval black objects from inside. He cupped it in his hand and closed his eyes, as he sank back on the bed. His mind connected with the device and was then swamped with the briefings, information and images, which had led up to his mission. Reports, photographs, data, theories and top-secret plans all replayed simultaneously in his head.

He homed in on the first of the classified reports, absorbing the information afresh. Dated fifty years ago, five top scientists, now known as the subversives, were discovered to be missing. Their absences had been covered up and it was not known how long they had been gone. They consisted of the best in their field. A picture of each of the faces, taken decades ago, was displayed in his mind with a brief description.

Firas Lateef: looking about mid-thirties in age; large figure of a man, with dark piercing eyes and bearded face, giving the impression of someone rugged and wild. He was an award winning artist and mathematician and it was he who had developed the highly secret *Tractus pusillus*, originally conceived by the legendary Tanastra Thut who had died at such a tragically young age.

Eshe Serq: a small, middle-aged, delicate boned lady, business-like but quite good-looking. Her renown was as a distinguished geneticist whose research had been responsible for some of the greatest code refinements enabling personality prediction.

Sefu Zuberi: expert in the bio-chemical communications sphere, photographed in his early twenties with his co-worker and younger brother, Nuru. Their dark hair, strong brows and roman noses crowned the wide smiles on the portrait, which had frozen them in time in what looked like an affectionate exchange. Araz momentarily layered a later report in his mind, naming Nuru as the scientist acting undercover for his brother and colleagues. Although originally put under house arrest, he had attested his innocence and appeared to be working with the authorities, assisting with developing their own Tractus marker, until his sudden disappearance thirty years later. He was now officially classified as the sixth subversive and it was suspected that he had recruited others within the empire to the insurrection. Araz was not involved with the domestic security search, but he knew the orders were to instantly destroy any found guilty of this crime. He had been advanced to the elite force to infiltrate and recover those who had escaped.

Returning to the fifty-year-old report, he looked again at the final fugitives: Rashida Omorose and Kasmut Akil. Young multi-talented technicians recognised for being able to translate the theoretical into the practical, they were rumoured to be 'tri-crypts'. They had a unique skill of turning concepts and ideas into reality. The blurred photograph showed Kasmut, tall, dark haired and strong, holding a protective arm around a young and clearly beautiful Rashida. Their bond was unmistakable, even in this old grainy snap.

Araz homed in on Eshe and Rashida's faces. They were not in good focus but one looked, yes, familiar. He flashed Imogen's sharp features, memorised in every detail, alongside the blurred images and had to remind himself that it could still be coincidence. No more assumptions. Looks could be deceptive. The faces all came from the past, sixty years out of date. No-one was sure what they looked like now, or indeed which of the six were dead or alive, although at least one of their number had been reported destroyed.

Araz opened his hand to disconnect temporarily from the black object, an imprint of the subversive emblem still circling in his mind. Why had they done it? He wondered. Why would six of the most trusted and intelligent innovators of their age take such drastic and extreme steps and turn their backs on their own kind? It was unthinkable, unless they had become deranged or their crypts had been corrupted.

Why had they used those symbols as their insignia? Barely seen now, they were from an age long gone, when the focus of progress had been sidetracked into searching for impossible solutions. There must be a connection.

Araz decided to re-visit the emergency meeting of the Supreme Council that followed the discovery of their absence. The meeting was not officially held on record, but Araz had persuaded his commander to let him watch the classified clip for background information. Knowing few had been given access to this data, he had surreptitiously taken a copy and concealed it with the other data. He now closed his hand over the device and allowed the full three dimensional view of the conference to replay in the inner recesses of his mind.

The impressive circular council chamber came into view. Bathed in red tinged light, the cameras began with the central figure pacing the black marble floor in an agitated manner. It was the illustrious person of their revered leader, entirely familiar, if some fifty years younger. She was a tall dark woman with jet-black hair that hung loose to her waist; deep brown eyes, a perfectly symmetrical and attractive face with large lips and bright white teeth. She was dressed from head to toe in gold, and as she paced the floor, her anger was plain for all to see. Those in front of her, all dressed in gold edged black robes, kept their heads bowed and nervously bit their lips or twisted their hands as they endured the loud reprimand directed at each one of them. Araz recognised all of them, apart from one. Most were still members of the Supreme Council today, a couple of them now very elderly. The ruler had not aged in the same way, he noted.

"Escaped!" she was exclaiming. "How could they have escaped? Who is responsible for this outrage?"

"I'm afraid it is worse than that, Kekara."

"Worse Odion? How so?"

Odion, completely bald and taller than Kekara, was now stooped in a subordinate pose, which looked at odds with his strapping muscular figure. He gulped quickly before continuing, "It would appear the insurgents broke away over nine years ago."

"WHAT?" shouted Kekara. "Nine years ago! You imbeciles! Why did we not find out until now? These were our most trusted scientists. They were working on the Tractus – that was Category One restricted. How could anyone escape undetected? They should not have been able to blink without our prior knowledge - this should not have been possible."

Sekhet, the light haired female official, whom he had not seen during his service – she was probably no longer in post - stepped forward tentatively to respond to their angry leader. "It is precisely because of their superior intelligence that they were able to fool us, Kekara. They duped the system into believing they were still present."

"Duped? Duped the most sophisticated security system ever invented? How could that be?" she raged.

Sekhet let her piercing blue eyes fall to the floor as she explained: "They intercepted the coding inputs which led to a false impression that they were still here..."

"They could not have done this without help!" Kekara retorted.

"We believe at least three others were involved. One, Sefu Zuberi's brother, Nuru, has been seized and is being questioned..." started Sekhet, before Odion interrupted her.

"Obviously, the five could not have escaped alone and a minimum of two others must have assisted in the subterfuge, Kekara," he began with authority. "As soon as we realised, we swept in and were about to track them, when Ubaid prevented us from doing so, saying we must call this emergency session of council first," he added with a sneer as he turned to the official who was the point of his derision.

"Your reasons, Ubaid?" Kekara asked, turning to the small delicate man with pale skin and a light pointed beard.

Araz paid particular attention to the reply. He had spoken at length to Ubaid, in private, and had an unswerving respect for his intellect and reasoning.

Ubaid stepped forward, giving Kekara a short bow. "Ma'am, we had been told that the Tractus was not ready. This was an outright lie. It would appear that they had not only developed a fully working model over twenty years ago, but had established an unauthorised link to... to…"

"To where?" she cried.

The response was given by Odion, who poured contempt into his words, and which prompted a complete and stunned silence: "To the primitives."

Kekara finally managed to mutter through clenched teeth: "No! The Tractus was not for their use. This is disgraceful. Links to the primal beings are completely forbidden; this could put our entire empire in jeopardy. They must be found. You should not have delayed. What were you thinking, Ubaid? They must be eliminated," she pronounced.

Ubaid advanced forward again, ignoring Odion's triumphant smirk.

"Ma'am, with all respect, we must ensure we retrieve the knowledge and advancements on the Tractus. It is crucial that we repossess the technology and it is not lost."

Araz remembered Ubaid's words: that the device was of such major importance that it could bring about the next technological evolution, which would benefit their entire society. He noted that not all the councillors shared this view as he continued to watch the interactions.

Kekara's eyes bored into the small face in front of her as he held her gaze, giving an almost imperceptible nod of the sense of what he said.

He had spoken to her too, thought Araz.

Kekara paused before turning and addressing the whole assembly. "Ubaid is right. We have to retrieve the Tractus and all its sequencing intact; for the greater good."

Odion snorted his objection. "Kekara, we should act now; swoop in before they have time to respond. They won't be expecting us. It will be swift and efficient. My team can do it."

"Yes, and in the process, destroy the greatest invention of all time. Still," Ubaid added, tone full of sarcasm, "it will only take another several hundred years to develop a new model…"

"Now look," started Odion angrily. "They are guilty of the worst crimes against our Empire; contamination from the primitives could be catastrophic! Who knows what they are planning. They must be stopped. They must be extracted and eliminated. They cannot be allowed to get away with this."

Kekara did a full circuit of the chamber again, before seating herself on a high gold seat. "Odion is right," she said. "No-one must be left in that place. All must be hunted down and returned and the utmost secrecy must be used. We must, however, be mindful of Ubaid's words, and the priority will be to retrieve the mechanism intact. Odion, send your forces as soon as you can, but surprise and capture is the mission. Elimination can come later. Use only our most trusted agents. We do not want these mutineers to realise they have been discovered. They have got away with it for so long they have probably become careless. We must not have them scupper the equipment; its safe return to the empire and their eventual eradication will be for the good of all and the honour of Ra."

As the image faded, Araz contemplated the recording of the meeting. Even now, only the select few had been advised of the Tractus and only on a 'need to know' basis. There was something that made him feel instinctively uncomfortable about the response of the council. Perhaps it was because it clearly demonstrated that mistakes would not be tolerated, or perhaps it was the use of the word 'elimination' applied to some of the greatest minds ever produced. The question again arose in his mind. Why? Going across to the primitives, especially sixty years ago, was like entering prehistoric times compared to theirs. The subversives had belonged to the highest echelons of the empire, trusted with the key restricted projects. They had status, respect and power. Why would these great minds conspire against their fellow men and women and desert? Their rebellion was inexplicable and left them a clear threat to the empire, putting in jeopardy the security and safety of all.

Placing the Data Encounter back in the box he decided to set out to do some more research. This time he would concentrate on Imogen's 'so called' Guardian. After all, he had a few days spare before the big party, when he was sure to see her again. Infused with a great sense of anticipation, he smiled inwardly before embarking on his task.

The Second Chronicle of Tanastra: Eshe Serq

I turn now to Eshe Serq. I cannot sing her praises highly enough. I suppose it was inevitable that she would grow deeply in love with Firas. Understand me it was not the way he looked! Such a fierce appearance, what with his size, his beard and facial hair; he had, what some of the locals would call, a mad 'Rasputin' look. No, Eshe was seduced by his amazing mind and she uncovered a gentle side to him not seen before by anyone else. She was herself a good-looking woman but very small. Goodness! They did look extraordinary together: he was wild and tall and built like a tank and she was delicate and very petite. It didn't bother them, and it was their teamwork that bonded the relationship. Eshe's talents perfectly complemented Firas' abilities and together they refined the Tractus to become what it is now; triggered only by our DNA. We thought it was foolproof and that no-one could use it outside of our group. Sophisticated genetic imprints alone could activate the apparatus. Eshe, of whom it was said, had the gift of prophecy, did warn us that it would only take a few clever changes to alter this, and that we should be on our guard. But we were so convinced that we were infallible that we did not listen and it is to my shame that it was not only proved that she was right, but also led to our current precarious position and, ultimately, to Firas' death.

Dear Eshe. The others would all have been floored by the news of the child. I have to confess I was taken aback; this was not part of the plan at all, but she took it all in her stride. It was one of the things she excelled in: being practical and adaptable. It was she who realised the child was extraordinary; she who urged complete secrecy and caution and developed a programme of special upbringing. She knew we had to protect this little one…

Now what was it I wanted to tell you? Oh yes, the first signs that the un-imaginable was happening and our illustrious leaders were interfering with the natural order were hard to believe, but Eshe had witnessed it first-hand. She realised a segment of the Supreme Council was developing a clandestine fighting unit: dozens of creatures forged from a rudimentary concoction of electronics and DNA. These beings, barely human, could not think inde-pendently but could be controlled remotely. Eshe had stumbled, unseen, upon the testing area where they were being drilled to beat and strangle their opponents. The general populace knew nothing of this militia, justi-fied by their creators, as a necessary defence weapon should our borders be breached. Utter balderdash! When they attacked us on that dreadful day in 1966, there was no question that they had been ordered to use their brutality to stop us, whatever it took. We were all shocked; this was a perverse use of genetic engineering. Human matter is and should be sacrosanct; it is not to be used like… like a form of moulding dough to fashion such aberrations. Totally immoral!

Also, it was Eshe who identified that one of our lines was being delib-erately diminished. She found proof that the regime was intent on phasing out certain traits of our race, anything that might challenge and threaten its power base at the top. So it had been decided, in the secret recesses of the high chamber, that certain personality types were not conducive to the 'correct' way of thinking. I can still barely believe it. This sort of psychology belonged to the dark ages, and what they were doing in the pre-expectant clinics under the guise of 'advanced evolution' was really a covert form of genocide.

It appals me to think of this growing wickedness. Our people had been a perfect synthesis of positive attributes; we had intelligence, rationale, vision and balance. Our genetic pool was a heightened multiplicity of all the best traits of humankind. Our differences were not only tolerated, they were encouraged and celebrated, so we could push forward and test the very boundaries of learning and progress. It was all to a higher calling. I still find it hard to believe how a thread of evil could not only seep into our populace, but also take power in such a sly and surreptitious manner. They have been stealthy and clever, and even now, very few suspect what is happening. It saddens me enormously that what had been our race's utmost accomplishment in refining our basic human form to be the beautiful beings Ra intended, is slowly being twisted and abused. Eshe predicted that this would eventually be the downfall and ruin of the entire race. And it was on this and Firas' warnings that we had to act. I only hope, my friend that you will be able to help undo the wickedness that has started.

My, I did miss Eshe's help and advice. She could always be relied upon to assist. If it hadn't been for her quick thinking when the child was lost, I think we would have all gone mad like her poor mother.

The first we knew we had been 'rumbled', so to speak, was that fateful day in '66. It was evening and father and child had come for their regular weekly visit to the church where I checked the girl's progress and she tried to teach me how to read Chroma. She may only have been seven but what a capable child; her skills were unbelievable. We can all play the 'cognitive link' game, where we transfer a selected thought or experience via the fingertips, but it has always been taken as read, that one person transmits whilst the other receives. There's no 'two-way' about it! It was therefore quite a surprise to find that she could see what a person was thinking at that moment, without them even knowing it. Quite amazing! Of course, this was not always a helpful gift. It got her into some trouble at school from what I heard. She was so young and innocent. It was Eshe who suggested she wore gloves to cover a 'skin complaint' when out and about, to prevent it happening again.

Anyway, back to the day that changed everything... It was such a shock when they attacked. We had been oblivious to the fact they had tracked and followed us and they launched their assault on our home ground, in our own base. They must have arrived at our marker, undetected, some weeks or months before, I am sure of it, and then set up a new base elsewhere. We should have been more vigilant, but hindsight is a wonderful thing…

How long had they been waiting their moment? We could only guess, but the first we knew, they were already upon us and a bloody battle ensued. We killed three of them and two others escaped. Kasmut is fairly sure one was badly wounded as he fled, and Firas had attached a tracking device to the other, quick thinking indeed. So we knew his movements, and that he had not returned to the empire, but we had no idea if he had managed to report back to the Supreme Council.

Stunned by the assault after nine and more years of thinking we were in the clear, we did not realise the girl was lost until it was all over…

I need to explain: Firas had been working on some modifications to the Tractus and had warned me that we should not go close until he had fine-tuned the key settings. How were we to know it would self-activate? It was an emergency and all so unexpected. Oh dear, Kasmut was beside himself with worry and I summoned all the others as soon as I could. Eshe instantly took control of the distraught parents and plans were made to change our locations and take immediate cover. Firas and the brothers removed themselves to a safe area and set to work without delay to fathom out how to overcome the problem, retrieve the girl, and detect the enemy marker, which was now an insecure link that led directly to our opponents.

It took several months for Firas, Sefu and Nuru to get to the bottom of it. The result of their researches was astonishing and gave us a new respect for the Tractus, a creation of the utmost magnitude! It turned out that it was capable of much more than even Firas had realised, and then they had to figure out a solution and a way forward. It was delicate, painstaking work and would prove to take not months, but years.

But, forgive me. I was speaking of Eshe. She was 'a real trooper', I think that is the term; she was tough and practical and helped us through the following years of trauma and reorganisation, but, alas, she just crumbled when Firas met his end. And so I must speak of this terrible incident.

It was decades later that a new force attacked. The battleground this time was not the site of our marker in the church, but the enemy base, which Sefu had discovered. They had chosen a perfect location, deep in the heart of London, completely hidden from city dwellers. We had set up a surveillance system and our own marker in a different part of the site in case we had to leave in an emergency. I was always told 'forewarned is forearmed' and so we waited and watched to discover what our enemy was up to.

At first there was little activity, but after years of observing and lying in wait, it was obvious they had developed the means to attack. Several of their trained forces, helmeted and clothed in black, had arrived in the space of a few hours on that July day in 2010. Under cover of darkness we gathered at the site and waited our moment for the advantage of a surprise pre-emptive strike, whilst they were still disoriented and unsuspecting.

I do not take any pleasure in the slaughter of others, but it was a matter of survival, and, if I am honest, it was satisfying to overwhelm such a group, barely human, bent on our destruction. We all sustained minor wounds, but Firas was, as it turned out, more seriously injured. He had a deep cut carved into his side, and it did not take long to realise that it would not heal. A poisoned knife had been used, a new and cruel invention by those in power to ensure slow and irreversible damage that our stem cells were unable to combat. Eshe and Sefu worked day and night to try and find an antidote, but its formulation came too late to help Firas. We could only watch, helplessly, as the toxins began to eat away at him mercilessly. Poor Firas, it affected his nervous system, his co-ordination and worse, his ability to think. Kasmut set up a hospital and home for him and Eshe stayed by his bedside for nearly six months, as he gradually deteriorated, eventually sinking into a permanent vegetative state. He could no longer move, talk or think and he lost all recognition of those caring for him. It broke Eshe's heart, and her spirit, and she was never the same again, when he finally died early the next year. Like the poison on the knife, the effects of his death continued to eat into her inner core, destroying what had once been one of our finest minds.

And so we had lost two of our number, two of our greatest architects, and there remained just a few to try and champion our cause and to fill the gap as best we could. Eshe and Firas had both paid the ultimate price and I mourn them daily.

The Manor

As Imogen drove, delighting in her newfound skill and exhibiting the ease and natural flair of an experienced driver, Leo received a message on his phone. Imogen could see the shadows of grey in his shading from the corner of her eye, as he sent a reply.

"Problem?" she asked, keeping her eyes on the road.

"It was Harr... your Grandad. Margaret has taken a turn for the worse. I said we were on our way."

Imogen nodded and, biting her lip, inched her speed up to the maximum allowable as they skirted the woodland area towards the Manor.

Poor Margaret – her strange behaviour and warning were probably just symptoms of her growing dementia.

Leo tried to compliment Imogen on her neat parking when they arrived at the home, but she was intent on getting inside, so he dropped the flattery and just followed her upstairs. Lisa had greeted him by name at the door, so Imogen knew he had been there before but then, she thought with resignation, he was probably in contact with her grandfather on a regular basis.

Another secret Grandad has kept to himself.

Leo remained by the entrance to Margaret's room, as Imogen entered and found Grandad standing over her bed. He gave a brief slow shake of his head to Imogen, a heavy grey-lavender etching sadness into his aura. Margaret was propped up in bed by pillows, looking frail and very white. Her hand rested on a framed picture, the face of it turned into her chest. The only movement was that of her thumb, which gently stroked the back of the frame, as she struggled to keep up her laboured breathing. She seemed even smaller, out of her wheelchair and Imogen could see that her body heat was pallid and her Chroma reduced to a dull blur of ashen colours that grew weaker as she approached the bed.

"She's been holding on for you," Harold whispered to Imogen, as he gently turned to Margaret and said softly: "Margaret, she's here."

Margaret stirred and Imogen leaned over the bed to her. As she bent towards her face, the old lady smiled weakly and a surge of faint cloudy orange and reds briefly rose in her aura.

"Iris, you've come. I have something for you," she said, in a barely audible voice.

"My drawer, in a box, it's yours." Her clouded eyes motioned to the bedside table, and Imogen quietly opened the drawer, and took out the small box. Margaret gave a drowsy smile, as Imogen opened the lid, and took out a beautiful, intricate necklace.

Hanging on a gold chain was, what appeared at first, to be a solid disc. But as she touched the centre of it, an inner, coin-like core sprang free and rotated full circle on a finely worked central bar, that ran from top to bottom. As the central disc was spun, it created the impression of a sphere, hanging from the delicate chain. Within the inner disc sat a five-pointed star, which also turned independently, on the same bar. This and the disc spun in beautiful balance, as she held it up, to examine it further. When the solid star was turned at right angles to the circles, it gave the impression of an additional and hollow star, and when the inner disc moved with the star, an empty circle was apparent. Aligning all the symbols, to flatten the pendant into its base shape, it was clear that the bar was, in fact, the shaft of an arrow, the arrowhead sitting outside of the main pendant, on top of the outer loop, pointing upwards. The gold was embossed with fine filigree detail, which caught the light and sparkled. Spinning the separate elements, in an ever-quickening motion, Imogen marvelled at the changing shapes, as it moved. In swift rotation, five clear elements appeared in rapid succession. They became almost three dimensional, like five holograms: a solid globe, translucent globe, solid star, and translucent star, with a full central arrow. She had never seen anything like it. The overall effect was quite dazzling.

"It's... it's beautiful, Margaret. Thank you," she responded, looking back to the wizened face, not knowing what else to say.

"Sanctus," whispered Margaret who feebly motioned for her to come even closer. Her weak eyes brightened as they held Imogen's for a piercing moment, and with one last effort, she added: "Sanctus Cryptus, to overcome, overcome them... Trust it. Trust, Iris..." Margaret, exhausted by this supreme effort to communicate, fixed her eyes on a far point above, and as they all watched, her breathing slowed. Her colours merged and fused into a dim wisp of pure white, which circled her head, ascended, and slowly powdered into a shimmering haze before vanishing on her final breath, as the light extinguished in her pupils.

No-one spoke for a good few minutes. Grandad kissed his fingers to his lips and then placed them on Margaret's lifeless brow, before gently closing her eyelids. He slowly turned the photograph over and placed both her hands across it, as he mumbled a blessing. Silent tears ran down Imogen's face, as Leo stepped into the room and awkwardly placed a comforting arm around her shoulders. She was barely aware of his touch, even though a different part of her mind registered his unmistakable red-gold surges of attraction that he was fighting to subdue.

"She thought I was Iris," she said with a small sob.

"To her, you were," said Harold.

"Well this necklace doesn't belong to me," she added, shrugging off Leo's arm and offering the chain to her Grandad. "It belongs to Iris, whoever she is..."

Harold and Leo exchanged a brief look, as Harold said, "Imogen, things are not always as they seem. Margaret was not her real name, and whilst Imogen is yours, to her, you were Iris. She had called you that since your birth. So this does belong to you." He pressed the jewellery firmly back into her hand. "You must take it," he asserted.

She let the chain hang loose as she closed her eyes. A few brief memories from her childhood jumped, unbidden, into the layers of her mind: Margaret, auntie, nursing her mother, holding her hand, reading to her, smiling, singing as she cooked her meals and then in quick succession, Margaret no longer there and then in her wheelchair, barely recognisable, suddenly aged and infirm. As Imogen forced her mind back to the present, there was one final sound of Margaret's shaky voice pleading inside her head: *Trust it - trust the Sanctus.*

Imogen blinked away a tear as her hand closed over the jewellery. "So what was her real name?" she managed to ask.

"Eshe," replied Harold softly as he and Leo slowly left the room.

Imogen looked at the now still, little figure on the bed and down to the smiling image of a large bearded young man, cradled in her dead hands. When she got to the door, she turned and blew a kiss with a soft farewell: "Goodbye, Eshe."

ARAZ

The central post office was easy to infiltrate. Araz, armed with high quality camera equipment he had borrowed from the college, and his captivating smile, had charmed the lady on duty by saying he was a young reporter doing a news round up on the hard working core of the community. All he required was her lovely face smiling in the foreground and the line of letter racks behind. No, of course he wouldn't touch anything.

"Wouldn't dream of it… How about over here by this? What's it called? This 'PO Box' rack. Oh I see… it can't be photographed due to security. Not a problem. Let's do the shot here. Lovely - smile. Thank you!"

He congratulated himself as he now used the college computers to locate the new postcode, swiftly memorised when he had scanned the box numbers. Whilst the primitives may be obsessed with references and electronically cataloguing every last thing, it did, at least, make his job easier. Even their old technology had its uses, he thought with a degree of condescension, as an address finally came up on screen.

Araz did an Internet search on the house name of the address, and mulled over the question, did Imogen's guardian live separately to her, or was this also her home? In the back of his mind he wondered how the Supreme Council had responded when they had later discovered that a child had been born within the escaped group. Forbidden, unauthorised and unchecked - the ultimate felony. He could imagine Kekara's fury and winced at the thought.

It was, of course, shocking to think that such a gifted group had allowed this to happen. What were they thinking? It put a whole new slant on the crimes they had committed against the empire. No-one had known when the birth had occurred, or if the illegal offspring survived, that is, until the breakthrough had come some ten years before, when they received information that the subject was female and much younger than they had assumed. Perhaps the unborn child was frozen for a number of years, as sometimes happened in the empire. To his frustration, it was unclear how this data had been reported, but Araz suspected an informer must have been planted in their midst.

As a result of the new knowledge, plans were put on hold, partly to ensure the insurgents were led into a false sense of security, and partly to uncover their identities and whereabouts. It had been sobering to find that far from becoming lax, they had all gone deeper into hiding, moving areas and shielding all outward signs of their existence. They had had the upper hand when an attempt had been made to send in troops, which had resulted in a crippling failure, destroying many of the frontline. Withdrawing to a safe distance, it was only when they got the recent tip off that the special taskforce was able to move. He had been honoured when he had been appointed to their select number, and having been trusted with an independence not enjoyed by the other agents, he was determined to make his mark. He smiled to himself. Now, thanks to his hard work and persistence, he may well be the first to have discovered her.

His attention was brought back to the screen in front of him. The painfully slow Internet search now showed some intriguing information. 'The Manor' had been a residential home for the elderly and infirm, but had closed several years before, after failing all the social services checks. An individual purchaser had bought the premises, it said he had saved it from the condemned listings, and it was now classified as a private residence owned by a Mr Harold Reiner. The number was ex-directory and the usual street view on the Internet map sites was strangely obscured, so it was impossible to view it online. More intrigue. Just what he had hoped, he thought with satisfaction.

With no small degree of self-congratulation, Araz set off to investigate further.

THE THIRD CHRONICLE OF TANASTRA:
THE ZUBERI BROTHERS

*I*t is here that I turn to the brothers: Sefu and Nuru Zuberi. My friend, as one of us, you probably already know that they were identical twins, born four years apart. This is not so unusual. After all, even in the primitive fertility clinics here, they can deep freeze several fertilised 'sibling-eggs' and 'thaw' them out years later. What you will not know is they were in fact triplets! Yes! We managed to hide the third, Amsu, from the moment he was implanted with Nuru. The mother became a supporter of our cause; she had good reason to suspect that her two previous female foetuses had been terminated for holding the wrong characteristics. They told her there had been 'genetic malformations', but Ruth was a medical practitioner of high standing and was right to be suspicious. Advised she could not produce a girl, and only one more male, the new rigorous council rules, she was more than willing to risk a dual pregnancy. With twin births being illegal, it was a high risk, both physically and politically, but Ruth took no persuasion. It was her way of protesting, plus the thought of producing two further boys as lovely as the loyal and intelligent little Sefu were all it took to decide her.

Eshe was still so young, but her remarkable technical expertise in the field of pre-expectant genetics meant that whilst she secretly investigated Ruth's worst fears regarding the 'ethnic cleansing,' she was also able to conceal the twins. She substituted all the information from Sefu's gestation, for that of the double conception, and she nursed and cared for both mother and babies during and after the birth. As far as the authorities were concerned, only one child was born and no-one even suspected.

We presented just one infant at a time, each answering to the name 'Nuru'. They were never seen together in public and were so physically alike, that even the mother couldn't tell them apart. It was only Eshe that had seen the difference, and she once whispered to me that it was the upper lip that gave it away. Amsu had a small dimple in the middle of his that looked like a tiny indentation, which glinted when he smiled.

Goodness, they were lively children. They would be termed naughty or 'challenging' here, but this was due to their bright minds and the way they spurred each other on. They all took to the subterfuge like ducks to water! Sefu delighted in his younger brothers. They were so like him! With the benefit of being older, it was only he who could keep them in order when they got carried away. Such positive lads, they were always ready for a challenge. The bond between the three of them was so close, they could often communicate without the need of speech. A mere gesture or wink would suffice.

So, they were nurtured to become experts in bio-chemical engineering which best suited their aptitudes and skills. Sefu helped refine those marvellous 'Data Encounter' devices, such clever technology! They could be used to teach all manner of things, like new languages and practical skills, train folk in areas such as the art of survival, relay a full history of, well just about anything in the universe… Oh dear, I am rambling again, but what you must know is that these brothers, triplets in all but age, grew with a different moral standing, thanks to our intervention. They developed an all-consuming and driving passion to undo the evil that was growing in the main power base, and they all committed their lives to this end.

As our leader, Kekara, and her compatriots had been trained from the very outset to take power, control and destroy, so our young team were trained to plan, retaliate and fight. We had learnt our lesson well from their tactics of our enemies!

Now where was I? Ah yes! Amsu Zuberi. So we finally had someone who would be as invisible as me: I ceased to exist when presumed dead, the third 'triplet' never officially existed as he was never officially born! Of course they were just young boys when I 'died', but ten years later, when the others were ready to move, they had matured and with Eshe and Firas' careful training, they and Kasmut and Rashida became the fighting team we had intended, and I couldn't be more proud of them. They were all like children to me.

We now had a means of moving between there and here. I could not risk going back and Amsu lived and acted as Nuru. He camouflaged the other absences: entering the daily imprints, compiling weekly reports, and to all intents and purposes our six brave comrades were living and working from deep within government. The counterfeit 'Nuru' reported constant failure on the progress of the Tractus, which appeared to have such innumerable setbacks that even Firas had no time to report to the council in person. And all the while, the seven of us were here and we had our working model, which we continued to refine. Yes, it had seemed the perfect cover.

We should have predicted that without his brothers, Amsu would lack company and recreation. He had been so close to them and although he and Nuru swapped places just once, for a few weeks, it was clear that Nuru's exposure to the primitive world had produced a marked change in his character and he was no longer 'up to speed' with daily life in the empire. It was decided, that in order to avoid these being detected, that Amsu must be the one to remain to mask our absences. He was downhearted at the news, but compliant, and continued to keep us all hidden for nearly ten full years. On that you cannot fault him.

No-one can be quite sure how it happened, but our communications were cut off abruptly when it was discovered we had absconded, and Amsu was arrested as 'Nuru: brother of the subversive, Sefu'. He was unable to warn us of the impending attack and did not manage to escape for thirty full years, during which time he attested his innocence of being involved with us. We were so glad to see him when he eventually arrived. And what would we have done without him when he so ably stepped into Firas' shoes after the fated attack in 2010. Even so, back in 1996 it was a huge surprise when he turned up with a young boy in tow, whom he announced was his son!

Don't get me wrong. It was quite understandable that he should have found a partner, although I am told it was probably several. Well, he missed the care and warmth he was deprived of when parted from Nuru and Sefu. It just surprised me that he was approved to have a child, as he was surely suspected of being involved with the rest of us. I imagine he must have demonstrated his commitment to the empire and all it stood for. But in truth, Amsu was not the fathering type and even for our race, he was elderly to be a father. I am sure he had little to do with this lad's upbringing. Just under nine years of age, the child had that look of mistrust and uncertainty in his eyes when his father was near. Amsu insisted he had no choice but to bring him when he escaped, saying the lad's life was under threat. It made me wonder at the reasons for this – very strange - but what could we do? Kasmut had lost his wife and child and it gave him some degree of comfort to take on the care of the youngster, who was, after all, a good-natured boy. Kasmut had taken pity on him the moment Amsu discovered he had smuggled a kitten in his hastily packed bag. Raging and shouting, Amsu had been beside himself with anger as he threatened to kill it. The child was so incensed; he opened his mouth and let out a deep roar in protest. It was Kasmut who put a stop to this and placed a comforting arm around the teary-eyed but defiant boy, whilst his scrawny kitten hissed and spat at the father. The bond was made and Kasmut's invisible arm remained in place for all the years thereafter.

Amsu was far too preoccupied with catching up on thirty 'wasted' years, as he termed them, and immersed himself in the projects his brothers had started, eventually taking Firas' place. Amsu was located a good distance from our new base so he rarely returned, and Kasmut told me he seldom asked how the boy was. I did feel sorry for the lad. Left to his own devices for much of the day, he watched endless television programmes and movies. I suppose this did enable him to develop an in-depth understanding of the new world in which he found himself, but it was a lonely life for someone of his tender years. By the time he was eleven, Sefu had managed to establish several new markers here, all linked to the ones hidden in the empire. After much pleading from his nephew, Sefu found a way for the lad to pay a brief visit to his former home. Amsu was dead set against it, and perhaps it was sheer folly to risk everything with a return to the very heart of the empire, but it was Sefu who took pity on the boy and pointed out that it was so reckless, that the enemy would not be expecting it. There was indeed truth in that!

When the lad returned a few months later, he had gained a new maturity and was adamant he wanted to be part of our revolution. He even said he was willing to sacrifice his own life for the cause. He may not have had the Zuberi physical characteristics, but he certainly had the Zuberi blood flowing through his veins! His birth title, Tarik, was most suitable. You probably know it means 'warrior', but of course we have always known him as our little lion after Eshe gave him the alias 'Leonard'.

As time had moved on, and everyone else was incapacitated, aging rapidly, or lost, like Kasmut's child, it was decided to allow this brave lad to become a protector for both mother and child, should we be able to restore them, and he readily agreed. I hope this does not cost him dear.

SANCTUS CRYPTUS

*L*eo suggested they took a long and circular route home, so Imogen could have a go at driving on the local motorways and get a complete change of air. He knew that the forced concentration would be a therapy for her after the emotion of Eshe's death. Doing something practical enabled Imogen to put her sadness and troubling thoughts to the back of her mind, as she automatically adapted to the new driving experience as if it was second nature to her. Although she intrinsically knew the increased dangers of driving at speed and the need to stay alert, she could not stop herself feeling a buzz as the car zoomed along the fast lane. The network of motorways played in her mind like an internal 'satellite navigation', and she effortlessly changed her speed and lanes in response to the traffic around her. She felt her emotions calm, as she became completely at ease. Realising the fuel was nearly on empty and her stomach suddenly feeling much the same, she pulled in at a service station.

They sat at the corner of the restaurant and as she had finished eating, Imogen slowly spun the central five-pointed star of the pendant as she held it to the light and Leo tucked into a large bowl of ice cream. In succession she admired the solid circle, outline circle, solid star, clear star and, through them all, the pointed arrow.

"It's so beautiful, what does it mean?"

"It was known as the Sanctus Cryptus. Each separate part is a symbol," he replied, mouth full of dessert. "Five symbols of the five genetic lines, you could call them the freak codes if you like!" he added, with an orange jibe of humour which left a small smile on Imogen's lips.

"Want some ice-cream?" he offered, holding out his spoon.

"What flavour is it?" she asked.

"Albatross!" he joked. "Seabird flavour..." Seeing her baffled look, he added: "Sorry it's..."

"Monty Python?"

"No, vanilla!" he smiled.

Shaking her head at both the humour and the proffered spoon, she continued: "So these freak codes, go on?"

"Well, each denotes a separate DNA personality coding. When all five are combined, they're supposed to make up the ultimate code. The old school called it sacred or sanctified."

She thought of Eshe's final words. *Sanctus Cryptus.*

"Explain?"

"You, me, our kind: we are a mixture of all the codes." Leo reached for the necklace with one finger; turned the star and stopped it when all the symbols were aligned and only the solid circle was showing. "This is Ra, the head, a solid circle." With a small adjustment to the angle, the hollow circle came into the forefront. "This is Iris, the eye." He then turned the star so it was first solid and then clear. "Nut is the hand, represented by the solid star and Hathor is the clear star and the heart. And finally Amon." He pointed to the arrow in the centre. "This line points the way forward, known as the base and also the feet."

When she didn't speak, but continued staring at the slowly spinning pendant, Leo continued, hoping to add more radiant blue-white shades to her already alluring and gleaming Chroma.

"Big-wig genetics experts discovered very early on, that they could fine-tune our race into five basic types. It took years of sophisticating and refining, as each line was genetically encrypted and advanced to achieve optimum results. It meant they could predict personalities, anticipate our characters, and match these up with our innate skills. It's how they found they could make the best of every individual and so benefit the entire race... Hey, are you listening?"

Imogen was staring at the pendant and seemed far away, on a cloud of yellows, blues and whites, the colours of quartz rock.

Where have I heard those names before? Ra, Iris, Nut, Hathor and Amon?

Her mind swept through years of schooling, television programmes and books that she had absorbed. As she continued searching on another level, she replied instantly: "Yes, I'm listening, Leo. Iris: the 'eye'. I suppose that's my line? Is that why Margaret, I mean Eshe, called me Iris?"

"Could be," he shrugged nonchalantly. "Iris is the rarest line, and you are pretty unique. No-one knows why, but it just occurs less frequently. Even freakier than the other lines," he winked, showing a sparkle of ginger-shaded teasing in his Chroma, which elicited a small smile from Imogen.

"As I said, we all have a smattering of each code, but one is always dominant. Very occasionally there may be two that are present in matched proportions – people with two lines are known as 'bi-crypts', and it has even been said that some rare folk have been found to hold three of the lines in equal measure: 'tri-crypts', but I've never seen it..."

"Got it!" She said suddenly, as her inner retrieval system focussed on a homework assignment she had completed at one of the many high schools she had attended. Names, descriptions and her orderly illustrations, displayed across the central pages of her project book unfolded in her mind's eye, as clearly as if the book was in front of her. "The names are Egyptian."

Does that mean the base for these hidden people is in Egypt?

"In fact, they're all Egyptian gods," she added. *Difference in spelling for a couple, but otherwise they match.*

"That's right," nodded Leo enthusiastically, noting her pursed lips and fleetingly wondering what it would be like to kiss them, before quickly subduing the flickers of red this prompted in his Chroma.

"I'm not sure I understand," continued Imogen. "You say these symbols represent personality codes? So what are the characteristics of each?"

"Well, the line of Ra produces strong minded, decisive and energetic people. Harry, your Grandad is from the line of Ra," he said as an aside before continuing. "That of Iris produces creative and imaginative characteristics. Sounds like you," he added with a smile. "Discipline and persistence belong to the line of Amon, that's me! - I'm an Amon, an Amon man, A-man Amon I am ..." he jokingly added in a sing-song voice, and when she remained straight-faced, he coughed, "Yes, well, never mind!" Whilst there was only a slight raise of the eyebrows from Imogen, he was gratified to see a small bubble of amused orange in her Chroma, before he continued.

"Those of the line of Nut are practical and calm, that was Eshe, and, finally, the compassionate and caring line comprises of those from Hathor. As I say, we are all a mix of each in different measure, but the one that holds the greatest ratio dictates which line you are from."

"And how do you know you're the line of Amon?"

"You're not going to believe this, but there is a mark for each line. So whichever one dominates your DNA is automatically… well… genetically inscribed on your body. Right from birth!"

"You're kidding me! So we come with a type of label?"

Leo smiled as he said theatrically, "Ladies and Gentlemen, my label: 'Leonard Newall: line of Amon; handsome, clever, witty, this way up! Batteries included!"

"Well, at least one of those is right," she replied.

"Handsome, I'm guessing!" he winked.

"I was thinking - batteries," added Imogen with a brief grin, before her sharp yellow probe and wide staring eyes subdued his smile and insisted on a fuller answer, with which Leo immediately obliged.

"So, in reality, it's a bit more sophisticated than a label. I guess it's not so much a birthmark, which is there by mistake, it's more like a hallmark…"

Leo's Chroma suddenly flared a bolt of blue inspiration, as he pushed his chair back, pulled off his trainer and sock from his right foot and lifted it up, resting it on the table so she could see the underside. A few other diners stared and gave disgusted looks, as Imogen stifled a giggle and put her hand to her nose, pretending to be overwhelmed by the smell.

"What are you doing?" she hissed, embarrassed by the attention from other people.

"Checking my shoe size!" he said sarcastically, before pointing to the area under his big toe.

"It's there!" he indicated. "Look! Under the toe: an upward pointing arrow, that's the sign of Amon."

"There's nothing there," she observed, "put it away!" But as she pushed his foot off the table, it was obvious that Leo thought he was telling the truth, as she could clearly see his snow-white honesty beneath a burnished copper indignation.

"Yes, well it would be far too easy if it showed in regular light," he said with a slight surge of purple annoyance, as he put his sock and shoe back on. "All the lines produce a mark on the relevant part of the body: head, eye, hand, heart and foot. It just doesn't show up in white light."

Imogen mused this over. "So, if I am Iris, where will this 'body stamp' be hidden?"

"Well, the mark of Iris, a clear circle, would be here." Leo leaned forward and gently stroked the area next to her right eye. Unable to mask his gold–scarlet swells of attraction, Imogen was quick to subdue an unexpected slight red flicker it produced in her colours.

She quickly pulled back and stared on the necklace in her hand, determined to suppress the strange surge of emotions triggered by yet another unknown male.

The mark of Iris - that's where Mum's birthmark is.

"So, tell me again. What is this 'Sanctus Cryptus'?"

"Well, it's complex, but I guess it has meaning on two levels. The sacred codes are the symbol of our kind: us freaks! On one level it means our entire race: all the genetic lines unified together, balancing and complementing each other, working for the good of all."

Imogen observed that the same gold-blacks denoting pride and righteousness that she had seen before in Leo, were also, interestingly, the same colour characteristics witnessed in Araz.

Leo continued: "Then on the second level, it means the one who holds all five lines in equal measure. It's considered archaic now, we've moved on from then, but it was once the ultimate objective: to combine all the codes evenly in one person. Bit like a 'super freak' I guess!" he added with a grin.

"So why haven't these 'super freaks' been engineered like everything else?"

"Look, it just doesn't happen. Geneticists spent eons working to find the right mix and with no success. It proved to be an enormous distraction from more relevant enhancements, and was finally abandoned. It used to be said, though, that when this equal balance is achieved, our kind will have reached the ultimate goal; the pinnacle of achievement, or something grand like that. Anyway no-one bothers with it anymore; it's a throwback to an age gone by…"

As he trailed off, Imogen set the inner star and circle of the pendant spinning in sequence and found her mind was also revolving with all the new information, as pictures of the Egyptian gods flashed in her mind for each line. Ra: solid circle and head; Iris: clear circle and eye; Nut: solid star and hand; Hathor: clear star and heart and Amon: upward arrow and foot. The five emblems then combined into one, and, mesmerised by the rotating ornament, she found herself launching into a deep and analytical deliberation.

So many things did not add up; her 'secret identity', the unknown incident that happened in her childhood, new disturbing information about her genetic make-up from Leo and a gut feeling that she had missed something key for most of her life. She started to pull all the threads together as several separate lines of thought began to interweave and build within her head, as the locket span.

Early childhood: bombsites, thin children in rags, discovering she was different. Playground taunts: 'you're not a fighter, you're a dirty little blighter' - that word 'blighter' she'd heard it before, but where? / Deep-seated fears: a crown in a candlelit church, shadowy figures, airless blackness, panic, the fog. / Eshe's gift and the warnings: 'they're coming – trust the Sanctus…' / Leo's random comments: 'your mum's in an induced state of unconsciousness', 'she has not aged', 'would you believe me if I said you were older than me'. / Grandad: 'things are not always what they seem…' 'It was essential that you were unaware of certain things for your own protection …' / Araz's red and gold colours also flashed across her thought: 'but you don't want to be seen', his lips near her neck and a flush of desire rippling across her inner core.

Concentrate on the other stands. Don't allow emotions to confuse.

All those years of veiling her existence at college: hiding, concealing, using the drills and shielding her colours. / The Reef's voice: '1959! – I ask you!'

Blighter! Got it - there in the wartime novel, the British spy used that term. Coward! It meant coward. Am I a coward? I'm always hiding…

The questions, facts, and possible theories all interlocked in her mind, and as she rejected all but the most logical explanation, the unbelievable gradually became incontrovertible in her mind. Suddenly closing her fist over the rotating signs, she put the brake on her thoughts.

Focus on the here and now.

Pushing the pendant into her pocket, she abruptly asked: "Leo – when was I born?"

Leo, who had been hypnotised by her reverie, which had produced a spectacular display of explosive sparks in every known shade in her Chroma, was floundered by both her sudden question, and the electric bolt of blue that ended her trance. "When?" he muttered. "Er… I dunno," he shrugged, "why?"

Imogen could see his rising yellow and mauve jagged edges of panic, and knew she had caught him unawares.

"I've figured it out Leo," she said calmly. "I know."

"Know what?" His flickers of purple alarm were completely contrary to his innocent response.

"Know that I was born in 1959 – not 1999 - in a different era." Imogen felt a calm she had not experienced for a long while as she continued, steadily analysing all those memories of years ago. She raised a hand to deter any interruption as she continued.

"The effects of the Second World War were still being felt. People spoke of it all the time. There was unimaginable poverty. My school was full of scrawny underfed kids who couldn't read Chroma and ganged up on me. I guess I was lucky, even if the word's not in Grandad's dictionary: I had much more than any of the other kids; we didn't go hungry. We had a nice home; we even had our own prized black and white television. No wonder I had never heard of programmes like 'Sesame Street'; I grew up with 'Watch with Mother'. It was a different world: no computers, no Internet, no mobile phones. My parents protected me; showed me how to shield my abilities. I can remember it just as it was, until my loss of consciousness. But now I know why, why I can't remember anything after that; why everything was so different when I woke." Imogen could not calm the surge of red anger and deep navy hurt that permeated her aura. "I know what must have happened," she said slowly, with complete conviction.

Leo's silence and rapid eye movement served only to heighten the swirl of his deep colours, as he rubbed at his ear, and appeared to undergo an internal struggle as to what to say in response.

"It's obvious, isn't it, Leo? I'm still only sixteen, when I should be fifty-six. Grandad did the same to me, didn't he? He put me, like my mother, in a suspended state of animation. He made me skip… forty - forty long years! He froze my life! All that time… Why?" Her angry sparks of deep red were accompanied by intense murky blue peaks of injury, as a solitary tear silently rolled down one cheek. She finished her revelation with one whispered question: "Why didn't he tell me?"

Leo was dumbstruck as he looked helplessly back into her enraged and miserable eyes, and not knowing what to do, he reached for her hand, which was balled into a fist, and squeezed it between his own.

When a few moments had passed, and he could sense her beginning to relax, he asked, "How did you know?"

"I didn't, not until now. I suppose I'd always trusted Grandad without question. It never occurred to me that he would… would…" she gritted her teeth and calmed the sparks of mauve-red anger that threatened to rise up again, before re-starting: "I guess I didn't delve too deeply, because I could see how it troubled him. But these last few days have made me see all sorts of new possibilities, and I finally put two and two together."

How could I have been so blind?

Disturbed by her realisation, and uncomfortable that she had been so open with someone she barely knew, Imogen stood up abruptly and announced that they needed to get home.

"Do you want me to drive?" Leo asked gently, as he trailed behind her towards the car park.

"Not a chance!" snapped Imogen

"Well, it's just that you're probably past it now!" he quipped, as he bent forward in a slow hobble, only straightening to dodge sideways and avoid Imogen's arm, as she took a mock swing at him.

"Don't get me wrong," he said with a grin, "I like older women! And you're quite amazing for your age!"

"So, you like walking then?" she retorted, as she unlocked the car, but Leo was relieved he had broken her dark mood, which could be seen both in the lightened edge of her colours, and a faint smile that curled on her lips. He raced to the driver's door first, and before she could object, he opened it wide and gestured for her to get in. Nodding assent, he couldn't resist saying: "Age before beauty," as he closed the door.

Sixty Years Earlier: The Final Briefing

The four young recruits, aged twenty-two or less: Sefu, Nuru, Rashida and Kasmut, waited nervously whilst Firas and Eshe took it in turn to address them. The small room, which had been secretly excavated deep into the rocks below the research facility, hidden by a labyrinth of false walls and buried passages, was long and narrow. At the far end of the space, a circular, opal-covered object glowed in a suspension chamber and all four glanced across to its alluring light throughout the talks.

The brothers grinned widely, evidently excited to be on the brink of a new adventure, whilst Kasmut and Rashida sat as close as they dared, without it raising eyebrows. Outwardly they focussed on the briefing and inwardly they indulged in the growing glows of attraction that radiated towards each other. Eshe was concerned that the budding relationship could detract from the mission, but she was unable to object as she, too, experienced the same overwhelming desire that she was careful to quell, when she was near Firas.

Firas was speaking in a hushed voice, which was not a necessary caution, as they could not be observed, but it seemed in keeping with the significance of the occasion: their final briefing before they set out on their mission.

"As you know, we have already placed someone of indispensable value on the other side. That person will be revealed to you upon our safe arrival, but I am unable to tell you who it is, as we cannot risk blowing such a crucial cover." Firas held up his hand to deter questions from the youngest member, Nuru, as he added; "Trust me, it will be a very welcome surprise!"

Eshe continued, "So you will be greeted by this person, who will update you on all the changes in the locality and provide you with new identities and disguises. Get used to your new names. They will protect you if we are followed; our birth names will become a thing of the past. Be prepared for anything. The world you are entering could have changed dramatically since our last communication of some five years ago, and you will have to use your wits and initiative to survive. There will be vast differences, as you are aware, living in the primitive world. You will have to communicate with little of our superior technology to hand, and learn new skills. But we are eminently adapted to this, and have the genetic advantage of quick thinking and survival."

Eshe did not wait for questions. "Now, I know you have been concerned about how we will mask our absences, once we are gone." She looked directly at the brothers. "But I can now reveal that we have a hidden ally who is not only trustworthy, but will be able to completely deceive the authorities." As she continued, Sefu and Nuru exchanged a conspiratorial wink and smile and Eshe, in a moment's realisation, raised her eyes to heaven and shook her head in exasperation.

"I was going to ask him to join us, but he is already here!" Eshe indicated Nuru with one hand, and as he stood and bowed.

"This is Amsu Zuberi," she announced with an aside to him: "always the joker!" Rashida and Kasmut looked stunned.

"You mean Nuru?" asked Rashida, very perplexed.

"No, I'm here," came a voice, as Nuru appeared from a concealed trap door that opened in the floor, and strode over to his siblings, clapping his arms around both of them.

Kasmut stood in shock, looking from one identical face to the other, as the brothers laughed loud and Rashida's face broke into a smile, as the realisation of the intrigue began to dawn on her.

"You produced twins; Nuru and Amsu are twins. Eshe, you must have done this. How incredible, and even we didn't know!"

"We couldn't risk anyone finding out."

"It's better than that," said Firas. "The lads are in fact triplets, but Sefu is a few years ahead! Eshe really is the best in her field." Eshe blushed and gave Firas a shy self-deprecating smile, as he beamed at her.

"You can never have too much of a good thing," laughed Sefu proudly, as he nudged his brothers.

Kasmut gawked at each Zuberi face in amazement, and then allowed a broad smile to spread over his face. "That means Amsu is unregistered. Everyone will think he is Nuru. Brilliant! No wonder you have got us into the habit of sending Nuru to the council with all the reports."

"Technically, we took it in turns, as we are both known as Nuru – I have rarely been called Amsu since the day I was born!"

"I can't tell you apart at all!" added Rashida in delight. "Which one of you is coming with us?"

"Nuru will go first, and we intend to swap on a regular basis – I don't want to miss all the excitement," said Amsu.

"Indeed," said Firas, "but now we really do need to continue, as there are a few final issues I need to address, so if I can have your full attention…"

Firas, twiddling his beard absent-mindedly with one finger, proceeded to give specific instructions on the use of the Tractus, explaining there was no room for error and that the tiniest mistake could be fatal. The mood quickly changed to a solemn and grim concentration, as the moment to leave came ever closer.

FURTHER TRAINING

*L*eo had gone to the Manor after their motorway trip, summoned by Harold, and returned later in the evening in a very different mood. He was not his usual jokey self; a pensive blue-grey permeated his colours. Even Sadiki seemed to sense he was preoccupied and didn't rub up against his legs, opting to sit upright in the middle of the room, eyeing him warily. Imogen knew some of this was to do with the task her grandfather had given Leo, to make arrangements for Eshe's funeral.

"Thing is," he had explained to her, flicking his hair and massaging the back of his ear, "she didn't theoretically exist. No birth certificate, plus, they require a death certificate - all necessary for a funeral. These pieces of paper are all important here," he added, with a snort of purple–red disgust.

"Tell me about it," retorted Imogen, an image of the Reef flashing unpleasantly in her mind.

"Well, unlike Eshe, and, come to think of it, me, you do officially exist," Leo said kindly. "Even if the dates have got a bit skewed. Harry told me it was Eshe who insisted on your birth being on the records here. She said it would conceal you better. And it would have done, well until you skipped, I mean missed all those years…" Leo tailed off with deep violets sparking in his Chroma, and avoiding eye contact. Imogen knew she had still not got the full explanation here, but resisted asking him more for two reasons. Firstly, he appeared clouded with a heavy grey tinge of worry she could not fathom; and secondly, she was not sure she could take any more disclosures right now.

"Anyhow," he added more cheerfully than his colours could muster, "I can sort you out a new birth certificate at the same time if you like," he offered. "How old would you like to be?"

"Think I'll stick to sixteen for now," Imogen replied, thinking of the false driving licence he had produced, and now knowing this was the sort of forgery her Grandad had meant by 'arrangements'.

"Okay, although age is not considered that important to our kind. Did you know Eshe was ninety-eight? Sounds so old, doesn't it? But for us, it's not. We live a lot longer than the people here. There's something to look forward to! See, we're built to last! If you want to work until you're well over one hundred or be a parent at sixty, it wouldn't be your age that stops you…" Leo broke off, as if he had said too much, intense purple flashes evident in his dark colours. Avoiding further conversation, he hurriedly said goodnight and shot off into his room.

Imogen checked the front door was locked, when Annie left, and as she passed his room she could hear the quiet murmur of him in muted conversation on his phone.

Sitting next to her sleeping mother, she mounted one of her paintings into a small frame and gift-wrapped it, as she spoke of all she had discovered and the confusion and pain it gave her. She was glad to note that more colour variation materialised in her mother's Chroma each time they were together. Imogen surveyed the equipment in the bedroom with an altered comprehension and frowned at all the implications of being biologically different to everyone around her. When she thought of being in the same induced state as her mother, completely outside of her control, her stomach knotted as she smarted from the hurt and betrayal it prompted deep within. She knew she must resist being swept towards the precipice, as dark thoughts enticed her to the edge. Fear, uncertainty, terror, nightmares… Once in their hold, they could spiral ever downwards, absorbing and overtaking her. She tried, instead to turn to other matters.

"So, what personality type are you, mum?" she murmured aloud. "I'm going to guess Hathor, caring and compassionate." She stroked the mark next to her mother's eye, "or maybe you're Iris and the circle is under here, or you have both, making you a bi-crypt?" As the possibilities circled in her head, the sense of yearning that had been with her for years, welled up and threatened to spill over. "Please wake up soon," she whispered as she gently kissed her cheek. "I need you." The surge of burgundy shades in her mother's Chroma was unmistakable, and that night, for the first time in weeks, Imogen slept a deep and dreamless sleep after curling up next to her, as she had done as a child.

The next few days passed in a blur. Imogen was in the mock Art exam for two full college days, and opted to have lunch in the art area, instead of going to the canteen. It gave her an opportunity to reflect on all she had learnt and immerse herself in her craft; giving her much needed displacement activity. She saw little of her friends and was thankful not to encounter Araz, although Chrissie kept sending her text messages to say he had been asking after her.

What does he want?

Danny was in the Art exam too, but between frantic bursts of painting, he spent his time staring out of the window, and didn't give her a second glance. Imogen was too wrapped up in her own thoughts to decide if he was either respecting her pensive mood, or just hadn't noticed it.

In the evenings, Leo concentrated for hours on her 'training', which she neither understood nor questioned. He seemed changed. He was distant and barely attempted humour. His Chroma was obscure, and he was absolutely insistent that she applied herself to the task in hand. Imogen assumed this was under her grandfather's orders, and still confused and aggrieved by what she saw as her Grandad's betrayal and lack of honesty, she opted to keep her own council and not ask why they were doing these strange new drills.

Leo wanted Imogen to communicate by colours alone. They sat opposite each other in the lounge, Sadiki watching proceedings warily in the seat next to Leo. He would suggest a word or action for Imogen to express mentally, and then he tried to copy her patterns and produce the same colour response.

"Silence?" he prompted.

Imogen produced a circle of cream calm, surrounded by a thin outline of authoritative black.

"Perfect," he responded, as he attempted to produce the same shape and shades in his Chroma. Imogen would have smiled at the wonky circle his effort produced, had she not been so aware that Leo appeared much more guarded and serious.

He's keeping something from me – again – but what?

"Run!"

"We've done that one," she said, bored and looking at her watch. This had gone on for over two hours already, and she wanted time at her mother's bedside.

"Again – run!" insisted Leo.

Imogen sighed and repeated the flashing yellow-mauve block, which Leo managed to copy almost perfectly.

"Go!" demanded Leo.

Imogen thought for a split second, traffic lights coming instantly to mind, she had already used a twinkling orange for caution and produced a green circle, which Leo then imitated.

"Okay – hide."

Imogen reflected briefly and then dulled earth colours into a slowly diminishing cloud, until it disappeared.

"Nice one," complimented Leo, as he tried to do the same, but only succeeded in producing a dull wash of brown that faded away.

"Now…" Leo started.

"No! That's enough. I mean, what is this Leo? Friend, foe, look, run, hide, go, jump, be quiet? I'm guessing crisis training? For when the enemy arrives, yes?"

Leo avoided eye contact and nodded affirmation, as flickers of embarrassed rust and irritated mauve spluttered in his Chroma.

"Well I don't buy it!" she exclaimed, standing and heading for the hall door. "If there is an enemy, it would be much more useful to be trained to recognise them, and know how to fight them!" she said with frustration, before leaving the room without looking back.

"There are some things you can't recognise, and some things you can't fight," Leo responded quietly to himself, as he pushed his hand through his hair, and the door slammed shut. Sadiki purred agreement and nuzzled into him, as Leo revealed his true swirling colours of conflicting emotion, which he had managed to keep subdued whilst Imogen had been in the room.

"I envy you your simple life," he said to the adoring cat, picking him up and taking him to his own room, as he turned in for the night.

Sixty Years Earlier: The Arrival

*T*he crossing went without a hitch. The six, now dressed in identical black bodysuits, were feeling heavy and disorientated. Once they were able to stand, they were quickly checked by a hooded figure in long black robes and escorted quietly in the dark, out of the large building. Into the night air and across open ground, they entered a much smaller building, went down a corridor and into a room where the lights were switched on as soon as the door was closed. They blinked in the fluorescent-lit space as they looked around, their nostrils still flooding with mingled odours and scents: incense, which had clung from the air of the other building, chalk, ink and a slightly musty smell. The brightly lit room contained thirty small desks and wooden chairs, facing a larger desk in front of a wall-mounted blackboard. Blackout blinds were down at each window.

"It's the classroom of a school – St Phillips," explained their guide in their own dialect, as he removed his hood, "which is quite apt for your arrival session – do please sit down," he invited.

The younger travellers, all feeling nauseous, stared at the robed man before them as they sank into the chairs. Recognition followed by disbelief showed on their faces.

"Tanastra Thut!" exclaimed Sefu.

"Not **the** Tanastra!" exclaimed Rashida, her face flushing with excitement, despite feeling nauseous from the journey. "The Tanastra who chronicled the rise of our race; who discovered the universal laws of relativity? Who…"

'Who modelled the Tractus,' added Firas with a grin.

"Who tragically died in his research facility," laughed Nuru, delighted with his realisation of a new incredible deception.

"I don't believe it!" exclaimed Kasmut with a broad smile. "I've admired your work since childhood."

"I told you it would be a welcome surprise," Firas added, twiddling his beard with pleasure.

"It's been said that Tanastra was the greatest mind of his time," pronounced Eshe, who rose and patted the man gently on his back as she added, "goodness, have we missed you!"

"Please," said Tanastra, self-consciously putting an open hand up in the air for them to stop. "I am not used to such accolade! My new profession demands humility, though I have to say, I am looking pretty good considering I was blown apart ten years ago! That still makes me chuckle! Now, do eat and drink, it will help with the motion sickness."

The trainees looked at the desks before them. Each held a small flat black oval shape, a plate of sandwiches and a full glass of orange liquid. Rashida had slumped back into a chair next to Kasmut, fighting back an urge to be sick, and Kasmut smiled sympathetically, as he winked at her and motioned for her to sip her drink. He also took a large gulp of the thick bright liquid, but found himself spluttering it back into his hand with surprise. "What is this?" he asked.

"It tastes wonderful," said Nuru and Sefu together.

"One of the greatest tastes on earth," replied Tanastra with a chuckle, "It's fresh orange juice! Had to beg and borrow to find oranges in the shops; supplies are still rationed, despite the last war being over ten years ago, but it's full of natural sugar and just what you require after your journey. You also need salt, so do have the food item, it is called a sandwich: slices of baked wheat dough, smeared with a dark yeast spread. You'll either love it or hate it!" he said cryptically, with a smile. "Now, eat and drink up and pay attention."

Gesturing for the newcomers to sit and take refreshments, Tanastra stood at the front of the classroom and began. "So my friends, welcome! You have been smuggled into the industrial Midlands area of Great Britain - a location you are only acquainted with from afar. The time is three o'clock in the pre-dawn hours and the year is 1956, close to the start of the autumn season. The information you were given is, unfortunately, out of date and not completely reliable, so I need to brief you in order to bridge this gap. I will start by advising you that the last two decades have proved a defining point here, as it has across the developed world. The conflict now referred to as 'The Second World War' has dominated recent history and accelerated the advance of industrial and technological developments ten-fold. Society has changed dramatically. You will need to familiarise yourselves with all that has happened: the history; politics; innovations and advances. Once you have finished your refreshments, please connect to the 'DE' in front of you."

"DE?" asked Rashida who was feeling much better, but couldn't place the acronym.

They all looked a little shocked that she had forgotten this, as Kasmut gently reminded her: "Data Encounter – Sefu developed them..." He crossed to her desk and ran his finger around the edge of the flat shape in front of her, which promptly sprang into a solid ovoid, perfect, but for the five indentations spaced at finger width on the surface.

"Oh yes, of course," she replied slightly embarrassed as she and the rest of the group cupped their individual DE's with one hand. As they connected, they sat back and their minds were flooded with the images of the previous twenty years. Facts, events, conventions, news reports, pictures, language changes, technologies, fashions; every conceivable aspect of daily life was impressed in multi-layers within their minds.

Tanastra observed them as they absorbed the information. These six were the hope for their future. The finest minds that could be found. They would have to be quick thinking and act intuitively in order to survive undetected. On them depended the salvation and liberty of their kind. The need for them to succeed was paramount.

The session lasted beyond daybreak, by which time a serious and focussed mood had descended on the recipients.

Tanastra had busied himself at the back of the classroom by sorting six neat piles of clothing on each of six travel bags, along with documents, carefully placed on the top.

He addressed the team again, switching to English: "You are probably wondering about my outfit. Well, my assumed name is Father Jonathan and I am, to all intents and purposes, an ordained Catholic priest attached to the church next to this school. This is the site of our marker and I am responsible for its secrecy and protection. The name, Tanastra Thut, must not cross your lips again."

He then indicated the piles at the rear of the room. "You each have here fresh clothing, a new name, valid identity documents and local currency. Jobs and accommodation await each of you. You will all claim to be refugees from Eastern Europe starting a new life here. It will explain why you don't have authentic English accents, or if there are gaps in your knowledge. You will be sent in pairs to different areas of the country. Firas and Eshe," he addressed the two eldest: "You will go to the capital of the country. Careers in university research await you, Professor Colin Wallace and Dr Margaret Proctor." The two smiled at each other as they changed into their new clothing and Tanastra turned to Nuru and Sefu.

"So," he spoke to the brothers, "Nuru, you will now be known as Nathan – Nathan Turner - and Sefu, your name will be Seth Turner. When Amsu finally joins us, he will be called Adam." The brothers nodded and Tanastra told them they were to go to the North of the country, working in research departments of key engineering firms.

Kasmut and Rashida had already looked through their papers, as Tanastra advised: "You will both be located here, not too far from me. Kasmut will teach basic science, here at the high school. Rashida will not have an occupation, as such, which is why we need you to act as if you are man and wife, to fit into this new life." Rashida blushed whilst Kasmut busied himself changing into his new clothing.

As they all dressed, Tanastra continued. "You will need to embed yourselves in daily life and assimilate to your new surroundings. Communication for those living elsewhere will be restricted to a monthly update, unless an emergency arises. Should this happen, you may use the devices, but otherwise they must remain hidden. Technology, as you have seen, is rudimentary here."

Tanastra glanced at each one as they sorted through their new possessions. "I must remind you that whilst we have access to unlimited funds in this primitive world, we do not want to draw attention to ourselves, so you will need to live frugally and exercise care and restraint. We need to be thoroughly absorbed into this new environment and blend in with our local communities. So, learn your new identities and backgrounds; immerse yourselves in the culture and your locality and observe, but remain unobserved. At all times stay alert. The world you are entering is one that was ravaged by war and is only just settling to a time of peace. It is a world of shortage where rationing has only just finished, and whilst there is optimism and hope, there is also prejudice and suspicion. Our presence here is, as yet, undetected, but we must be prepared for all eventualities and stay watchful in case we are discovered. Remember, exercise caution at all times."

Rashida, fresh and eager as any nineteen year old about to begin the adventure of a lifetime, placed the gold ring from the bottom of her pile on her third finger and smiled shyly at Kasmut. He nodded approvingly at her new outfit, a full calf length skirt belted at the waist, over a white crisp short sleeved shirt, with a small bright scarf tied at the neck. Tanastra had quickly given Kasmut a neat haircut, on which was placed a felt grey fedora, which went with his casual shirt over white vest and dark trousers. Rashida put her hair up in a ponytail to look like the image of a modern day model she had seen during the DE download, someone called Audrey Hepburn.

Firas shaved off his beard, which had Eshe in fits of laughter, as he scratched at his exposed chin and swore under his breath to re-grow it at the earliest opportunity. Nuru and Sefu donned identical grey flannel suits and matching dark hats as they exchanged amused winks.

"Looking good Seth."

"You too Nathan."

Rashida looked admiringly at Kasmut's muscular figure. She couldn't imagine being separated from him. They had been drawn to each other from the moment they had met, a year or so before. The magnetism between them was so powerful that they knew then, without speaking, that their futures would be forever entwined; and here they were, finally about to begin a quest of monumental importance. Her face was flushed with excitement; his was more tempered, with a calm but keen apprehension.

"So Rashida – what is your new name?" he asked.

She looked at her papers before replying, "Eli – no Eliza-bet."

"Pronounced Elizabeth," corrected Tanastra.

"Elizabeth - it sounds so strange!" she laughed. "How about you?" Without waiting for an answer, she took the papers out of Kasmut's hand to scan his details and smiled as she returned them to him, before he placed them in his bag.

Putting on their coats and taking their luggage, they turned to the others for a final goodbye as Tanastra concluded: "I do not need to remind you that your assignment will be fraught with danger and, in truth, some of you may not survive. Our future, our salvation depends on your training, your conduct, and, ultimately, your success. May the blessings of Ra be upon you all."

The Day of the Party

The next day, Imogen was glad to excuse herself from going to The Manor, as she normally did on Saturday morning. She did not feel ready to speak to her grandfather face to face, a combination of deep hurt and uncertainty rising at the thought of what he had done. She had given no indication of this when she spoke to him by phone and explained that she had promised Chrissie they would meet for her birthday and shop for outfits for the party. He sounded pleased she was going out and said he would add more money to her account for some new clothes. He had checked where she would be, arranged for a carer to stay over, despite her objections, so she did not have to worry about getting back early, and he encouraged her to have a good time, reminding her to 'act the part' with Araz. Imogen gave a sigh when the conversation was over. Leo was not around and there was no noise outside his room when she left.

She wished she could be as light-hearted and innocent as Chrissie, as they travelled together to the town centre on the bus. Chrissie was brimming with warm happy hues mixed with random red sparks of excitement. Imogen divided her mind to chat on one level and summarise all the disclosures on another. She realised, for the first time in her life, that she had doubts about her grandfather's motives. She felt totally unsure about who she was and what this meant for her future. She was repulsed at the idea of being genetically modified and worse, being put to sleep for a lifetime with no say in her own destiny. In another part of her mind, she acknowledged that it would have been nonsense to have grown to be older than her own mother whilst she recovered from whatever damage she had suffered. However, the realisation that her entire life, no, her entire being, was part of someone else's plan in which she had no say, caused her to be deeply hurt and suspicious of those she had so implicitly trusted. It had completely undermined her sense of self. The word 'why' went round and round in her head. With more questions filling her mind and no answers, she decided to put it all to one side for the time being, and gave her friend her full attention.

Imogen rarely went shopping and was not very confident buying clothes. She had even agreed to let Chrissie choose an outfit for her, although this was not without some trepidation. Imogen did not really 'do' fashion. She had neither the time, nor the money. Her allowance, which hadn't increased for years, only gave her enough to replace her basic wardrobe of jeans, tops, underwear and trainers, when they had worn out. But Grandad had been true to his word, she conceded, and her bank balance had now been healthily increased, although a belligerent part of her mind said it was the actions of a guilty conscience.

Chrissie was determined she would transform Imogen for the night and homed straight in on party wear. Not wanting to spoil her fun, Imogen allowed herself to be trailed around town all morning and ended up with a pretty, and thankfully, reasonably-priced, flared floral dress with an impossibly tall pair of shoes. She would have liked the neckline to be a little higher, but Chrissie had assured her that she looked amazing and when she added that the look was really in, very 'fifties', she could not hide her smile at the irony of the remark.

The era in which I was born!

Glad to please her friend, Imogen was really happy with the flattering choice of clothing. With her world turned upside down, she felt that Chrissie was the only person left that she could be sure of. They returned to Chrissie's house after the shops and, as it was a pleasant day, sat out in the garden.

With her parents preparing food for the party, Chrissie's three brothers kicked a football around the garden, shouting mock abuse at each other in friendly banter. Imogen quietly gave Chrissie her present, the now framed portrait she had been working on in her Art class. Chrissie shrieked in delight and called her family to come and see the picture. It showed Chrissie's smiling face in striking and unusual blends of green, brown, pink and orange watercolours; her Chroma had been caught in each brush stroke, resulting in a captivating picture of lightness and warmth. Much to Imogen's embarrassment, the family clustered round. Chrissie's dad said it was extraordinary and demonstrated a real talent and her mum dabbed a tear from her eye when she admired the painting.

"This is incredible," marvelled Callum, echoing his dad's praise and glowing ruby hues as he beamed at Imogen. "I mean, it doesn't just look like Chrissie, it, well, it feels like her too!"

Imogen flushed as they all looked approvingly at her. In another part of her mind, she could not help thinking she should be the same age as Chrissie's parents. *I was probably born before them!* Shaking off the unwelcome train of thought this started, she turned to compare their Chroma, noting the close family resemblance in the base tones which blended the mother and father's in differing measures, in each of their offspring. Chrissie and Ben had a stronger rust-orange, like their mother, whilst Callum and Rory, the two eldest, had a slightly larger measure of their father's sage-green. A fleeting sadness crossed her mind - *I wonder what happened to my dad* - but she quelled this too, determined to try and be positive.

"It feels like her too," mocked Ben, the youngest sibling, fluttering his eyes mischievously at Imogen.

"You idiots!" added Rory, as he thumped both Ben and Callum on their backs, knocking them to the ground, and ran off, hotly pursued by the other two who caught him up where they all fell, rugby tackling each other, on the grass.

"Careful!" called Chrissie's mum, "You're too old to mess about like that - someone could get hurt," she gently admonished, as she and the dad went back to the kitchen, rolling their eyes to heaven and shaking their heads in exaggerated despair.

Imogen, feeling embarrassed at the unwanted attention and the sharp contrast between her homemade gift and the shop-bought presents heaped inside, stammered quietly: "Sorry I couldn't buy you something."

"Oh my God! Gen – it's wonderful – I love it!" Chrissie responded, her Chroma glittering with a sapphire edge, echoing the awe and honesty of her words. "It's me, but it isn't me, if that makes sense. You've made me look lovely!"

"Well, you are lovely, and anyway, I could always add a moustache," joked Imogen, as she pretended to pull back the picture.

"Hands off!" laughed Chrissie, protecting the frame with both hands.

The doorbell rang and as Chrissie went to answer it, Imogen could not help but envy her friend's happy and loving family. Not for the first time, she wished her life was more straightforward and she was accepted for who she was.

But who or what exactly am I?

Richard was at the door, glowing gilded reds. He insisted the girls walk with him to the local school to see his surprise and Chrissie's was delighted to find his birthday gift was a driving lesson, arranged with a young person's driving school. The car didn't leave the parking area of the grounds and most of the lesson was spent with the instructor explaining the controls, but Chrissie was finally given a try at the wheel. Imogen and Richard looked on from a grass bank that bordered the car park, and Richard's colours blazed with a scarlet heat and a deep green pride as he watched Chrissie clearly enjoying the experience. Imogen had to bite her lip when the car kangarooed and stalled in quick succession. *Ouch! The engine won't like that!* She was very glad she had already mastered this skill, as the primitive way looked painfully slow. *Did I just use the word 'primitive'?*

On the way home, Chrissie linked arms with both friends. Imogen was pleased to see that her orange glow of appreciation for Richard was now rimmed with a few red-pink sparks whilst he was practically radiating burgundy adoration as he casually rested his hand over Chrissie's forearm.

They spent the rest of the afternoon preparing for the party, setting up the band equipment, lights and buffet table, and dressing the local church hall with balloons and streamers. The effect of spending the day with Chrissie and her family was to entirely lift Imogen's mood and she found herself looking forward to the evening and her plans to change her outward attitude to Araz, should he bother to come. It gave her butterflies in her stomach just to think of it, but also a sense of excitement and anticipation.

When they finally got ready, Chrissie took charge.

"Now, you just need a bit of make-up. Don't screw your nose up, Gen, I promise I'll give it a light touch! Close your eyes… Perfect!"

Chrissie applied the eye shadow as she happily chattered. "Danny said a funny thing yesterday."

"What?"

"He said you had a stalker!"

Imogen's colours prickled internally as she casually asked, "Really? Who?"

"Oh, you know Danny – makes a random remark and moves onto something else without explaining. He is funny. I did wonder if he meant Araz. A couple of people said he was acting a bit strange and Katie swore he tried to catch you up at the gate the other day, but who knows? Anyway it looks like you may have struck it lucky with him, although if you ask me, he's the lucky one."

Imogen was surprised Chrissie had detected this, acknowledging that without being able to see Chroma, there were other ways to determine someone's feelings, but there was no glint of jealousy and only the softest yellow enquiry. She decided to say nothing and her friend sensitively moved the conversation on.

"It was a bit of a result getting him to come to the party. I'm not sure Richard likes him, but I guess I can probably keep him occupied," she smiled shyly. "It was so sweet of him to get me that driving lesson. He's so tall, and quite good looking, isn't he?"

Imogen sniggered as Chrissie exclaimed, "What? Well he is. Hey! Stop laughing! Gen! Pack it in, or I'll smudge your lipstick!"

THE PARTY

*O*nce the party started, it didn't take long for the decorated church hall to fill. Chrissie's brothers had set up their band equipment on the stage. Her parents manned the kitchen, allowing beer to the older age group and a single glass of buck's fizz to the younger ones as they arrived. Imogen was glad Chrissie had not heard Leanne sneer at this arrangement with obvious disdain. Chrissie was blissfully unaware of Leanne's grumbles and cryptic remark to Katie: "We'll soon see about that."

Callum, seeing Imogen transformed in her new outfit, gave an approving smile and wink as he turned off the lights and the DJ began the music. Bright disco lights flashed in a multitude of colours, in time to the bass beats. Laser beams and spots of light from the glitter ball above moved around the walls and floor of the room, changing the rather drab hall into a vibrant dance floor. Callum's red hues of attraction immediately disappeared and Imogen remembered, in an instant, that the effect of the artificial multi-coloured lighting was to obscure Chroma. She hadn't been to many discos, not liking to leave her mother often, despite carers being available later in the evening when required. She realised, with relief, that she could no longer detect the thoughts and emotions of others and furthermore, her own colours were blocked. If Araz were able to read Chroma, he would be unable to do so in here. She felt liberated, as she thought through her act of swooning over Araz in her attempt to look 'normal', and smiled within at the thought that no-one was able to observe her red-gold sparks of intrigue and anticipation.

Araz slipped in unnoticed soon after the start. Slightly breathless and agitated, he calmed himself, unseen in the shadows at the back of the hall, whilst he waited his moment. As soon as Chrissie was whisked off to dance by Richard, he made a beeline for Imogen, who was momentarily taken aback as she had not seen him arrive. Quickly changing tack, she launched into her 'besotted' act and was pleased to see that he seemed a bit disconcerted as she fluttered her eyelashes at him and flashed him a dazzling smile.

"You look nice," he said, after a brief pause and even without being able to observe his Chroma, Imogen could tell from the way his eyes flickered quickly around the others in the room, that he was unsettled.

Determined to take advantage of this, Imogen giggled, "So do you," which she knew sounded silly as he was still dressed in the same leather jacket and jeans he had worn at college. She grabbed his arm to lead him to the buffet table across the room. It was wonderful to know that the red electric thrill produced by touching his muscular arm and breathing in his scent could not be detected, unlike his awkward body language, which clearly showed how ill at ease he was.

Leanne was standing at the refreshments table, her back only just evident, as Katie and Danny shielded her. She jumped around guiltily when Araz and Imogen got there. Leanne was dressed in a tight black strapless dress, which was not a good fit around the bust. This resulted in her hitching it up every few minutes as she laughed nervously and smirked at Araz. Imogen could detect a strong mint smell on her breath and without being able to see them in the disco lights she knew instinctively that, were they visible, her colours would be quite hazy. Leanne giggled and attempted to pour several ladles full of brightly coloured punch into some plastic glasses, which resulted in a large quantity being slopped over the table.

"Want some fruit cocktail?" she slurred to Araz, proffering a full glass, as she dropped her bag to the floor and kicked it out of sight under the table, the sound of an empty bottle was faintly heard, chinking out onto the floor from within.

Danny, dressed rather absurdly in a dark dinner jacket with a vivid yellow bow tie, shaped his hands into a camera, framing Leanne's flushed face and observed loudly: "Subtle as a kick in the teeth!" which set Leanne off, laughing uncontrollably.

"Not for me," Araz politely refused. "Do you want some Gen?" he asked, taking the glass and passing it to Imogen.

"It's looks very orange," replied Imogen, with a giggle, perfectly mimicking Leanne's flick of the head and raising of the eyebrows as she held the drink up to examine it.

Leanne, vaguely aware she was now competing directly with Imogen, tried to look seductive and said in a garbled voice: "That'll be the man… mango," and then sniggered hysterically.

Imogen was about to purse her lips, but remembered she was supposed to act like Leanne and instead attempted to copy the titter, which, rather too loud, sounded more like a cackle. Araz raised an eyebrow and Imogen, suddenly feeling embarrassed, quickly downed the drink in one. This only caused Leanne to snort with more laughter, spilling her own drink over her dress. Katie quickly dragged her off to the kitchen to mop it up.

"So," asked Danny in a booming voice and turning the 'camera' onto Araz. "Do you think Leanne drinks too much?"

"No," replied Araz sarcastically, "she spills most of it!"

Danny roared with laughter and, to Imogen's surprise, dropped his camera hands and clapped Araz on the back. Araz looked shocked and a bit flustered at this contact. In fact, had Imogen imagined it, or had his hand made a quick fist which he promptly un-flexed? Imogen, feeling more unnerved and slightly heady, poured herself another glass of the fruit punch, which she sipped as she tried to chatter about anything of no consequence. Araz appeared decidedly dejected after several minutes' mindless talk of the weather, the sales in the shops and the colour of her nail varnish and shoes. Imogen had to admit it was all going to plan, as she trawled her memory for every puerile sentence ever uttered by Leanne and regurgitated each one in turn.

I'm even boring myself, she chuckled inside.

As she finished the drink, Callum joined them and made a flourish of pouring another, handing it to her whilst giving Araz a territorial look. Not wanting to be rude, Imogen took the cup, muttered thanks and took several large slugs, as Callum faced Araz.

"So, not seen you before, mate. Where are you from?" He gave a polite smile as he asked the question, but there was a clear challenge in his eyes.

When Araz just stared back, face defiant, Imogen found herself stepping between them and answering: "He's new to college, and Chrissie asked him to come…" She trailed off awkwardly, as they continued to stare each other out. She was unsure why she felt the need to defend Araz, although she was annoyed that Callum was behaving as if he had some kind of possession rights over her. She was very relieved when Danny broke the confrontational stance as he suddenly took out his mouth organ with a flourish, and gave a loud blast on it, followed by the trill of a well-known cowboy tune. *The gun showdown - from the Good, the Bad and the Ugly! Honestly, Danny!*

Callum relaxed and laughed out loud and a small tight smile crossed Araz's lips as the moment passed. Relieved, Imogen drained her glass and absent-mindedly poured and drank two more, as the lads started to talk about music. Araz seemed keen to join in the conversation. *Probably fed up with the tedium of mine,* she smiled inwardly.

In no time Callum, Danny and Araz were engaged in an animated discussion about their musical likes and dislikes and, as Imogen gulped the drinks and listened, she began to feel decidedly queasy and found herself unable to work out what they were saying. *Maybe it's because I can't see their colours.* Imogen couldn't be sure, but she thought Araz had mentioned that he played guitar. *No – does he?* And Danny was shouting something. She thought he had asked Araz to join them, but he had firmly refused, whilst Callum maintained a stoic silence.

Danny persisted obstinately, despite an obvious lack of support from Callum and Araz remained adamant, recoiling slightly from the strident tones of Danny's sonorous voice. It was a relief when Katie came and interrupted, looking for Leanne's bag. Leanne was unwell and needed to go home. Callum bent down to retrieve it just as Ben and Rory came up behind, exchanged a mischievous nod, and, in unison, jumped down on top of their older brother, pushing him flat under the table with a thump. There was an ominous sound of breaking glass and their laughs quickly turned to a shocked concern, as

Callum yelped with pain. They hurriedly moved off him, and he scrambled up from the floor.

"Arghh! Crap! Look what you did!" he shouted as he hopped from one foot to the other, cupping his left hand with his right, revealing a bloody wound on his palm, from which protruded a jagged piece of glass.

"Well, which idiot put glass down there?" shouted Rory. A flurry of activity ensued, where Katie pulled back the tablecloth to reveal Leanne's bag and sharp pieces of broken bottle scattered across the floor. Callum was led to the kitchen by his concerned brothers and Imogen, quelling a bilious feeling, stooped to help Danny pick up the glass. She was surprised when a shard sliced into her finger and thumb drawing a blood red weal across the pads. She didn't really feel it, but instinctively dropped the fragment, closed her hand and stood whilst others rushed to clear up the mess. Araz grabbed a serviette and held it out to her.

"Are you alright?" His eyes showed concern, but he also seemed excited, his breath having quickened. Imogen struggled to respond, but knew, even through her haze, that he was testing her in some way. She grabbed the serviette and pressed it over the injured digits, mumbling that she was fine.

Focus, why can't I focus? Sugar — need a boost - drink more juice.

Araz helped to clear the broken glass, glancing at Imogen every few minutes, as she held tightly onto the square cloth and swallowed more bitter-sweet fruit punch.

Callum's brothers reappeared, Ben looking close to tears, as they announced that whilst Callum was fine, he would be unable to play guitar with a bandaged hand, so the live music would have to be cancelled. Imogen could see Chrissie consoling her brother in the distance, as the disco continued regardless, and Danny, who did not cope well with change, came up with a plan and insisted vociferously that Araz played instead. When he commandeered the younger brothers to join in the persuasion, Araz eventually gave in, with great reluctance, and they hurriedly discussed which numbers he knew and rushed round to get him printouts of the chords and riffs needed.

Imogen, automatically tucking her injured hand protectively under her other arm, a habit she had acquired from infancy, so others did not detect her rapid healing, was unable to finish the half cup of sickly liquid in her other hand. She could not quite work out what had been decided, but thought she should say something… something close to a Leanne phrase, so she urged: "Oh, do play Awaz…" She could not understand why speaking had become so difficult. It felt as if her mouth was stuffed with cotton wool. The disco beats were starting to bang in her head and she was glad when it finally stopped and the DJ announced the 'band of brothers'.

Giving her a piercing, quizzical look, Danny then turned to Araz, who was staring in the direction of her hidden hand. *The cuts, he's trying to see them.*

Danny remarked with volume: "Ah well, the power of speech is not everything," before rolling his eyes up and down and indicating for Araz to follow him to the stage.

The main lights went back on, briefly, for the lads to tune up for the live music. Imogen could see Callum reluctantly giving Araz his guitar under the instruction of Danny, and although he looked a bit annoyed, she could not clearly see what he was feeling. She was surprised to find that everyone's Chroma appeared blurred. It also seemed to take a great deal of concentration to balance on her high heels. She did notice Araz give her a last intent look, which ended with what she could only describe as a dismissive shrug, as the lights went down.

It was a welcome respite to obscure all those fuzzy Chroma she could not bring into focus. After a short tuning up which produced a glimmer of a smile on Araz's face, the band struck up a well-known number, Rory on the drums, Ben on bass, Danny with harmonica and Araz on lead guitar. The sound flooded the hall and nearly all the guests cheered and got to their feet to dance. Imogen steadied herself against a nearby wall and watched. The band was good, and even though she had a buzz in her head and her mouth felt so dry, she could see the dexterity of Araz's hands as he played chords in perfect rhythm and harmony with the others, as if he was a long-standing member of the group. Even Callum seemed to approve as he watched from the edge of the stage.

As the guitar instrumental section started, Imogen was intrigued to see Araz's face glow with a deep concentration and innate pleasure and she became so captivated by him, she hardly noticed when the ultra violet disco lights were switched on. In fact, the glowing whites and radiant blues highlighted on sections of clothing in the crowd blended with the Infrared white heats from each body and they all quivered and span in front of her, as if part of a moving ethereal trance.

It took her a few moments to realise Katie had come up to her and was trying to tell her something.

"Hey Gen," Katie yelled over the loud music. "Love it! That was my surprise, to get the make-up. Where did you get yours?"

"Sorry? What?" she mouthed back, feeling a lot worse to try and focus on lip-reading Katie's words. Katie smiled and closed her eyes, showing her eye makeup, which was now glowing bright in the UV light, revealing iridescent flowers and butterflies she had carefully painted on.

"The neon paints," she shouted, as she pointed at her lids. "They're great – I did Chrissie," Katie nodded across the hall and Imogen followed her look to where Chrissie was happily dancing with Richard. Her face, lit by the same UV rays, now had a large white-blue 'L' shape on each cheek, with a '17' on her forehead. These had not been visible before.

Imogen managed to splutter, "Mmm?" as she tried to make sense of what Katie was saying.

"It's not as artistic as your efforts!" Katie laughed. Still feeling woozy, Imogen didn't know why she was being complimented and shrugged her shoulders.

"Think you've had too much fruit punch Gen!"

Imogen blinked in response, looking genuinely blank.

Katie giggled and shouted over the noise in the hall, "Anyhow, just saying, love the circle," she pointed next to Imogen's eye. "And that star, on your hand, amazing!"

Slowly raising her hand to look at it, Imogen barely noticed that Katie was whisked away to join the dance. She could do nothing but stare at the perfect five-pointed star, which clearly glowed as a solid silver shape between her thumb and first finger. She instinctively rubbed at it but it didn't change.

What the? Solid star – what does that mean? Ra – no - Nut?

Feeling increasingly wobbly on her feet, Imogen, unaware the bloody serviette had fluttered to the floor, made her way around the heaving dance floor to the wall mirror behind a line of chairs. She peered at her face, lit by the ultra violet light. Next to her right eye was the outline of a perfect circle. She gawped as she traced the circle with a fingertip.

Iris.

As she moved her head back and forth she noticed a glimpse of another mark behind her ear. Pushing her hair out of the way and turning her head to one side, she could just about see the solid circle under her right ear.

The mark of... of Ra? Three! Star – solid circle - clear circle. Three marks. What had Leo called those with three equal codes? Tri-scrypts? Why can't I think straight? Could I be a tri-thingy?

Imogen then recoiled from the mirror. It was just visible at the chest line of her dress. She felt faint as she bent forward to reveal the full mark placed centrally, the clear shape of an outline star glowing mystically.

Hathor, the heart.

With a sudden sense of urgency, she stepped out of her right shoe and bent her leg back from the knee to look at the underside. She swallowed back a gag reflex. The arrow. *Amon.*

It was there under her big toe, gleaming in the glow of the bluish-purple disco light. The song came to an end and as the crowd cheered and the band started another number, the UV light was turned off. The mark disappeared at once. Imogen lurched and steadied herself by pressing her hand to the mirror.

She had all five marks.

It just doesn't happen. Leo's words rang in her head.

Super freak!

Feeling faint, she sank into one of the chairs as she slowly put her shoe back on.

Your true identity came Grandad's voice, and then Eshe's: *Sanctus Cryptus.*

She fumbled in her bag and took out the necklace and stared at the symbols, dangling at the centre, as she held them up and they turned in the bright lights. Feeling a surge of nausea, and not realising Araz had ceased playing and was staring intently at her and the sparkling pendant; she stood and ran shakily to the toilets, just in time to be violently sick into a sink.

Chrissie, who had seen Imogen race out, came dashing after her, full of concern for her friend. Imogen was already feeling a lot better; the clammy feeling was receding and her head, which had thumped violently inside her skull a few moments before, was now starting to clear. Chrissie made her sit in a chair and drink some water, as she cleaned up the sink.

"Bloody Leanne! She only went and emptied a massive bottle of vodka into the mix," she was complaining angrily. "It was her fault Callum cut his hand. Silly cow! She passed out in the kitchen and dad had to take her home and then I got the blame," she added in an offended tone.

Plucking a piece of jewellery from the vomit and holding it with the edge of one finger and her thumb at arm's length, she gave Imogen an enquiring look before saying: "Do you remember eating this?" They exchanged glances before bursting out laughing, and Chrissie washed it under a running tap before drying it on paper towels. She briefly held it up to the light to examine the spinning stars and circles, and then returned the necklace to Imogen.

"It's beautiful," she admired. "I've never seen anything like it. Well clever, the way it changes when it's wet. Where did you get it?"

"Oh, it was a gift from an old friend of Grandad's," she answered truthfully, as she put the pendant back in her bag, making a mental note to check it out in water at home.

"So, is that really what being drunk is like?" Imogen shook her head as her mind finally returned to full clarity. "Horrid!" she groaned.

"Well, you couldn't have been that hammered," retorted Chrissie. "If you were, you wouldn't make sense now, and you'd have woken tomorrow without knowing how you got home. Then, you'd have the hangover from hell for at least two days, as you tried to piece together how embarrassing you were!"

Imogen did not enquire how Chrissie knew this, but was never as grateful as now, that her body repaired at high speed. Remembering the broken glass, she glanced at her previously cut thumb and finger, rubbing the soft pads together and noting all trace of injury had gone.

Chrissie, glowing red-pink hues, talked about Richard, which prompted a flutter of red embers in her Chroma. Imogen smiled and squeezed her hand, and, as their fingertips briefly touched, an image of Chrissie's recent experience of kissing Richard skimmed across her mind.

"He's liked you for ages," said Imogen, knowing Chrissie could not realise she had shared this intimate moment.

"Well, Araz likes you!" responded Chrissie. Imogen then remembered her ridiculous act and inebriated responses in front of Araz, and the clear look of utter disappointment he had given her, as the lights went down. She was surprised to find that she felt a little saddened to have repulsed him so successfully.

"Thought, for a minute, you were going to blow it with him," chirped Chrissie.

"You mean, I haven't?" asked Imogen very bemused.

"Well, he's waiting for you outside," she smiled. "Very concerned about how you are, and if he can help, so, suck this mint, and let's get a bit more lippy on," she said, as she forced a sweet into Imogen's mouth and applied some new make-up.

Imogen felt a surge of conflicting emotions: how did Araz prompt her to spark crimson attraction? And why should she feel relieved to think he may still like her? She was supposed to have put him off. She seemed unable to control her emotions when he was around… She cautioned herself - he could still be 'the enemy' and she needed to watch out. But surpassing all of these questions was the sense of horror that she had all five marks. Touching the area next to her right eye, she asked hopefully: "Chrissie, did you use those special face paints on me?"

"The UV ones? No! Katie brought those. Her surprise was to plaster them all over me! Although, I reckon you can still see the outline in normal light," she added, as she rubbed at the faint 'L' shapes on her cheeks with a wet finger. "There! Now we're both looking more like it!" she smiled approvingly.

Imogen swallowed hard and found herself quickly checking her face in the mirror, both relieved and disconcerted, to find her marks were now completely invisible. She used the drill and internally dulled down all the clashing colours that permeated her Chroma and, taking a deep breath, she followed Chrissie out.

Araz was waiting just outside the cloakrooms and gave her a seductive smile as he crossed to ask if she was okay.

"Not playing?" she asked, glancing at the band, the three brothers were on stage, as Callum attempted to strum guitar with his bandaged hand.

"Not one I know," he responded. "How's your hand?" he asked, with an intense look at her.

"What happened to your hand?" asked Chrissie, immediately concerned and grabbing Imogen's arms to turn her hands over and back, to examine them.

"Nothing," replied Imogen, as she quickly pulled them back from Chrissie's grasp. "They're fine!"

"Oh sorry, I thought you'd been cut," said Araz, his smile almost a sneer and his voice full of accusation. "Glad to see nothing is damaged." With a slight flick of the hand, Araz transferred a tissue to the top pocket of his shirt and slowly pushed it down inside, two small bloodstains visible for just a brief moment, all the time staring into her eyes. In a fleeting glance, she saw the serviette and Imogen felt as if she had been kicked in the stomach, her emotions surging purple peaks of panic. Although the disco lights hid her colours, she knew he could see it in her face. Her mind simultaneously layered all the times she had encountered him, his voice echoing in her head: *But you don't want that, do you? - To be seen – Clever!* And Grandad's voice: *Trust your instincts.*

She looked into his dark eyes and there, in the depths, she could see his gold-yellow-black spikes of challenge and power. In an instant, she realised that her worst fear was right.

He knows – he's looking for me. He is the enemy.

Imogen froze, unable to take her eyes off his, as Chrissie looked confused at their unspoken exchange. Not for the first time that evening, Danny broke the spell, as he arrived and placed an arm around Araz's shoulder, causing him to recoil and break eye contact with Imogen.

"Gen - your lift's here," he announced loudly, giving her the tiniest wink.

"My lift? Oh yes… Er, thanks Danny," she responded gratefully and muttered, "got to go," to Chrissie, giving her a squeeze.

Chrissie, who knew there was some issue she had missed, but full of loyal support for her friend, nodded and put her arms through Imogen's, as they headed for the exit together, leaving Araz squirming under Danny's arm.

"What's going on?" she asked. "Danny wouldn't touch anyone, unless it was extreme circumstances. Was Araz being a creep?"

"Something like that."

"Why is it the fit ones are always creeps?" Chrissie complained.

"Look, I'll call you tomorrow, don't worry," said Imogen, "I've got money for a taxi home," she added, as she swung the hall door open and stepped out, rummaging in her bag for her purse.

"Danny said you had a lift."

"He was just covering for me, could see I was in a bit of a fix. Reckon he's got a sixth sense!"

At that moment, headlights dazzled them as a rusty red car swerved into the road, braked sharply with a loud screech, and came to a standstill in front of them. A tall lad, with curly blonde hair jumped out, his face full of alarm. Even in the moonlight, Imogen could see that his grey-mauve sparks were flashing so brightly they were close to ignition.

What on earth?

When Leo spotted Chrissie, he carefully toned down his anxiety and gave her a quick nod as he casually said: "Sorry, got to rush. Get in Imogen. Cheers!" He dived back into the driver's seat and revved the engine.

Imogen looked apologetically at Chrissie, whose eyes were urging some explanation, and hugged her, saying in her ear: "Look, I didn't know he was coming. He's just a friend. Tell you tomorrow," as she got into the passenger side of the car and they sped off.

Chrissie gave a small wave, with a dumbfounded expression on her face, as Danny and Richard came out of the church hall and stood next to her. As the car turned a distant corner, a motorbike with helmeted rider shot past, and disappeared in the same direction.

"Told you she had a stalker."
Chrissie and Richard looked at Danny.
"The bloke on the bike?" asked Richard.
"No. The bloke in the car."

Araz

When he had arrived at the disco, Araz had been in a high state of tension and needed to compose himself in the shadows at the back of the church hall. He reviewed the events of the day with confusion and annoyance. Things should not have gone so badly wrong. Someone else must have interfered. But he was the only one in the near vicinity, wasn't he?

He had reported the location of the Manor to his superiors at the end of the morning; delighted his initial investigation of the premises had shown the presence of sophisticated defence shields. The shields had clearly been disguising and deflecting the subversive communication signals proving the old house was being used as a base, but, incredibly, they had been turned off. Why? Was this a deliberate ploy or a stupid mistake?

With Imogen's undeniable links to the owner, this clearly pointed to her being the illegal child for whom they searched. However it was not corroborated and until he knew for sure, Araz decided to only advise the facts, as he knew them: "Signal jamming devices of a kind that could only have been developed in the empire, evident at the address. Current status of owner to be ascertained."

Uneasy he had, yet again, not included any mention of Imogen, Araz argued to himself that he could add more once he had full evidence and at which point he would recommend an appropriate course of action. This was his project now. He decided to ignore the deep-seated turmoil and stirs of arousal he was unable to shake off each time he thought of the young woman.

He had returned to the home at the end of the afternoon and entered in the guise of being a gas engineer doing an annual maintenance check. The worker at the door had, initially, been reluctant to admit him but Araz had poured on the charm, flashing gold-reds, which he now realised had more than the desired effect, even if these blind primitives could not see Chroma directly. The chunky crooked-toothed woman in her drab clothes appeared disoriented and had blushed deeply, mumbling something about getting him a drink before he left. All it took was a wink and a seemingly sincere compliment. These low lives are so deluded, he had thought contemptuously; how could such a specimen think anyone would find them attractive.

The home had seemed ordinary and unexceptional. A musty aroma assaulted his highly tuned senses, as he noted the decrepit state of the residents sleeping on worn furniture or moving hesitantly around with the help of an assortment of wheelchairs and frames. How could anyone live in this state? They were barely human, he thought to himself, as he headed for the stairs.

What happened next had been a shock. He had heard the front door being smashed inwards; an almighty crash of splintered wood and broken glass. Gruff shouts and heavy footsteps sounded from the open doorway and the residents caught in the entrance screamed in alarm. Araz had instantly dived under the stairwell to observe events out of sight. He was acutely aware that what he was witnessing was, without doubt, the unanticipated action triggered by his own report.

He had only seen the secret 'Repro' warriors once or twice, during his early training. Like the Tractus, knowledge of their existence was restricted, but he had never seen them operational until today. Their gratuitous brutality confirmed in his mind that their tactics were crude and vicious and whilst he fleetingly regretted sending his last report, he realised in a flash that this was a clear message that he had suddenly been discounted. Someone had decided not to await his detailed findings, but to take action without his involvement. Why? Who had ordered the Repros into a situation he was handling perfectly well by himself? It meant his predicament had now become precarious and as soon as he managed to exit without being seen, the corridors echoing with angry shouts underpinned with wails and sobs, he hastily returned to the safety of his bedsit to check his device.

The communication that was awaiting him sent a jolt through his body. Something was not right. He had been recalled to base immediately. Why? After all, it was he who was ahead of all the others and he who had led them directly to one of the subversives. If his intuition was correct, and he was ninety-nine percent sure of it, the girl was the one and he was just a stone's throw from confirming it. Perhaps he should have sent a preliminary report when he first suspected it. Could someone else have found her too? Had they reported on his failings? If so, he would need to do something to redeem himself and go directly to his own commander. As Araz layered all his options in his mind, he quickly came to the conclusion that there was only one course of action he could take.

He knew he would be disobeying orders to continue, but figured he could argue he had not seen the instruction until after he had the girl safely in his grasp. He was glad he had invented a way to open the messages undetected, so the automatic 'command read' signal was overridden.

Shuddering at the raw violence employed by the Repros, he felt an overwhelming sense of protection towards Imogen. He could not rationalise why; he did not know her, they had barely spoken, but there was an inexplicable attraction he could not subdue and a prodigious sense that he alone should be in control of her safe passage. He had set off for the party in a determined frame of mind. He needed to justify himself to his superiors and it was now imperative that he make a final attempt to substantiate her identity and then seize her.

He had not expected to find Imogen so changed. It threw him to see her behaving like one of her insipid friends and she had even proceeded to get drunk in front of him, losing all self-control, the evidence of her intoxication in her ridiculous giggles and slurred speech.

When her hand had bled on the cut glass and she continued to hold it protectively, he had been too quick to assume she did not possess curative stem cells, plus her colours had appeared hazy and indistinct when they switched on the normal lighting. He had more or less decided it was all a massive mistake when chance, or was it luck, came into play again. In that split second in which he had looked up from the stage, he had caught sight of it in her hand, shimmering in the spotlights: the forbidden emblem used by the subversives. Unmistakable. And whilst no further confirmation was necessary, he had received it none-the-less, when Imogen had rapidly regained sobriety and it was clear her cuts had completely healed.

He was unsure what had prompted him to taunt her with the blood stained serviette he had retrieved from the floor; he surely hadn't meant to warn her? Perhaps he just wanted to get an uncontrolled reaction from her? She did evoke the strangest feelings in him. He knew this would be a sign to her, as much as the pendant had been to him. As they made eye contact, he saw her realisation. It was written in the depths of her clear blue-green eyes and in her fearful but defiant silence. He knew then that she would not go with him willingly.

Prepared, he had transferred the pen-like shot from his back pocket into the palm of his hand, pressing the activate button ready to jab, as he was interrupted. Maybe the defective, Danny, had seen the mechanism and that's why he had intervened, who knows? But thanks to that imbecile, he had missed his chance to sedate and capture her and knew he could not mess up again.

When she had dashed off, he had ducked under Danny's arm and raced for the rear door and his motorbike, to set off in hot pursuit. He would not be accused of failing in his duty a second time.

The Manor

as Leo raced along the roads at a dangerous speed, his face set like flint, he confirmed what Imogen had already surmised, saying through gritted teeth: 'Something's happened.'

Imogen, heart racing, did not press him for further information, and instead used the drill to calm her swirling emotions and rising panic as they sped along the roads. At the point where they should have turned in the direction of her home, they continued straight on and Imogen, only partially relieved it was not her mother, steeled herself as they took the route she knew would lead to her Grandad.

The flashing blue lights of the police cars and ambulances crowded on the roadside by the Manor, strobed like the disco lights she had just left behind and as Leo stopped the car at the rear of the emergency vehicles, Imogen leapt out and stared at the scenario in front of her, her heart pounding.

There was a great deal of confusion, as police officers and suited officials called to each other and spoke on their mobile phones and radios, whilst supervising the gradual evacuation of the home. Elderly people, some moaning, were being led out in their nightwear, draped with blankets, and taken to the waiting vehicles. A few were on stretchers; others in wheelchairs and a number walked with the help of frames or sticks, accompanied by nurses and people wearing badges indicating they were from Social Services.

A plump lady in a grubby blue uniform, wearing a sling around a limp arm and holding a bloody pad against her cut and bruised mouth, stood forlornly just inside the broken front door, next to two police officers. When Imogen saw her, she set her Chroma to a steely authoritative white-blue; marched up to the back of an open ambulance; lifted a white coat from the shelf inside and put it on as she walked confidently towards the brightly lit entrance.

She passed officials as they talked into handsets and caught snatches of conversation: "Eighteen residents in total, roger that. Four of the staff sustained injuries that will require further treatment; two had their legs broken by what appears to be heavy implements like baseball bats…" Imogen shuddered as she advanced up the crowded driveway and Leo came alongside her, also wearing a doctor's coat he was hurriedly doing up. They both caught more snippets of information.

"No sir – no CCTV – nothing," and "the descriptions of the attackers suggests they looked more like an army unit dressed in black and wearing helmets. Yes, I repeat, helmets."

An image from Imogen's nightmare flickered briefly into her mind. *The dark figures in the church – I can see them now - they wore helmets.*

Imogen muted any outward response, as the police officer continued: "Most witnesses are not of sound mind – no sir. How many assailants? Well, the accounts range from two to twenty! And sir, they appeared to have been organised. One said they were paratroopers, another old chap said: 'Nazis' and one even described them as dark forces…" Imogen restrained the jolt that threatened to convulse through her body.

They passed two badged women taking notes, and heard them say: "For an illegal care home, the residents look surprisingly well cared for. And given the shock they've had, it is amazing there has only been one fatality."

Who's dead? Imogen's chest tightened as she quickened her pace to reach the door, dropping her head downwards and indicating for Leo to do the same to shield them from Lisa's sight. She forced her colours to exude an innate calm and authority she did not feel.

The police officers were quizzing Lisa who, between sobs, seemed incapable of answering any question to their satisfaction. As they got to the door, Leo was forced to step in ahead of Imogen and she hesitated as Lisa suddenly looked up and right into her eyes. Momentarily holding her breath, expecting Lisa to blow her cover, it was to Imogen's complete surprise that Lisa simply glazed over and turned back to the officers. Imogen noted two key points:

the carer she had seen almost every week for the past five years clearly did not recognise her, and amidst her hazy, navy- grey colours of troubled confusion, Lisa did not have a single trace of silver in her Chroma; it had gone.

They passed into the house, the police merely nodding them through, believing they were two more medical staff, as Lisa was saying "I dunno - I've never met 'im - the owner - not once. I just come in and help get 'em all washed and settled. Them yobs were asking that too and I told 'em the same." She broke into more sobs as she added: "and then they punched Doris in the stomach. I mean she's ninety-two, 'eaven knows if she'll recover, and then they twisted me arm and thumped me in the face…"

As soon as Imogen and Leo were further down the corridor and out of sight, they dashed up the stairs and raced to Grandad's room, flinging the door wide open. Imogen gasped. It was empty, but for the bare furniture and a few scraps of litter on the floor, amidst a fine and strange powdering of dust. Her grandfather was gone, his clothing, his heaps of books and boxes, all his knick-knacks, they had all vanished. It was as if he had never been there.

She turned wildly to Leo who, deep in thought, had stooped to touch a small mound of the sand-like dust. "I heard them say there was a fatality." She didn't realise she was shaking all over until he advanced and held her shoulders tight.

"It's okay. They found Eshe. The funeral was going to be tomorrow, she had been transferred to the back of that ambulance."

Her mind replayed the image of a small sheet-covered body in the vehicle, which had registered briefly in a sub-conscious layer of her mind and confirmed it could not be her grandfather, who was much larger.

"So where's Grandad? What's happened to him?" She barely realised she was shouting, as she pushed Leo away.

Leo started pacing the floor, his face a deathly white, his colours still flaring yellow-mauve anxiety. "He said this might happen."

"What? What might happen?" she demanded, her heart thumping.

"That they might come for him. I never thought they'd actually use 'Repros' though," he added, almost to himself, before giving Imogen a weak smile of reassurance.

Use what?

"Look, he may have escaped," he said hopefully, before grey clouded every other colour, indicating how unlikely he thought this to be. A black authority began to infuse and strengthen his resolve as he added, "But he may not have. Imogen, we have to assume the worst and follow the crisis procedure."

"Assume the worst? Leo - No!" her voice dropped to a low murmur. "This is my Grandad we're talking about… he can't be… I didn't even see him today; I was so angry with him… Please, please don't say he might be dead." Tears escaped down her cheeks as she tried to rationalise everything, but nothing made sense.

"Imogen, we need to stay calm and work out what to do." Leo's voice was strong and compelling. "Tell me, what was it you noticed about that carer at the door? You saw something."

"No silver," she quickly answered, unsure why he was asking this.

"Harry said you could see his hypnosis threads."

"Hypnosis? What the hell are you talking about Leo?"

"I'll explain later, but if the carers no longer have silver, he must have broken the connection, which he would only have done in the worst emergency but more importantly, if he had time. He may be oaky. Come on, we have to go."

Imogen then noticed the small photograph of her mother as a child, still stuck in the mirror, and went and pulled it out, barely noting a date and place were scribbled on the back. Clutching it to her heart, Leo grabbed her other hand and led her to the emergency exit and the fire escape at the back of the first floor. She forced herself to quell her fears and try to analyse the new information. *Silver = hypnosis. Lisa and the other carers at the home – all hypnotised – Annie, Cath, the team of home carers. That's why they simply accepted the equipment in her mother's room. Broken connections? Leo had said this happened only in the worst emergency. Lisa no longer knew her. And what about the others?* She glanced at the photograph. *Her mother!*

Imogen gasped again and came to a standstill, fumbling for her Multi-Com to bring up the home camera, a different layer of her mind noting Chrissie's strange message, which had appeared briefly on the screen.

"No!" urged Leo as he quickly closed his hand over it. "Not here, it can be traced." Glaring at Leo in frustration, she bit her lip, shot past him to the end of the corridor where she pushed open an old door onto a rusty fire escape. Leaping the steps two at a time, she raced for the car ahead of him, as if her life depended on it.

Leo didn't argue when Imogen got in the driver's seat, threw off her high heels and started the engine. They pulled away from the kerb as soon as he was inside.

"Imogen… about Harry, your Grandad…" he started to say, as Imogen hit the accelerator with her foot and hissed back at him as she drove.

"Not now Leo, I'm using the drill. We need to get home."

What did Chrissie's warning mean? Leo: the stalker?

Leo tightened his lips shut and looked back at the Manor, as all the vehicles and swarming people outside diminished behind them, and saw that a motorbike had pulled away, just after them, and was following at the same fast pace. He was about to say they were being tailed when it dropped back and turned off down a side road, as they continued ahead at breakneck speed.

THE FOURTH CHRONICLE OF
TANASTRA: RASHIDA OMOROSE

So I now come to Rashida: Young, intelligent and quite beautiful - such deep green eyes. We were all a little in love with her, but Eshe had warned she was a wild card. Incredibly bright and artistic, she was also unpredictable and prone to dramatic outbursts. She was only accepted into the group after her parents pleaded with Firas. After all, they had hidden that she was not only a Tri-Crypt, but held the line of Iris. A special dye had been used at her birth, to permanently obscure the mark. Iris! So few remained. We were left with no choice when events overtook us.

Firstly, her parents publicly challenged some of the 'new rules' made by the regime, then her mother suddenly died. She was reported drowned, but I can tell you that such a thing is unheard of in the empire, however the authorities insisted her death was a freak and unfortunate accident. Secondly, her father was 'relocated' to a remote research facility and we lost all contact with him. We hurriedly named Rashida, their daughter, as an essential part of the restricted Tractus team; she was after all quite brilliant in adapting theories into new technologies, and she therefore became exempt from the same exile.

It would, perhaps, not have been so bad if she had just fallen in love with Kasmut, but she fell in love with the primitive world and desperately wanted to be a permanent part of it. It was, perhaps, her artistic side that felt a freedom that she had never experienced in her lifetime. It should have been no surprise when she fell pregnant. After all, our fertility was no longer being suppressed by the carefully calibrated dietary controls. Our bodies were left to their own devices. But it was hard. There were no checks for the unborn child, even by today's standards. This was, after all, only 1959. There was no way of eliminating illness or disability and she would not be persuaded to take any action, being quite determined to keep it. Of course, Kasmut supported her. He loved her unconditionally, some would say blindly, but we could not risk telling anyone else, and so we kept it secret. We only informed Eshe just before the birth so she could deliver the child, a precious little girl with a unique genetic make-up.

Rashida, really, I should call her by her local name, Elizabeth, but I seem to have reverted to our birth titles in these chronicles. No matter, where was I...

So, Rashida launched into a doting and claustrophobic relationship with the infant and would not part from her, even when it came to the time to send her to school. This may not shock you, my friend, not if you are used to the primitive, and dare I say, restrictive manner of child rearing. But our form of parenting is much wider reaching and not confined to a mere one or two adults. Our children are cherished by all; they learn from a variety of other age groups, young and old; they are assimilated into the social side of society right from the word go. Whilst 'bonding' as it is called here, is usually with several key figures, including the permanent partnership that was approved for the child, everyone takes a part in its upbringing. It is after all, essential in the early, most formative years. No one person can supply all of a child's needs and it needs to grow up with a sense of respect for others and for society at large.

Anyway, I am wandering again. The child... Yes, Kasmut had to insist that the girl was registered in a local primary school to widen her horizons, and Rashida reluctantly agreed, but only if it was the one attached to my church, so I could keep an eye on her. Such a poor area of the city; swamped with rough and ready families that had emigrated from Ireland and other parts of the world; hoping to find work in the industrial Midlands. The hardship and privation she was to witness was bound to be a culture shock for this adored and protected innocent girl. Unbeknown to the mother, Kasmut brought her to me regularly, so I could check her progress and, as I have explained, it was after one of these sessions that the tragedy occurred and she was lost to us.

Rashida was inconsolable. She paced the floor, tore at her hair, went from crying to screaming and eventually had to be sedated. She seemed unable to exert any control over what had once been a gifted mind, entirely in the grip of explosive emotions. She lacked any rationale and behaved like a disturbed human being, rather than a superior scientist. It seemed to a number of us that the primitive world had infected her in way that a virus could not, and we did not have any cure.

Over the next several years, whilst Firas, Sefu and Nuru looked for a solution, Rashida paled to a shadow of her former self. She only brightened when a concrete plan was made to attempt to retrieve the child and it was at her insistence that she was allowed to undertake the first try, although we all knew it was highly risky.

The failures were devastating, doubly so to Kasmut, as years and years passed. Indeed, the solution was not discovered until thirty years after the calamity occurred and it would take another decade to see if it worked. The small opal multi-faceted device was made on the inspiration of Nuru, who had become as expert as his older brother in bio-chemical triggers.

And, as you will now know, it did work. Thank the heavens! The return came some ten years ago. I should have been angrier with Kasmut, who had secretly arranged for Leonard to follow a back up plan that had not been passed though me; but he had been blinded by grief and longing. By the time I knew of the plan, it was too late: Leonard had gone. I was shocked that Kasmut was prepared to sacrifice this young man, should Nuru's gadget not work. We should not risk the lives of our youngsters so carelessly, but Kasmut was nearly broken with it all… Anyway I am again wittering and need to tell you of the rescue.

As Leonard was sent on his perilous journey, they arrived back, together. An emotional moment, I can tell you. But we feared the worst seeing them lying there, so still. My heart was in my mouth as Eshe and I set to work on the girl, whilst Firas and Sefu attended to Rashida.

Kasmut was devastated. He paced the floor, crying out: 'It's too late, they've been gone for too long,' and 'it's all my fault.' Firas was the one to quickly bring him to his senses forcing him to support Rashida, whilst he and Sefu administered the stimulants.

Eshe and I had to work hard to revive the child. She was a deathly pale colour and barely breathing. It was thanks to Eshe's medical skills that we finally got a response that reduced us to tears when at last, she blinked open her eyes and said: 'Where am I?'

Rashida was a different matter. My friend, I have to tell you that when she eventually came to, she had a deranged look in her eye and did not seem to recognise her daughter or anyone else around her. It was when she started screaming at an ear-piercing pitch that we decided to tranquilize her and take a full analysis of the damage. It was worse than we imagined. Nerve connections, cell synapses all controlling mental function, needed repair. Poor Kasmut. He had waited years for her final return and here she was, in nearly all respects, still lost.

Despite this, Kasmut adopted a 'hands on' approach and took over the care of his little girl, doing everything in his power to formulate a rehabilitation programme in order to repair the damage to Rashida. He developed the most sophisticated equipment to nurture and restore her. At the time of writing these chronicles, even I do not know if he succeeded, but I can only pray that all his efforts are rewarded, we have already lost too many of our number.

BACK AT HOME

$\mathcal{L}$eo put the handbrake on, turned off the headlights and retrieved the keys from the ignition and the photograph that had been left on the driver's seat, as Imogen leapt out of the car, barefoot, without a backward glance. He gave her a small smile of reassurance as she called from the front door, the relief clear in her voice: "It's locked, the door, it's locked." She turned the key, opened the door and stepped in, switching on the light.

Leo then heard her give a short scream, which was immediately stifled, and he sprinted up the path, pulling a small pen-like object from his pocket and brandishing it in front of him. When he reached the door, Imogen was being held from behind, wide-eyed and startled, by the arm of an older tall man. He had dark peppered grey hair and a prominent nose and, with one hand over her mouth, was urging her to be quiet by placing the forefinger of his free hand to his lips. The cat was hissing and scratching at his legs as he tried to shake his foot at it.

He and Leo stared at each other for a few moments, before Leo lowered his arm and closed the door behind him. The man released his hand from Imogen's jaw and hissed at Leo: "You fool! Why did you come back here? The forces have arrived. They've probably tracked you, can't you follow simple instructions?"

The cat hissed loudly, snarling at his legs. Leo glared back angrily and set his mouth in a steely line. Giving a click with his fingers, Sadiki ran to Leo and rubbed around his legs purring furiously. Imogen, who felt an odd but unmistakable familiarity with her captor, could see that he was no stranger to

Leo, whose defiant amethyst spikes of anger and resentment throbbed strongly above the russet recognition in his Chroma.

Before she could speak, Leo started to soothe these into calmer tones and put the pen back in his pocket as he said sarcastically: "Nice to see you too!"

Pushing his hair aside and holding out his open hand towards the man, he added: "Imogen let me introduce my delightful father. I apologise that instead of saying hello, his first greeting was to try to cut off your air supply, but hey! Who needs niceties?"

Imogen turned and looked properly at the man, who looked nothing like Leo. It was hard to judge his age; he could be anything from sixty to eighty. Although he had fine lines etched around his strong features, he was trim and muscular with only a smattering of grey in his hair.

Leo's father? Well, they do have the same chromatic base shades.

She trawled her memory until she found a similar visage from the past.

"I've met you before? Is it Seth?" she asked uncertainly as a photographic record of a younger look-a-like talking to Grandad flashed into her mind.

"Close," came the warm reply, showing none of the annoyance he had directed at Leo. "Seth is one of my brothers. I am Adam, Adam Turner. And you must be Imogen, grown up and lovely," he winked.

He's got some of Leo's mannerisms too.

"I hope I didn't hurt you, but really, there is no time for 'niceties'," he said, glaring briefly at Leo. "…The hour is upon us and we must make haste."

"Very poetic, father, but we're ahead of you. We've just come from the home and Harry's gone. Sounds like Repros."

Repros? That word again. Imogen could only guess at what he meant, but could plainly see the yellow-mauve ripples of fear and foreboding that accompanied the statement.

"We thought as much," said Adam.

"Our communications were cut and when I got here the carer was leaving in a state of confusion; she had no idea where she was. It can only mean one of two things: Harry has been captured or…" Adam trailed off as he glanced at Imogen's anxious face and he gave her shoulder a comforting squeeze of reassurance.

"Don't worry; there's been no indication that he's been injured, or worse, and he has every chance of making an escape. However, we can't bank on it, and we can't stay here. So now, I'm afraid, we must follow procedure."

Imogen's heart sank and, employing the drills he had taught her, she pushed the fears and dread for her grandfather to the back of her mind and forced herself to focus on the here and now.

"Mum?" she started, with a rush of anxiety as she looked up the stairwell.

"Elizabeth, your mum, she's fine. In fact she's more than fine. She's awake," he said gently and Imogen recognised another of Leo's traits, as his eyes sparkled kindly. The ice-white truth of his statement was unmistakable and her heart lurched. Turning to race up the stairs, Adam put a hand on her arm to stop her.

"Imogen, she needs gentle treatment, no shocks. Don't alarm her in any way. Don't mention Harry or what's happened. She must stay calm."

Imogen nodded agreement, took a deep breath to stifle the grey anxiety of worry and, taking two steps at a time, she bolted up to her mother's room, as she heard those long awaited words calling:

"Imogen – is that you?"

Her mother was sitting up in bed, her cheeks pink and healthy and her Chroma glowing jade-orange hues, which surged with intense emeralds and reds as she saw her daughter. She opened her arms wide and Imogen hurtled across the gap and fell, weeping, into them. They clung onto each other, rocking to and fro, smiling as tears cascaded down their cheeks, words unnecessary to express the deep emotion of being fully reunited.

Eventually, Imogen sat back and wiped her tears, grinning and staring into her mother's open eyes - her Chroma glistening with deep greens of adoration. Glancing past the monitors, now turned off, she noticed her sketchbook open on the bedside table, showing her depiction of her mother's smiling face, which perfectly matched the reality before her.

"My darling, you're so grown up! So accomplished. You're every bit as perfect as I imagined," her mother said, stroking Imogen's face and hair and squeezing hard on her wrists. "And I've watched you, from my sleep, I can remember every word you've ever said to me, seen every experience you've transmitted to me. I've shared your hopes and your fears. Bless you for never giving up on me. I may not have had voice or sight, but even so, you have allowed me to watch you blossom and mature. My lovely, darling Imogen."

Leo appeared quietly at the doorway and caught his breath when he saw the glow and rhythm of the bright dappled hues of mother and daughter. They looked so close, so in tune. Imogen's colours soared and shone and as his heart welled, he realised in that moment that he wanted nothing more than to prompt the same reaction, to trigger those feelings of joy, to bring unimaginable happiness to this beautiful young woman.

He coughed awkwardly, breaking the reverie between them. "Sorry to interrupt…" he started.

"So you're Leonard," said the mother, a note of anger creeping into her voice. "Imogen has described you as a joker, but I'm not so sure. That could just be a clever disguise…" Imogen looked quizzically at her mother who linked one hand with hers and pulled it protectively towards her, tightening her grip with the other.

"I don't trust anyone I haven't met," she glared at him, purple barbs rising in her colours. A confusion of dark suspicions and fears glanced across the tactile touch into Imogen's mind, as her mother asked: "Where have you come from? Can you answer me that?"

Imogen, who for ten years had been unable to discern clear thoughts from her mother, realised in that moment that she was far from well, her thinking being chaotic, blurred and overwhelmed with anxiety and paranoia.

"Mum, it's ok. Leo's a friend," soothed Imogen, her fingers starting to hurt under her mother's grasp. She smiled apologetically at Leo, before noting that he was attempting to form a circle of green in his Chroma.

Go! We need to hurry.

The simmer of anxiety about her Grandad threatened to surface in her own colours, and mindful of keeping her mother calm, she smothered these as her mind layered together the immediacy of the night's events: *assume the worst / dark forces / danger / we can't stay here / follow procedure / do not cause alarm.* She knew instantly what was planned, even though she didn't know how it would be accomplished.

Sending a brief surge of black to indicate 'okay' to Leo, she released her hands from her mother's hold and gently stroked her mother's arm, as she projected tranquil greens.

"Mum, Leo's going to help us move to a new place where you can fully recover," she announced calmly, as Leo nodded approvingly.

"Don't leave me," cried Elizabeth plaintively, pulling Imogen's hands back as she tried to release them.

"It's ok mum, I'm here…" she replied, noting the increasing pulse of grey in her mother's colours.

"We need to go very soon," added Leo, as Adam entered the room and Elizabeth recognised him and gave a faint smile.

"Here he is, the man who woke me. I've been trying to figure out if you're Seth?" she asked, "Or is it Nathan? I could never tell the difference! And now you're so much older…"

"Unlike you, Elizabeth…" winked Adam, as he added: "who remains gloriously young. I'm afraid I am neither Seth, nor Nathan. I'm Adam." When Elizabeth looked blank, he added softly: "You may remember me as Amsu, Rashida."

Imogen silently noted, with resignation, that both Adam and her mother had names she had not heard before. *Like Eshe.*

"Amsu! The hidden triplet!" exclaimed Elizabeth. "But you were imprisoned… how did you escape? In fact, where is everyone? Where're Sefu and Nuru?" She looked from one face to another, a frown starting to furrow on her brow. Imogen could not make sense of what she was saying.

Isn't he Leo's dad? What does she mean, hidden triplet? And who had imprisoned him and why?

Her mother continued her questioning with a faltering stutter and a growing fear in her eyes: "Where's Eshe and… and Firas?" A dark cloud of deep foggy greys began to spread in her Chroma and when, instead of replying, they exchanged awkward glances, she took on a frightened look as she mouthed, "Kasmut? – Amsu, where is Kasmut?"

Kasmut? I know that name.

Adam approached the bed and took her hand, saying: "All in good time…"

Elizabeth gave a loud shriek as a look of terror took hold: "No, not Kasmut - no!"

To Imogen's alarm she began to thrash about on the bed lashing out at Adam who calmly revealed a long thin object, which he pushed firmly against her wrist as he pressed a button at the end.

"Sh. You need to rest…"

Elizabeth's eyes slowly closed and her head slumped back onto the pillow. Imogen jumped back in bewilderment.

"Wh… what have you done?" she stammered.

Adam replied calmly, as he tenderly lifted Elizabeth and carried her to the armchair on the other side of the room. "Imogen, don't worry, it's a mild form of sedation so we can transfer your mother without distressing her."

"Transfer her?"

"We are changing location and need to move quickly. I take it Tarik, I mean Leonard, has explained the Tractus?" Adam raised an enquiring eyebrow to Leo.

Tarik?

Leo's colours burnished a bronze frustration followed by hues of violet as he lowered his eyes, with a slight shake of the head.

"So that would be a no!" Adam frowned at his son.

"Right, well there's no time to explain in detail, but Imogen needs to know the basics so she is not shocked."

Imogen looked bemused. *What is going on here? Who are these people with their false names?*

The questions bombarded her mind as the magnitude of all the unknowns hit her simultaneously. Her grandfather was gone, possibly captured or injured or worse; her mother had woken only to be put back into unconsciousness; the carers had all been hypnotised; she had been put to sleep for forty years; she had marks she had not known about and did not understand. Nothing was what it seemed; Leo - *was he really stalking me?* - had clearly withheld key information from her and they could be under attack from an enemy who wanted her… *what? Dead? Why? Did Araz want her dead?* She just couldn't make any sense of it.

"Look," she said, fists tightly clenched and feeling angry and sidelined. "I don't know anything about a 'Tractus', or why Grandad has been taken, or who the enemy is, or why they are after mum or me, and for that matter, I don't even know who the hell I am… so will someone please explain what's going on?" She had not realised her voice had increased in volume and pitch with each declaration, and as she looked from Adam to Leo, eyes full of accusation, she could feel a rush of raw emotion threatening to erupt to the surface.

Leo found himself closing the gap between them, placing a protective arm around her shoulders and leaning in to touch his lips lightly to her forehead in a comforting gesture. It had been an instinctive response and he was unable to suppress the surge of scarlet attraction that Imogen could not fail to perceive, as she found herself briefly taking comfort by leaning into his embrace, despite her misgivings, and blinking back a tear.

Adam started to advance towards Imogen with the sedation pen poised, but Leo put a hand up to stop him and waved him away.

"No! It's okay, Imogen is strong, she'll be fine. I just need to explain how the Tractus works so we can get going… Imogen, come with me…"

Leo grabbed Imogen's hand and pulled her from the room, onto the landing. "I was supposed to explain, but Harry didn't want me to go too quickly."

Imogen pulled her hand out of his and stared at him long and hard. "I don't know if I can trust you, Leo."

His colours danced copper and violet, *indignation and lies,* before a deep shadowy blue hurt filtered into both his Chroma and his eyes, which appeared to darken.

"What do you mean?" he asked.

"You've been keeping things from me for a start and you've been following me?"

Leo paused, as he looked for the words to deny this, but then he shrugged his shoulders with resignation, saying: "I had to follow you; I was supposed to protect you. I had to make sure that other bloke wasn't sniffing around, or posing a threat to you. Look, there's no time for this now, we have to go." He rubbed at his ear, adding: "You should get changed and I'll try to explain the next step."

Imogen, unable to see any violet smudges, regained her composure and stepped into her bedroom, pushing the door to and taking a deep breath. As she changed out of her dress, Leo spoke from the landing and she was only too glad to focus on just his words and not the swirls of distracting colours he seemed to be producing every time they interacted.

"So, the Tractus is a travel device which instantly transfers you from one place to another. No need for cars or planes, no need for luggage or passports…" Leo paused to check she was listening.

"Go on," came Imogen's response.

He continued: "Think 'Star Trek', and transporter room and you kinda have it, although it's a bit more complicated than that."

"A lot more complicated than that," snorted Adam contemptuously, who had joined Leo on the landing. Adam continued, as he glared at Leo: "The device is an intricate creation, employing the laws of sub-atomic physics. The existence of infinitesimally small gaps in the space-time continuum is a well-known fact, but, simply put, we have been able to isolate a specific type of gap, which has allowed us to achieve spatial compression. This, in effect, enables us to jump across large distances using these 'voids'. Your scientists call them worm holes."

Imogen, who had changed into shirt, jeans and trainers, and was glad to have a new focus for her anxious mind, was pulsing concentrated yellow-blue-whites as she tried to comprehend the explanation. She threw her bedroom door open wide as she fastened the Sanctus necklace around her neck.

"I've heard Professor Hawking talk of those," she responded, a brief image of the disabled scientist speaking with a mechanical voice on TV, flashing through her mind.

Adam nodded and continued, "Indeed. Well, once isolated and held in a specific electro-magnetic state, all that is required to activate the connexion are two markers to briefly open the so-called 'wormhole' at either end. This enables the instantaneous transfer of matter from one place to another. Up until now, the markers have been sited in set locations, but my brothers and I have been working on a portable marker and we have one of the only two working models right here."

He held up his hand with a flourish and opened it to reveal a shiny black globe, the size of a plum, which turned in his fingers as flickers of yellow light pulsed rhythmically around the surface. Imogen stared at the device. It seemed vaguely familiar, but also unnerving. The hairs on the back of her neck began to rise whilst beads of sweat broke out on her forehead and goosebumps prickled her arms.

"Is it safe?" asked Leo anxiously, moving his hair out of his eyes and showing that his brow was also perspiring.

"As safe as it can be for a device of this complexity," Adam replied, with both a glow of emerald pride and a touch of purple irritation.

"Where's the other end?" asked Imogen, quelling her fearful reaction. "... Of the void? Where will it take us?"

"Now that is a better question!" Adam said, with a slight sneer towards Leo. "The setting is a delicate precision exercise and must coincide with the true centre of one of the permanent markers. We now have them all over the planet: Europe, Asia, Africa, the Americas, and Australia. Unfortunately, there are limitations with a portable mechanism. It disallows jumps of more than ten thousand kilometres."

"Ten thousand kilometres?" gasped Imogen.

"That's just the portable markers; much further distances can be jumped with the fixed ones," Adam added.

How much further?

"Yeah, it's rubbish, isn't it!" quipped Leo, with a forced levity as his colours pulsed dark grey and he dabbed at his forehead with the back of his arm.

"You can only get a quarter of the way around the Earth with these, max!"

"You could still go all round the Earth," corrected Adam, giving Leo a withering glare. "...Theoretically, but it would have to be in four separate jumps, which is not recommended."

"Why not?"

Why is this making me shiver?

"Imogen, what you have to understand," said Adam, "is that this is an incredibly powerful device, relatively untested. Every leap involves the compression of all matter that enters the portal, human or otherwise. Whilst it emerges completely intact on the other side, it invariably takes its toll on the more complex human cells and tissues. We are still examining the effects…"

"What he's trying to say is, that whilst it won't fry your brains, it could make them hurt for a while," added Leo matter-of-factly, but with a pulse of grey evident in his colours.

"Comments like that are not helpful, Tarik," admonished Adam sharply. "Being flippant about such a miraculous discovery serves only to denigrate the work of others."

Leo gave his father a wounded look, thinking belligerently to himself that his father had never once understood him. He rubbed his ear and lowered his head as Adam turned again to Imogen.

"So, you need to know that there is usually a degree of disorientation after a crossing, and recovery time is a necessity. This is why the Tractus should only be used in exceptional circumstances. A lot more research is needed to fully comprehend the long-term consequences. We have also limited the jumps to just one person at a time, just to ensure no further unforeseen accidents are triggered…"

"Accidents?"

"Yes, like the one you were involved in…" Adam trailed off, realising Leo was motioning for him to stop, finger to his lips and urging silence with his eyes.

Imogen looked from one face to the other and the images from her nightmare sprang unbidden into her mind: *the church, Grandad – no, not Grandad - urging me to run.* She saw the grasping hands, the crown, the glint of a black globe amongst the jewels as it flickered yellow light, the utter black-ness and then the fog. The thumping of her heart filled her ears, but before

Leo could speak, she silenced him with her hand, as she held Adam's eyes and said: "Go on."

Adam was unable to look away from her piercing scrutiny, as a strange sensation overtook him and he found himself blurting out a summary of what had happened...

THE SUPREME COUNCIL

*K*ekara sat on her high throne, her elbows resting on the smooth black marble armrests, the interlaced fingers at the top of her hand touching the centre of her forehead, whilst her thumbs pressed against her closed lips as she listened to the report.

Odion held the floor, the gold of the ornate carvings in the council chamber reflecting off his bald head, as half a dozen key members sat in the next tier of chairs down from their leader.

He completed his account: "So, my fellow councillors: in conclusion and thanks to our informants, we now know that the subversives, Firas Lateef and Eshe Serq are both dead; Rashida Omorose no longer poses a threat and can be easily dispatched. The Zuberi brothers, Sefu and Nuru, have, by all accounts, fled – a typically cowardly act – but rest assured, we will find them. I have just had news that, as we speak, Kasmut Akil is being tracked and will be captured shortly." Odion sneered as he added with distain: "The old fool was utterly predictable. He will be transferred directly to us. The illegal child, a girl who has now been reported to be of inferior intelligence, has been located and will be terminated before further contamination can take place. I will advise the council as soon as this is accomplished." He added with an air of pride and satisfaction: "All in all, a good result."

A young fresh-faced councillor stood nervously, giving a slight raise of his hand as if to ask a question.

"Ma'am" he started, uncertainly, as he addressed Kekara. "I had understood that our intent was to capture and return all those planning to subvert the council. Elimination, including that of an innocent child, seems somewhat…"

"Yes? Somewhat?" Kekara prompted, as she looked up with what appeared to be an enquiring smile.

"Well, extreme Ma'am… and…" The youth took courage from what seemed to him to be a genuine look of concern on the beautiful face of their leader, so continued: "…and also against the basic ethos of the empire?" The pause that followed was laden with tension.

"It is Halim, is it not?" enquired Kekara, with a set smile upon her lips. Halim nodded, unsure if the reaction was quite what he had anticipated.

"Halim joined our council but a few weeks ago, when he came of age," advised Ubaid quietly, turning from the young man to the throne and giving a slight shake of his head, as Odion snorted loudly in disgust.

"Pray Halim, do continue," prompted Kekara, leaning forward, her hands now tightening on the arm of the throne, her eyes fixed on the young man who was growing increasingly uncomfortable, as her smile began to take on the look of a grimace.

"Well, it's just that, I thought… I mean, I understood, that all life was counted sacrosanct and that termination was part of our dark and distant history; that we are above using such methods in this day and age. I mean, these people were valued scientists, were they not?"

"The best in their field," answered Odion, his cold eyes boring into Halim's, which now fluttered uncertainly.

Halim gulped as he continued, "and maybe… perhaps they should be questioned as to why they acted in such a way… I mean, they could be made to realise the error of their ways…" Halim trailed off as he shrank from the look of contempt that had spread across both Odion and Kekara's faces, and decided he had said too much.

"So, Halim," began Kekara in a whispered hiss. "You wish us to preserve our enemies? To save and forgive those who have plotted against us and put into jeopardy our entire race? You, perhaps, think we could reason with them? Hmm? These rogue scientists who have conspired together over sixty long years and tried to overthrow our society and push it into disarray."

"I didn't mean, that is, I wasn't saying…" Halim's voice faded.

"These rebels have eluded justice and broken every law imaginable. They have crossed to the primitives, risked contamination of our perfect society, bred without any reference to our strict and careful principles and continue to conspire to topple our government. Yet, you think they should be preserved?" Rising from her throne, Kekara's eyes bored into Halim's, as he froze to the spot.

"Tell me, Halim. What line are you? No! Let me guess. Hathor? All heart?" Kekara spat.

"Yes, I mean no, I mean, I am a bi-crypt, from the lines of both Hathor and Amon, Ma'am, and I had only meant... that is, I was only trying to say that the child... well she might not... I mean... may not have wilfully conspired against us..."

Odion interrupted. "That we cannot know and anyway, she is no longer a child. I understand the girl is nearly seventeen, close to your own age of supposed maturity, young man."

Halim stared down at his feet, unable to find any further words as Ubaid stood. Despite his small frame, the thin elderman with his carefully clipped pointed white beard had an air of authority and strength acknowledged by all. Ubaid motioned to Halim to sit back down on his seat, which he gratefully did, looking as if he wanted the floor to swallow him up.

Ubaid addressed Kekara: "Ma'am, we digress. May we ask Odion how he has managed to achieve this success, after all these long years of failure? Also, how does he propose to capture the Zuberi brothers?"

Odion snorted his response: "We have a reliable source who led us to the heart of the group, though I must say, Ubaid, your chosen agent would appear to be acting entirely at odds with our main forces and, it would appear, can no longer be trusted. He will be made to answer for his actions," he added, with a spray of saliva as his eyes conveyed loathing for his fellow councillor.

"I see," answered Ubaid. "How unfortunate. It would be a great shame to lose such a useful soldier, but they all know the penalty for disloyalty."

Ubaid then glanced from Halim to Kekara and added: "I must, however, also question the elimination of the 'Falsebred', at least not until we have an opportunity to test her. Even if she is flawed, she needs to be captured and examined before that decision is made." Ubaid ignored the growing red angry look in the face of Odion as he continued.

"There is something else to consider. We have surmised that Kasmut Akil is the father of the girl. Perhaps we should anticipate how he would react to his offspring being slaughtered? It may be wise to preserve her life, until we have all the information and technology we require from Kasmut. Otherwise, it could be 'Akil' too soon." One or two council members laughed nervously at his quip, as Odion fumed.

Kekara gave him a steely stare.

"Always so correct, Ubaid," sneered Odion in contempt. "Heaven forefend that we should miss out on key knowledge! We all know what is important to you."

Ubaid shrugged at the accusation, as Odion announced: "Well, as it happens, I'm afraid you're too late. The Falsebred is being dispatched as we speak."

"A pity," remarked Ubaid. "She could have been very useful. No matter…"

The Accident

*I*mogen's eyes blazed bright as she stared into Adam's, saying, "Go on – tell me - the accident?"

Adam, eyes fixed on hers and unable to stop himself, began, as Leo bit down on his lip.

"I'm told it was no-one's fault. There was an attack. You were only seven years old and, in the struggle, you ended up right next to the marker. You had nowhere else to go, so you 'jumped'. It was Firas who realised that the Tractus was not set to another marker, and we had to figure where you'd gone and how to get you back…"

"So, where had I gone?" she asked, her voice barely a whisper.

"You don't know?" asked Adam, perplexed.

"Enough," interrupted Leo, "We have to…"

"No, Leo, it's not enough. Where did I go?" she demanded of Adam, ignoring Leo's protest. Her hesitancy was gone and her Chroma gleamed bright azure and white as silver strands glided from her aura and infiltrated Adam's.

"You went forward in time," he answered, the threads of silver now entwining around his colours, unnoticed by him, as he shrugged his shoulders to signify it was no-one's fault. The words reverberated in her head: *forward in time – an accident.*

"Imogen, I was going to tell you…"

"No, Leo! Or is it Tarik?" she spat. "I'm not sure you were." She briefly glared at him, before demanding a further response from Adam: "How, Adam? How did I go forward in time?" The silver threads twitched at the sapphire truths in Adam's Chroma.

Adam could not have stopped himself telling her if he had wanted to. Her eyes, her colours, had him mesmerized and the words just flowed from his lips. "My brothers and Firas worked on the problem non-stop for the next seven years. They discovered that if the marker was not linked to a second one, the 'wormhole' just continued on and on, transversing vast, unimaginable, distances across space and time. Eventually, it comes full circle and arrives back at the starting point – it set back to itself."

Imogen's filaments continued to tug gently and he continued, "It was a chance discovery, but the Tractus actually became trans-dimensional. It turned into a 'Tempus' as opposed to a Tractus. It meant, that instead of jumping a distance, you vaulted time. The transfer was almost instantaneous for you, the 'vaulter,' who in effect, was travelling beyond the speed of light. Firas did the calculations and then realised it would take approximately ten full years of our time for you to re-emerge. So we had to wait, and when you didn't return after the first ten years, your mother vaulted too." Adam did not notice Leo, who was holding his head in his hands and shaking it slowly from side to side.

Imogen continued to stare at Adam, her cold sharp crystal colours insisting on the complete explanation, which was teased from him as, hooked with her silver filaments and spellbound, he felt compelled to finish.

"The thing is, the wormhole formed into a continuous loop and you remained within it. We had to find out why, in order to try and get you back. Another ten years of research and troubleshooting passed, and only your mother returned at the end, opting to immediately vault again. We didn't even have time to assess the effects of time propulsion on her. Hope of getting you back was fading. Then finally, we had a breakthrough with a new tracking device containing a coded imprint of your DNA. It was, in fact, my brother, Nuru's discovery," he added proudly.

"On her third vault, your mother took this with her and you finally both emerged some forty years after you had first gone missing. Neither of you had aged, but both of you were in poor shape. Maybe it was because you were so young, or because you did it in one vault, but you recovered quite quickly. Your mother, however, needed time to heal and repair. The rest is history…"

Imogen broke eye contact; the silver fibres in Adam's colours slowly evaporated and he blinked rapidly, not quite sure what had happened to make him give this full account. Leo looked anxiously at Imogen's flushed face, chewing his lip, and trying to catch her eye. But she walked past him back to her mother's room and stared at the sleeping figure in the chair. Her Grandad's words echoed in her head: *You and your mother were involved in the same incident / None of this was ever meant to happen / It all went wrong / Oh Imogen, if only I could turn back time.*

Leo and Adam followed her into the room and stood in the doorway, lost for words.

Imogen felt strangely stronger; her senses were heightened and she could feel the new facts interlocking with everything she had ever experienced, as deep layers of logic and rationale were tested and proven, before settling in her intellect. She knew the truth when she saw it, but there was still something niggling away at the back of her mind. She spoke again to Adam. "So, I take it, it is not possible to travel back in time?"

"No, it is a universal impossibility. Time flows in one direction only," came his definite response.

She turned to Leo and, looking fiercely at him, said: "So, Grandad did not put me to sleep. None of this was his fault…" When he went to answer, flushing deep crimson and violets, she stopped him by holding up her open hand and saying dismissively: "It was a statement Leo, not a question."

A few minutes passed where Imogen stared intently at her mother, saying nothing. Leo could see the wild collision of multiple hues leap and clash in her vibrant colours. Adam could see it too and looked on in wonder, but only Leo knew, when she surged a bright bolt of electric blue overwhelming all other shades, that she had experienced another revelation. He could see her using the drill, calming each shade in turn, and waited anxiously for her to disclose her thoughts. However, she ignored him and turned slowly to Adam, a gold-black edging of authority underpinning her still quartz whites and calmly said: "Right, well if this contraption is sound, you'd better transfer my mother to a place of safety." Her voice was devoid of any emotion.

"Show me how it works."

Adam, clearly relieved that Imogen had not developed anything of her mother's psychosis, launched into an explanation of how to use the marker, as Leo looked on, miserable and dejected. Just as he realised he wanted nothing more than to protect Imogen and win her love, he was now quite sure she hated him. She had hardened and he couldn't read her whilst she was in this frame of mind, so he had no idea what she had now concluded.

"So," Imogen was saying to Adam, "This is different to the permanent markers which have a separate activation sequence."

Adam nodded eagerly, interjecting with, "Oh, and you can't, of course, jump to a portable marker. Only to a permanent marker as…"

"…As the portable ones are not in any fixed place," she finished for him, which produced a broad smile from Adam. Imogen continued: "So, with the portable marker, you just need to activate it with a thumbprint in the indentation…" she indicated the small groove at the base of the device.

"Yes, that's both start and stop," enthused Adam. "And then?" he prompted.

Imogen recited his instructions: "You then select the desired location on the surface of the globe, squeeze down on the chosen one, and wait the one minute gap to the portal opening?"

"That's right! You learn quickly," smiled Adam, glowing bright greens of satisfaction.

"It's what Grand… I mean Harry, would call intuitive," she said sincerely, "the way all the markings are set on the globe like a map, in the same spatial position – like a mini-Earth."

"Precisely," enthused Adam, adding proudly: "That was my idea."

"I can see there are two markers in the UK, but no other country?" she questioned, as she rotated the globe round and round in her fingers.

"This one," he pointed to the centre of a tiny etching of the United Kingdom, "is our first marker, but it was found by the enemy. We believe they used it only once in the 1960's, when they initially arrived. It was after this that we were attacked and you were accidentally caught in the Tractus. So we suspended its use and set up an alternative here." He pointed to the south of the country. "The only problem with this location is it is practically on top of an enemy marker, but at least it's accessible any time of the day or night, as it's sited in a disused area of the city."

"So, when the marker is activated and the destination selected, will it only transport the person directly next to it?" Imogen asked, a yellow intensity encircling her Chroma.

"Well, it homes in on human tissue, detecting the closest in proximity. We call it 'DNA triggering'. All other matter in contact with that flesh, like a person's clothing, or items being held, are absorbed and also transferred. You can even take the marker itself. In fact, the last person must. You must be holding it at the precise second the gap opens."

"And if two or more people were linked, say holding hands, would it take both? Theoretically?" Imogen glowed white and the intense yellow subsided.

Leo stayed quiet, but listening to Imogen's detailed questioning and how she chose her words, he began to suspect she was planning something. He watched her closely, but her colours just gleamed a glassy concentration, betraying nothing to confirm his suspicions.

Adam was quick to answer Imogen. "Yes, if linked, it would take them both. In fact we used to regularly travel together like this, several at a time. But, as I explained, since your accident, we are careful not to take any more risks than are necessary and that's why we have restricted the jumps to just one person at a time."

Imogen nodded understanding, before asking: "So, which marker are we going to?"

Adam pointed to a spot on the sphere and she summoned an atlas inside her head, to bring the coordinates into focus and smiled. "Somewhere I've always wanted to visit, New York, yes?"

Adam, delighted, clapped her on the back, and called out: "Eshe said this one was special, she wasn't wrong." He seemed to expect someone else to be there as he turned, absentmindedly with a smile, but seeing only Leo, he coughed and turned back to Imogen, keen to answer her questions.

He explained that most of the markers were situated in churches, or other public buildings that were only used infrequently. "If in doubt, we always check that it is night time, or the early hours where we are going, so we don't arrive in the middle of a crowd; that would be catastrophic." He added that carefully hidden next to each marker were items that may be needed: clothing, food, local currency, Data Encounters to educate the traveller with the regions' languages, history, politics and social customs.

"Look for the symbols," he nodded, indicating Imogen's chain, which dangled in front of her. She nodded, as she touched the pendant and pushed it inside her shirt.

Looking at his watch, Adam said in excited tones: "Ok, it's early evening in New York and I've had the all clear from Sefu, my brother."

"You mean Seth?" she checked.

"Yes, Seth," he corrected, clearly animated by the speed with which Imogen picked things up and the thrill of using his creation. "He is already there, waiting at the site, St Patrick's Cathedral, and it's been locked up for the night. We'll send Rashid… I mean Elizabeth, first, then you next, Imogen. Tarik and I will join you after we have laid a false trail for the enemy."

Imogen nodded agreement, reached for her drawing pad from the bedside, and scribbled: 'I love you' on the open page, placing it gently under her mother's hands and kissing her brow lightly. She then watched as Adam activated the marker and placed it on the chair arm next to her mother. They all stood back and after exactly one minute there was a bright flash of yellow light, which blinded them for an instant. As they regained their sight, Elizabeth had gone and the glowing marker remained on the empty chair arm.

Looking at the space her mother had occupied, Imogen was aware that her stomach had knotted and that her heart rate had rapidly increased. She forced it to slow, taking a deep breath of genuine relief, as Adam received a confirmatory signal, on his Multi-Com, that Elizabeth had arrived safely, and gave her the 'thumbs up' sign.

"Perfect transfer. Okay, Imogen, you next," said Adam, indicating for her to sit in the armchair.

Imogen told them to wait a moment and ran to her bedroom to collect her phone. She briefly clenched and unclenched her fist, set her resolve and returned to the room, pausing a moment.

"What about my friends?" she asked.

What about Grandad? I need to find him.

"You can call them from the states," reassured Adam. "It's not like you're leaving the planet! You can say, quite truthfully, that your mother has come out of her coma, and you've gone to a rehabilitation home with her."

Imogen nodded, Chrissie would buy that. There was no college for over a week with the Whit holidays starting, so she wouldn't be missed there. She punched in a quick message to her friend, to say she was fine and would be in touch, and put the phone into a small pocket in her shirt, before tentatively sitting down in the chair and wiping her clammy hands against her jeans.

Leo tried to catch her eye to give her a reassuring smile, but she was studiously avoiding him and, as he watched her, she appeared to flare a brief surge of gold edged black, but he couldn't be sure, and he didn't know what it meant. Anyhow, it had gone as quickly as it had appeared.

Imogen picked up the marker, looked at Adam and asked: "Can I?" Adam nodded 'yes'. She pressed her thumb into the indentation, and then squeezed the globe at the same point that Adam had activated for her mother. Placing the device on the arm of the chair, she silently started counting down to herself. As she reached the last few seconds, she suddenly flared a cobalt blue, grabbed the marker and deliberately rolled it along the floor, watching it spin towards Leo's feet.

Three – two – one…

Ten Years Earlier

They were sitting in a small alcove, in a quiet pub opposite the church: the 'Plough and Harrow'. Kasmut had told Leo everything, despite it being against the wishes of their leader, Tanastra. They spoke in low voices as Kasmut put his request to Leo. It was perilous and could prove fatal, but how could he refuse? Kasmut had been like a father to Leo, and he was eternally grateful for this.

He looked into the tired eyes of the closest person he had to a parent, and Leo could see the pain of years of worry, etched into the lines around them.

"I know, I should not ask you to do this, Leonard. It is very dangerous, but I can see no other way. Rashida will not be able to vault again, so you are my only hope."

"What if Tanastra, or Firas, or any of the others see me?"

"I have a plan. I intend to occupy them, in the countdown to the marker. You can get into position and by the time you rush out to the altar, it will be too late for anyone to stop you."

"And you're sure I can't wait to see if they return? I mean, for the sake of a few seconds…"

"Firas will be closing down the Tractus the moment Rashida appears, with or without Imogen. They do not feel the same as I do. They are more detached. They have decided that the marker needs a complete overhaul and, against my wishes, they voted for immediate shut down, regardless of what impact that may have on Imogen." Bitterness was etched into his voice. "If we delay, the opportunity will be lost and I fear that will be the end, the end of…" Kasmut put his hand to his forehead and shook it disconsolately. Leo, who rarely saw him at such a loss, felt compelled to comfort him.

"I'll go, of course I'll go," he said, with a forced cheeriness. "They won't shut it down once I have entered it, will they! And, with a bit of luck, I will return in ten years' time, yes?" The slight wobble in Leo's voice was the only contradiction to the bright manner of his question.

Kasmut recovered himself and looked with grateful eyes to the young man opposite him, saying: "You know what I always say about luck, Leonard…"

"There's no such thing as luck!" they chimed together, smiling.

"And it will feel instantaneous to me?" Leo gulped.

"Completely! You will return in just under ten years' time. Our calculations are precise. It will be three thousand, three hundred and sixty-three days from now. You will step out of 2006 today and straight back into 2016, in what will seem like a split second. Unlike Rashida, you should not require too much recovery time. You are young and it is just one vault."

Leo inwardly gawped at all the assumptions and the phrase, 'just one vault', but outwardly nodded enthusiastically.

"And Leonard, rest assured that whatever happens, one of us will be here to meet and revive you," added Kasmut kindly.

Leo swallowed hard and nodded, wishing Kasmut had used a different word to 'revive'.

"So, if I arrive back alone, I can assume either the first attempt was successful and Imogen was returned, or we have failed…" Leo faded out as he saw the pain etched into Kasmut's eyes, as he solemnly nodded agreement.

"Well, let's hope it works today, or I succeed in my mission!" Leo declared with far more confidence than he felt, as he patted the small opal covered item inside his top pocket with one hand, whilst unconsciously pushing his hair to one side and scratching his ear with the other.

They left their drinks untouched and exited the pub to go across to the church where they entered a side door into the dark building. Leo nodded to Kasmut and flattened himself against a recessed doorway to the side of the altar, as Kasmut stepped into the church and greeted the others. Eshe had a medical bag open, the contents spread across the front pew. Firas was in deep conversation with Sefu and Tanastra, which stopped abruptly when they saw Kasmut approach.

"I appeal to you one last time," started Kasmut, his hands open in supplication. "Wait before you close down the marker. Let us allow some time for consideration, if Imogen is not returned."

"And let Rashida vault again?" questioned Firas. "You know we cannot."

"It would kill her..." started Eshe.

"If it has not already done so," added Sefu gravely.

"It has been decided, Kasmut," said Tanastra kindly, as the robed priest put a comforting arm around him. "Our theories may be wrong. The child may have been permanently lost to us forty years ago."

"It has been the focus of our work for too long," added Firas. "Our main purpose has nearly been forgotten in the attempts to recover her – it has to stop." Firas rubbed his beard slowly, as he shook his head sadly.

"Let's not give up hope yet," soothed Eshe, as she patted Kasmut's arm. "Nuru's device may well work. Come, it is nearly time."

The group lined up in front of the altar, Firas' hand poised over a small opal-covered square as the globe, high above, pulsed and glowed in ever brightening colours, and the countdown started.

As the first flash of light came, a shadow of a figure was momentarily seen dashing from the doorway and disappearing, but before anyone could react to this, the light dimmed and the two figures of mother and child lay, apparently lifeless, on the floor before them.

Firas replayed the split second in his head, the image frozen on Leonard's anxious face as he vanished, and with a momentary glare at Kasmut and a heavy sigh of frustration, he lowered the device in his hand and put it to one side. They could not now shut down the marker. He would not be able to change the sequencing. But he suspended all such thoughts, as the urgency of revival forced him and the others into hasty action.

The Marker

$\mathcal{L}$eo saw the globe roll towards him and rapidly jumped back to the door in alarm, whilst Adam, utterly astonished, stepped forward and instinctively reached out his hands to retrieve his precious invention. As his fingers stretched out, the flash of light came on the last count. Imogen blinked to re-focus; Adam was gone and the sphere glowed on the carpet where he had stood.

Leo stared at Imogen from the doorway, a look of horror on his face, as all his colours blazed disbelief, confusion and dismay.

"What the f…" he started, but Imogen leapt to her feet, grabbing the marker, and advanced towards Leo.

"Give me one good reason why I shouldn't send you away now?" she demanded, flaring scarlet fury, her finger poised to activate the device again.

"Well how about: you've already jettisoned the only other person in five thousand kilometres sworn to protect you, so you'd have no-one at all, without me!" he said angrily.

"Why the hell did you do that?" he added, ignoring the ringing that had started on his phone.

"Don't you dare accuse me," retorted Imogen, the merest trace of uncertainty in her voice. "It was supposed to be you, not Adam! I know I can trust him, or at least force him, to be honest, but you've done nothing but give me half truths or lies."

"That's not fair!" Leo protested, quickly stabbing a button on the phone to divert the call, before glaring back at her.

"No? Well how come, when I realised I was born in a different era, all you said was 'how did you know'? You clearly wanted me to believe I had been put into a coma, when it was blatantly untrue…"

Leo paused and shook his head, "It wasn't a lie. I just didn't want to overwhelm you with what really happened." His indigo-edged white did not completely convince her, but she had to acknowledge he had not so much lied, but allowed her to believe in her own conclusions by not contradicting her.

"No-one knew if you would go deranged, like your mum had. I mean, she went right off the rails as soon as you went missing. And then it's taken nearly ten years to get her right since she arrived back. What if that had happened to you?" Leo shook his head in despair, a genuine flutter of grey anxiety apparent in his Chroma.

"Oh please, spare me the violins," Imogen retorted angrily, pulsing livid reds. "You expect me to believe that you didn't tell me the truth for my own protection? You have no idea what it feels like to have been catapulted forward in time…"

"Well, actually, I do! And I don't think you're being very fair to me," Leo responded in a belligerent voice, a navy-blue wave of hurt quite clear in his Chroma.

"After all, I had promised to shield you – I even risked my life on your behalf!"

"What do you mean?" she demanded, flaring copper indignation, but also slightly taken aback at the bright sapphire truth that accompanied his statement.

"I agreed to do a time vault, to make a second rescue attempt, in case you didn't return." She continued to give him a piercing look, but there was no denying that his colours exhibited crystal truth as he continued.

"I mean, there was no guarantee either of us would come back," he said, with a gripe in his voice and a clear smoky-green wave of sacrifice circling the navy blue. His phone rang again, but he silenced the ring and threw it on the bed.

"So you went forward in time too?" Imogen said in a sarcastic voice, her colours flashing purple derision. "And how many years did you skip? No, don't tell me, let me guess, you were actually born the same time as who, Eshe? Grandad?" As the words left her mouth, Imogen's anger evaporated and she went silent.

Leo sat at the edge of the bed, flicking his hair back. "It was just ten years. I was, that is, I am, eighteen. Ten years went like that." He clicked his fingers and thumb. Eyes briefly glazing over, he continued. "So, we are both younger than we should be, although, theoretically, I was born nearly thirty years after you." He looked beyond Imogen, as he added: "It was such a weird experience – ten whole years – they just went in a flash! I can only imagine what vaulting forty years must have been like…" He then focussed on Imogen's stare as she sat down in the chair, and slowly moved the marker from one hand to the other and back, her eyes boring into his, clear yellows demanding more details.

"Look, I only arrived back last month. It took a few days to recover, but since then I've been madly catching up on events: ten years worth of news and changes… until I was ready to come and help you." Leo rubbed at his ear and pondered the meaning of the grey-navy background behind the bright yellow chromatic demands for more information.

"It was a sort of back up plan," continued Leo, in the face of her silence. "Harry gave me a refined version of the recovery mechanism that was given to your mother, on her third vault. But there was a catch - I had to go ahead - just seconds before your mother returned. So I didn't know if you had reappeared when I stepped out of 2006. Anyhow, as it turns out, you had, and as you can see, I came back too and was, thankfully, unharmed…" Leo then added, with a grin: "If you don't count the twitching," Leo started to jerk and flutter his eyes in a mock lunacy manner, "the screaming fits…" he opened his mouth into a silent scream, "the…"

"Shut up, Leo!" Imogen retorted, red-blacks pulsing in her colours. "If what you're saying is true, I was just a little girl and I was lost in time. Why the hell would you risk your life for me? You didn't even know me!" she challenged.

"For the love of Ra!" he exclaimed, as he stood up with his hands out-stretched upwards, the frustration clear in his face and his bronzed colours.

"Look Imogen, give me a break. You might have been hurtled forty years ahead, when you were seven, but I was also torn from my home, when I was only aged eight. I was put in a world I had never heard of, let alone experienced, with nothing but my cat. Yes – Sadiki - I named him when he was a kitten. And it was thanks to Harry that I survived. No, I didn't know you, but it was for him that I did it. He was like a father to me, and I could see that the only thing that would make him truly happy was to have you and your mother back. I remember it as though it was yesterday. You see, to me, this only happened less than a month ago. The leap of ten years was instantaneous and suddenly, everyone was a decade older and you were no longer a snapshot of a little girl in the 1960's…" He retrieved the photograph she had left in the car from his pocket and held it out to her. She took it from him with a tentative hand and the realisation: *It's not my mother – it's me!*

"You'd transformed into a sixteen year old," he continued, "Nearly the same age as me, in all but chronology."

Imogen felt another piece of the jigsaw slotting into place. It made sense. She recalled all the things that had baffled her: Her Grandad saying he had known Leo from long ago, Leo being so familiar with the house, Grandad's words - *things are not always as they seem.* Even Sadiki, who had been there from the moment she woke from the fog, was never hers. He had been pining for his true owner.

Leo took a small step towards her, hands pleading in front of him. "Imogen?" he softly asked.

"What?" she snapped.

He paused, before saying: "Is this the five minute argument, or the full half hour?" a small twinkle appearing in his eyes.

Imogen glared at him, then bit her lip and rolled her eyes to heaven, as her remaining anger started to subside. She had nothing to confirm that he had deliberately lied. She regained her composure as she stood and walked about the bedroom, before finally turning to Leo and saying: "In the car, on the way here, you were going to tell me something about Harry…"

Leo started to colour violet and then looked her straight in the eye, as blue-white infused his Chroma and the purple shades disappeared. With determination in his voice, he started: "I think you should know Imogen – your Grandad, Harry – he is in fact…"

"My father!" she finished ahead of him. "I know."

My dad – he was there all the time. He kept my photograph and I stayed a little girl whilst he grew older and older.

She breathed deeply and quashed the threatened onset of emotion before it could start, pushing the photo into her shirt pocket, next to her phone.

Leo said nothing for a few seconds and then: "I knew you'd figure it out," clear admiration in his voice, colours glinting deep emeralds. "Even without seeing Star Wars! Superior brain and all that…"

"Don't push it Leo," she retorted, but in calmer tones, as she transferred the marker to the pocket of her jeans. Glancing out of the window into the dark street to Leo's red car parked outside, she thought aloud: "Mum called him Kasmut – it came back to me - she'd called him that occasionally when I was little – I suppose that was his real name, like hers was Rashida and yours is Tarik. It's no wonder it didn't bother me, where my dad was. I must have known, deep down, that he had always been with me. He was just so much older, that I accepted him as Grandad."

"He did it to protect you, Imogen," explained Leo in a tender voice. "You were so young. Can you imagine explaining why your father has aged forty years, to a child who is already traumatised by her mother being in a coma, and has entered a world completely changed from her childhood years? You had come from a place where a calculator would have been considered high tech, to one swamped with electronic and digital gizmos, and buzzing with instant communication. Your dad, he had aged beyond forty years, what with all the worry and such an enormous sense of loss. It really took its toll on him. He was incomplete without his daughter and wife. I know; I saw him. Seems like yesterday…" A glimmer of russet, intermingled with sepia shades, revealed the sincerity of his affection and compassion, which Imogen could not help but warm to.

Imogen contemplated it all and began to feel an overwhelming sadness when she realised that, whilst she had only 'lost' her mother for, in effect, ten years, during her 'coma', her father had been without her far longer. It was clear now, that her mother had been completely unhinged when the accident happened and then, on top of the three separate vaults, she had taken nearly ten further years to heal, which had suspended her ageing process. Imogen knew her mother was about forty, but her father was now in his eighties. A picture of his despondent expression and his deep colours of hurt and loss, on the occasions he had looked at her sleeping mother on her Multi-Com screen, flared into her mind with a new meaning.

No wonder he didn't want to stay in the house looking at his unconscious wife, forever young. He was bereft and had been utterly heartbroken. And I was so angry with him. She cringed from the injustice she had done him, as she heard his words again: *None of this was meant to happen.* The words went round and round in her head.

A swirl of emotions enveloped her mind and she found herself saying: "What's happened to him?"

"We'll find him," said Leo decisively. "If he escaped, I think I know where he will have gone…"

"Where?"

"Back to the first marker, to Birmingham. We'll go there to look for him, but not by Tractus. The marker is not in use and anyway, any form of transport is better than that," he nodded fearfully towards her pocket, adding: "We'll drive there."

Imogen indicated agreement and recalled Adam pointing to the centre of the country on the globe. *Birmingham, my town of birth. The church and the site of my accident; my nightmare.* She shuddered involuntarily, but her concentration was interrupted as she sensed the familiar prickle of infiltration. Looking back out of the window she noted that a large black transit van was now parked opposite the red car. As she searched for the signs of the Infrared glow of others, the phone, which Leo had thrown on the bed, finally reached the edge, having inched its way across the cover with each vibration, and dropped to the floor with a thump. Leo picked it up and answered.

"Daddy!" he said sarcastically, before pausing, briefly holding the phone away from his ear, allowing Adam's angry voice to be broadcast to the room, and finally responding in an offended tone: "What? Look, calm down! No, of course I didn't plan it… Well don't get mad at me! Yes, I'll pass you over to her." He put the handset into Imogen's hand, a small grin curved on his lips, as he mouthed: 'You're in trouble!'

Imogen put the Multi-Com to her ear, closing the curtain quickly with her other hand, and listened as Adam ranted at the other end for several minutes. Leo could hear the odd word like 'reckless, stupid, irresponsible and priceless device', and Imogen remained silent before finally replying: "Adam – or Amsu – I appreciate your concern, but I don't want to be hidden, or looked after. I can't sit back and do nothing. I am going to try and find my grand… my father, with, or without your help. From now on, I intend to be in control." She listened for a further few minutes before turning and looking intently at Leo, making him feel very uncomfortable, before saying, "Okay, well, I will try to trust him – if you say so." Leo blinked, his colours swirling a conflicting array, but predominantly copper indignation, as Imogen finished by saying: "Please take care of mum for me. What? Yes, of course I will take care of the marker." As she listened to Adam, she shook her head with clear frustration but quietly responded: "I know – invaluable. Yes – the enemy must not know about it. I will - with my life. Tarik? Yep - here he is." She handed the phone back to Leo, who watched her go across to the window again, as he attended Adam's instructions. Imogen pulled back the curtain a fraction of an inch and her colours started to spark purple-yellow bursts of alarm.

Leo hurriedly finished the call saying, "He wants you to follow your mother, as soon as…" when Imogen swung round, pressing her back against the wall next to the window, her face drained of colour.

"What is it?" he asked anxiously.

"Dark forces, in helmets – they're here," she hissed, details from her nightmare replaying in another part of her mind: the clarity of the figures grabbing for her in the church, long ago. They were one and the same.

As the words left her mouth, they heard scuffles from the front door.

"Repros," said Leo in a grim voice. "We've been here too long – we need to go," he said in hushed tones. "Have you got the marker safe?" Imogen nodded, her eyes wide with trepidation. "We can't risk using it here. It will take too long to transfer us both and, besides, we should only use it as a last resort," he said, clearly deeply worried about using the Tractus.

Jumping into action, he took the pen out from his back pocket and pulled Imogen out of the room, along the landing to the bathroom. Loud systematic hammering began at the front door, accompanied by the sound of splintering wood.

In the bathroom, Leo knelt on the toilet and quietly opened the narrow window, nodded to Imogen in the direction of the garden, his colours forming the approximate yellow circle they had devised for 'look'. She knew immediately what he wanted her to do, and she joined him, peering into the dark using her Infrared sight. She could only see the heat from a small cat, hiding in the hedge. *At least Sadiki is safe.* She nodded the all clear to Leo and, to Imogen's surprise, he lifted the windowsill to reveal what looked like a rope ladder, which he threw over the edge where it transformed into light rigid steps with a thin handrail. *No doubt another of my dad's inventions.*

They hurriedly climbed out, one after the other, closing the window behind and descending to the darkened patio. Leo tugged the bottom rung of the ladder, and it softened and dropped noiselessly into a flaccid heap on the ground.

From inside the house, they could firstly hear a thump, as the broken door crashed open against the inner wall, and secondly, the stamps of booted feet racing up the stairs.

"This way," hissed Leo, grabbing her arm as he jumped a low hedge and slipped into the narrow passageway at the side of the house. They edged their way to the front corner of the house, but Imogen took a step backwards as she saw the heat of a large figure move behind the trunk of a tree in front of them. Grabbing Leo's arm, she shook her head furiously, to indicate 'no', and they edged back to the garden and pushed though the shrubs into the rear of the house next door.

Heart racing, Imogen picked up speed to keep up with Leo, as they dodged through gardens and passageways, until they came out in the street that ran parallel to Imogen's.

Leo looked down the road and Imogen double checked there was no sign of life, before they both dashed across the road, round to the next street, getting further and further away from the house. Had she looked back to a higher level, she would have seen the Infrared image of a small cat, as it chased them from tree to tree and over walls and fences.

Breathless, Leo slowed to a quick walk and giving a half smile, said: "We've outrun them! Imogen, I've been thinking, we'll definitely go after Harry. We can't just give up on him. We can join the others later. Now we have the portable thing, we can pick our moment."

Imogen nodded agreement, only slightly puzzled that Leo seemed to announce this as a new decision.

He already said we would look for dad, didn't he? Or was that insincere?

She patted her pocket to check for the outline of the marker, which was safely in place. She shivered as she internally remembered Adam's words, almost a plea: *this device could make all the difference to defeating the enemy, it must remain secret, this is absolutely critical,* along with the implicit danger associated with using it, which seemed to reverberate in her bones.

They hurried across the street to cut through an open park space. The gate was wide open. Looking back to ensure no-one was following, they entered when Imogen suddenly stopped. The body heat of three large figures, crouching in the bushes, caught her eye and as she turned, pulling Leo back to the opening, more figures appeared, walking towards them from the street.

How many now? Eight? Where in hell had they come from?

They looked desperately in both directions, but they were now surrounded and as they backed up to a tree inside the park entrance, the figures advanced, stepping in time together, moving as one.

They must be seven feet tall!

Faceless, she could see the street lights reflected in the dark visors of the advancing helmets, until one of them lifted his visor and signalled the others to encircle them. Imogen's breath caught in her throat. The eyes that met hers were huge and a deep blood red, as they stared out at her from pale sunken sockets.

They're not human!

Imogen's heart hammered in her chest as she came to a halt, back pressed against the solid tree trunk. Eshe's words *they're coming - they've seen you* sounded in her head. Leo grabbed her hand and squeezed it hard, passing the pen-like object into her palm. Imogen carefully pushed the pen up the sleeve of her shirt. Each attacker held what looked like a large black truncheon in one hand, which was repeatedly tapped into the other gloved palm, back and forth, in unison with the others. Imogen was frozen with fear. The implied threat of violence in this action, accompanied by the red-black jagged flares that pulsed in their Chroma, was stark and terrifying. They were cornered. Rigid with fear, childhood memories jumped into a deep layer of her mind. *She's not a fighter – she's a dirty little blighter...*

Gulping hard, Leo let go of Imogen's hand and stepped forward into their path, hands held in an open show of submission. He started to speak in a language she had not heard before. It sounded like 'Aquieseratt' and she knew, without translation, that it meant: 'we submit'. But before Leo could finish, the assailant with the open visor raised his weapon and in a swift move, crashed it down on one of Leo's outstretched arms. The sickening crunch of his bone shattering was immediately followed by his deep groan, as he slumped down to the ground, nursing the limp and now useless limb.

Imogen stifled a scream and braced herself, as it then moved towards her with a raised club. As she crouched in a tight ball and quickly shielded her head with her hands, waiting for the impact, a loud yowl filled the air and she looked up to see a rust coloured ball of fur, teeth and claws on top of the brute's shoulders. It proceeded to bite and maul, lashing out at the red eyes inside the helmet and forcing the figure to swirl and flay out its arms, dropping the cudgel. Imogen made a split second decision to seize the moment. She rapidly uncoiled and made a grab for the cosh, using it to whack the figure across its legs, with greater force than she knew she possessed. The blow sent it to the ground, as two further Repros moved forward towards her. Leo reacted quickly and shot out a leg, tripping them in their advance. More of them swooped in on Leo and rewarded him with vicious kicks to his stomach and further blows to his legs, making him cry out in pain. Sadiki snarled and clawed at their legs, before being grabbed by the scruff of the neck and being tossed into a bush.

As Leo was being beaten, he glanced up and for a fleeting second, his eyes met Imogen's as his Chroma, infused with the green-black of self-sacrifice, flashed a bright yellow-mauve block – *Run!* With a renewed energy, he spun on the ground and kicked out at the attackers, who redoubled their efforts to strike him again and again. Imogen, rooted to the spot, flinched as one struck a ferocious blow across Leo's face, breaking his nose and cheek bone, as blood splattered across his head and blonde hair, and they piled on top of him.

No!

Imogen surged with a blind rage and ran towards the attackers angrily, lashing left and right with the baton, trying to stop them. She was about to smash the weapon down across the back of the nearest brute, when her legs were pulled from beneath her and she felt a large hand grab her hair and start to drag her backwards. Pain screamed from every follicle as she grasped the clenched glove that was pulling her, and tried to hit it with the cudgel and wriggle free, her back being scraped over a gravel path. As they neared the gate, the Repro let go and made a grab for her neck. Imogen briefly distracted him, raising the weapon with one hand, but swiftly slipped the pen out from up her sleeve with the other. With a sudden upward movement, she jabbed it into the exposed bit of flesh under the helmet. The pen lodged in its throat as she intuitively pressed the button at the end and it crumpled to the ground. Imogen then saw two more Repros racing towards her, coshes raised.

With close to supernatural quickness, she managed to dart out of the way of their clutching hands and swinging weapons, and out onto the street where, heart thumping, she ran as fast as her legs would carry her. Her nightmare replayed elsewhere in her head - *the grasping hands, dodging towards the altar, the leap* - Only daring to make a backward glance when she reached the corner of the next road, she continued at high speed and, as she looked back over the wall, she could see the tops of several of their heads giving chase. She came to a sudden halt as she slammed into the chest of a waiting figure – another hard helmet. She dropped the truncheon in shock and would have screamed if she could, but her voice would not surface above her terror. Her hands were seized and forced to her sides in a vice-like grip, trapping her arms, and she felt her legs being lifted from the pavement as she was swiftly hauled up a driveway and pushed flat into the side of a dark porch. A strong arm fastened around her middle, keeping her immobile and a gloved hand clamped around her mouth, the cold of the helmet pressing into her cheek.

A number of the Repros raced past the house and on down the road and Imogen's heart lurched in confusion, as she watched them sprint out of sight. Tightly held from behind, her rapid breathing was forced through her nose and as she breathed in the scent - a light musk barely detectable under the smell of the leather glove - she realised that she knew her captor.

He reduced the pressure of his hands and gently touched a gloved finger to her upper lip, as she turned her head. He lifted his visor, dark eyes serious and gleaming, as he whispered in deep tones into her ear: 'Imogen. I'm sorry...' Waves of fear, confusion, dread and unwanted sparks of stimulation coursed through her body, as Imogen opened her mouth to respond. She felt the cold of the pen against her wrist too late, and his captivating dark eyes faded slowly into blackness, as she mumbled: "Araz…"

THE FIFTH CHRONICLE OF TANASTRA: KASMUT AKIL

*A*nd so, my friend, I come to Kasmut Akil. Such a remarkable techni-
cian, he had the brilliance of visualising mere concepts and convert-
ing them to practical appliances. It is thanks to him that we remained so
hidden from our enemies. He developed a shielding device for our homes,
communicators for the group that could not be detected by the primitives or
those that chased us. Such clever things – the Multi-Coms can change shape
and function, and remain hidden, disguised as rudimentary mobile phones.
Rashida's artistry was also evident in the design, but, of course, you know all
this. Forgive me. I digress.

So, the equipment Kasmut formulated to help Rashida recuperate was
also a marvel: an integrated system of nourishment, repair, exercise and healing. It was he who devised a way to employ local help to nurse his wife and
child. Here, they would call his methods a form of hypnosis, but it was far
subtler than that. He merely sought out those who had a caring nature, along
with a deep-seated need to be used in a positive manner. He then subdued
their curiosity, whilst enhancing their need for a purpose in life and deploying
their complete loyalty to assist his friends and family. He found folk who had

been lonely, bereaved or abandoned and gave them a fresh rationale, whilst providing a reliable and trustworthy care team. A small organic trigger was implanted behind the ear, another wonder of a gadget (I can assure you they didn't feel a thing and were unaware of its presence). Kasmut then gave daily instructions, remotely, and ensured that his 'silver threads' were tightly entwined in their minds. I suppose some would say that they had been used, but if truth be told, they were oblivious of the intrusion; they were happy and were paid handsomely for their time.

So, where was I? Dear oh dear, what it is to get old! Yes – Kasmut. He really did combine in one person, the skills of inventor, doctor and innovator to the highest degree. I have to say, his incentive was the return of his wife and child. He was driven by this and this alone; such was his deep love for mother and daughter.

Poor man, he had not realised that I had been watching that evening twenty years ago when Rashida briefly returned after her second vault. He managed to give her the device Nuru had created, in the hope it would enable the child to be retrieved. He was so utterly heartbroken, not only to find she had come back alone, but to see her so young, so unchanged, whilst he had aged and grieved for the twenty years she had been missing, and the thirty years his daughter had been gone. I did not have the heart to make my presence known as he openly wept when she had gone, but I have recorded those moments elsewhere.

After the girl's disappearance, it was decided by all concerned that we needed a new centre, somewhere away from Birmingham. We also needed to access the Tractus from a new site. Firas had managed to attach a microscopic tracking device to one of the attackers, that dreadful night in 1966. He then discovered that the enemy was setting up its own portal, down in the capital of the country. It would take them many years to succeed; after all, they did not have our advanced expertise. So, Firas and Sefu were able to rig up an observation post to spy on their progress, along with a new marker in the same location.

Able to monitor events from afar, the team moved north, where Sefu and Nuru were established in research facilities. I remained in the Midlands, at the church, to guard and keep watch on the Tractus, on the outside chance that Rashida and the child might return out of sequence. It was the only way we could persuade Kasmut to move. He came back when the time came for the marker to reactivate, but spent the rest of his days and nights developing ways to nurse his family back to health should they be returned.

I'm afraid it wasn't just me who saw his loyalty to our mission beginning to take second place to their retrieval. He seemed to have 'lost the plot' with regard to our purpose and the plans to overthrow the evil growing in the empire. It caused more than one argument amongst our number, who began to wonder if he could be relied upon. Nuru said Kasmut had been infected with the primitive mentality of self-interest, but I feel this was a little unfair. He and Sefu began to question why we continued to expend our energies on a child who could have been long dead. Eshe told them that the child was more important than they realised, but I don't think that either Zuberi brother was convinced. She could not say more; our pact of secrecy had even excluded the mother from knowing her pedigree.

Once Amsu arrived with his son at the London portal later in 1996, it was the triplets who began work on developing the new movable markers and setting up sites across the world, whilst Kasmut reluctantly took on the care of Amsu's child. It proved a welcome distraction from his grief and helped him to form a rehabilitation programme for his wife and daughter, as Tarik knew nothing of this world and, if returned, his family would also know nothing of the years they had missed. Tarik proved to be a kind of guinea pig for this preparation.

As it happened, Tarik – I really should call him Leonard - was a good-natured boy, ready to learn and desperate to be given the love of a parent that he appeared to have always lacked. We had no inkling that Kasmut would force the lad into a time-vault. Such a reckless act.

If I am truthful, the rest of the group no longer trusted in Kasmut's judgement. It was Firas who said he was operating on a sort of autopilot. Without Kasmut's involvement, we agreed to turn off the Tractus at the exact moment Rashida reappeared, regardless if it meant the girl was lost. I appreciate that this sounds harsh, but we had practically given up hope and it was necessary to realign our focus to higher things. Forty years is a long time to be thrown off course. In hindsight, I should not have informed Kasmut of our decision, but I felt duty-bound to be open with him. Little did I know what action he would take.

When Leonard vaulted, we had no option but to leave the marker operational. Even his father, who lacked any close relationship with the lad, agreed on this. It was most unfortunate and would mean the marker could not be shut down until he was safely returned, and we knew this would take ten years. Firas was furious about it and could only continue to work on theories for its eventual overhaul. Little did we know that he would be dead by the time Leonard re-appeared and it would be down to me to attempt the necessary adjustments. As I write, I have no idea if these have been successful, but back to Kasmut…

Once we had Rashida and the girl back, Kasmut's only focus was their recuperation. After all, Leonard was gone, having been catapulted forward in time. In the early days he tried, once or twice, to awaken Rashida, but it proved to be more damaging than helpful.

Unlike her mother, the girl appeared completely unharmed, apart from a little memory loss. She was such a delight. She absorbed new information and the change in her surroundings with a logic and thoughtfulness I have never witnessed in a child so young. She took it upon herself to communicate with her sleeping mother in the only way she knew how, despite this being entirely one way. She intuitively knew to shield her many talents and employ logic and reasoning in everything she did. When frustrations rose, she used her incredible artistic talents as a form of therapy and rejuvenation. She was a true prodigy!

Kasmut taught her to use the various drills that had been instilled into the rest of us from birth. He ensured that when she did go back to school, that she changed on a yearly basis to hide her from any unwanted attention and it was decided that Eshe would take over her tutoring, once she got older.

This plan, however, was never put into action, my friend, as, just a few years later Firas was fatally wounded in the attack of 2010. With him out of action and Eshe fully occupied with his twenty-four hour care, the workload on the others doubled. Sefu's time was spent trying to find an antidote to battle the poison eating away at Firas' body. Kasmut did his best to contribute, but sadly, as we had so few resources at our disposal, progress was slow and the eventual remedy came too late for Firas, and Eshe's resultant demise, as I have explained elsewhere.

The team, now greatly depleted, struggled to keep up with all the commitments. It was Nuru who was the least happy. He did not like working alone, a decision made when Amsu returned, so the third triplet would remain hidden, even in the primitive world. And it was he who was called upon to cover up any mistakes and ensure we did not attract any undesirable notice that might be spotted by the enemy. We needed to blend into our surroundings; 'keeping a low profile' is what I think is said here. This fell heavily on Nuru's shoulders and I'm afraid I have begun to detect a deep resentment in him that I had not seen before.

Nuru was also irritated with Kasmut's apparent growing disinterest in keeping himself concealed. As his daughter grew older and he moved into the care home he had set up to look after Eshe, he became more withdrawn. The home grew more and more dilapidated and Kasmut appeared to lose his sense of direction. I was shocked when I learned that he had not told his daughter about her accident, or her lineage. I mean, I understood that Kasmut was worried she might descend into the same madness as her mother, but it is wrong to keep such essential information from one so bright.

It was left to me to greet Leonard when he arrived back, just a few weeks ago, and in need of revival and rest. Once I had educated him on all the events he had missed during his ten-year absence, I insisted that Kasmut allow Leonard to train and enlighten his daughter, which would finally permit her to make her own life choices. As I write, I am aware that progress is slow, but positive.

In the meantime, I have attempted to make the necessary repairs to the Birmingham portal, so future accidents and time vaults are rendered impossible. I pray that the enemy does not discover this unanticipated capability of the Tractus, as I am sure it would be put to evil use. Heavens! It does not bear thinking about: a strategic usage for vaulting ahead in time – what havoc would they choose to reap? I shudder at the very thought…

But I am wandering again… So, my friend, you are nearly up to present day with these chronicles. You will see, that from our original number, we are diminished. We have lost Firas and, as I now understand it, Eshe. Dear Eshe – it was probably a blessed release. We are also unable to rely on Rashida and, as I have explained, there have been concerns about Kasmut's focus.

On the plus side, however, we have the Zuberi brothers, all on board and working non stop to expand our network and plan our next moves, and we now have Amsu's son, Leonard, thankfully unharmed after his vault.

I'm afraid I must also tell you, that it is a major concern of mine, to hear reports that the enemy is closing in. We have been so careful to cover our tracks that I have had to come to the conclusion, painful as it may be, that one of our number must have collaborated with the Supreme Council. Yes, a traitor, a Judas in our midst. I cannot bear to contemplate this treachery, but how else could our defences have been breached? I hope that I will be proved wrong, but never before has it been so important for us to follow procedure to the letter and be wary of anyone acting on his or her own.

I finish by telling you that we do have one huge asset: someone who may turn out to be the key to any future success. It is, of course, Kasmut's daughter, Imogen. Eshe knew she was exceptional from her birth and with her quick thinking and innate skills, she could be the one to tip the balance in our favour. However, she will need to be made fully aware of her situation, as it is only she who can decide her own destiny and if she is willing to join our cause and the possible sacrifice that could entail.

ABDUCTION

*I*mogen's hearing returned first and, as she slowly regained consciousness, she was aware of a soft rich melody being strummed on a guitar. It was not a tune she knew, but it resonated deep within and seemed to express a heavy sorrow and longing that connected with her innermost feelings.

She lay perfectly still, eyes closed, as her other senses roused and despite a deep sense of grogginess, she attempted to analyse where she was and how she had got there.

Still dressed, she thought with relief. *No restraints. No trainers on my feet. Pendant still round my neck. There's a blanket over me - what am I lying on? A bed?*

She detected the sound of light rain against a window pane, just audible underneath the guitar tune, and judging from the way the sound travelled, she sensed the room was small and the musician was sitting fairly close to her. Remaining as if asleep, she set her outermost Chroma to pale slumber hues and, hidden beneath these layers, she ran through her memories to retrace what had happened. The disco, the marks on her body, Araz, the Manor and the empty room were her grandfather had been. *No - my father,* she corrected herself, quelling her fears for his safety lest they erupt into her cloak of colours. Her mother - finally awake. *Safe, safe with Adam and Seth, far away,* she soothed. The Tractus marker! *Is it still there?* She heightened her senses at the top of her leg and perceived the impression of the small globe nestled inside the pocket of her jeans, with another sense of relief.

Leo! The thought of his broken nose and face covered in blood as the Repros attacked him on the ground, caused a surge of anxiety to ripple above her disguise, and, simultaneously, the guitar playing stopped and a deep, rich voice gently murmured her name.

"Imogen?"

Feigning slow awakening, stirring her colours to calm and clear earth shades, Imogen's final inner thoughts raced through all she had seen of her captor.

He's the enemy, but why did he protect me from the Repros? Where has he taken me? And why does my stupid body want to turn to jelly in his presence? It's probably some sort of ploy. Caution, she urged herself. *Stay practical – focussed.*

"Araz," she said coldly, as she blinked open her eyes to find him standing over the bed, dressed in his leather jacket and leaning towards her, the guitar now resting on the floor, steadied with one hand.

As she threw off the cover, swung her legs over the side of the bed and sat up, she touched her shirt pocket to confirm what she had sensed, that her Multi-Com had gone. *The photograph is still there, though.* Her head felt heavy and unresponsive, in contrast to the calm clear shades she forced herself to project. Araz propped the guitar up against a wall and dragged the single chair next to the bed, sitting facing her, his expression unreadable, but his colours blazing the gold flame shades of confidence and power.

"We have to talk," he said.

"Do you normally drug and kidnap people to get a conversation?" she asked, in an icy tone.

His reaction was unanticipated, as he grabbed her arm by the elbow, pulling her forward towards him and responding with an angry: "I don't think you realise what kind of trouble you are in!" Imogen caught her breath and recoiled in surprise at his forcefulness and the close proximity of his face. Their eyes locked in a confusion of challenge and anger and she was sure she detected red sparks, like hers, surge briefly in his Chroma.

"Besides," he said with a burst of gold-back scorn, "you were not drugged, merely placed in a state of non-awareness by electrical impulses. The use of drugs is considered prehistoric by us…"

"Well, drugs or no drugs," retorted Imogen, reflecting the same scorn in both her voice and colours, "it would seem you still had to knock me out to get my attention…"

"Get your attention? Is that what you call stepping in to save you life?" he snapped, although his chromatic response was closer to a burning desire rather than anger.

Appearing flustered, he released her arm and looked away, before turning back to her with resolve.

"You are in grave danger. There are people out there who want you dead." Imogen noted the clear sapphire truth he exuded, as a chill went down her spine.

"Who? Why?..." Imogen started, but Araz silenced her with a hand.

"You just need to know that it is my intention to give you safe escort to neutral territory, but it won't be easy."

Safe escort to where?

Imogen quickly glanced around the room, to gauge her chances of escape. There were two doors beyond Araz, both possibly locked, and a small window, which only opened at the top. Besides, this may not be on the ground floor; the window was covered in raindrops, so she could barely see through it. It did not help that she felt so tired and weak. *Take stock - stay calm.* She returned his stare, expression guarded, as Araz continued.

"There's no way out," he said flatly, "if that's what you're thinking. Even if you got away from me, that armed unit you saw will not stop until they've hunted you down and believe me, you will get more than the beating your friend received, if they succeed."

Leo – is he alive?

"They do not question orders," he added. "Not ever, and they have been instructed to eliminate you."

"Why?" she began again, but he disregarded her question and continued at pace.

"We are going to have to avoid their detection and there are only a finite number of ways to do this. I have decided on a strategy. We will leave in a short while and must prepare."

"To go where? And why on earth should I trust you?" the words burst out angrily before she could check them. Her disdain for Araz burnished scarlet and copper in her Chroma, but she allowed them dominance, as this veiled her white blue analysis of all her possible options in another level of her mind. She knew Adam and his brothers would know what to do. *So would Grandad – dad - if he escaped. I need to get to one of them. I have a marker right here! I could jump in just one minute, but I would have to be clear of him.* She knew she couldn't risk retrieving it from her pocket. *He's too close – he mustn't see…*

Aware only of her indignation and hatred, Araz lowered his voice to a deep murmur. "Let's get this clear, Imogen Reiner. You don't need to trust me. You are my prisoner and I am taking you in for testing. Should you be legitimised, you will then face justice."

Legitimised? Justice? What the hell…

"The only choice you have is this: you can come with me awake, or I can take you 'drugged', as you call it." He picked up a pen-like tube, identical to the one Adam had used to sedate her mother, and dangled it between his finger and thumb in front of her.

"What is it to be?" His eyes sparked with intense superiority and Imogen knew she had to comply.

I can't let him find the marker – I need to think - wait my moment…

"It seems I don't really have a choice," she replied, lowering her eyes in a dip of submission. "Where are you taking me?"

"No questions," he snapped. "You have to eat and drink. You've been out for hours…"

How many hours? What day is it now? Imogen sensed it was no more than twelve hours, but as her stomach grumbled, she realised she had not eaten since the party, and then she had been really sick. *No wonder I feel faint.*

Araz thrust an unappetising small, pale square, the size of a stock cube, into her hand and a glass of water.

"The tablet contains all the nutrition you will need for the next few hours," he said matter-of-factly. "Eat!"

Imogen gingerly put the rubber-like substance to her nose and sniffed it, before nibbling off a small corner. It had little taste, but was not unpleasant; she thought there was just a hint of vanilla, but her body responded instantly, as energy surged into her blood stream and coursed around her body, immediately making her feel stronger, wide awake and refreshed.

What's the worst that can happen? If it's poison, I'll recover quickly.

Under his gaze, she popped the rest into her mouth, chewed, swallowed and washed it down with the water. She felt revitalised, as if a mountain spring had magically flooded her entire being, bringing clarity to all of her thoughts. She smiled inwardly, as she remained outwardly subdued and compliant.

Thanks, now I can plan to get away from you so much better.

Araz pulled her trainers out from under the bed and indicated for her to put them on, which she dutifully did.

"My phone?" she asked, knowing he must have seized it, but using the strong yellow of her question to mask the quartz of her scheming.

Need to know the day and time. She heard Adam's words: *Check that it is night time or the early hours where you are going; arriving in the middle of a crowd could be catastrophic.*

"You won't be needing it," he sneered, as he patted his own jacket pocket, indicating its whereabouts, adding cryptically: "not where we're going."

"But I don't even know what day or time it is?"

"It's now Sunday afternoon, 2pm, if it makes a difference," Araz said sarcastically.

Oh yes – it makes a difference – 2pm? Wrong time for a church in New York – Sunday morning it will be busy... Where else?

"There will be people looking for me," she challenged.

I need to find dad. She remembered Leo's words: that he may have gone back to the first marker, *but hadn't Adam said this was not in use?* She knew she could not risk being vaulted forward in time again. *Keep talking, Araz Vikram...*

"Really? I don't think there are many left," he said with sarcasm, but as Imogen winced, he could see her flush deep grey anxiety as she fought back the tears that pricked at her eyes.

He regretted the tone of his remark immediately and awkwardly put a hand on her shoulder, but as she stiffened at the gesture, he quickly removed it. Perplexed at his overwhelming urge to comfort her, he stood and set about gathering items around the room and placing them into a small backpack.

Imogen sensed his regret and persisted with her questioning, concealing her internal scheming.

"So, this armed unit, what are they called? Repros? Where are they from?" she asked. *Are they a different enemy to you?*

Araz gave a sigh, as if weighing up whether to answer her, before saying: "They are a reproduction primeval life form." As he spoke, he carefully transferred the contents of a small box into the bag. "They are unsophisticated constructs, programmed to follow orders without question."

Constructs?

"They are brutal, crude, but above all, efficient."

"I saw their eyes," said Imogen with a shiver, glad she had managed to prompt Araz into talking, so she could not only find out more information, but also distract him whilst she planned her getaway.

"So, they're not human?"

Araz paused from his task and gave her a long hard look, before saying with a shrug: "Of course they're human, but only on the most basic level. They do not think independently. In fact, they don't really think, they just act, rather like most of the primitive people here," he added, with a glower of disdain.

"What do you mean by that?" Imogen responded, with a sense of frustration riding on a parallel plane to her escape planning. "Who exactly do you consider to be primitive?" *Leo was always using that word.*

"This entire world is primitive!" he said, now packing up the items on a small table. "Uncultured, greedy, self-satisfying, coarse, violent and blinkered." Imogen noted his intense disgust and hatred as he spat out the words, and found her stomach had knotted.

"Is that what you think about me?" she asked, the words tumbling out of her mouth unbidden, as she found herself unable to subdue the green-bronze flutter of hurt indignation. *Why the hell should I care what he thinks? Block it...*

Araz closed the bag, threw it over his shoulder and sat back down in the chair, staring at Imogen, who was biting her lip. His eyes sparked an amused interest, but under the bubble of orange, his colours betrayed a surge of powerful scarlet's. Imogen struggled to smother the same response that threatened to rise within her.

"I don't know what to think about you," he said slowly. "I can't work you out. For a Falsebred, you seem to have all your wits about you."

Falsebred?

"But there again, you have been brought up in the art of deception and dishonesty, so this could be a ploy."

Imogen flushed deep red, as much by his accusation as the thought that she had considered him in exactly the same light.

"And is this something that will be determined by 'legitimising' me?" she asked angrily.

"Possibly," he grinned, prompting a purple annoyance that pulsed through her Chroma. "We shall see, but now we need to go."

Imogen recovered herself and squirmed from side to side. "I need the bathroom," she said quietly, projecting earth colours to emphasise the innocence of her request.

"Over there." He indicated one of the two doors, adding: "but be warned, there's no lock and no exit…"

That's what you think.

Once in the small bathroom space, Imogen closed the door and fumbled to get the marker out of her pocket. Her hands were shaking as she glanced over the globe to make quick calculations in her head, remembering the maximum distances possible, and narrowing down the choice of location with the differences in time. In a matter of seconds, she decided where she must go and, heart racing, she pressed her thumb into the indent below. Her stomach filled with dread at the thought of using something that had once had such a catastrophic effect on her life. *I have to trust it – I've no option.*

As she squeezed down on the selected destination, she started to count, perspiration beading across her brow. One minute suddenly seemed like an eternity.

She had got only twenty seconds in, when she heard a loud noise from the next room, followed by shouts, the sound of fighting and objects being smashed. As she froze to the spot, still counting down mentally, the door was flung open with a crash. Araz was tossed in by a helmeted figure, which began to slam a cudgel down towards his head. Her heart lurched.

Dark figures racing down the aisle…

Araz ducked as the implement caught the side of his skull, and he reeled and started to sag at the knees, making the Repro stand back in satisfaction and raise the cosh for a further blow. Araz then suddenly sprang forward and, with what seemed like a replay of Imogen's own battle, he retrieved a pen from up his sleeve and jabbed it into the throat of his adversary, who groped to try and remove it before crumpling to the floor.

Eyes wide with fear, the blood thumping the seconds of the countdown in her head, Imogen froze.

They're coming…

Another Repro started to climb over the first, now blocking the narrow doorway, brandishing a large knife that gleamed in the light. Araz, blood seeping from a cut above his ear, swerved unknowingly from the blade and staggered towards Imogen.

Her words would not surface as her mind screamed: *Behind you…*

The sharp metal rose in the air above his head, as the Repro summoned full force to sweep down with an almighty strike.

No…

Araz saw the glowing orb in her hand, and a mixture of panic and indecision in Imogen's eyes, as his eyes, shocked and puzzled, met hers. His hand reached out involuntarily towards hers as time ticked… He barely noticed her Chromatic flare of intense blue, as she grabbed his open palm and in a split second and a bright flash, they were gone, and the razor-sharp knife swung through nothingness.

NURU

Nuru checked his outfit in a glass reflection outside the hospital entrance. Like his brothers, his age was indeterminable and, despite his advanced years, he could easily pass as a fit middle-aged man. He gritted his teeth and set about his task with grim resignation. Disguised as a hospital porter, he slipped into the mortuary of the local hospital, flashing an agency card at a flabby porter sitting behind a desk.

"Nathan Turner," the heavy man read from the card, before adding, "So, they've sent another one?" with a sarcastic sneer. He gave Nuru a dismissive look and returned to his newspaper, saying: "Last one was a complete waste of space! Well, you better make yourself useful as you're here. They're taking 491 for cremation, so get her out ready." Let the idiots from that agency do the work, he thought to himself, as he picked his nose. They get paid more than me.

Nuru nodded complacently and entered the cold storage area. He had checked beforehand that the undertaker was due to collect an old lady, who had died on Ward E. As no relatives had come forward, a public cremation had been authorised. It took only a few minutes to find what he was looking for and switch the bodies of the two frail old ladies, both as light as a feather, and swap their identities. He wheeled the trolley to the pick up point; the grumpy obese porter checked the tags and grunted, as the undertakers arrived and transferred the body to a coffin, before signing papers and moving it to their hearse. Nuru said a farewell in his head; he had always been fond of Eshe and was saddened to think she had wasted away so quickly. He was then ordered to fetch another corpse.

"Did you hear about that old folks' home that got raided by thugs? Well, this one is from there. Don't know why they need to establish cause of death, though. If you ask me, she dropped dead of extreme old age…" When Nuru just shrugged his shoulders at the man, he mumbled irritably, "don't know why I bother. Just go and get her up to the examination area." He glared at Nuru, thinking sulkily, 'I bet the bloke's on double time for a Sunday, unlike me,' and then sat back in his chair for a snooze.

Nuru did as he was told, leaving the lady from Ward E in the post mortem area, complete with tags denoting she was an unidentified victim from the raid on 'The Manor'. The head porter hadn't even checked the body. Nuru slipped out of his overalls and exited the hospital unseen.

Another clean-up job done, he thought dourly to himself. It would stop any discovery of Eshe's genetic make-up, and the furore that would have been initiated. By the time the authorities realised there had been a mix up, if indeed they did, Eshe would be fine ashes and they would just be grateful that neither of the deceased had any relatives to kick up a fuss, so they could bury the whole sorry incident in obscure paperwork. After all, it would not be the first time there had been an unsolved episode.

He had been at the same hospital nine years before, then disguised as a doctor in the Accident and Emergency department. That had all been Kasmut's fault, he thought with irritation. He had attempted to revive Rashida within days of her return, completely against Eshe's advice, and, screaming and shouting, she had fought him off, dashing out of the house into the path of an oncoming car.

It was a good job the child had not witnessed it. The driver was dealt with, but they had not realised he had already called an ambulance and before Kasmut could get her back in the house, it arrived. They had no option but to let the hospital procedures take their course and Nuru - as usual, he thought angrily - had been sent in at the earliest opportunity, to fetch her and remove any records. The overworked and weary members of staff were baffled when they found her cubicle empty, but too busy to stop and make further enquiries. In fact, a junior doctor, exhausted after a duty of over thirty hours, convinced herself that she must have been hallucinating or, more likely, had been the subject of a bad joke, played by other young medics. Nuru could still recall the reports that he had flicked up on screen, before deleting all traces of the event:

Junior Consultant report, 4pm:
> Discovered in the middle of the road at 3.30pm in the outskirts of Stockport, in her dressing gown, this unknown woman, thought to be approximately forty years of age, was in a semi-comatose state, with major injuries to the legs and arms, a possible victim of a hit-and-run? She had no identification; her right leg was crushed and there were severe cuts to her arms and hands. Arriving by ambulance, she presented symptoms of anterograde amnesia and was unable to give any information about who she was. She became very distressed when questioned. Skin was cyanotic and she was hyperventilating. Admitted to A&E for treatment of shock. Sedation necessary.

Second Report, 6pm:
> Blood type inconclusive after several tests. Contusions seen on patient's arms and legs on arrival are no longer apparent. There was no evidence of any crush injuries on either leg. Lacerations recorded as being on the patient's arms and hands, appear to have healed. Repeated X rays do not show normal skeletal make up – bones are of a density not previously seen. Referral to senior consultant recommended as a priority.

> By the next check, Rashida had been taken from the hospital and all records and samples had been destroyed. Another mess avoided, thanks to him, Nuru reflected with annoyance.

So much for being a Zuberi brother, he thought sardonically, as he made his way back to his car. His brothers, Sefu and Amsu, were known as the inventors, the innovators, the ones at the forefront of their game and he was just the one who cleaned up after others had fouled up. No-one seemed to notice that he worked just as hard as his siblings. It was exasperating that he could only remember being acknowledged once. The device that finally got the child home was his, but this seemed to have been forgotten, along with his hard work supporting Sefu with the other innovations.

He had been so close to Sefu until Amsu returned, and when his lost twin had first arrived, he had been as delighted as any of them, even if he had brought with him that nervous child he claimed to be his son. But he soon realised that this was going to alter everything. It had been decided that the presence of the third triplet must be concealed, even amongst the primitives, so that in the event of capture, the enemy would not know they numbered three. Ridiculous, he had thought, but no-one had listened to him, as usual.

Amsu, renamed Adam, had argued that having been alone for the best part of thirty years and a prisoner for nearly all that time, it was only right that he was at Sefu's side, whilst Nuru was deployed elsewhere. This meant that he had been sent far away from Sefu, who had become his closest brother and friend. He had had no choice but to agree. It was a choice of working alone in the field, or looking after the dumb boy and, thankfully, Kasmut agreed to that.

He had now been alone for nearly twenty years and had begun to brood on everything he had once taken for granted. For instance, it was never made clear why the boy's life would have been in danger, had he been left in the empire. Nuru suspected he had been falsely bred, but had never had the opportunity to ask Amsu. Whilst Nuru knew Imogen was considered to be in this category, it was clear that, despite this, she not only appeared normal, but highly intelligent. However, he could not forget that illegally born children were historically known to be impaired. Nuru was annoyed that Amsu may have been complicit in bringing a possible defective into the world, although in all honesty, the lad looked nothing like his supposed father.

Yes, it was true, he told himself, that his own birth as one of triplets was prohibited, but he reasoned to himself that at least Eshe had ensured that he and his brothers had been subject to full genetic scrutiny. The more he thought about Amsu's thirty years' imprisonment and lack of explanation as to what he had done in that time, the more he distrusted his brother. However, what exasperated him the most, was that Amsu, who had at one time been inseparable from himself, seemed to have replaced him in Sefu's affections.

In the last few years, he was rarely asked to engage in research and instead was put to travel the world, to set up new marker sites. He had to use inferior forms of travel and spend long lonely nights by himself, in squalid little guesthouses, eating cheap unappetising food. It seemed ludicrous to him that they were not allowed to use the unlimited funds he knew they had at their disposal. He was sure he could have travelled first class and lived in better conditions, without drawing attention to himself. It was a ridiculous measure, in his opinion, to be so frugal. That said, he would have put up with the worst conditions imaginable, if he had been there with Sefu, or for that matter, Amsu. He did not like being by himself and felt incomplete and isolated.

As Nuru headed for Imogen's house, to clear up yet another mess, he grumbled to himself that it was always he who had to cover their tracks when needed, he who had to sort out any disorder.

The door to the property was badly split, but a bit of joinery would fix it, so it would lock again. He could turn his hand to most things, after years of experience. He would need to check that he removed all trace of their kind left in the house. Rashida's medical equipment, the hidden cameras and deflector shields, they would all have to go; a few blasts and they would all be dust. As he finished clearing the place out, he became aware of primitive voices outside and a knock on the door. Watching from behind a curtain in an upper room, he saw three youths, a girl and a tall thin lad in conversation and a chunky chap stood at some distance from them. Their voices drifted up to where he hid.

"She's not here, and anyway, she said her mum had woken up and was being transferred to a rehabilitation home in the States," Chrissie was saying. "But what I don't understand, Richard, is why it's all happened in such a rush. Is she coming back? Something just doesn't seem right and I'm worried about her."

Richard nodded in agreement and peered through the window of the front room. "Well, the furniture is still there, so it looks like they plan to come back…" he started to say, as Danny interrupted:

"Isn't this her cat?" He pointed to a bedraggled creature, crouching under a bush.

"Yes, he's called Sadiki," replied Chrissie. "But he's dead unfriendly." The cat hissed, as if to prove the point and went to run off, but was unable to go more than a short distance as it had a bad limp.

"Oh, poor thing, it's got a bad leg. I wonder if there's anyone to look after him?"

Danny, without hesitation, stomped across to the bush, swept up the cat, which looked too surprised to complain, into his arms and announced: "I'll sort it. I like cats." He headed off as the other two shook their heads, before following him down the road.

Nuru heard the other lad say: "Don't worry, Chrissie. Imogen will be fine; she knows how to take care of herself."

Finishing up in the house, Nuru received a message on his device. Trying to contain his anger at yet a further order to help those who couldn't help themselves, he slipped out to head for his next assignment, in an irritated frame of mind

On The Run

The absence of all things was so momentary, that the hair on the back of her neck had not even started to rise. Quelling the urge to be sick, Imogen released the limp hand in hers, got gingerly to her feet from a hard concrete floor and felt all around, arms outstretched in the pitch black. She could feel that there was a strangely sticky cold wall to one side. The air tasted stale and smelt musty as if she were in a cellar, and there was a distant but muffled noise of machinery that came and went as if passing close by on another level. A cool draft blew around her legs, giving her goosebumps all over.

Hearing a deep gasp of breath beside her, she pushed the marker back into her jeans and reached down to the figure on the floor, which glowed Infrared to her eyes. She felt for his leather jacket and into one of the pockets, as the owner groaned quietly. Once she had her Multi-Com in her hand, she traced its outline so it flattened. She then rolled it into a tube, switched it to torch and illuminated her surroundings.

The filthy concrete floor was encrusted with mud-coloured dirt. The wall, covered in grimy white ceramic tiles, curved upward and away as the low arched ceiling went full circle to the opposite wall, blackened metal work and brick exposed in the gaps where tiles were missing.

Not a cellar, an underground tunnel.

Sweeping the torch around she could see the platform edge and the track bed below that used to house rails. There were old angular maps set in sections of the tiles and circular red signs, some with blue labels reading: 'Aldwych' and 'Platform 1', others bearing black arrows pointing: 'Way Out'. The layout was familiar enough to be recognisable but the dated signage and eerie sense of abandonment made it quite alien. The station couldn't have been used for decades. She shivered as she realised that the muted noises were underground trains passing unseen above and around them. Above she could just discern the dying glint of a black globe as the permanent marker switched to standby.

The enormity of the jump and their close escape washed over her and she exhaled slowly with relief. *We made it!*

A sparkle high in the nearby wall caught her eye and she illuminated the area. She saw, painted in gold on the tiles, the same star, circle and arrow symbols as her pendant.

First things first.

Imogen turned the torch onto Araz. He struggled to his feet and blinked at the light shining in his face.

"Where are we?" he asked weakly, touching the injury beside his ear, which had already stopped bleeding.

"No questions," she promptly answered, both smiling inwardly that the tables had been turned, but also trying to justify her instantaneous decision to bring him with her. *I had to save him – I couldn't just leave him to die.*

Imogen wished she could contact her father, or Adam for help but she could not even activate her phone to see if there were any messages. Adam had been clear that this location was right on top of the enemy marker and they could be close. It had to remain 'silent'.

"I require you to hand over your device and to keep still," she ordered Araz, sounding more in control than she felt and grabbing the rucksack that was still over his shoulder and pulling it from his arm, transferring it to hers. *My mouth is so dry.*

Surprisingly, he allowed her to take it without resistance. He just stared back at her, his expression unreadable, his Chroma, only just visible in the torchlight, tinged with grey swirls.

Perhaps he's been badly affected by the Tractus. Her stomach felt as if it had been twisted in opposite directions.

Cautious not to turn her back on him, she kept the torch shining in his face and backed up to the wall, reaching up to the symbols with her other hand. As she touched the centre of the arrowhead in the insignia, a section of the tiles below it sprang open revealing a drawer at eye level. Inside, there were items of clothing, vacuum packs of food and cartons of drink, a large quantity of money, a pen-like device she recognised as a tranquiliser, and a small flat black oval, like the one Leo had used for the driving lesson. *Data Encounter* she reminded herself, mentally thanking Adam and his brothers for their forward planning.

"Sit down," she ordered Araz, who gradually sank back down to the floor without taking his eyes off her. With her free hand, she took two of the juice cartons and gave one to Araz and drank one herself, making her feel instantly better. She then picked up the DE, inflated it, and felt for the familiar indentations and connected with the information, forcing it to a parallel area of her consciousness, as she spoke to Araz. Images flooded into the separated section of her mind, as she spoke aloud.

"It seems we are now equal."

"Really?" said Araz, flashing purple derision and yellow questioning.

The data flashed up the figures in her head: the year, date and time, which confirmed she had only jumped, and not vaulted, and was just a few minutes further on than when she left Araz's bedsit. *No accidents - thank goodness!*

A three-dimensional world globe then turned before it zoomed in firstly into Europe, and then the United Kingdom, as a set of detailed London maps circled in her mind. The layers of street views, satellite images, and photographs confirmed her precise location. *Amazing! Although Adam could have said the London marker was hidden in an old tube station.* She felt the outline of the globe in her pocket with a new admiration; delighted she had used it without any mishaps.

"Yes, equal: you saved me from the Repros the other night; I saved you from them today, which makes us 'one-all'," she added matter-of-factly, her mind equally divided between the exchange with Araz and the information pouring into her other faculties.

A set of architectural plans, showing her exact location in the underground complex and the possible exit routes, appeared along with a red warning sign indicating where the enemy marker was located: the other disused platform linked to theirs by a common corridor leading to old escalators. *So close…*

"Saved me? That's pushing it," retorted Araz, pulsing copper-black. "I had it in hand…"

"Really? Is that so?" she challenged.

A telephone number with strict instructions as to what to do in the case of emergencies, imprinted into her mind, then the images moved on to a summary of current news, as the device connected with local TV & radio channels. There were directions to libraries and Internet cafes, if further research was needed, lessons in basic spoken and written English and information Imogen did not need. She released her hand, broke the connection and put the DE back in the drawer, now focussing fully on her involuntary companion.

Picking up the sedation pen from the storage area, she idly swung it about as she added: "I realise your graze has healed quickly…" pointing it at the side of his head, a smear of dried blood the only sign of any injury. "…But your brain might have taken a bit longer, had it been cleft in two!"

"What do you mean?" he asked, before reaching out his hand, with fingertips wide and the request: "Show me!"

"Show you?"

The words along with Araz's outstretched open hand prompted missing thoughts from her childhood: a large black robed figure with a kindly face and the same open hand, saying 'Show me'. *Father Jonathan! I had forgotten about him.* She ran through how she had tried to transmit her thoughts to him by fingertips. He had wanted to read Chroma. She had laughed to see the priest's thoughts, confusion as to which colour meant which emotion, and a clear admiration for the intelligence of her young self. But she hadn't used this method in years. She had learnt to avoid touching others, tip-to-tip, knowing that it was dangerous to see their thoughts, which entered her head uninvited. She had only used it to 'speak' to her mother as she slept, when there were no images to bounce back. No-one else had prompted her to try, not even Leo.

'What? What do you mean?' she started.

Araz looked askance. "Cognitive link? You've surely done this before?" he questioned with a slight sneer, gold-black hues rising.

"Not for years," she responded honestly. *What if it's a trick?*

"Well, you show me what you saw," he said in a patronising tone, "and I will decide if I agree." He held his hand up, opened wide. She remembered how it was supposed to work. One of the party decided on the experience they wanted to project, the other would receive an accurate image directly, via the nervous system, and compare it to their own. Father Jonathan had called it the 'mirror' game and it was supposed to be one-way, but it led to her seeing thoughts that were not projected. She shuddered at the memory of shock and hatred on Oonagh's face, when she had relayed that she had stolen the teacher's money. Father Jonathan had decided it was not a good idea to employ it's use; 'everyone's entitled to his or her private thoughts' he had said. *But will it be one-way with Araz?*

"Okay," she responded, unable to completely remove the uncertainty from her voice. Taking a deep breath and soothing her colours, she put the pen in a side pocket of the rucksack and reached out her fingertips to touch Araz's. She concentrated her focus to ban the instantaneous surges of attraction, so that the only image in her head, at that moment, was her view in his bathroom before they jumped.

As their fingertips touched, Araz saw the replay of him being thrown through the doorway, the Repro striking him on the side of the head before he counteracted with the pen, and then the image he had not seen: a second Repro raising a large knife behind him, ready to slice him down with full force, as Imogen grabbed his hand and they disappeared. Pulling his hand back, Araz made a fist, putting it to his mouth as swirls of bronze, black and grey darted around his Chroma. Imogen barely noticed his change in mood, as she digested the thoughts he had unwittingly transmitted to her.

In the few seconds they had linked, she had seen, through his eyes, his experience of the same moment and his reaction to her account. An image of herself, startled and holding the glowing marker, and his multiple thoughts had slammed into her head, giving her a glimpse of his state of mind. His deliberations were confused and, like her own, happened simultaneously in different levels of his mind. She separated them out, along with each conflicting emotion as she compared his 'reality' with her viewpoint…

Who is this girl? *Wonder, reluctant attraction.* The object she's holding – it must be a Tractus device! *Disbelief.* But it's not fixed - how did they create it? *Admiration and thirst to know more.* Why would the Repros turn on me? *Bewilderment.* That knife was meant to kill - they want me dead! *Shock.* Who gave the command? *Confusion and a flood of alternative names Imogen could not distinguish.* It must be because I didn't report finding her? *Guilt mixed with stubbornness and pride.* I was her captor, so why did she save me? Why am I so drawn to her? *Incomprehension, along with a rush of raw desire, which triggered a deep reciprocal pulse within Imogen's own body.*

Imogen steadied herself against the cold wall, shaken at the honesty of his thoughts and mollified by the sense that he, too, did not understand everything and was unclear about his situation. *What does that mean - he didn't report me?* She found she was unable to fathom it further, as her immediate challenge was to quell a deep burning current of thrill and yearning, triggered by the realisation that he held an equally intense attraction for her. *Maybe he can't control it either?*

As she used the drill to remain outwardly calm, she watched Araz ponder his situation in a swirl of multiple shades. There was no indication that he was aware he had revealed any of his inner thoughts to her. She decided to set this aside as she said quietly: "So, you see, they want you dead too, and if I hadn't grabbed your hand, they would have succeeded."

He gave a slight nod and got to his feet, a faint flash of blue rising in his colours.

What have you decided?

Imogen, for the first time feeling safer with Araz who, it would appear, was also a target of these forces and didn't know why, crossed to the opening of an interlinking corridor she had located from the plans and reached up to a high box and pulled a black lever which turned on dim lighting above the wall. *Well the electricity is still on!*

Turning off the torch, she put the Multi-Com back to standard mode.

"So, what's the plan?" he asked, as he joined her at the opening, with a genuine yellow-white question.

"Not sure," responded Imogen truthfully, "but it looks like we both need to avoid those Repros."

"We're going to have to work together," announced Araz decisively. "You have equipment I don't have," Imogen winced internally, "and I have knowledge of these fighting units you don't have." She did not need to see his clear sapphires to know this was true, but it prompted a grey surge of worry, that the portable marker was no longer secret. Araz had been intensely interested when he realised what it was. She needed to contact Adam, but would the Repros detect her signal if she used her phone? Araz saw her glance at her device and guessed her thoughts.

"You can't use that: we could be detected; we can't take any risks. I need to know precisely where we are." His black-gold colours made this more of a command than a request.

Imogen, with a slight hesitation, nodded as she replied: "Abandoned Underground Station, in London. Used to be called the Strand, then Aldwych."

"No! So, there's a subversive portal here too?" Araz exclaimed in genuine surprise.

Subversive?

Imogen saw the location of the enemy marker on the floor plans, in her head. Araz's white-blues told her that he had not known they had a marker here too, and now she had inadvertently revealed more key information to the wrong person. Her stomach lurched and she could not help but feel resentful that she had not been trained to know more about 'the enemy', by either her father or Leo.

Stay practical! Imogen decided that if she couldn't contact Adam from here, then there was a double reason to get to the first marker. Firstly, Leo had said her dad might be there, if he had escaped (she felt a combination of dread for her father and a stab of guilt that she had been unable to help Leo. *Please don't be dead.*) Secondly, it would have a deflector, preventing enemy detection so she could call in safety. *I can also try the emergency number, when I get a chance.*

Putting the phone back in her shirt pocket, she felt the photograph, pulled it out and glanced at the writing on the back. Next to the faded date, *"May 1966"* was a note written in a different pen: *"Little Rome, Birmingham"*. Well, she reasoned to herself, Birmingham was a big place, but probably had very few areas known as 'Little Rome'?

Before Araz could interpret the meaning of the brief blue flare in her Chroma, Imogen replaced the photo and announced: "We need to travel – the old-fashioned way!"

"Where?" asked Araz.

She was not going to give him any more information than necessary, so she responded with her father's stock answer: "All in good time," as she crossed back to the hidden storage.

Taking a quantity of money and some food stores, which she packed into the rucksack, she closed the tiled drawer and walked ahead of Araz, as they both made their way down the linking corridor. They emerged at the bottom of an old escalator run that disappeared up into darkness and were about to climb upwards when they heard a clatter from above and mumbled voices getting closer to the top of stationary steps heading straight down towards them.

Imogen and Araz dived against the wall to one side of the stairwell and pushed into a narrow recess where they froze. The footsteps of a group descended, heavy and mechanical. *Sounds like six, maybe more.* Imogen held her breath and her ears prickled at the sound of a quiet groan with each downward step, one step being taken slowly and painfully, at variance with the military-style stomp around it.

Could it be? She felt a surge of both hope and fear.

As the unit reached the bottom of the escalator and came into view, Imogen could see the backs of six large Repros marching away towards the other platform. In the middle of their number, being pushed and prodded, there he was; a shorter, blond-haired figure, his t-shirt splattered in old bloodstains as he limped to keep up. *Leo!* She could not see his face, but his body language and poor mobility spoke of constant pain. She remembered her father's stern counsel that whilst rapid healing was miraculous it could also be problematic and that dislocated bones and torn tissue must be joined and straightened instantly so it could knit and mend correctly. His warning that without this, cells may repair 'out of joint', causing serious trauma, rang in her head. *Poor Leo…*

As if he had heard her thoughts, Leo suddenly glanced back taking in his surroundings, a pained grimace on his face, his misshapen nose flattened to one side. Was it her imagination or had he seen her in the shadows?

Shoved sharply in the back, a helmeted figure forced Leo forward and the detachment along with their prisoner disappeared into the far corridor.

Imogen and Araz stepped into the dim light as Araz's eyes motioned they should quickly go up the steps. Imogen stood her ground, whispering urgently: "We have to help him."

Araz, his expression filled with questioning and impatience, gave a shrug asking: "why?"

"That was Leo – I can't just let them take him," she hissed.

"I know who he is," spat Araz in a low voice of contempt.

What? Imogen was surprised at the vehemence in his tone and unable to read his Chroma. *What is that? Jealousy or something else?*

"There's nothing we can do - they're going to the portal," he declared adding: "we must go!" Araz reached for her arm but, infused with indignation, Imogen pulled away and folded her arms decisively, staring Araz in the face.

"Well you run if you want but I am going to try and help." As the angry words escaped her mouth, her heart sank. *What can I do in face of so many Repros?*

Araz shook his head slowly. "I am trying to help you," he said with a deep frown, purple annoyance clear even in the gloomy light.

"There's such a thing as loyalty," Imogen blurted out, conscious not to raise her voice.

"And there's such a thing as foolishness," countered Araz, voice full of aggravation. He glanced to the distant corridor and back before lightening his tone.

"Do you not see?" he pleaded, "if we go within a few yards of them, they will detect us. They want us dead, remember." He could see the conflict begin on Imogen's face, as well as in her colours.

"Look, he's safe for the time being," he reasoned softly. "If they had wanted to eliminate him, they would have done it by now. They're taking him back."

"Back where?"

Araz gave Imogen one of his long stares, before answering: "Holis, of course."

Holis? More mystery. Well I'm not going to abandon him again…

Shrugging her shoulders, Imogen replied, "I have to try and help him… you do what you want," a set determination fixed on her face, as she darted across the hall space and headed for the corridor. Araz pursed his lips in annoyance, clenched and unclenched his fist before following her with a grim resignation.

As she moved along the walls of the linking passage, Imogen surveyed the architectural plans in her head and saw that the enemy marker was positioned in a service subway on the next level, accessed by a spiral metal staircase behind a doorway at the edge of the old train tunnel.

Sensing Araz close behind, Imogen emerged on the other side of the abandoned station to see the far door on the platform lit up by torchlight as one of the Repros unbolted and opened it. Pushing Leo ahead they all disappeared inside.

Imogen ran swiftly to the door, left ajar, and pulled it open. Araz joined her, touched her arm and nodded for her to be cautious as they both began to creep down the spiral steps and into the growing doom. They heard voices; Imogen did not recognise the language, but somehow understood what was being said.

A gruff voice was telling Leo that he was lucky to be alive and to have been given a reprieve. As she concentrated, the words became clearer and translated in her head, a part of her mind acknowledging that this was a language she did not know, but seemed to be rooted in her cells.

"We have orders to send you back and place you under the direction of the Supreme Council," spat the harsh voice. "Your claim that the Falsebred is an imbecile, is a lie. She has evaded capture and kidnapped an agent. What do you say to that?"

Falsebred? Does he mean me? Why would Leo say I was an imbecile?

Imogen turned the stairs and peered just over the edge of the metal rail, looking down the stairwell. Lit by a bare bulb hanging from the low ceiling, she could see the back of two of the Repros and the top of Leo's head, his blonde hair streaked with dried blood. She was unable to see who was speaking and started to lean further over but Araz put a hand on her shoulder to deter her.

Leo's voice, somewhat shaky, responded: "now, let me think – what do I say to that? Well an imbecile has the advantage on you bunch of thugs who, if you had more brains, would possibly make the grade as half-wits." There was a loud thump as a cosh impacted on his back, followed by a deep groan and Leo dropped to all fours on the floor, wincing as he protectively pulled his broken arm into his body. Imogen flinched as she stared down from her hiding place and mentally urged Leo to be quiet.

"Subtle…" began Leo, sarcastically, as, with some effort, he turned over, rolling onto his back, eyes shut tight with pain. "Where did you learn such classy moves?" He was rewarded with a sharp kick in the ribs.

Leo – Shhhhh.

He looked completely dishevelled, pale and exhausted, his nose horribly distorted; his lips were dried and cracked and his arm had set at a strange disjointed angle, which was clearly causing great pain as he tried to protect it with the other hand. Imogen gave an involuntary gasp to see him so disfigured.

Leo continued, with dogged determination: "Hey, it's only a scratch! Just a flesh wound… I've had worse," opening his eyes and briefly looking up.

What's he doing? In a glance, he saw Imogen's face. His Chroma responded by twinkling orange – *Caution!* Imogen realised that he had shown no flare of surprise, *he had seen us, he's trying to keep them distracted,* but as he awkwardly got to his feet, he displayed no outward sign that he knew she was there and continued his Monty Python monologue.

"Okay, let's call it a draw…"

Imogen could see the effort he needed to force a change to his colours, to a dull wash of brown, that gradually faded away, followed by a flashing green circle. *Hide - go!* She stepped back next to Araz, out of sight, as Leo tried to finish: "You just got lucky, but if you don't believe in luck..." they heard movement from the steps above as the harsh voice from below grunted:

"Shut up! I heard a noise!"

A Repro started up the stairs. They were trapped!

"...then where would you be?" finished Leo, loudly. Imogen's heart thumped as the footsteps from above got louder and a figure below climbed the stairs. *Don't believe in luck: dad! Where will he be: the first marker, Birmingham. He's telling me where to go.*

"Who's there?" came a rasping cry below them.

"It's your last two half-wits," shouted Leo at the top of his voice, emphasising the word, 'two', before another groan indicated he had been hit again. Imogen and Araz both knew this was a clear warning to them.

Imogen stared wildly at Araz who put a finger to his lip and started to climb back up the stairs, silently urging her to follow him. They increased their speed and heard a shout from the Repro below as it caught sight of them. Leaping upward, they beheld the helmeted figure standing in their way above. Without hesitation, Araz slammed into the legs of the stationary figure with full force, and as it lost its balance, Araz got next to it and pushed it down the stairwell, Imogen pressing herself against the wall. The Repro fell on top of those coming up.

Araz and Imogen raced up the remaining steps, Imogen pulling the rucksack round her body and grabbing the pen from the outer pocket as they moved. Araz saw the shadow of the second Repro, running to the doorway, as he got to the top and rapidly dropped into a tight roll, as he attempted to collide with its moving legs from the ground. With surprising agility for its large size, the Repro dodged out of the way and before Araz could stand, it had reached down and grabbed him by the throat, lifting him high in the air. Imogen, unseen behind the huge figure, hurriedly closed the door at the top of the stairs and bolted it firmly as the Repros from below launched into it, shouting and banging on the wood. She darted around the back of the dark form, as it turned towards the commotion, holding its captive tightly at the neck, Araz thrashing about helplessly, his face losing colour. With a lightning move, Imogen leapt, swung the rucksack into the back of the helmet and, as the Repro's head went forward exposing the rear of the neck, she rammed the pen into the top of its spine, pressing the button. It instantly let go of Araz and collapsed.

Araz, breathless and rubbing his neck, gave Imogen a brief smile and in a strangled voice said: "Two: one!" a red admiration and sage-green gratitude, sparking in his Chroma.

With unspoken agreement, they each nodded towards the exit corridor and both broke into a run. The stairway door behind them smashed outwards onto the platform and booted feet pounded loudly, in hot pursuit.

HAROLD REINER

*T*he deflectors were down. He had not disabled them. It could only mean one thing. His location had been discovered and he had limited time to get out.

Harry had always known that this moment would come, even after years of hiding so successfully. It had just been a matter of time. We could not have gone on any longer, he thought sadly; we had expected to achieve so much here, but all it has brought is heartache and loss. The faces of Firas, Eshe and Rashida fluttered in his mind; death, pain, mental illness... The primitive world had, in the end, taken them all. Everything he ever cared about, apart from Imogen, was lost and no longer under his control. It is time to return and face the enemy, he thought.

With a heavy resignation, he began the task of disposing of his effects. As he pointed a fine light pulsating cylinder at each file and database with a short blast, they disintegrated and powdered on impact. The speed of destruction, he reflected sadly, was far more rapid than that of creation. He was, however, thankful for a number of things: firstly that Imogen was now under the protection of Leo. He is young and competent and has lived in both worlds, so should be able to safeguard her in either place. Plus, his loyalty to me is complete, he reassured himself. Secondly, he was thankful to have time to get rid of anything that would put the others in danger and break all the hypnosis connections, rendering his loyal staff incapable of reporting on either him, or the rest of the group. Leo and the brothers would know that communications had been cut. They would know to start the emergency plan. Yes, all in all, things could have been a lot worse, he reasoned.

With the new portable Tractus devices, Amsu and Nuru could be mobilised in seconds. Their bases were only a few hours travel from the closest markers. Someone would have to dispose of Eshe's body; they could not risk her genetic differences being discovered. Nuru was gifted with this sort of thing. Amsu could move Rashida to the place of safety organised by Sefu, and then he could assist his son, Leo. It's about time those two got on better, he decided. Yes, the Zuberi family would launch into action. Imogen would be protected.

Imogen's smiling face sprang into his mind. It was strange, he had got used to thinking of his daughter as his granddaughter. She was so young and so capable. He was truly proud of her, but very sorry that he had not been able to explain things to her directly. He went to remove the black and white photograph of her First Communion from the mirror edge, but promptly realised he could leave a clue here. Writing the reference to the church on the back, he blinked back a tear, as he placed the corner back in the mirror frame. In his mind, her trusting, smiling, little face grew to that of a young adult, her eyes now filled with anxiety, her expression questioning and distant. She thought she had hidden her resentment and anger on the last occasion they had spoken, but he knew her too well. He did not need to see her Chroma to know she was suspicious and confused. He gave a sigh. They had been so close.

He was unsure how much she had found out about her true identity. If only Eshe could have handled this, rather than an inexperienced young lad, he mused. But he had had no choice; he would just have to trust in all the drills he had taught her over the last ten years. She was strong, logical, creative… she would use her powers of analysis to figure it out. Deep within his mind, a small voice asked, 'what if she develops her mother's instability?' Determined not to follow this through, he shook his head and forced himself to put these thoughts aside and to focus on the disposal of his effects.

Retrieving a large quantity of money from under the now bare mattress and swapping his sophisticated device for a primitive cell phone, he called a taxi to take him the seventy-five miles to their leader. Tanastra would also know he was coming. Their emergency procedures were watertight. Times have changed, he thought. Where once he would have driven, or caught a train and shirked from spending large amounts of money, for fear it would draw unwanted attention, he felt it was no longer important. What does it matter now? he asked himself. We have been found; the final chapter has begun.

He left, unseen, from the rear fire exit, just before a growingly confused Lisa, acting on auto-pilot, admitted a dark charismatic figure who claimed to be a workman, at the front door. It was only a matter of minutes before a large, black van had then pulled up outside.

LONDON

*I*mogen and Araz flew up the non-working escalator, two steps at a time.

"Get out in the open, they won't follow us there," urged Araz.

A glance back from the top saw several Repros burst out of the corridor below, right on their heels. Imogen's heart thumped. They were coming for her and fast; they would be up the flight of steps in no time. Forcing back her terror, Imogen summoned the maps of passageways, service link and exits imprinted on her mind by the Data Encounter as they ran.

Araz headed for a far door as her scan confirmed it would lead to a deep circular ventilation shaft with a steel wall ladder ascending several floors to ground level. They would only be able to climb the narrow ladder one at a time and the hatch mechanism at the top would not be quick to open. Her intuition kicked in; they could not go that way, they would be caught.

Instinctively she grabbed Araz's arm and veered off in another direction, as the corridor grew darker. She could sense a slight resistance in the tension of his muscles but this faded as they picked up speed, the pounding footsteps of Repros behind them. They raced towards a seemingly dead-end, rusty metal shutters barricading an old passage, only just discernible in the shadowy light.

Araz looked wildly at Imogen as they slowed, his gesture imploring: 'where now'?

Imogen darted into a hidden inglenook to the side of the barred entrance. *Please let these maps be accurate.* To her relief she could feel a 'locker style' door set in the wall. As she fumbled for the handle, Araz sprang next to her kicking the door open and they entered the dark space beyond, their assailants rushing for the shutters behind them.

As they moved forward, barely able to see a few feet ahead, Imogen grabbed her Multi-Com and switched it to torch. They were in a circular metal-lined passage, old bundles of dusty cables drooping from the side of the walls and a raised metal walkway that twisted and turned into darkness ahead. Imogen swiftly plotted their course as they ran towards the corner. *We have to reach the ladder down to the platform service door.* Grabbing Araz by the hand as they moved, she sent an image of the route to him via fingertips, ignoring his anxiety and his worry for her safety that he had unintentionally transmitted back.

Temporarily slowed by the narrow doorway, the Repros were now pressing in, one by one, as each picked up speed to follow them. Imogen knew they must not falter and rapidly sprinted for her goal, Araz matching her pace.

As they reached the promised ladder, off to one side beyond the bend of the tunnel, she flicked off the torch, launched onto the top step and, feet either side of the rungs, slid quickly to the bottom. Araz followed suit landing next to her as she felt for the opening that showed on the plans. Above they could hear that their pursuers had raced past the hatch, but it would not be long before they discovered their mistake and backtracked.

A metal grate covered the exit opening, through which they could see Imogen's dim platform lights and they both pulled and pushed until it came loose and moving it aside they edged out onto Platform 1. *Back to where we started.*

Araz went to make for the first corridor again but she jumped in front of him and shook her head vigorously. "No," she mouthed, indicating "this way" with her head. Loud stamping rang around the empty station as Repros appeared both at the end of the corridor and at the grating simultaneously.

Imogen pulled Araz back to the platform edge, then leapt off onto the track bed and dashed for the tunnel, Araz right behind.

Pitch black ahead, she narrowed the beam of her torch as they ran, so it just picked out the track bed below as they sped around bends and the tunnel began to slope downward. The sound of their pursuers reverberated in noisy echoes around the walls, giving the impression they were being chased by dozens upon dozens of militia and Imogen had to quell the rising panic she felt inside. Looking at her internal maps she could see that the track stopped only half a mile ahead, and they would have to drop into a smaller parallel shaft to reach the nearest exit that gave them any chance of survival: Charing Cross. The link had never been enlarged and was just a rudimentary channel made during the original excavations in the early 1900's. It burrowed below the live underground lines running close to old riverbeds and sewers and she just hoped it was still navigable.

Concentrating on the uneven terrain of the track bed as they careered down the inclines, she could not grab Araz's hand to show him the way; he would just have to stick close to her. The ring of footsteps and angry shouts told them both that the Repros were in hot pursuit and gaining on them.

As the end of the tunnel came in sight, completely blocked with concrete and scree, she spotted the small circular opening that heralded their way. Rushing to the hole, Imogen ducked down and pushed forward, bent low as Araz urged her to hurry. The Repros were just metres away.

Please let them be too big to fit in.

Grunts of frustration resonated around the grimy metal channel from the entrance behind them as they ran in a half-crouched position; it was clear the unit were forcing their way in, squeezing through the aperture and barely slowing their pace.

"Faster," insisted Araz, steering her from behind to increase their speed.

The shaft descended steeply ahead and it became soft and wet underfoot, a fetid smell rising from the darkness ahead. Whilst Imogen's key focus was to maintain her high velocity and point the narrow beam of light ahead to ensure they didn't stumble, her senses were heightened in every respect. Besides the sound of the booted feet that ran after them there was the sound of a train passing just the other side of the tunnel which temporarily drowned Araz's fast breathing as he ran, awkwardly stooped, at her heels. Imogen also had a growing awareness of water dripping ahead of them plus the regular Infrared glow of small creatures at ground level that could only be rats scurrying in and around them. At any other time she would have shuddered or even screamed, but her survival instinct had overridden all other reactions and she knew they must race ahead regardless.

The tunnel began to open out and they were able to straighten up as they rushed forward. *We must be close to Charing Cross,* she thought, mentally praising the accuracy of the diagrams she had been given.

Their feet were starting to splash in murky water that was beginning to puddle beneath them and within metres they were up to their ankles in a musty smelling stream, fluid pouring down the sides of the shaft and lightly showering them as they ran. Running became more problematic and the splashes from behind confirmed the Repros were nearly upon them. The torchlight flashed ahead to a sight that made her heart sink: the tunnel descended as the water rose with only shoulder and headroom in the upper part of the ceiling curve. With their adversaries just yards behind she knew there was no way back.

We have to go on – I can... I can do this!

With grim determination and getting in deeper by the second, Imogen pulled the rucksack off her back and held it above her head with one hand, torch in the other. Araz came alongside her, looking briefly into her eyes to question the route. She shrugged imperceptibly indicating 'there's no other way' as they trudged forward with as much haste as possible. Within metres they were wading against the filthy water. It was now up to her chest and his waist and she raised her chin high in order to breathe.

Imogen could feel the panic bubbling away inside her. *What if it's completely submerged ahead?*

Araz reached up and took the torch from her to light the way. In doing so he deliberately brushed his fingertips to hers and his message slammed full force into her psyche: 'We can do this,' it reassured neurologically, in an echo of her thoughts and accompanied by a wave of respect and admiration he could not know he had sent, but which, nonetheless, swamped her fears instantly giving her a renewed determination.

Despite the icy cold fluid dragging at their clothes, they ploughed forward, the murky pool now up to her shoulders and his chest, as they kicked up thick sludge with every step. Slowed by the resistance of pressing against the flow, cold seeped into every muscle and a decaying stench filled the small air space threatening to choke them. Imogen intuitively cut the messages her from smell receptors switching off the disgusting odour. *That's better!* With no time to wonder how she had done this, she struggled on; there was far more to worry about. Their chasers, although slowed by entering the waterlogged channel, were still gaining on them and the effort to stay ahead was beginning to wain.

Please let it be no deeper, Charing Cross station is just a few hundred metres away.

The culvert floor beneath their feet thankfully began to rise as they ploughed ahead and the water gradually dropped as they started to pick up speed and put a little distance between them and the Repros who they could hear gasping with the effort of pressing through the flooded channel, still up to their armpits.

As the tunnel emerged out of the water, Imogen threw the sodden rucksack onto her soaking back and she and Araz put on a final burst of speed as best they could with heavy wet clothing dragging them down as they located their exit ahead: another shuttered gateway.

The bright lights beyond the opening proclaimed a station platform that was completely deserted. Only stopping when they hit the open metal work of the shutter, Araz immediately began to force the catch at the bottom with his wet boot. It broke easily and he dragged the shutter up to form a gap just wide enough for he and Imogen to roll below onto the well lit platform. Once through, Araz forced the shutter back down and kicked in the side so it burst out of its metal housing, distorting the frame so it could not be lifted up again.

Springing around the corner, Imogen mentally reviewed the maps and charts. She could see that this platform was no longer used by passengers, but acted as a siding to stable trains. The tube tunnel would provide a way out, but it was risky: a moving train might hit them plus the live rails would be treacherous. She searched for other options.

The noise of angry grunts and shaking metal reached their ears as the frustrated Repros grappled with the twisted metal shutter; temporarily halted. Araz had bought them valuable time and Imogen hurriedly decided that the safest route up to the operational platforms would be via the linking ventilation shaft. Shaking the surface water from her dripping hair she broke into a run for the shaft door, Araz jogging next to her with a slight grin on his wet face, his Chroma flaring cherry admiration. Imogen shook her head in disbelief. *Amazing! Life and death chase and he's still pulsing desire like crazy. Must not get distracted – we're not out yet!*

Closing the shaft door behind them, they began to climb the steel wall ladder, Imogen ahead of Araz. Thirty feet up, the sound of running boots alerted them that the chase was back on and as the door below was flung open, her soaking wet trainers slipped and Araz quickly caught her legs.

"Careful," he snapped, placing her feet back on the rungs, adding more encouragingly: "Not far now."

Reaching the top, Imogen stepped onto a small metal landing area and pushed at the closed door of a circular hatch. It would not budge.

Araz joined her and they both pushed together. The first Repro was now only several rungs away. Imogen's heart thumped with fear.

Steeling themselves they thrust at the door with all their might and it finally sprang open. Araz swiftly dived through and started to pull Imogen through the opening by her arms. A massive hand suddenly grabbed her foot and she squealed in terror.

"Let it take you – briefly - then kick," commanded Araz, as he stopped pulling for a few seconds. Imogen felt herself being dragged back into the shaft and as the Repro clumsily released her ankle to grab her knee she kicked back with full force thumping it in the chest. The creature screeched as it toppled backwards and before they heard it hit the bottom of the shaft, Araz had hauled Imogen out and shut the door as they turned and bounded down a small corridor to join the jostle of travellers in the Charing Cross passages

"Think that makes it 'two–all'," smiled Araz, catching his breath as Imogen looked back in alarm.

"They won't come out here," he added, glowing gold and black surety. "Too many primitives."

"I'm not taking any chances," she retorted as they dodged in and out of the throng of people.

Northern Line: northbound to Euston. Imogen, checking the underground signs, pressed on glancing back intermittently as they weaved their way to the platform just as a train pulled in. The doors slid open and the other passengers moved aside, giving them a wide berth. Their reflection in the windows of the train confirmed the reason why. Filthy, dishevelled and still sopping wet, she realised they also stank to high heaven as she re-engaged her sense of smell. *Yuegh!*

The doors slid shut with a hiss and ignoring the distasteful look of the few others in the carriage, she and Araz sank with relief into the nearest seats, hair and clothes still dripping, as they allowed themselves a quick exchange of a small smile and nod.

"So, we're even again," she said to Araz as she squeezed the water from her hair. "Although that was my route that got us out."

"Your route nearly killed us…" he started to say with a haughty sneer but he then stopped in mid sentence. Imogen realised he was staring at the centre of her soaking shirt, an incredulous look on his face. Looking down quickly, she saw an intermittent flash. It was coming from her pendant, stuck with water between her shirt and chest. Sheepishly, she pulled it out and stared down at the wet symbols. The central arrow was aglow with sparks of gold and silver. As she rubbed the inside of her sleeve over the face, wiping away the surface liquid, the light paled to a glimmer and died away. She remembered Chrissie's words: *Well clever, the way it changes when it's wet* and wondered what it meant.

Araz looked from the necklace to Imogen's damp face, bright swirls of yellow reinforcing the question in his face. When she merely looked away, unable to fathom its meaning, he asked: "So what does it unlock?"

"Sorry?" she mumbled.

"The key?"

"Key?"

The tube pulled into Leicester Square station as Araz persisted with his questioning, slight annoyance in his voice, traces of purple-black disdain visible in his Chroma.

"Yes, it's a key. Electro-chemical in origin, old technology now. I've only ever seen one like this…" Araz faded out as he recalled, with a snapshot from the Supreme Council Chambers, that the chain he had glimpsed was around Kekara's neck and was normally hidden. He realised, on reflection, that he had no idea what that unlocked.

"Well, if you're so clever, you tell me!" retorted Imogen, pushing the chain and symbols back into her wet top and mentally calculating how many stops before they got to Euston. *Four more.*

"I think it's more important we plan our next move," she added, tensing as the doors opened and only relaxing when no-one got in and the tube moved off again. She had to stay in control. The mystery of the pendant, or key, or whatever it was, would wait until she got to her father, or Adam. *Got to think straight.*

"So what exactly is our next move?" Araz asked, a slightly annoyed curl appearing on his lips and a plum shaded sarcasm in his Chroma as he drew slightly away from her.

Imogen thought long and hard about her answer. She could jump off the tube, lose him in London and be free of him. However, they had escaped together and he had protected her. Plus she had no idea if she was being tracked and Araz knew about these Repros, their tactics and weapons. She was frustrated she knew so little. *Is he still the enemy or not? I just don't know...*

Deciding to stay with him she reasoned that at least she had glimpsed his private thoughts and she knew he was just as unsure about his predicament as she was. Whilst Araz projected a front of surety and confidence, this was clearly a cover for all his uncertainties. She also knew, from her vantage point that he burned with a mutual desire for her. It somehow made him more acceptable.

Looking him in the eye and repeating his words from the bedsit, she slowly said: "well, it's my intention to give you safe escort to neutral territory. Then we'll decide what to do next."

"Touché," applauded Araz, a flash of gold respect barely surfacing above a calculating base of ice-whites and a vein of deep red attraction he was unable to suppress.

"Araz?" she added, now facing him square on, colours alight with bold yellows. "If I take you with me, I need to know you won't... won't try anything..."

The words had not come out as she had intended. She had wanted assurance he would not drug or imprison her, and now she had coloured the same red shade of his allure, trying consciously to subdue her own deep pulses of crimson. She forced herself to scan his face, concentrating on his colour responses.

"Well, that's something you can't be sure of…" he replied, with a brief flicker of burgundy and a glint in his eyes, as they acknowledged a brief unspoken exchange of their reciprocal attraction.

"We are, after all," he continued spiking black-red hues, "opponents."

"Enemies," whispered Imogen, her face clouding over as misgivings filled her mind.

"Enemies! Huh! A typical subversive word…" began Araz, scorn and annoyance clear in his voice, but as he watched her pale further and noted her chromatic grey eddies, he relented and his colours softened as he added: "Look, I have little option but to stick with you, so let's get to your neutral territory and take it from there. In the meantime you have my word that I will comply." The sapphire blues rang true, as Imogen nodded assent.

"I just hope it doesn't involve using that mechanism you keep in your pocket! I never dreamt it would turn out to be a Tractus device," he added, shaking his head, causing droplets of water to spray around him. "Gave me such motion sickness…"

Imogen gasped as she felt for the marker, checking it was still there in her soggy jeans. *Let's hope it's not affected by water.*

"You knew about it before we jumped?" she asked nervously, his slight nod and dismissive shrug confirming this, along with a white flash of truth.

She drew back away from him. "You knew I had it, and yet you didn't take it from me – in your flat." Imogen's innards lurched. *What else does he know? I was sedated for hours – could he have seen my marks?*

"Well, I could only guess at its purpose, but as for taking it, I have been trained never to mess with something I don't understand," he said dispassionately, but he could not fail to observe that her Chroma had started to infuse with shadows as he continued, "and, as it turns out, it proved to be an inspired decision." The warmth of his smile and emerald of his gratitude was unmistakably genuine, but again Imogen's stomach folded on two counts: the first due to his untypically tender response and the second due to the worry that, besides now knowing about the highly secret portable marker, he could possibly know about her genetic peculiarity as well. *I have to find my dad – he'll know what to do.*

Trying to give no indication of her troubled thoughts, Imogen looked away from Araz, and lowering her voice, said with more honesty than she'd intended, "I really hadn't planned on bringing you with me, but... well, when I saw they were going to kill you... I just... I..." she faded out, as conflicting emotions suddenly rose within and started to engulf her.

Her impossible predicament and the flurry of new information suddenly bore down on her like a tidal wave: she no longer had a home to go to; her mother was thousands of miles away and far from well; her father was captured or dead; Leo had been brutally beaten and taken prisoner; she had the unwanted genetic makeup of a 'super freak'; she was apparently labelled a 'subversive' and 'Falsebred' and was clearly seen as some sort of threat. *Why?* She had in her possession, a key - to - to what? *None of it makes any sense...* As the numerous facts and possible theories bombarded her from every angle, Imogen felt powerless and exhausted. She had no idea where to start to try to sort it out, and there was no-one she could turn to. All this, with the thought that someone wanted her dead... Large vicious figures entered her mind... Sharp knives – heavy coshes - gloved hands clamping down on her... squeezing her heart... choking the life out of her... her breathing started to shorten. There was no time to think it all through – her mind began to spin in turmoil. *Tangled mess – so black... They're coming – they've seen me - What should I do? What if I can't find the others? What will happen to Mum? Dad? Leo? Me?* Imogen bit her lip and as a pale drop of blood surfaced below her teeth, she started to shiver and began to feel faint.

Araz had been watching her closely and aware of the random quartz glints being dulled by churning greys, which threatened to entirely engulf her Chroma, he realised beads of perspiration had sprung up on her brow and she was shaking, having paled to a worrying white. He quickly took off his jacket, wrapped it around her shoulders and pulled her close to him, holding her cold clammy body tightly in his arms.

"It's okay," he soothed, "Shhh - stay calm - you're in shock – you'll be okay."

Imogen initially stiffened as his strong arms encircled her, but his warmth began to penetrate through her damp clothing and gradually she relaxed and leaned into his chest, forcing every conflicting thought to diminish and sink to the recesses of her mind. Araz stroked her dank hair away from her face and continued to whisper "Shhh" in her ear, with each caress. She shut her eyes and allowed her sense of smell to concentrate on his musky aroma as the invisible hands, one by one, began to release her heart, allowing it to slow to a steady beat. The knives and coshes faded as the metabolism of her cells progressively rebalanced, repaired and healed, and her circulation and breathing gradually returned to normal. They remained locked together for the next several minutes, silent and as one, until Imogen realised they had arrived at their destination, Euston, when she reluctantly opened her eyes and separated from him to stand and exit the tube.

"Thank you," she mumbled, a tinge of crimson-edged embarrassment clear in her Chroma, as she handed back his jacket and they ascended the stairways.

"You're welcome," he responded gently, adding: "Your restoration rate is truly remarkable," a deep jade respect evident in his colours. "No wonder you were up on your feet so quickly, after using the Tractus."

Imogen noted this praise internally. *Do I heal quicker than others of my kind?* Now recovered, and feeling somewhat guilty to be infused with a strange, inner warmth from a person who was undoubtedly her adversary, they ascended to ground level and she headed for the sales booth where she used some of the wodge of money to buy rail tickets, whilst Araz kept a lookout for any sign of danger.

Quickly choosing a new set of clothing and trainers and nodding for Araz to do the same from the forecourt shops, she then ushered him up to the priority lounge, where she showed their tickets before using the separate cloakrooms to shower and change. Imogen threw away her old clothes – *thank goodness the marker appears undamaged* - and hurriedly blew hot air around the rucksack, before going out to the reception desk and asking to use the desk telephone. She dialled the emergency number imprinted on her memory from the DE in the abandoned tube, and got an automated message. It was a familiar, deep, male voice she couldn't quite place, but it gave her comfort and she listened intently to the brief recording:

"Welcome, my friend. If you are using this number, you must have lost or been unable to use your communicator device. Do not worry. Leave your name and location and we will attempt to reach you as soon as possible. Stay hidden…"

The tone beeped and Imogen said just four words: "Imogen / Little Rome / Birmingham," before hanging up and sitting in the lounge area, where Araz re-joined her.

Now dry and refreshed, they ate packets of biscuits and drank hot tea, keeping to their own thoughts whilst they waited until it was time for their train to depart. Checking the concourse was clear, they headed for their platform, and once aboard, got into their first class seats, Imogen forcing Araz to the other side of the table by putting the rucksack on the chair next to her. *I need to keep him at arm's length.* They both looked out at the platform, scanning for any helmeted figures and only relaxed when the train finally pulled out of the station.

"So, what shall we talk about for the next hour and a half?" Araz asked, eyes glinting with mischief, as he lent forward on the table with his arms crossed. "I take it we get off at Birmingham. The first subversive base?'

"Will you stop calling us subversive!" retorted Imogen in irritation. "And yes, we are going to Birmingham, but I've no idea which part, unless you know the area 'Little Rome'." Araz looked blank and shrugged his shoulders.

"We thought the Birmingham base was no longer in use," he said matter-of-factly.

"Don't you know where it is?" Seeing her glare and a flash of red-purple annoyance, he quickly added, "I'll take that as a no!"

"Well, our reports," he continued, "say it was a church."

"You don't say!" said Imogen sarcastically.

"Tetchy!" sneered Araz.

"Right – if you want to talk," Imogen said leaning forward on the table between them, "tell me who you work for, why you took me captive, and why we are considered to be subversive."

"You surely know that?" Araz jeered, before seeing the warning in Imogen's eyes and the flare of yellow-black. He altered his tone, a genuine russet empathy surfacing in his Chroma, as he said: "I guess you don't," in a quieter voice.

Araz sat back and studied Imogen's face, looking deep into her eyes. With a wave of quartz-whites that told Imogen he had decided to respond in a truthful manner, he said: "It's a bit difficult to know where to start, without knowing what you know, if you see what I mean?" he began.

"Let's just assume I know nothing, and you can start at the beginning."

The next hour and a half passed in a flash. Araz talked, Imogen gave him an occasional nod to continue and other than a quick prompt, or question, she listened in silence. By the time they reached New Street Station, Birmingham, Imogen had more of the jigsaw pieces in place.

EITHER SIDE OF THE ATLANTIC

*I*n Birmingham, Tanastra paced the marble floor of the altar area, his black priestly robes clinging to his light frame, now slightly stooped and clearly aged although no-one would have guessed his advanced years numbered well over one hundred. He was in a dilemma, heart heavy and troubled. They had been discovered. Reports were incomplete and the procedure had not gone exactly to plan. Now Kasmut was insisting on returning to the Empire, to challenge the Supreme Council.

He glanced at Kasmut, who sat with his head in his hands in the front pew. Even in the dim candlelight, the man looked broken and ten times older than his age. This is the result of living so long with worry and fear, he reflected shrewdly.

"I cannot re-activate the Tractus from here, my friend," he reasoned softly, hands open in supplication.

"It remained unset for fifty years: a time trap for Imogen and Rashida and then Leonard, until his return last month. Yes, I have made the adjustments recommended by Firas, so in theory it should not be possible to initiate another time vault; however it is untested..."

As Kasmut went to interrupt, Tanastra cut him off adding: "also, we cannot forget that our enemy will have a tracer fitted at their end and will know the moment it is triggered. Their forces will arrive directly – to switch it on would mean suicide."

"Yes, but it is my plan to jump the moment it is activated and hand myself over," Kasmut argued. "They would not dare dispose of me outright. They would want answers, updates on the technology we have created, you can be sure of that. That will be my negotiating point. Besides, once my concerns are made public, they will have no choice but to call a full hearing. I will take my chance with the populace judging. The Sanctus laws will still stand."

"Kasmut, you must realise the council was beyond following procedure before we left over sixty years ago; they are driven by self-interest, self-protection and who knows what? Their rule is not one of honour. Amsu described the growing dictatorship they had become. What will it have grown into, in the twenty years since his escape? They will not hold with the laws of long ago; you know this deep down, my old friend."

Kasmut shook his head, "I have no other option. It will give the others a chance to re-group and conceal themselves better. We cannot allow Imogen to fall into their hands."

Tanastra sighed, "We may already be too late." Pain sprang into Kasmut's eyes as he put his fist to his mouth.

Tanastra continued: "I have learned that Amsu was inadvertently sent to New York, just several hours ago, so there is only Leonard. But in all honesty, this young protector has been absent for ten full years; he is barely up to date with events. He only found out about Firas' death a few weeks ago and then witnessed the demise of Eshe. Yes, I have briefed him, as have you, but he is too young, and worse, I believe there is a traitor in our midst. For all we know, it could be him."

"A traitor? No, there can't be! And if there were, it would not be Leonard. Aside from the fact he has been missing in time, I trust him Tanastra," insisted Kasmut, with a vigorous shake of his head. "He is true, I am sure of it, he would do anything for me."

"Kasmut, he may do anything for you, but he barely knows Imogen and he is inexperienced. Had he remained here ten years ago, we would have put him to work with his father, or one of his uncles, and by now he would have matured to be a fully-fledged member of the group, but as you saw fit to vault him ahead…" Tanastra could not keep the censure out of his voice, as Kasmut lowered his eyes, "he remains unprepared and is not in full possession of the facts."

Kasmut put his head back in his hands as Tanastra relented and added kindly: "Forgive me, my friend, I do not wish to sound so negative. After all, Leonard has one clear advantage: that he is of the Zuberi blood, which should count for something."

Kasmut was silent for a while, then slowly stood, seizing the rail in front of the pew for support, as he pleaded for the last time: "Tanastra, you know our enemy now has a firm foothold in this world, we cannot be sure if they have other markers besides the one we have monitored. You must face it; we may never be safe again. They have no respect for the people here. They will kill these 'inferior' beings without thought and it will not go unnoticed. Our presence, hidden all these years, will finally attract all sorts of unwanted attention. It could escalate into an unimaginable mess. For the sake of the innocents of this world, for the sake of the future of ours, we must take this fight back to Holis, where it belongs and justify our cause. I beg you, re-start the marker, let me be our envoy, or the cause will be all but lost…"

The frail old priest resumed his pacing, deep in thought and Kasmut witnessed his intense quartz colours flash and spark, as the elderly statesman ruminated on all the options and possible outcomes. As a clear blue permeated his Chroma, Tanastra stopped and gave Kasmut a piercing look, as he slowly nodded his head.

"We will try – if you insist. I can do some testing without fully activating the Tractus, but I will need several hours. This evening, after the last mass, when the church is clear – we will try. Come, let us rest now." Tanastra led Kasmut out of the church, throwing a brief, but worried look, back to the crown-like canopy that hung above the altar, before locking the door.

In New York, five hours behind Birmingham, in a private apartment off Central Park, Sefu spoke with his brother as his patient lay in a cataleptic state.

"Amsu, we must decide a course of action. We cannot leave Leonard's fate to chance…"

"Now I know you are being serious, Sefu," responded his brother, with a twinkle in his eye. "You have called me Adam for the last twenty years, but suddenly you revert to my birth title."

"You were not given a birth title, my dear brother," was the teasing response. "Remember, Amsu, you do not exist, you are but a facet of Nuru! As for sticking with our primitive names, it suddenly seems irrelevant. We have been discovered, regardless of our lengthy masquerade… Now, one of us must go and help. Unlike Nuru, your Leonard is young and inexperienced. He cannot be expected to manage alone…"

"I will go," declared Amsu. "You, my dear brother, may be able to help Rashida. Someone needs to…" he added despondently, giving the sleeping woman a despairing look and Sefu no chance to object.

"I just wish we had crafted more than two portable markers." Amsu bemoaned. "Our brother has one and Imogen now has our only other device. Foolhardy girl! To play stupid games with such a delicate instrument, especially after demonstrating such intelligence. I can only think that Tarik's idiocy must have rubbed off on her."

"We've had no trace of her, or Leonard, since your call," cautioned Sefu, worry lines etched deep in his heavy brow. "I fear they have been captured."

"We must hope they have not. If the marker has fallen into the hands of the enemy…" Amsu trailed off, the consequence unspoken.

Sefu shook his head and frowned, as he admonished: "**If** they have fallen into the hands of the enemy, brother? You realise, if they have been captured, they will both be classed as Falsebreds? The consequence of this could be grave indeed. It is they who are irreplaceable, not the device…" Amsu had no time to react, as the primitive telephone suddenly rang loudly.

"It's Tanastra," exclaimed Sefu as he glanced at the screen on the device. "Perhaps he has news?" He answered and listened in silence, until Amsu heard him respond: "Yes, I see. Well, if you think that's for the best. I can hear you have considered all the options, Tanastra. When will you reactivate the marker? Tomorrow - Sunday? Right - 7pm local time. Amsu will come. Yes – for the good of Ra." He shook his head and turned to his sibling as he ended the call.

"Well, on the plus side, Kasmut is not captured, but on the minus side, he is to go back to the Empire as some sort of emissary," Sefu announced sombrely. "I hope this is not a mistake. Tanastra will re-activate the Birmingham Tractus tomorrow, but we cannot risk using it from our other sites. It is recommended that you jump to the Paris marker and catch a flight to Birmingham from there. Apparently there is no embargo on what we spend any more."

Amsu rolled his eyes to heaven, as he quipped, "Well, at least some good has come from this. Nuru will be delighted, he loathes second rate travel!"

Sefu gave his brother a faint smile as he continued: "Nuru has already transferred to the north of England via France. He will be dealing with Eshe and removing the evidence left in the house occupied by Imogen and her mother. He will then go to Birmingham, to make plans to find Leonard and Imogen."

"Good for Nuru: we can always rely on him. It will be good to see him again," nodded Amsu. "If only all three of us could work together," he said wistfully, "but I doubt that will be possible for a good long while," he added with resignation.

"Eshe's advice was harsh, but right, we cannot risk the enemy finding out we number three, but I also share your sentiments." Sefu squeezed Amsu's shoulder in a brotherly gesture, as they began making ready for his departure.

On Sunday, once Amsu had jumped to Paris, Sefu was left alone to tend his charge. There was nothing he could do to help the others at this distance, so he turned his mind to Rashida's recovery. He was using an ancient hypnotic technique that Kasmut had refused to try, to calm and soothe the deep-seated veins of irrational worry. It was true, there was a risk of memory loss, but Rashida could not remain in this disturbed state. With Kasmut returning to Holis and possibly never to return, it was he who was now her protector as well as her doctor, he reasoned: the responsibility was his. All other noises were subdued, so he did not notice the brief flash of the message light on the primitive mobile phone. The four words 'Imogen / Little Rome / Birmingham', would not be heeded, until it was too late to warn the others of her intentions.

BIRMINGHAM

*I*t was late Sunday afternoon and despite being the centre of one of the country's largest cities, there was little open in the shopping arena next to the station concourse. They managed to find an Internet café just before it was due to close and Imogen logged on to a computer.

After a few minutes, she sat back in satisfaction. "Well, that was easy!"

Araz raised an eyebrow as his creamy yellows asked the question, "What?"

"I only had to search Little Rome, plus Birmingham and Church and there it is!" she pointed at the screen as Araz lent towards her, setting off the inevitable sparks of electricity between them.

Araz gave her a fleeting look of desire as he took a deep breath and turned to read the screen: "The Oratory Church… Its classic domed design gave rise to the term 'Little Rome'. So, its location is Hagley Road, Edgbaston." Imogen had already committed the address and routes to her memory, as Araz silently moved the cursor backwards and forwards and eventually looked up at her. "It says, the last Sunday mass is 5.30pm. Mass?"

She glanced at the time at the top of the computer display, 6pm.

"It's what they call the church service. We need to get going, so we can get in whilst it's still open. Come on – taxi rank is that way."

Araz, as a matter of habit, quickly clicked on the mouse and erased all the links they had opened in the computer, before following Imogen. They got into the first available cab and headed across the city.

They travelled in silence, as Imogen analysed all the information she had gleaned from Araz on the train, and summarised the new facts. This separate race she came from was clearly some distance from Europe and hidden from humankind. She surmised that 'Holis' was probably underground. Araz had said they shielded their presence from 'primitives' and she remembered Leo saying something about the light not being conducive to reading Chroma, so they had not grown up with this skill, unlike her. This, and the tetra-chromatic make up of their eyes, made her think they must live in a type of artificial, or shadowed light, that did not reveal colours, so underground seemed as good a guess as any.

The Supreme Council was the governing body of the people and it seemed that Araz answered directly to one of them, although he was very cagey when she had asked why they had wanted him dead.

"It's probably a misunderstanding," he had replied, flashing violet grey flares of denial and worry.

"You asked why you were called 'Falsebred'?" he had said, changing the topic quickly, leaving his death sentence unexplained. "Well, quite simply, you were born illegally." Araz had stopped the protest on the tip of her tongue, by raising a hand before continuing: "I appreciate you may not understand this. After all, you did not ask to be born. But bringing a new person into our world is considered to be of paramount importance. It is given the most serious consideration on every level. You cannot simply just have a child, as your thoughtless mother had done."

Imogen had suppressed the urge to retaliate and had listened intently to the explanation, as Araz told her that producing children had to be pre-authorised on all sorts of social and political grounds. A desire to be a parent was the least important factor. Personality and suitability to nurturing the young was paramount. Even then, consent could not be given, unless the entire process was genetically screened and approved. Illnesses, disabilities, personality flaws, were all eliminated. Imogen managed to hold back her response - *you mean, anyone not up to scratch is stopped, before they are started* - and inwardly shuddered in disgust. It seemed that only 'perfect' children were born into this perfect society. Thoughts of the 'master race' from her war time History lessons, scuttled uncomfortably across another part of her mind.

Araz had added that incidents of 'Falsebreds' in the past (he claimed it never happened now) had proven their system to be right. He described those born without the official 'care and control', as being mentally defective, or carrying genomes that could threaten the entire race and which could not, under any circumstance, be allowed to contaminate the nation's genetic pool. Imogen picked up on the implication that these 'Falsebreds' had been eliminated. *So not being legitimised basically means a death sentence.* She winced internally.

Araz had not mentioned the five personality codes Leo had told her about, so Imogen had not alluded to them either. She had squirmed to think of the markings on her body, showing that without any outside genetic interference, she nonetheless held all five lines in equal measure. *Who else knew about the marks? Leo didn't seem to know. Did Araz?* If her existence was already deemed to be an offence against the nation's ethical code, what would be said if they knew she was, what Eshe had called, the 'Sanctus Cryptus'.

It had been Araz's snappy response to one of her remarks that had made her keep her own counsel on the subject. She had commented, "It's just appalling, to think that the state control reproduction and everyone is moulded into a pre-conceived idea of perfection. Talk about 'Big Brother'!"

He had swiftly risen to defend this, with angry bolts of purples and gold-flecked blacks, as he had sarcastically retaliated: "I suppose you think it's better to allow the population to grow unchecked? To allow children to be born with inherited illness, disabilities or birth defects? To allow the creation of unwanted children, or children condemned to a life of abuse, poverty or want? Better to allow children with a predisposition to cause death and destruction in their adult life? Perhaps you think that is preferable?"

Without allowing her to answer, he had proudly added, "Those born to Holis are healthy, wanted, treasured individuals, who all grow to know the value of belonging to a superior race and preserving its beliefs. It is our race which reveres and safeguards life, whereas the primitive race, here, cares only for itself and is intent on the destruction of others."

Imogen had felt like retorting, 'well, your precious council wants to destroy us,' but checked herself in the face of Araz's tirade and his deeply held sapphire-gold pride and conviction that he was absolutely right.

There was no sign that Araz knew about her forty-year time gap. He did not seem to question her age, or date of birth. Perhaps he believed she had been born just seventeen years ago, or maybe he thought she had been placed in a coma, like her mother. Whatever he knew, she realised it would be impossible to ask him about this, as it would involve information about the Tractus. He may not be aware that it is capable of catapulting someone forward in time and she could not risk divulging any more than she had already done, bitterly regretting that he now knew about the portable marker. She had decided, instead, to prompt Araz on another unanswered question.

"Okay, I can see why I am labelled 'Falsebred'. Is that why my parents are branded subversive? Because they produced me without permission?" she had asked.

Araz had assured her that their subversion dated back to an earlier treachery, and that her birth had merely added to the catalogue of their crimes. His account made Imogen glimpse an alternative view of her family. It would seem that their most heinous crime, was to turn their backs on Holis and spurn their idyllic world. He told her that five of the greatest scientists, including her parents, had covered up their exit for over nine years and a sixth 'subversive', who escaped at a later date, was found to have been complicit. Imogen had matched the names he spoke with the 'others' of her race that she knew about. *Kasmut: dad; Rashida: mum; Eshe: Margaret. Who is Firas? Father Jonathan perhaps? Or, maybe Eshe's bearded man? He hasn't mentioned Tarik, Leo's other name, but I guess the Zuberi brothers must mean Leo's father and uncles.* She recalled her mother had called Adam, or Amsu, the hidden triplet? *What exactly did she mean?* Imogen showed no outward sign she was correlating all the information into logical interrelationships, but she now knew Araz's count was wrong. She knew they had numbered more. Careful to subdue her colour reactions, she had focussed on sharpening the clear yellows as she had asked the question: "What was their subversion?"

Interestingly, Araz could not explain it fully. He had not seemed to have a clear notion of why the council so disapproved of what they termed, 'the subversive six'. He surmised that they would be accused of stealing the highly desirable technology of the Tractus, away from the empire and risking contamination from the primitive world, any contact with which was completely forbidden. But he had not seemed to know why, or what their motivation was. "They have to return and answer for their desertion, so peace can be restored…"

"Unless the Repros get them first," Imogen had added coldly. She had then fixed Araz with a piercing look, her Chroma shouting bold colours as she had challenged: "What about the not so perfect, brutal 'reproduction life forms', created by your high and mighty council? Are they part of this faultless world?"

Araz had bristled, as he attempted to dismiss the use of Repro forces. He showed both a cold disdain in his voice and surges of purple hatred in his Chroma, as he had explained that most of Holis was unaware of their existence, which had been completed in secret. He had added, with annoyance that their creation had only come about, as a direct result of the subversive action.

Imogen smiled inwardly, as she acknowledged the skewed logic. *So it's our fault they created Repros, because we didn't follow the rules!* She had kept her gaze steady, as he had then implied Repros would not be necessary in the future and were merely a short-term measure. *So whilst he thinks it necessary to defend their manufacture, he clearly disapproves of them in essence. Interesting.*

"Do they have guns?" Imogen had asked, her stomach lurching as an image of the hollow red eyes beneath the helmet flickered across her mind. Araz had given another of his steely stares, as he had replied that Holis had no need for the 'vile weapons used by primitives'.

"Even the Repro forces," he had explained, "for all their crudity, used only basic hand-to-hand combat rather then the remote, lethal weaponry used by lower life forms." Imogen had kept quiet, but had wanted to point out, that they seemed pretty lethal in their use of coshes and knives. *Hardly an advert for a superior force,* she had thought wryly.

As the taxi neared their destination, Imogen filed these thoughts away, and turned to what lay ahead. She felt a surge of apprehension judder through her body, as the taxi drew up outside the church and a shiver went down her spine. *The place of my nightmares – of my accident: we are here.*

"Okay?" enquired Araz, who had seen her Chroma spark worry and fear. He placed a reassuring hand on her shoulder.

"Fine," she replied, running through the drill and quelling both the purple-greys and the red embers of attraction, still prompted by any touch from this enigmatic male she barely knew. "I haven't been here for years," she added truthfully, paying the cabbie. *In fact the last time I remember being here was fifty years ago.*

"Let's go."

They stepped out and intuitively Imogen ran around the corner to the rear of the church and a side door, Araz on her heels. The large wooden door was all too familiar; her father had used this entrance every week for years when they had visited Father Jonathan. Childhood memories cascaded into her mind. She took a deep breath.

Someone will have got my message. They will meet me and know what to do about dad, Leo, Araz, everything! At last, someone else can take charge.

Feeling a sense of having nearly reached the finishing line, she turned the chunky metal handle that opened the door, as they entered the dark church, the smell of incense flooding their senses.

Leo

*L*eo was glad he had not been conscious for the jump. He hated the disorientation and the sickness with a vengeance; aside from the terror he associated with the whole weird process. The Tractus may be one of the greatest inventions ever, but he was not a fan of using it; it had not only been one of his scariest experiences, it had taken weeks to recover from his ten-year time vault. No, it was much better he had been out of it for the latest jump. He guessed he must have passed out with the final kick to his head. Boy, those Repros had not been happy to be thwarted in their attempt to grab Imogen. He would have chuckled, but the slightest movement of his mouth caused pain to shoot into his head and stab sharply down his neck.

For a few blissful hours he had been unaware of pain… of anything, but now, as he regained more and more feeling, his head, stomach and arm began to groan and throb. His cells were self-repairing as best they could, but his fractured arm, split spleen and broken nose would require some external help to be put back into place. He stayed motionless, cushioned by what seemed to be a quilted hammock that held him, suspended, in the recovery position. He knew without opening his eyes that he was back. Apart from the warmth that now permeated his skin, he had the same sensation of weakness and light-headedness that he had experienced on his previous return. The difference this time, he mused regretfully, was that instead of slipping in and out unseen, he was now under the full spotlight of those in power. He knew his position was precarious.

"Tarik," came a soft male voice from near his head, "you are in a mess young man, we had better get these wounds looked at by a practitioner…"

"The prisoner sees no-one until he has talked, Ubaid," a harsh voice from the outer edge of the room decreed. "Open your eyes," it ordered harshly, as it moved closer to Leo.

Leo gradually flickered his lids open, knowing the influx of light would obscure his vision for hours and make him feel doubly sick. Until his brain adjusted to the red filter, everything looked shadowed and blackened. He could barely make out the figures next to him as he blinked, other than the larger man had a bald head and the smaller man a beard that looked puce in the strange glow. Their long gowns marked them as councillors and behind them he could see the glints of a row of dark helmets standing on guard. Bizarrely, a comedy sketch jumped into his mind.

"No-one expects the Spanish Inquisition," he mumbled aloud.

"Silence! On your feet," commanded the bald man.

Ubaid helped Leo to sit, swing his legs over the side of the hammock and place them down to the floor. As he attempted to stand, Leo nearly crumpled. The searing pain, sickness and lack of clear vision sent a rush of vomit up to the edge of his windpipe that he just about managed to gag down, as he sank to his knees.

The bald man glared down at his prisoner in annoyance as two Repros stepped forward to grab Leo.

Ubaid put his hand in the air to stop them. "Odion, give him time," he started to reason.

"We do not have time," spat Odion, "I have just received a report that changes to the defunct portal have been detected. The subversives are about to use it, but we will get there first." With that he signalled to the Repros, who grabbed Leo by the shoulders and hauled him to his feet, as he groaned with pain. Manhandling him to the door and closely followed by the councillors, they part walked and part dragged Leo down stone corridors and roughly hewn passageways before forcing him through a narrow opening.

"You will witness their capture," Odion barked at Leo before turning to a suspension chamber in which an opal globe turned.

Leo's mind was racing as he tried to hang onto consciousness and force his brain to think above the nausea and screaming wounds. This must be the portal to the Birmingham marker, he realised, and his heart sank. No! I told Imogen to go there. She'll think I set a trap, I have to stop them… warn her.

As the globe brightened, Leo feigned collapse, sinking to the floor as he pumped blood into his leg muscles in a crouch position. The Repros turned away from him, formed a tight group with others and started to unsheathe their knives. As the yellow light intensified, Leo, with supreme effort, suddenly sprang up, pushed the guards aside and raced towards the chamber as the portal opened.

The Oratory

The mass was concluding, and Imogen and Araz were unable to see the interior from their position just inside the small inglenook next to the side doorway of the church. They crept along the shadowed wall until the raised altar area was in view. Imogen stifled a gasp. The richly painted dome rose above them; saints gleamed in the smoky light, smiling down at her in virtuous detachment. Gold-framed paintings, carved wood depictions of the stations of the cross, tall thick candles reaching to the curved roof, rich-red marble panels contrasting with wide creamy columns, all sprang out with an overpowering sense of familiarity. She knew every detail. Yet, somehow, it all seemed much smaller than she remembered.

I was only seven.

Imogen looked to the raised marble steps below the altar and the large gold, jewel-rimmed canopy that hung above it. *Not a crown,* she thought. *But it looks like a crown to a child's eye.* Her drawings from her nightmare were more accurate than she had realised. *It's here – this is where I was chased and then catapulted through time.* Images of the black figures and grasping hands, her father's eyes urging her to run, the all-engulfing fog, they all crashed into her mind. Araz must have sensed her agitation, as he gently reached out and stroked her cheek, forcing her to look at him. Unable to subdue the electric spark it prompted, Imogen swallowed hard and motioned for Araz to drop down into a crouch position, as she did.

Must stay calm. Need to think straight.

Her eyes and the black authoritative glints she managed to summon, urged silence from Araz. He nodded agreement as they both put their colours to camouflage and crawled further in, able to observe the end of the service from a low position, concealed by a statue of the Virgin Mary that towered above them.

A white robed priest was blessing the small congregation of about twenty people, his hands mildly disturbing the floating cloud of incense that hung in the air. After this he turned and knelt before the altar, crossing himself, rising and walking down the central aisle. Followed by two young boys in chorister robes, the priest led the worshippers, now talking in hushed tones, out of the church via the front entrance.

When they were all out of sight, Imogen hurriedly rose and motioned Araz towards a small curtained booth standing against the side wall. Imogen remembered the confessional from her childhood days, a wardrobe like item of furniture divided in the middle, with a small grid connecting the two halves. The priest would sit on one side and the confessor on the other, each side barely bigger than a broom cupboard. She had intended that they would take a side each, but as voices came back into church she urgently indicated for Araz to squeeze into the tight space with her, as she closed the heavy curtain and whispered "wait". They froze in the dark, motionless, barely breathing and unable to move, as their hearts beat in unison. The muffled sounds of the priest locking the door, walking back down the aisle and chatting to the altar boys as they blew out candles and switched off lights dwindled, and the group eventually left via the side entrance, locking it as they went.

All was quiet, as they listened for any other sound and breathed a little easier in the pitch black, confined space. Their bodies were pressed against each other, her face just inches away from his neck, his musky scent filling her nostrils, making her feel heady and distracted. Unsure why she was drawn to do so, she slowly raised her head in the dark and saw the Infrared glow of Araz, as he bent his head towards hers, mouth slightly open. Her lips parted instinctively, as she felt his hot breath against her face. It seemed as if time was suspended, as his mouth gave hers the briefest of touches, sending peaks of desire flushing through her body. Araz gave an almost inaudible groan, as he pulled her even closer and kissed her deeply and fully. Any misgivings evaporated, as Imogen found herself returning his kiss and embrace, pulses of longing coursing through her entire body.

It probably only lasted moments, though it seemed much longer to Imogen, but when they broke away, she felt a flurry of emotions: warmth, yearning, wonder but also confusion and guilt.

Opening the curtain and clumsily stepping out, slightly breathless, Imogen, face and Chroma burnished red, was more flustered than she knew, as she started to say: "That, that was a mistak…" but Araz put a finger on her lip, as he leaned into her ear and his deep voice prickled her skin and reverberated in her head:

"No apologies, no regrets."

His lips touched her earlobe, sparking electricity through her whole being, and he paused, as if reluctant to move, before giving a low sigh, drawing back and turning away. His Chroma was also pulsing deep burgundy sparks and she could see he was calming and smothering these feelings, with clear blues and greens, as he turned full circle to take in the church in the half light that entered the skylights set into the arched ceiling.

Deep within, she knew they had crossed a line and he had unleashed feelings she barely recognised, but there were more urgent things to think about. Would her father be here? At last she could finally speak to Adam or one of his brothers. She had to smother her shimmering thoughts about Araz, bringing to the fore a fresh analytical layer of planning and action. *Stay focussed.*

Araz whistled his amazement at the interior of the church. "This place is something else," he said in admiration. "So rich and ornate."

"You should see the real Rome," smiled Imogen, who had been there on a rare school trip, a few years before. "Then you'll know why this place is dubbed 'little'…" she petered out, as the sound of a key turning in the side door came sharply into focus. Exchanging a quick look with Araz, they both stepped into the confessional, either side this time, behind the curtains as voices were heard entering the church. Moving to the front of the altar area, the voices became less muffled and more familiar.

Imogen concentrated hard on the speaker who was saying: "My friend, can I not persuade you to give up this course of action? I am not sure what will happen, if you are not accepted as an envoy…"

She knew that voice. *Father Jonathan.* But an inner caution made her decide to remain hidden until she had heard more, so she could identify the others in the group. She sensed there were more than two. Another then spoke and she could not place him…

"I cannot emphasise enough, that you will not get the treatment you expect, or deserve. The regime is rotten to the core. If Imogen and Leonard have been captured, as seems the case, they may already have been eliminated." Imogen's stomach churned. *They didn't get my message.*

There was a short anguished cry from another member of the group, as Father Jonathan quickly soothed: "Please, can you not see that your words cause much pain. It will do us no good to speculate. They are both gifted young people, with a lot of initiative…"

'They are both Falsebreds, in the eyes of the council…' spat the unknown voice.

Imogen was puzzled. *Leo a Falsebred too?* Although another part of her mind acknowledged that he had never mentioned his mother, or his early childhood.

"It is no good claiming otherwise," the voice continued, as if preventing another from interrupting. "Why else would Leonard have needed to escape Holis, as only a young boy? I am not stupid…" the voice took on a belligerent tone, as he added: "…although I am treated as if I am."

"That is just not true," responded Father Jonathan in a slightly exasperated voice. "No-one has ever thought you stupid. It will do us no good to make assumptions. What we must do is find out what has happened to Imogen and Leonard. Until then, we need to continue with the plan."

What plan? Imogen was acutely aware that Araz was listening to all that was being said. His very presence compromised the situation. She needed to reveal herself, but something stopped her, as there was a sound of shuffling, denoting that the group was moving up the marble steps.

The voice of Father Jonathan said: "All is ready. You know you will surface at the captured marker in Holis? Be in no doubt, my friend, they will be alerted instantly, as I activate the portal. We only have a short window of opportunity…"

A small pulse was audible and the hairs stood up on the back of Imogen's neck, as she heard the group starting to say their farewells. *Someone is going to jump or vault!* Her stomach folded. It was then that she heard his voice: "If you find Imogen, please take care of her and say... say that I am sorry."

Imogen's heart surged. *He's alive! Grandad – My dad!* Without hesitation, she flew out of her hiding place and ran blindly towards the altar, now glowing in an eerie red light. In the back of her mind, she wondered at the red light, but gave it no further thought as she launched herself into the arms of her father, who was standing dumbfounded, rooted to the spot.

As they held each other tightly, tears of joy streaming down both faces, Father Jonathan hurriedly ushered them away from under the canopy, as the other member of the group looked to where Imogen had emerged and silently went down to investigate further.

"Imogen!" Kasmut and Tanastra exclaimed together. She held onto her father like a limpet, as he and Tanastra's questions flooded out, on top of one another:

"Are you alright?"

"How did you get here?"

"Clever girl to have found us."

"Where's Leonard?"

Before Imogen could compose herself and answer, they heard a loud voice order: "Step out now! Do not engage your communicator or weaponry..." as Imogen saw what looked like Adam - *he looks like him but he doesn't sound like him?* - force Araz out of the other side of the confessional, his hands in the air, a sedation pen pressed to the back of his neck.

As his finger went to press the button she shouted: "Stop!" without thinking and as all faces turned to her in surprise, she added, in a slightly faltering tone: "I... I promised him safe passage and the enemy is trying to kill him too."

The group descended the steps towards Araz, who was staring intently at Father Jonathan. Imogen saw a bolt of blue recognition flare in his Chroma and wondered what she had missed, but before anything further could be said, the air prickled, the red light intensified for the briefest of moments, and a deep groan of pain echoed around the church.

They turned sharply to the altar to see the crumpled figure of Leo, disfigured and stained with blood, as he raised his head and managed to blurt out, "They're coming…" before being violently sick down the marble steps.

Kasmut pushed his daughter away, as he shouted, "Run," urging her with his eyes, then rushing across to Leo, who had lost consciousness.

Imogen's heart raced, as she stepped backwards into the central aisle. She was vaguely aware that the one that looked like Adam had got Araz in a firm arm-hold, as he dragged him backwards, struggling, towards the side entrance, but she could not take her eyes off the scene which unfolded before her, accompanied with an intense foreboding and Eshe's words in her head: *they're coming – they've seen you…*

Another flash of red light and her nightmare began to replay in front of her. Dark forces. Four, no five, in helmets, armed with knives, appeared next to the altar. They shook their heads groggily, before standing tall and advancing down the steps, raising heavy sharp blades as they moved. Kasmut was bent over Leo and Imogen saw the gloved hands of the nearest Repro grab her father and place the blade against his neck, as he forced him upright.

Imogen screamed "No!" and ran towards him, as another Repro bore down on her, knife raised high. With surprising agility, Father Jonathan rushed out next to Imogen, pushing in front of her at the last minute, as the blade came slicing down, glancing the back of her right hand and carving deep into his torso, as he tried to avoid its arc. As he sank to the floor, Imogen could see blood pouring from his wound, but had no time to tend to him or her injury, which was smarting painfully, as the Repro raised his knife for a second blow and two others jumped towards her. She turned and ran down the central aisle, dodging left and right, as they swooped down on her, the sharp skimming knives missing their mark by only inches. Increasing her speed, heart bursting in her chest, she veered around the last block of pews towards the side aisle and raced blindly back to the front of the church, her attackers in hot pursuit.

Adam appeared ahead of her and as soon as she came level with him, he pointed a cylindrical device beyond her, at the three advancing Repros, and fired what seemed to be a flash of noise. A cacophony of ear-piercing sound filled the church, but was doubly intensified in the direction of the assailants, who fell to the floor screaming and holding their heads, before passing out.

Imogen gulped a breath and ran back in the direction of the altar area, her ears buzzing with white noise, her hand on fire. Her father was in the grip of the Repro holding its knife firmly against his neck, as it tried to shake off the blaring sound in its head. She saw the warning flashes in her dad's Chroma too late, as she turned and spun straight into the last Repro. It lurched, quickly righting itself and grasped Imogen by her neck with one massive hand. Lifting her from the ground, it gave a deep-throated cackle, as it pulled back its knife with the other hand, ready for the fatal blow. Air supply cut, Imogen could just see Adam, through the corner of her eye. He was racing towards her, but she knew he would be too late, as the razor sharp blade made a stab for her heart. Her final thoughts flickered from her mother and father, to Leo and Araz and as her life should have closed, she fell through the air, in, what seemed like, slow motion… Araz, who appeared from nowhere, had jammed a pen under the helmet and up into the neck of her executioner.

"I don't think so," Araz snarled, as he kicked the collapsed form to one side and swept Imogen up in his arms, placing her gently on the front pew, before turning to the final, and somewhat disconcerted, Repro, who stood firm with Kasmut its prisoner, regarding the carnage before it.

Imogen, barely conscious after her strangulation, gasped for breath. She felt nauseous and searing pain was coming from her hand. Glancing down she saw the gaping cut, which was now oozing puss. Confused that it was not healing in the usual way, she looked up and thought the lack of oxygen was making her see double. Adam had come up from one side next to Araz and then also from the other side. Both gave Araz an enquiring but approving look as they all turned to face the last Repro, who held Kasmut and stood over Leo. She could only look on, as her body rapidly circulated more oxygenated blood and swiftly started to heal the crushed tissue in her neck, but instead of a sense of relief, she began to feel feverish and faint. She could not think straight.

Kasmut managed to choke out a plea, "Stop – no more…" The Repro tightened its grip as Araz stepped forward and spoke in a different dialect. The words translated deep in Imogen's head, which was beginning to ache. He was instructing it to release her father. It responded in a barely translatable grunt, that it had orders to return the prisoner and, failing this, he must be killed. It pulled Kasmut's head further back, as if to slice his neck.

Imogen gasped in horror, but Araz, in a voice of command, spat out his instructions, which partially translated in her head:

"You will not harm… the… You will… the prisoner directly to… Supreme Council… me to answer to…"

She could no longer concentrate on his words but thought he had said something to the effect that his chain of command was the higher authority and, with this, the Repro had nodded reluctant compliance. It still held the knife to Kasmut's throat, but more as a warning rather than an immediate threat.

The others did not appear to have understood the exchange, but Araz turned to the two Adams and said he had guaranteed Kasmut's safety, and now needed their help. Without waiting, he dragged the drugged Repro at his feet, up the steps towards the canopy and indicated that they should do the same with the other forms, collapsed in the side aisle. The two Adams, smiling in accord, heaved the large figures, one by one into the altar area, the voice of the Adam she knew, congratulating himself on the use of his new 'decibel weapon'. When all four were draped across each other, they stood back. One of the Adams pressed a hidden button under the altar table and quickly stood back. There was a pulse of brightened red light and the bodies disappeared.

"That will warn them to hold back," stated Araz authoritatively as he indicated for the remaining Repro to move back towards the altar with Kasmut. Leo gave a groan, as he regained consciousness at their feet.

"What's happening?" he mumbled.

Without warning, the Repro dropped its knife, made a grab for Leo with its spare hand and with surprising strength, hauled both he and Kasmut under the canopy. Swiftly lunging for the button under the table requiring it to briefly release Kasmut before regaining a firm hold, the red light flashed and Kasmut, who made no attempt to move whilst giving his daughter a fleeting smile of reassurance, vanished with Leo and his captor.

Imogen, shaking violently, gave a cry and would have leapt to her feet, but she could not feel them, or her legs. Something was horribly wrong…

Araz rushed to her side as Adam made a dash for the altar and reached the marker, pressing it decisively, as the red light disappeared. The other Adam raced to the still black-robed figure, lying prostrate on the floor, in a growing pool of blood and turned him over, noting the gaping wound carved into his side.

As Araz examined her swollen hand and the twins tried to tend to the priest's injuries, Imogen could just see an increasingly blurred picture of the pair as they tried to administer first aid. Father Jonathan appeared to stir and mouth something, as he weakly touched the end of a chain that hung around his neck. She could not focus on it, or catch their exchange. Her body was burning up and she could not find the muscles to move her tongue to speak, but even in her haze, she knew the significance when the brothers shook their heads and knelt down prayerfully either side of the still figure, each holding a limp hand. As she desperately clung on to consciousness, she saw Father Jonathan's colours swirl, merge into a dim wisp of pure white and circle his head. Her heart screamed, but her body stayed limp and as she looked up into Araz's fearful eyes, purple shades of worry darting in every direction, she could see his mouth clearly shouting 'Imogen', but there was no noise accompanying it. Her nightmare then came full circle, as the thick, all encompassing fog, took her completely.

FADING

Night plummeted. Dense fog swirled thicker and thicker.
Wisps of hands formed in the vapour and reached towards her, nails clawing.
Red eyes glared into hers.
Blades slashed.
Pain – intense pain.
She screamed at full volume in her head, but her voice would not surface,
her lips would not move, her body was like lead.
Paralysed.

A gloved hand clamped around her neck, squeezing, choking. The fog shot
up a tendril of black smoke, which formed into a pointed knife. She could
only watch, as it drew back, then raced down on her, piercing her chest,
entwining its threads around her heart, as it began crushing her chambers,
slowing its beat, stalling…

A red light growing - pulsing.
Penetrating heat, a scorching sphere, above and around, burning, blistering.
As her heart compressed, her throat burned, inside and out.
No breath, unbearable thirst...
Escape – must escape.
Colours detaching, lifting and twirling, into a higher and higher eddy.

The scalding red spread into a large, bubbling, glutinous quagmire. As it darkened to black, it began to engulf her.
Spiralling and twisting downward into the swamp, bottomless. Dragged down, hot, bleak, nothingness, sucking at every fibre. Deeper and deeper into its depths.

Resist – imperative – get clear – lift – join the rising spectrum...

A bright white light shone high overhead – *release – reach up...*

Soaring skyward, colours faint, white...

... barely there...

Suddenly, a rush of water. Cool, pure, flowing love, washing over ever part. Floods of tenderness, purging away the pain; sweeping away the clamps; cleansing wounds; releasing waves of hope; invigorating deep within her soul.
White light split into a rainbow of promise, the pit cracking and shrinking. Heat dampening, thirst quenching...

Awareness...

Him...

His fingertips, touching hers. His strength; his desire; his kiss.
Araz............

Imogen floated on the comforting wash, melted into the swell of affection and sank into the strong currents of esteem and adoration. With a sense of utter security, she uncoiled and, muscle by muscle, relaxed.

An overwhelming exhaustion infused her body, and she lapsed into a deep and dreamless sleep.

RECOVERY

The first thing she was aware of was the sound of distant voices. Barely audible, it took a while for them to sharpen, but she was reassured to know she was amongst friends. *I'm alive! Adam... and Araz - he's here.* Random words like 'antidote' and 'recovery' were repeated, but she was drifting and unable to make sense of them.

When she finally opened her eyes, she was amazed to find herself in a luxurious hotel bedroom, with floor-to ceiling windows, giving spectacular views over the city. The sun was low in the early evening sky, its warm glow bouncing off the iconic buildings of the skyline. *The Eiffel Tower? Paris!* Lying in the middle of a very large bed, propped up by pillows and wrapped in a thick white dressing gown, she took in the opulent room in front of her and glanced down at her hand, which was tightly bandaged, a wide, ominous, brown-red stain apparent on the dressing. Before she could fret, a deep voice came from the doorway of the adjoining room.

"Awake, at last! We thought you were going into hibernation!"

Araz's smile shone down at her, as he quickly crossed the room and sat on the side of the bed, his dark eyes twinkling and his Chroma alive with reds, burgundies and golds.

He's trying to smother the greys – he's been worried about me. There's something different about him too – but what?

Imogen returned his smile with a shy nod, and eased herself up into a sitting position, as she looked around. Adam also emerged from the other room, and upon seeing Imogen awake, strode purposefully across to her, sitting on the other side of the bed. Imogen was aware he was looking much older, as if troubles were laid heavily upon him. *He could almost be the same age as my father.*

"Imogen, are you a sight for sore eyes! You had us so worried back there. No, don't speak, not until you're fully revived." Adam handed her a small cube, not dissimilar to the one Araz had fed her in his bedsit, and a carton of juice. She chewed and drank, infusing her body with nutriments, as Adam launched into an explanation.

"Poison!" he said, with certainty. "The Repros used poisoned knives. But thanks to my brother, we have the antidote and fortunately your cut was not too deep, although I thought we'd lost you there for a moment." Adam glanced up at Araz, significantly, as he added: "And, something more powerful than the medication appeared to make the difference..." Adam paused, as if battling what to say, before shrugging his shoulders and continuing calmly: "You have made quite an impression on this young man." He smiled, looking from Araz, back at Imogen, with a raised eyebrow, as he added more seriously: "In truth, your end had, at one point, seemed inevitable, but, well, you just suddenly improved. Quite the most dramatic change I have ever seen."

Imogen looked at Araz, who gave her an intense stare, glowing hues of scarlet and briefly putting his hand up to his mouth, as if to cough, but with the slightest movement, she saw him touch his fingertips with his lips and knew he had used the cognitive link to pull her back. Adam did not acknowledge this, but Imogen knew he must have witnessed what Araz had done, even if he had not known the essence of the exchange.

"I could not lose you," Araz said, simply and quietly, as he held her eyes. Her Chroma flared crimson, as her heart surged and she caught, in Araz's aura, a colour she had not previously witnessed. Here was the difference. A burnished red, of a deep hue that rippled gold and white. She knew those intense shades – the colour of love. Flustered, she forced her stomach not to fold and turned to focus on Adam, who, appearing somewhat embarrassed, hurriedly continued with other matters.

"Sadly, we could not save Father Jonathan. His cut was too deep; he had lost too much blood." He gave Imogen a significant look, as there was an almost imperceptible nod towards Araz. She could see, from his leaping violet blacks, layered with a flash of red warning, that he did not want her to question this further. *There's something Araz mustn't know.*

Adam continued without pausing: "Araz here, has assured us that Leo and your father will be safe, for the time-being, but things have changed and we must plan our next move." Araz nodded agreement and Imogen could see that there was a degree of trust between the two of them, although clear shuttered shades were apparent in their distinctive colours.

So is Araz still considered to be an opponent? Surely he has proved himself?

"First things first, we need to remove your bandage," Adam said, reaching gently to unwrap Imogen's hand. To her surprise, when the last segment was lifted, there was nothing but a pale wide groove showing where the cut had been. She examined her hand closely, feeling along the long indentation that ran across from one side to the other, in between her knuckles and her wrist. It was like a cross section had sunk inwardly, forming a small valley. She held it up in the air and flexed it, examining it from every angle. She was unable to make a full fist, her hand would not stretch into the move, but there was no pain and she was fascinated to see the way in which her flesh had healed, into her one and only scar.

Good job I can write with both hands, as I'm not sure I will be able to hold a pen with this one.

"Hmm – not bad," Adam nodded in approval, before adding: "Afraid we couldn't prevent a small amount of scar tissue, but given that your hand was slowly being eaten away, and the poison was beginning to devour the rest of your body, I guess this is a good result." As he casually stood and walked away from the bed, to dispose of the dressing, Imogen gulped at the thought of her lucky escape.

"Impressive," said Araz, clear sage admiration accompanying his nod, as he used the moment to reach for her hand and tenderly stroke the blemish. Imogen could not subdue the embers that flamed in her Chroma, as he stared intently into her eyes, the new colour pulsing bold and proud in his aura.

"My brother is something of a genius," added Adam proudly, unaware of the exchange, as he picked up a tiny glass tube from the table and turned to hold it up in front of them, a split second after Araz had released her hand.

"We all carry a phial of the antidote wherever we go. It's just as well, or we may have been too late. This was a much stronger dose of poison than that used in the past."

"They have used this before?" asked Araz in genuine surprise. "I had no idea they would stoop to using venom-tipped blades," he added angrily. "It goes against every one of our principles..." he started to say, but quickly stopped with a self-conscious glance to Adam. Imogen could see, as he grappled with subduing his crystal honesty, that he was forcing himself to exercise restraint in the presence of what he must see as an adversary.

"I'm not sure there are any principles left when it comes to your commanding officers, young man!" Adam quickly retorted, blazing purple-blacks. Araz rose to his feet as, for a brief moment, they flared livid bolts of challenge, staring directly at each other.

Imogen quickly coughed and broke the moment with her enquiry, "How's mum?" as Adam's glare subsided and the two of them sat back down beside her.

"She is making a slow, but what looks like, a promising recovery. You can speak to her soon," he said, the tinge of warning again evident in his Chroma. *He doesn't want me to mention Seth or New York.*

Adam then turned to other matters, as if to prevent further questions. "Imogen, I need you to check your memory banks, looking for any signs of damage. Use the drills – verify everything."

Imogen nodded and momentarily glazed over, as she slowed her breathing and internally inspected her memories for any missing links. She checked her capacity to reason, her mental analysis and calculation skills. Complex exercises, devised by her father, were now second nature to her, as she arrived at the outcomes and answers that matched those embedded in her psyche. She then ran through the key moments in her life and the events of the previous week in swift 'fast forward': from the day Araz had arrived at college, to her training with Leo, the party, her capture, escaping the Repros, her mother, her father and the latest developments, ending with her current situation. Everything tallied. The only questions and missing information were, although reduced in number, still the same as they had always been. She could not help shaking her head at the end of the process. *That was one hell of a week!*

Araz was staring, mesmerised by the chromatic cyclones she had produced during her recall and thought to himself that her beauty was truly captured in her Chroma. She calmed the spectrum swirls slowly, but gently, until there were just steady earthen blues and greens. Re-focussing on both the younger and the older man either side, Imogen gave a slow nod.

"All ok?" asked Adam.

"Just the same questions as ever," replied Imogen.

"Well, this might help," said Adam, as he reached to the bedside table upon which her pendant and a heavy chain lay. *That was the chain around Father Jonathan's neck.* Adam unlatched a flat disc, from the end of the chain, and handed it over to Imogen.

"It's faulty!" Araz blurted out, with a slight sneer.

Adam gave him a hard, disdainful stare. "It's encrypted," he stated, with a heavy sarcasm and flare of gold-black.

"You don't say?" answered Araz, with equal derision.

"No, this is an encryption not used before. It is of my own making and completely foolproof." He spat the last word out, clearly intending Araz to think he was the 'fool'. Araz looked as if he would retort angrily but, staring from the object to Adam, he seemed to think better of it.

"In that case, I think the term used by the primitives here applies: respect!" he slowly nodded, giving Adam an admiring dip of the head.

Adam bowed his head graciously and folded Imogen's fingers over the piece saying: "Well, Imogen can unlock it." She was sure she had observed a short burst of cobalt accompanying the brief intensity in Adam's eyes, unseen by Araz.

"Come," Adam said turning to Araz. "Let us leave her for a while."

Araz nodded reluctant agreement, as he gave Imogen a brief smile and he and Adam left the room, mistrust evident in both their colours.

Giving an audible sigh, and forcing herself to suspend all other thoughts, Imogen instinctively ran her finger around the edge of the disc. It popped up into an ovoid shape but unlike the Data Encounters she had used before, there were no indentations in this one.

Examining it closely, she noticed a glint at an outer edge of the device. A small area appeared to be of a different material. Scarcely visible, it looked translucent, as if concealing a bubble of fluid under the surface. *'Imogen can unlock it,'* Adam's colours had flashed blue as he had said this. *Unlock? There must be a key.* Her eyes darted to her pendant next to the bed as Araz's words from the tube train reverberated in her head *'It's a key – electro-chemical origin'* *Of course!* Reaching for Eshe's gift and, grasping the symbols at the end of the chain so they were flat and the central arrowhead was pointing outwards, she pressed the tip against the area. As it pierced the surface, the arrow instantly took up the hidden liquid and glowed with moving sparks of silver and gold. At the same moment the familiar notches slowly recessed into finger indentations, the spacing of her hand, around the DE. She would have smiled to herself had she not felt so apprehensive about what further information was going to be revealed.

Taking a deep breath, Imogen settled back against the pillows as she pressed her digits into the grooves and images flooded into her mind. A turning set of holographic symbols that matched her pendant: solid and outline stars, circles and the arrow, all twirled. The familiar voice of Father Jonathan began to speak in her head, accompanied by an image of the face of his younger self…

"Welcome.

If you are studying these chronicles, then two things are absolutely clear. Firstly, you must be a friend, not a foe, as I ensured that the encryption can only be lifted by a trusted minority; and secondly, I must, alas, be dead!"

She listened and watched, intently, to the unfolding story, as film clips, photographs and the commentary played out in multi-levels in her mind. She absorbed all the new information greedily – noting all the connections between her parents and their colleagues; grasping the facts; filling the blanks. She discovered how this group of scientists had been a team, how they were united in a struggle against an empire that was growingly corrupt and attempting to eradicate certain people in the population. She was shocked to think her mother was amongst them. She began to understand how they felt so desperate and why they had left in secret for the primitive world way back in the 1950's.

The crimes against the empire were clear. Mixing with the human race, which was considered abhorrent, was categorically forbidden. Primitives were seen as a source of contamination. Escaping with the technology of the Tractus seemed to be the bigger crime. It was obviously immensely important to the empire. Her parents and the group appeared determined to safeguard what was originally Tanastra's invention. Imogen was entranced to see her parents so young, so in love and full of life as three-dimensional film played, showing their departure and arrival.

The group had managed to stay hidden for nearly ten full years, with Amsu covering up their absence in the guise of his brother. Then Imogen watched how events had overtaken them with the attack in 1966 when she was vaulted in time and how, as the years had gone by, they had lost three of their number through poison and mental illness. A tear escaped her eye as she watched the film of her mother's final vault: her father heartbroken and bereft. She now understood who Eshe and Firas had been and their part in the team, and how her father had done his best to care for them, for Leo, and for herself and her mother when they had finally returned. She learnt about the secret triplets, thought by the authorities to be two brothers, and she could only wonder at the strained relationship between Leo and his father, who had been held prisoner in the empire for the equivalent of a lifetime. Like her own father, she was in no doubt that Amsu/Adam had also suffered untold troubles, cut off from those he loved for so long.

As she absorbed all the new information, she grew to know the character of Father Jonathan, the Tanastra behind the chronicles. His intelligence, compassion and tenderness were all evident in his narration. *He died saving me,* she realised with awe and gratitude. *This great man sacrificed himself for me. Why?*

As the sky outside darkened with the onset of twilight and lights began to flicker into being across the Paris skyline, Imogen realised she was almost at the end; the puzzle was nearly complete. She suspended the deeply uncomfortable feeling she got when there was mention of her destiny and possible sacrifice, as she forced herself to concentrate on Father Jonathan's shaky and faltering voice as he announced the sixth and final chronicle:

"This last chronicle has been recorded in haste. My apologies..."

The photographs and film clips stopped and the turning symbols of her pendant were the only thing in view. Father Jonathan's voice, sounding much older, rang clear in her head and was tinged with worry as he announced:

"This final account is about Imogen Reiner."

Imogen's heart skipped a beat as she sat forward and hung on every word.

"And so you have now got to the final chapter and it is about you. Yes, my dear Imogen, I have always known, it is you. Only you could break the encryption. It is for you that I have compiled these chronicles. Forgive me for not mentioning this before. I spoke as if to a third party; you were but a child; it was hard to think of you grown up… My dear girl.

I know these accounts would have only been given to you on my death. It had to come and it is pointless to dwell on it, so I must give you the final information you require. It will be up to you what you do with it. You could choose to ignore it, or to use it for the good of Ra, and the good of all.

Where should I begin? Well, perhaps I should turn to history, if you can briefly indulge an old man.

I need to tell you that for centuries, the focus of Holis was to try to genetically bring about a person with equal amounts of each of the five hereditary lines. Your father, or Leonard, may have spoken of this, I am unsure… We had so little time to see what progress was being made with your induction… It should have been done long before, in my opinion, but then I was not in charge. You will have to ask them about the five lines, if you have not been told my dear, I do not have time here.

Now where was I? Ah yes, it was considered to be the search for perfection. The creation of someone so balanced, so internally harmonious, that it would herald a new age for our entire species. To begin with, it was thought not only possible, but highly probable; I mean, we were skilled practitioners. We were able to eliminate disease and personality defects and refine our bodies to self-heal and live longer, but when it came down to it, we were not able to produce a Penta-Crypt – not for love or money, as they say here.

As time went on, it became almost a religious fervour to produce a 'Sanctus Cryptus', the sacred mix that would compose the highest pedigree. Other research was suspended and eventually, centuries after it started, it became clear that the quest had attracted undue concentration that deflected from more important matters. A great debate was held and concluded that the hunt for perfection reflected badly on everyone else and devalued all of us as worthy and vital people. In fact the whole emphasis of the mission became the subject of ridicule; derided and scorned. There was a realignment of priorities. Sanctus Cryptus came to mean a balance across the entire race and eventually it was forgotten and consigned to an age gone by.

Eshe was a geneticist and one of the few who still thought there might be some value in this line of research. It was she who insisted the 'Sanctus' was our emblem – all five lines equally upheld and respected - but she turned from genetics to put her energies into fine tuning our group and assisting all our efforts. Dear Eshe…

And then, Imogen, you were born. Unplanned, untested, unforeseen… can you imagine our astonishment, our disbelief, when we discovered that nature had done what thousands of our finest scientists could not do. That, without any intervention or planning that you would arrive with an equal balance of all five lines! Yes my dear, you are a Penta-Crypt! The first ever, the Sanctus Cryptus! Eshe was beside herself with excitement and also worry. Here you were, born in a world with barely any of our highly advanced technical systems at the mercy of the primitive environment. To all intents and purposes you were unprotected. This seemed an outrage for one so rare.

Your mother was in a delicate state of health. She had to be calmed when she was told you held the line of Iris. She already feared for your life, because you were born illegally. Knowing that you held the 'undesirable' line doubled her sense of protection for you. We could not add to her worries.

So Eshe and I decided only to inform your father of the full truth. He was mystified but, as you know, he does not believe in random chance, luck as it is called here, and thought this must be preordained. He was convinced that geneticists could have only been a stone's throw from their goal in their last attempts. After all, he and your mother are tri-crypts, unusual enough in itself, but probably a result of the scientific enhancements made in the previous generations. He was pleased, but remained stoic. You had to be given every chance to grow normally. He did not even want you to know about your unique heritage in case it influenced your upbringing. In this he was insistent. We dared not tell the others in the group; it may have placed all sorts of conflicts in their minds and we needed to be unified, to develop and refine the Tractus in complete secrecy.

So what could we do? Well, we watched and we waited, and as you grew, we realised just how extraordinary you were. Such a delight to us all - my dear girl - you could not have been cherished more.

You were both completely normal and completely brilliant - at the same time! The speed with which you absorbed information was astounding. Eshe even managed to teach you several of our languages, before you could walk! We discovered your ability to cognitively see the thoughts of others; your amazing skills at both reading Chroma and altering your own, to change the way in which others saw you. No-one of our race has such advanced skill, but, after all, we do live in a different light. You had such prowess when it came to multi-tasking and an eye for what was logical and right. Imogen, as you developed, it was clear that you had abilities in every sphere, strengths in all areas: science, art, mathematics… and despite your mother's incarceration, or maybe because of it, you had an intuitive empathy with all those around you.

Now, what you may not know is that, whilst the search for a Sanctus has long ceased, the genetic make up of a person is still of paramount importance. From birth it is clear which individual will be suited to which occupation and they are encouraged in the right direction, to use all of their gifts for both their own good and the good of all. Had you been born amongst your own people, there would have been great excitement and, as Eshe believed deeply, you would have been destined for higher things. Although, my dear Imogen, I have to temper this with the question: would your existence have been sanctioned had they known you held strong the line of Iris? It is possible that you might never have been given the chance of life, a sobering thought.

But I digress, and all of this is just speculation… After all, you were not born there, you were born here! Thank Ra for that!

So what should you do? You are unique. You could go to Holis, claim your entitlement, but please remember there is nothing inevitable about your future. Imogen - you have a choice.

We made our choices long ago: to give our lives to exposing and defeating the growing evil in our empire and, in the process, to develop a technology with universal implications without the influences and demands of a corrupt leadership. In the creation of the Tractus, we have succeeded thus far, but, as regards overcoming the wickedness that has continued to grow in the government of Holis, I'm afraid we have made little progress.

Imogen, I feel sure, as did Eshe, that you could use your 'Ra-given' talents to assist in this fight; to make a vital difference to our people and prevent what could be the downfall of our entire race. But this would mean you going to Holis. Only you can make this decision.

If you decide to go we could not, in all honesty, guarantee your safety and I am unsure of the reception you would get. True, you have in your favour the fact that you are a Penta-Crypt, but against this, you would be considered falsely bred and worse, contaminated by your association with the primitives. The people of Holis, sadly, only see the negative side of the human race, but you and I know another side…

I am quite sure, Imogen that you will use your talents for immense good whether you stay here, or go there, but it will be up to you to decide where your future lies. It will not be easy and, I suspect, having been earthbound, the thought of engaging in an unknown world whose leaders appear to want you dead, must hold little temptation for you. But I do have to say that your arrival could reverse the direction Holis has taken and be the saving grace of all our people.

Eshe said that you came into being for a purpose and for the good of Ra. She thought, she said she knew, you could be the key.

Now, no-one can force you to do anything against your wishes, but I beg you to use all your skills and intuition to help you decide. I realise this may be a daunting prospect, but rest assured, that every person, whether from Holis, or Earth, faces the same choice: firstly, to live life either using or squandering the gifts they have been given; and secondly, to live life just for themselves or to make a difference for others… I had not meant this to put you under any pressure; I only meant that it is you and you alone, who can decide what to do with your life.

Imogen, I fear I will not see you again, my dear. Time is so short. I pray that you are, and will remain, safe. May the blessings of Ra, and indeed all the Gods here, be upon you, my dear girl…"

Imogen released the DE as if it were sizzling hot. Her mind was in turmoil. She could barely take in the implications of what she had learnt. *How can I make a difference? I am only one person, and barely seventeen! What's so important about being a 'Penta-Crypt?' And what does he mean by 'claim my entitlement'? Why would I want to take up a fight in a world about which I know nothing? It's all well and good Tanastra saying the choice is mine but how can I make a choice without knowing more?*

As the information buzzed around her head she found her thoughts energising and automatically launching into a deep analytical exploration as to what it all meant. She downed a glass of water, steadying her breathing and heart rate, and rose to go to the window and look out over the darkened city of Paris, lights twinkling ethereally. As the stars grew more apparent in the clear night sky she scrutinized all the facts, went over past conversations with a new hindsight and tied up the possibilities and likelihoods as they careered to a new and terrifying conclusion.

It was Leo's half-truths when he had attempted to explain 'her kind' – '*a group of individuals, greater in intellect to anyone around them, sealed themselves off in a place hidden to the rest of the world…*' This, and Adam's explanation of the Tractus, along with snatches of Tanastra's last words, swirled in her head and finally convinced her that she must be right: '*we live in a different light… having been earthbound… every person, whether from Holis or Earth, faces the same choice… the blessings of Ra and all the Gods here…*' Her focus then flashed back the church and the eerie light from the canopy. Red. The portable marker had only produced yellow/white light when it was connected to known sites around the world, but the light she had witnessed from the permanent marker in the church as Leo had arrived and then been taken prisoner with her father, had been tinged red.

As all these thoughts layered and combined, she realised there was only one logical deduction to be made, startling as it might be.

Imogen blinked and sat in the window chair. She was amazed she felt so calm. Infused with a tranquillity derived from arriving at the only rational conclusion available, she called to Adam, raising her hand to stop Araz from entering the room as well. *Not yet Araz – all in good time.*

"I need to speak to Adam alone," she said calmly, giving Araz a reassuring smile as he paused, then nodded, unable to calm the grey flurries evident in his Chroma as he retreated back to the other room.

Realisations

$\mathcal{C}$raz waited in the lounge area of the hotel suite unable to sit still. He paced the floor, stopping to look out at the night sky from time to time. How he wished he had an instrument he could play, which would soothe and calm him.

He could have easily listened in to the conversation in the next room, but could not bring himself to eavesdrop. Something that would have been a natural response only a week before now seemed intrusive and unworthy. His priority was no longer to look after just himself. For the first time ever, he cared deeply for another.

He was unclear how such a dramatic change had occurred, but he did know that his fate would forever be interlinked with the amazing young woman in the adjoining room. He had never experienced such an intensity of feeling and it altered his entire perception.

When did it happen? He thought back to the moment he had first seen her in the exam room, colours blazing in iridescent hues that had him captivated, even before he had seen her beautiful face. He had been drawn to her since then and could not deny the unspoken chemical - no spiritual - connection. It appeared, unsolicited, with every encounter and had overwhelmed him when they had finally kissed in the church.

She was such an extraordinary mix, strong and consistent at times, vulnerable and erratic at others. In his head he replayed the moments in his flat. Her defiant and determined challenges to his way of thinking, her instant decision to save him when she used the portable marker, her change of attitude in the underground station when she no longer seemed to view him as a threat. She had saved him a second time when he was being throttled in mid-air, when it could have been her chance to abandon him. He recalled their chase under London, their escape and her deep fears surfacing as she went into shock. Holding her close as she shook, he had softened further towards her, inflamed by her close proximity; irresistibly drawn to protect her.

On the train to Birmingham, she had insisted that he gave her information about the empire and its workings. It was an eye-opener to find that things intrinsic to all of their kind were a revelation to her. She simply did not know. It was then obvious that she had barely any knowledge of her homeland or its government. Did she even know where it was? He realised as he thought it, that she did not, and glanced at the door behind towards the unheard conversation. Is this what they are discussing?

Araz gave an impatient sigh as he stared out of the window at the darkened city, picking out the shapes of pedestrians far below, looking like ants moving on rote. She could no more be blamed for the transgressions of her parents, than these unfortunates could be blamed for their primitive state. And, whilst the extermination of one of these lowlifes would pass practically unnoticed, to destroy her would be an aberration. He realised he could not bear to think of it.

How strange, he contemplated, that in the course of just a few weeks, he had gone from seeing her as a trophy to take home to someone he deeply cared about. And he had nearly lost her. The thought made him shudder.

At the church he had been held in a fierce arm lock and could only watch on, helplessly, as she ran from the Repros. To see the priest fall was enough, especially as Araz had recognised him as one of the greatest scientists and historians of his race. He was quite sure his superiors did not know about Tanastra's involvement; after all, he was supposed to have died seventy years before. If this great man's life was worth nothing, they would not hesitate to slaughter all the others, including him. As Imogen was then grabbed by the Repro in the church, ready with a blade, his mind had screamed 'no!' He would not watch her cut down by the brutal forces of his so-say commanders. He had used a supreme effort to free himself from the surprisingly strong grip of that Zuberi brother and had called on every fibre in his body to launch himself into her attacker and put a stop to it. Any sense of relief quickly subsided as Imogen had lost consciousness and began to fade.

He had felt so helpless, watching the brothers attempt to revive her, knowing she was going rapidly downhill and drawing nearer and nearer to death. As they shook their heads and one gave a powerless shrug as the other beat his chest with his fist, Araz knew in that instant; he knew he could not live without her. His life would be in shadow if she died. He had acted on autopilot, sweeping the others out of the way, reaching for her limp hand and pressing his fingertips to hers as his declaration of love and need for her poured into her being.

Had that made the difference? There was no scientific reason that could uphold it, but she had begun to breathe again and her subsequent recovery was now a matter of fact. He blinked rapidly. Her glance with death still unnerved him.

So, what now? His life was also now in jeopardy. He would be seen, at the very least, as a collaborator and, at the very worst, as a traitor. How could he resolve matters?

Imogen needed to be taken from this backward, primitive environment. She must experience the marvel of living with her own people. The contrast would be immense. Araz was certain that she could not fail to see how wondrous her life might be. She would be inspired and would surely want to stay. It was inevitable, to his mind.

As Imogen had recuperated, Araz had thought long and hard and had now made up his mind. He could not live in this world – that was absolute. He would, however, do nothing without her agreement, but he would help her to formulate a plan to return to the empire. He was sure she would want to attempt to free her father, although the man would have to answer for his own crimes - that was not his concern. She also seemed to have some attachment to that blonde boy, and whilst this made him bristle with an irrational irritation, it would give Imogen more reason to make a rescue bid. He had seen this 'Leo' or 'Tarik' before, just fleetingly, in the secret depths of the council area and he could not be sure of his role but if Imogen agreed to try and free him, he was sure he could force himself to subdue any feelings of envy. He probably means nothing to her, he said to himself, in consolation.

The most important goal, to his mind, was to ensure the empire rejected the ridiculous claims made against Imogen. If she was exonerated of all faults and he could justify his actions, they would be free to unite. He was not usually prone to flights of fancy but the thought caused him a delicious tremor, which pulsated strongly in both his body and Chroma. Realising Adam was returning to the room, he quickly toned it down. Right now, there were more important things to think about.

Whilst Araz had been left to his own thoughts, Adam, in the meantime, had sat on the edge of Imogen's chair, taking in her calm aura and quartz Chroma as he looked out of the window.

"I love to look at the night sky. Beautiful, isn't it?"

"Yes, it is." Imogen stayed looking out of the window, as she asked: "Adam, fill me in on events since I was poisoned."

Adam, seeming somewhat relieved with this line of questioning, gave a quick account: "Once your condition stabilised, we got you to Paris by private ambulance. We could not risk using the Tractus; you were too weak. I was surprised Araz knew about the portable device, but he has told me you saved his life with it… anyway, that was a week ago." *A week! What will have happened to dad and Leo in that time?* She stifled the rising worry and stilled her colours. *Remain focussed.*

"I looked after you, Araz drove." Adam continued, adding as an aside, "Your new admirer was very helpful and appears to be cooperating with us for now."

Imogen nodded before asking, "You must be worried about Leo?"

Adam paused, looking slightly askance, before answering. "Yes, I suppose I am." Sepia shades of sadness and possibly regret crept into his Chroma as he continued: "Forgive me, I hadn't seen him for over ten years and I keep forgetting he is still only eighteen, not twenty-eight. But I'm sure he will be fine, he has your father to protect him…" Seeing his awkwardness and aware of a navy tremor of hurt, Imogen turned the conversation to the events in Birmingham.

"My brother was left there to take care of Tanas… Father Jonathan, you now know his true identity?" Imogen slowly nodded and put the brake on the thoughts of his ultimate sacrifice for her. *Concentrate on getting Adam talking.*

"You will also know that we need to keep this fact hidden from the enemy." Adam bobbed his head in the direction of the other room.

Imogen turned to him and responded, "I think Araz already knows. He showed signs of recognition when he first saw him in the church."

Adam's Chroma flared, with a mixture of mauve annoyance and bronze frustration. "We need to get that young man on our side," he muttered, as if to himself, as Imogen, eyes now fixed on Adam, asked about the 'second Adam'.

"That's Nuru, known as Nathan here. He was to check that the church marker was completely disabled before joining Seth and your mother in New York. There should be no mention of a third brother in the hearing of others. Sefu and Nuru are the only two as far as others are concerned. Araz thinks I am Sefu," he added. Imogen nodded understanding as she started on the real focus of her questions.

"So, Leo and my father cannot return to the marker in Birmingham?" asked Imogen, unable to quell a flurry of deep grey worry.

"That's correct. It had to be immobilised. The risk of opening that particular portal is just too high. Aside from it having turned into a tempus, which we still do not quite understand, it is clearly being watched and gives direct access to the very centre of Holis and its corrupt government. Personally, I think it most improbable they will attempt to return here, but in the unlikely event that they do escape, they could use one of the markers sited elsewhere. Even then, they would not want to lead the enemy to any of these."

Imogen knew her moment had come. Adam was relaxed and speaking freely. She had him off his guard, as she had when he had explained the Tractus to her, that night in her house.

"Adam, tell me, when you said the portable markers meant the Tractus was restricted to jumps of just ten thousand kilometres, you did not explain the maximum distance that can be travelled from the permanent markers?"

"Did I not? Well that's because, well it wasn't relevant…" Adam's colours showed the start of a rising influx of tell-tale violet - he was preparing to speak falsehoods as he rubbed his ear. *More in common with his son than he realises.* He slowly petered out, as Imogen faced him head on, fixing him with her gaze. He could not break contact. Silver threads filtered across to his Chroma and teased and pulled at the pure white truths, as they took precedence in his colours. Spellbound, he poured out the facts.

"Well, I... distance? So, the maximum we have jumped is about twelve trillion miles – approximately twenty light years. We have not tested further distances, but there is no reason why a much greater expanse could be achieved..."

"Twenty light years." repeated Imogen slowly.

"Yes."

"Is that the distance to Holis?" she asked in barely a whisper.

"Yes."

"So Holis is a planet in another solar system?" Imogen swallowed hard.

"Another solar system, yes, but still part of the same galaxy, the one you call the Milky Way." He gestured to the night sky, as if pointing to a far off location, as he elucidated: "Also, Holis is technically a moon, not a planet. It is one of two moons – Holis and Ankh - that orbit a large but dead planetary mass. Holis does not turn like the Earth; it has a dark side and a light side, but the light is mainly red from the closest star which is, what they call here, a red dwarf."

The red light of Holis.

"Twenty light years," Imogen said slowly, forcing the truth to sink in. She had surmised that Holis could not be on Earth, but to hear the stark facts being voiced felt like being thumped in the stomach.

I come from a different planet – another part of the universe.

The revelation, whilst it matched her conclusions, was still staggering and she had to quell the sudden urge to be sick.

"The distance may seem incredible, but it is only a jump by Tractus," Adam said gently, seeing Imogen's face drained of colour.

"Just a jump," she whispered, as she lost focus and the hypnosis strands began to withdraw. It was hard to assimilate this resounding confirmation and realise her deductions had been correct. Adam shook his head and looked at Imogen as if disbelieving what he had just told her.

"I had to know, Adam," she said apologetically. "Forgive the intrusion." Adam nodded, shrugged acceptance and gave her shoulder a gentle squeeze as Imogen continued: "I should have guessed – I was so different – It should have been obvious…"

"What should have been obvious?" asked Adam who, although disconcerted, was concerned with Imogen's presentation and swirling dark grey clouds, interwoven with veins of deep blue hurt.

"It should have been obvious that I am not human."

A freak and an alien.

Adam stood and instantly answered with quartz clarity and a slight copper indignation: "Human / Holan – it is all the same. You could call the people of earth 'primitive Holans' or our race 'advanced Humans'. Imogen, it is an indisputable fact that all matter in the universe comes from the same source and we discovered long ago that all evolved life forms have the same basic make-up. Universally, intelligent life is carbon-based and a variation on the same theme. Yes, there are differences, but it is a star-wide fundamental pattern."

Imogen concentrated on his words with a faint sense of relief, as he continued, gesticulating with his hands to illustrate his points:

"It is the environment that alters shape and form but we are made in the same prototype of perfection as ordained by Ra. We do have differences, as you know. So, for instance, we have denser bones, as gravity is slightly heavier on Holis; we have a different make-up of the eye, as our light is from both a white sun and a more dominant red star. These differences are due to where our human form developed, not our basic DNA; we all share the same building blocks of life. In addition, the people of Holis have been in existence long before humans began on earth, so we have evolved to a higher state of being, in addition to having fine-tuned our race using sophisticated genetic alterations."

Imogen fell silent for a few minutes and could not combat the navy tinges of hurt that rose in her Chroma as she asked: "Why was I not told?"

Adam studied her face for a long time before he finally answered with clear white truth: "To be honest, I am not really sure. My brothers and I were involved in the Tractus project and had little to do with your upbringing. Plus, you were lost in time all those years and key members of our group were killed or put out of action. Perhaps your father thought you were too fragile to take this on board. There is a lot of nonsense talked about so say 'alien' races here on Earth."

She thought back to when Leo had given her a skewed account of her 'race' and wondered how she would have reacted if she had been told the truth. Maybe it would have thrown her, but surely her father should have said something during all those years of her mother being asleep.

A deep swell of anger, hurt and incomprehension began to bubble away inside but another part of her mind suddenly replayed, unbidden, the faces of her mother, sedated in a chair, Leo covered in blood with a broken arm and nose, her father giving a faint smile as he vanished in the church and Father Jonathan bleeding to death in front of her having taken the blow intended to kill her.

This is no time to be precious – not when others have given up so much for me - I must remain strong.

Realising self-pity and resentment would lead nowhere; she determined that she could not go down this route. She had not been told and that was that. Now she did know and so must decide what, if anything, she was going to do about it.

"I need to talk to Araz," she declared.

"Well, all in good time. First you need some gentle exercise and to have a proper meal. Just walk around the suite, have a bath, dress and we will order food for the room. I will leave you to talk with your devotee alone, but be careful Imogen, he may be cooperating with us at the moment, but we do not know his position with regard to the empire on Holis and we certainly do not know his intentions."

Imogen nodded and Adam left the room, closing the door so she could gently stretch her legs as she ambled around the room and ran a bath. She removed the pendant's sparking arrow from the DE, which instantly stopped flickering as the device itself flattened to its former shape, no grooves apparent. She held up the chain and turned all the symbols, so the alignment showed them unified, the solid circle most apparent: Ra, the head, and clearly some sort of God.

Was my being preordained as Eshe said? Am I really the Sanctus Cryptus?

Her thoughts calmed and soothed as she bathed. She relaxed her aching muscles and infused warmth into her stiff joints. Later, as she dried herself, she thought about her physical being. The five marks had always been there, whether or not she had only discovered them recently. Her extraterrestrial background was a fact, and had not impinged on how she saw herself up until now. She had always known she was different. Normality was not changed, merely her perception of it. It was still her face in the mirror – she was still herself. *It's going to be okay* she told her reflection.

She dressed with care. Someone had hung new clothing, of the right size, in the wardrobe. It was to her taste - casual jeans and tops - but they were in beautiful fabrics and of a very high quality. *Chrissie would approve of these designer labels,* she had smiled to herself. In the mirror, the effect was just what she wanted. She looked normal, but somehow rather classy. She stepped into the next room to be greeted by Araz who ushered her to a candlelit table filled with silver dome-covered dishes, which released delicious smells as he lifted off the covers.

"Mademoiselle, your dinner awaits." His smile was so wide and the gold white flashing reds so warm that she could not stop her heart leaping, as she crossed to the table.

"Monsieur Zuberi has left us in peace for a while," he said, sitting opposite Imogen and staring intently at her across the table, his devotion sparking like a firework display in red-white-golds of vivid intensity.

Imogen found it hard to stop her body and Chroma reacting with equal fervour but there were too many unknowns about him. She lowered her eyes and enforced a drill to keep a lid on her feelings.

"Please, don't look at me like that – I won't be able to eat!" she smiled, as she avoided his look and put food on her plate.

"Sorry, but this is a new experience for me," Araz answered, with no apology in his voice. "I will try to comply, but it is very difficult for me to take my eyes off you."

"Try eating instead," she insisted. They ate in a companionable silence, glancing out at the fairytale view of Paris and exchanging unspoken smiles between mouthfuls.

Eventually Imogen spoke, choosing her words carefully as she moved the last of her food around the plate with a fork.

"Araz, I am going to have to go to Holis – I must speak on behalf of my father and Leo. But...' she hesitated slightly, 'but I will need you to take me." She looked up, relieved to find that he was nodding full agreement.

"If you had not asked, I would have insisted," he responded decisively, adding, "I do not intend letting you out of my sight."

Imogen flushed; she was still a little disconcerted to find this arrogant foreigner was now full of unerring devotion. Granted, he had saved her life, and he prompted a deep ardour within, but she barely knew him and she could not afford to let herself go. There was too much at stake.

"We will need to leave as soon as possible," she said authoritatively, looking away to avoid his admiring gaze. *Be still my heart.*

"Well, we can't leave for a week or two – you have not yet come of age."

"What do you mean?"

"It is only when you have reached seventeen that you will have a voice in our world. Not before." Imogen was intrigued.

"Surely a week or so will make no difference?" she quizzed.

"There are strict rules on Holis: when you can, and cannot speak and reaching seventeen is one of these rules." Imogen could not help thinking to herself, with some amusement, that she was, by birth, closer to fifty-seven, but knew she could not share this.

"Will my father and Leo be safe, in the meantime?" she asked anxiously, grey fluttering at the edge of her aura.

"I cannot completely guarantee it, but it is my strong belief that they will be held for analysis and questioning, which I know to be a slow process," he responded darkly, eyes flickering away from hers, a brief surge of purple-greys evident in his aura.

Imogen gulped and chose not to interpret his meaning. *There's nothing I can do to help them from here - focus on what I can do.*

"In the meantime, we can make plans," he said positively as he went to take her hand and leaned forward as if to kiss it, flaring deep red-golds. Imogen recoiled and pulled her hand back. *I have to stay firm.* The blue hurt was evident in his colour response.

"Sorry – it's too quick…" she started, in a faltering voice.

"Are you denying you have the same feelings?" he asked, unable to keep some aggression from his voice.

"No," answered Imogen quietly. "But…" Imogen held her hand up to stop him, responding, "but I cannot think straight when you, when we… look I just need to be able to think."

Araz stood and walked to the window. After a few moments he turned and said.

"You can take all the time you like. My feelings will not alter and I intend to protect you, no matter what." His statement was accompanied with open palms and the quartz truth of his declaration, as unsaid words seemed to leap into her head: '*With my life, if need be*' and hung in the air between them. Had Adam not re-entered the room at that moment, she may have weakened and instinctively responded to the passion evident in his expression, body language and Chroma. *How I would love to fall into those arms.* As it was, Adam arrived just in time to prevent this.

Maintaining an external composure she did not feel inside she told Adam of her intentions expecting him to argue, but he merely nodded acceptance.

"You will need briefing," he challenged. She nodded, biting her lip. "And I have not been on Holis for a long time, so our friend here, what do we call you?" he addressed Araz quizzically. "An ally?" Araz dipped his head in a form of agreement. "Well you will need to bring us both up to date and tell us all that you know about the Supreme Council."

There was a slight hesitation and a troubling surge of violet on the perimeter of his Chroma, but Araz replied positively, falling silent as Adam sat down declaring, "We will start tomorrow," before tucking into the remains of the meal.

A pensive mood descended on the three of them with no further conversation. Imogen was glad to escape to her room to speak to her mother in New

York using a face-to-face Internet link. She was pleasantly surprised at how normal her mum had seemed, although there was no way of observing her Chroma to check her condition. She did not speak of her brush with death or her plans and, whilst she hated being dishonest with the only person she had always shared everything with, she did not wish to cause any deterioration in her mother's delicate health.

Imogen had also managed a brief chat with Chrissie, who assumed she was calling from New York. Describing Leo as a distant cousin who had assisted with her mother's move to the States, she played down his involvement and hinted that the relationship with Araz was still a possibility but on hold until she came home. Having reassured her friend, she feigned a bad line and promised to call in a few weeks or so. *If I manage to return,* she thought to herself uneasily.

Sitting in the seat by the large window, looking out at the night sky and concentrating on a group of stars low on the horizon, she twiddled the symbols of her pendant in mid-air.

Somewhere out there, twenty light years away, is my home planet, my father and Leo. I may not be accepted, I may be considered to be a Falsebred, another subversive, a threat or who knows what, but I have to go there. It could mean my death, but I cannot stay here and pretend it does not exist. As a distant star gave a barely perceptible flare, as if in beckoning, she made a fist with her good hand. *If there is such a thing as a destiny for me, I will find out what it is.*

Appendix

Chroma

The aura of colours we all unknowingly exude which show our deepest fears, emotions and thoughts. The aura can only be seen in visible light and then, only by those who possess 'tetra-chromatic' sight, like Imogen. Those with tetra-chromatic sight (having a fourth light receptor in the eye) are able to see not just seven, but twenty-one distinct colours. Imogen has learnt to read Chroma as a form of extra sensory perception. She can distinguish the varying shades of each colour and is able to understand what each means. For example the red of anger is a shade different to the red of excitement or the deeper shade of love, or the red of fear.

The Chromatic range of emotions and feelings:

White & Quartz: Honesty / Logic / Reason / Truth / Clarity
Reds – Hot colours: Passion / Fear / Love / Attraction / Anger
Red flickering white gold: Intense Love / Devotion
Oranges: Humour / Laughter / Calm
Yellows: Enquiry / Prying / Questioning / Searching
Blues – Cold colours: Logic / Reason / Aptitude
Cobalt Blue: Inspiration
Sapphire: Genuine
Navy Blue: Hurt

Purples – Dark colours: Worry / Suspicion
Violet: Lies / Untruths / Injury
Greens & browns – Calm earth colours: Relaxation / Trustworthiness / Loyalty
Russet: Recognition
Sepia: Sadness / Grief
Deep Greens: Pride / Adoration / Sacrifice
Sage Green: Admiration
Grey: Worry / Confusion / Anxiety
Black: Authority / Power
Copper: Indignation
Bronze: Frustration
Silver: Hypnosis Threads / Control
Gold: Power / Intrigue / Seduction

Characters:
Imogen Reiner.
Harold Reiner, Imogen's grandfather
Elizabeth Reiner, Imogen's mother
Father Jonathan, confident to Harold
Margaret, elderly resident in Harold's care home
Leonard Newall (Leo)
Seth, Nathan and Adam Turner (brothers)
Araz Vikram

Friends at Forrester College:
Christine aka Chrissie (brothers Callum, Rory and Ben)
Danny / Richard / Katie / Leanne

Renowned Scientist:
Tanastra Thut, author of the chronicles and inventor of the Tractus.

The Scientists labelled as subversives:

Firas Lateef: Scientist, artist and mathematician who developed the Tractus, originally conceived by Tanastra.

Eshe Serq: Distinguished geneticist.

The Zuberi Brothers: Sefu Zuberi / Nuru Zuberi (named subversive at a later date) / Amsu Zuberi (the hidden triplet) – all experts in bio-chemical communications

Rashida Omorose: Scientist and artist

Kasmut Akil: Scientist and inventor

Tarik Zuberi (son of Amsu Zuberi)

The named members of The Supreme Council:

Kekara – Supreme Leader

Odion

Ubaid

Sekhet

Halim

Repros: Reproduction Life forms used as a fighting force by the Supreme Council.

The Five Lines or Crypts of Holis:

Ra – the Head: Symbol: Solid Circle

Mark found at the back of the head below the ear

Personality type: Strong minded, decisive and energetic

Iris – the Eye: Symbol: Clear Circle

Mark found to the side of the eye

Personality type: Creative and imaginative

(Iris are reported as being surreptitiously phased out as they are considered to be a challenge to the Supreme Council)

Nut - the Hand: Symbol: Solid Star

Mark found on the hand between the thumb and first finger
Personality type: Practical and calm
Hathor – the Heart: Symbol: Clear Star
Mark found on the centre of the chest
Personality type: Compassionate and caring
Amon – the Feet: Symbol: Arrow
Mark found at on the sole of the foot below the big toe
Personality type: Disciplined and persistent

Uni-Crypt: most common – one line is more dominant than all the others so only one body mark is visible.
Bi-Crypt: Two of the five lines are held in equal measure
Tri-Crypt: Three of the five lines are held in equal measure
Tetra-Crypt: Four of the five lines are held in equal measure
Penta-Crypt: All five lines held in equal measure (known as the Sanctus Cryptus or sacred crypts and not considered possible after many failed attempts to genetically engineer a Penta-Crypt)

About the Author

B Fleetwood: The third of six children, I grew up as part of the baby boomer generation in the late 1950s and 60s in Birmingham, UK, where I attended a primary school not that dissimilar to the one described by Imogen.

I met my engineering hubby, Julian, when studying Sociology at the University of Bath, a mix that was always going to make for an interesting life! We have lived in Stockport (North-West, UK) for over thirty years, bringing up our four children and now have four granddaughters to add to the collection.

I have worked as a waitress, barmaid, dinner lady, secretary, exams officer and school timetabler and also ran a cub pack. I still run a toddler group at my church, and sing and dance whenever I can. Life has always been at breakneck speed.

My love of writing started when I was only eight, the consequence of winning a stack of chocolate in a Cadburys competition "the life story of a Cocoa Bean"! Since then I have had a burning ambition to write a fantasy series, grounded in everyday existence. I have only life to blame for taking so long to finally do it.

I hope you have enjoyed Book 1 of the Chroma Series. If you are able to write a short review, I would be most grateful – they are the life-blood of authors. Thank you.

www.bfleetwood.com

Made in the USA
Charleston, SC
17 November 2016